Restoration Day

Deborah Makarios

© 2018 Deborah Makarios
deborah.makarios.nz

OI
MAKARIOI

A catalogue record for this book is available from the National Library of New Zealand.

ISBN (paperback): 978-0-473-41519-8
ISBN (ebook): 978-0-473-41520-4

Editor: Sara Litchfield, http://rightinkonthewall.com
Original of cover image: George Becker (CC0 license)
Front cover typography: Evelyn Doyle, http://evelyndoyle.com

To Anna
without whose early encouragement
this book might never have been more
than a seedling

Trouble Brewing

One day, Lily promised herself, *I will walk down the stairs alone.*

She stood at the head of the castle's grand stair, trying to wait patiently, and counted off the days: Martday, Launderday, Fallowday, Sunday, Mūnday, Landday, Middweek—only one week until she would be eighteen. Were it not for the War, how different things would have been!

A grand coming-of-age ball, at which *no one* would prevent her coming down the stairs on her own... Her magnificent entrance, the cynosure of all eyes... (She wasn't sure of the precise definition of a cynosure, but it sounded impressive.) The hall, full of guests in their finest...

She swept the hall with her gaze, populating it with a glittering throng. At the foot of the stairs stood her parents, King Frederick and Queen Celandine, greeting their guests and looking remarkably like their portraits in the gallery upstairs. Her imagination laboured to animate their oil-and-canvas features, and moved on. A flourish of trumpets, an expectant stir in the crowd, and all faces turned upwards, seeking a glimpse of their young princess.

Lily's simple white day-dress was invested with swathes of lace, frills, and exquisite embroideries on tissue of silver. Her head went up. One hand delicately reached for the balustrade, and the other swept up her skirts as she prepared to descend. A dancer's light grace carried her down to the landing, where she turned, bathing the hall with the warmth of her gracious smile. After a nicely-judged pause, she put forward one dainty foot to continue her triumphal progress down the stairs.

"Lily!"

The glittering crowd disappeared, along with the lace, the grace, and her parents. Instead there was only Aunt Hortensia, sweeping across the hall like a storm-front, purple-grey in the half mourning she still wore after fifteen years. Lily froze, one foot still hovering over the step.

"What *do* you think you're doing, child?" Aunt Hortensia moved up the stairs with a rapidity surprising in so stately a woman, and took firm possession of Lily's arm.

"I had my hand on the railing all the way, Aunt Hortensia," Lily said. "Just as safe as in someone's arm. Safer, really, because the railing—"

"Young ladies do not talk back," Aunt Hortensia said firmly, descending the stairs with aggravating slowness. "You know the rules. Just think if you had slipped and fallen! And not a soul present to come to your aid."

"But—"

"You must not take these risks with yourself. Arcelia depends on you."

"I was imagining my coming-of-age ball," Lily said. "I remember you saying that you entered alone at yours, and since I'm practically—"

"That was entirely different. *I* was not heir to the throne of Arcelia."

"But Aunt—"

Having reached the foot of the stairs, Aunt Hortensia released her death-grip on Lily's arm and turned the full force of her pale blue eyes on Lily's face.

"That is quite enough, Lily. We shall not discuss the matter further. After the evening observance, you may wish to remain in your room and consider your motives for spurning the care others go to so much trouble to give you."

"But that's when I have dancing!" Lily cried.

"I am sure Master Sennet will not object to excusing you on this occasion. Now come along. It would not be appropriate for you to be late."

Lily trailed across the hall and out the solid oak doors after her aunt. She didn't want to miss dusk in the garden, but her usual enthusiasm was dampened by the loss of the evening's dancing. Aunt Hortensia *never* said "you may wish to" if it was something you might actually wish to do.

Lily risked a scowl at her aunt's perfectly straight back as it led the way across the terrace. And she *knew* how much Lily loved to dance! Which was probably why she was only allowed two dancing evenings each week—young ladies ought not to be enthusiastic, Aunt Hortensia held, and to be enthusiastic about something so potentially *vigorous* as dancing was suspect indeed.

Lily sighed, and gave her arm to her aunt. Together they descended the stone stair which led from the terrace to the eastern lawns and the ceremonial garden. The steps weren't even slippery. Winter ended tomorrow, and it had been unusually mild this year: wet rather than icy. But it was no use arguing the case with Aunt Hortensia. "Young ladies never argue," was one of her favourite maxims.

Master Sennet, Lily's tutor, and Holly the cook (still wearing his apron) were already waiting at the entrance to the ceremonial garden, as was Burdock the gardener. The three men ducked their heads respectfully as Lily and her aunt approached. Holly flashed Lily a cheerful grin, which made her feel a little better. Holly was like that.

"Good evening, Master Sennet," Aunt Hortensia said formally. "Holly. Burdock."

"Good evening, Lady Hortensia; Princess Lily," Sennet replied warmly.

"Lovely evening for it," Holly observed, as he invariably did if it wasn't sleeting down in a gale.

"Eh," said Burdock, which, while not strictly in line with the etiquette of the situation, was as much as he ever contributed to any conversation.

He was, Lily privately felt, a little odd, but he kept himself to himself and since Aunt Hortensia apparently thought him harmless, he must be less dangerous than a staircase.

Aunt Hortensia led the way into the ceremonial garden, and silence fell. The beauty of the moment never failed to have its effect on Lily. The green, growing hush. The sinking sun bathing the grounds in that unearthly golden light seen at no other time. Best of all, the earliest of the bulbs were in flower, and the garden was full of their intoxicating scent, a promise of wonderful things to come after the cold sterility of winter.

She stood in silent gratitude for the good things of the day— Holly had made her favourite cake, for one—and resolved to be a better, more dutiful niece and pupil henceforth.

Aunt Hortensia gave a genteel cough, her accustomed signal that the prescribed time of silence had ended. It came, as usual, far before Lily was ready for it. She gazed off into the distance, so as not to be drawn immediately into conversation.

The distance was composed, as always, of the Hedge: the great wall of privet that encircled the Castle of Candra and its grounds. Privet in the language of plants meant *prohibition*, and Lily felt the force of it. The Hedge had no gaps, no arches, no breaks. It was a solid, living barrier between her and the world outside—she couldn't even see over it unless she was up in one of the towers. It was the green boundary of her world. Except it didn't look entirely green, not today. Perhaps it was the light.

She wrinkled her brow, trying to focus more clearly. *That can't be right…*

"Lily, do not squint. It is most unattractive."

"Aunt Hortensia, isn't privet supposed to be evergreen?"

"Of course it is, child, what a silly question! You know—" Her aunt fell silent.

By now they were all looking at the Hedge, and the dull brown patch that had formed on it.

"Probably just the light," Holly said, but even he sounded uneasy.

"*Lily,*" came a whisper on the chilling air.

Lily turned. One moment she was looking at Burdock, who was leaning on his stick, one hand stretched out to her, and the next, she was looking at a dandelion. She blinked. Burdock hadn't moved; he just wasn't there any more. There was only a dandelion, leafy, green and puffy-headed, in his place.

"Burdock!" Aunt Hortensia trumpeted, appearing at Lily's side. "Where is the man?"

"He...he..." Lily couldn't quite find the words.

"*And* a dandelion seeding! I shall have to speak to him quite severely."

"He was here a moment ago," Holly volunteered.

"He turned into a dandelion," Lily said, her disloyal throat abandoning the gentle tones of a proper lady's diction for a childish squeak.

Aunt Hortensia's head snapped round. "What?"

"He was there, and then there was a dandelion! He just vanished!"

Aunt Hortensia stood swelling for a moment, and then, with a visible effort, controlled herself. "Don't be ridiculous, child! You are far too old for such make-believe."

"I'm *not* making it up!" Lily said, stamping her foot.

"Master Sennet, will you kindly check the gardener's cottage while I escort Princess Lily to her room?"

"Of course, my lady." Sennet bowed slightly and moved away, his rheumatic limp more noticeable in his hurry.

Lily cast an appealing look at Holly, her last remaining ally.

"Did you actually see it?" Holly asked, clearly interested. "Did he go all green first?"

"Holly, I will thank you not to encourage Lily in her foolishness," Aunt Hortensia said frostily. "I am sure you have some duties to attend to in the kitchens."

"Oh—well, yes. Yes," Holly mumbled, avoiding Lily's eye. "I'd better…" He rolled away at remarkable speed for one of his bulk.

"Come along at *once*," Aunt Hortensia said, taking Lily's arm and clamping it to her own well-corseted side.

As she was towed away, Lily looked back. The dandelion was still there, a little tuft of white in the gathering darkness.

⚜   ⚜   ⚜

Lily rose the next morning determined to find answers to the questions that had troubled her all night. She knew her aunt well enough not to waste time with a direct approach, but she tried a solicitous inquiry as to Burdock's health at the breakfast table. The reply came straight out of Master Sennet's lessons on diplomatic vagueness.

Her necessary morning attendance at the ceremonial garden was closely supervised, and she discovered only that the dandelion had gone. Had she imagined the whole thing? Aunt Hortensia wouldn't have been so upset if that was all. But, then, what…? And what was happening to the Hedge?

The time spent in the ceremonial garden each morning was supposed to help you think of bad habits and errors that you needed to pull up by the roots, just as you pulled up weeds in the morning so as to have them wither in the heat of the day. Privately, Lily thought it much easier to resolve to be better henceforth in the evening, when you were going to be asleep soon anyway, and had a fair chance of being good for several hours together. Her repeated resolution to be good was difficult enough to keep on an ordinary day, sitting down to hour after hour of lessons in the library, but today…today it would be particularly hard to be the docile young lady Aunt Hortensia required.

Lily chafed inwardly as Sennet discoursed on the geographical formations caused by the movement of water. What had happened to Burdock? She'd seen no sign of him this morning, and—

"Do try to attend, my lady," Sennet said wearily, rubbing the spot on his temple where the hair was entirely grey already.

This was his habit when a headache was coming on; and now she looked closely, he had dark rings around his eyes as well.

"Dear Master Sennet, you aren't unwell, are you?"

She was seized with a sudden premonition of all the castle's residents being carried off one by one by this mysterious ailment of Burdock's, leaving her alone in what would no doubt be, henceforth, a *haunted castle.*

"Quite well, I thank you," Sennet replied. "I am perhaps a little fatigued—I did not have so much repose last night as I am accustomed to."

"Are you sure you wouldn't like to take a rest? I'm sure I can find some way to pass the time before my walk." Her pulse quickened. Would he take the bait?

"No, no. Let us not be shirkers of duty. As Arcelia's future queen, it is vital for you to have a working understanding of the land and the forces at work upon it."

Lily gave up that line of attack. When Master Sennet got onto the subject of Duty, there was no moving him.

"I am sure some fresh air would do you good," she said solicitously. "Perhaps we could continue the lesson on the terrace."

Whence there would be a better view of the Hedge. She did not say it, but Sennet's look suggested he heard her anyway.

"I think not, my lady. It is still winter, after all, and I am sure your aunt would not like you to catch a chill."

That wasn't the only thing Aunt Hortensia wouldn't like about the idea, and they both knew it, but you would never get Master Sennet to admit as much. He was a diplomat at heart.

He cleared his throat. "Now then. As the water descends in the form we know as a waterfall, the rock and soil over which it passes are eroded by the passage of the water—the principle of friction."

Lily stifled a yawn, allowing no sign of it to appear on her face—possibly the most useful lesson she'd ever learned from Aunt Hortensia's discourses on the art of Elegant Conversation.

"This is particularly the case at the foot of the waterfall, which receives the brunt of the water's force as it falls from above. Thus, natural rock pools are formed, which are frequently of much greater depth than the rest of the river's passage. It is also by no means uncommon to find a cave behind the waterfall, another effect of—"

"Caves behind waterfalls?" Lily exclaimed, her interest diverted for a moment. "How exciting!"

He gave her a wry little smile. "I can assure you, my lady, that there is nothing at all exciting about the gradual erosion of rock by water. Tens if not hundreds of years are involved."

"But it seems so magical… The sort of place one would find buried treasure."

"The sort of place one would find a great deal of slime, I am afraid," Sennet said. "Now, if you will turn to—"

The door opened, and Aunt Hortensia entered. Sennet scrambled to his feet, and Aunt Hortensia gave him one of those looks which mean a great deal, but only to those who already know what they mean. Lily was familiar with those looks, and loathed them, since she was invariably the one who *didn't* know.

"Dear me, is it that hour already?" Sennet said. "We have

entirely lost track of the time in the fascination of geography."

"I'll just go up and change my shoes," Lily said, rising and arranging her books neatly on the table with exemplary docility. Aunt Hortensia mustn't suspect why she was so eager to go out...

"No need," said Aunt Hortensia. "We shall have our promenade indoors today—I fear it is coming on to rain."

Sennet unsuccessfully tried to conceal his surprise. The day had dawned crisp and clear, and with hardly a cloud to be seen.

Lily's heart leapt for a moment. "In the ballroom?"

"The portrait gallery," Aunt Hortensia replied, turning away.

Lily fumed inwardly. The ballroom windows looked out towards Burdock's cottage, but the portrait gallery would tell her nothing.

⚜   ⚜   ⚜

"It's so *unfair*," Lily said.

Elegant Conversation had continued until luncheon, a semi-formal affair from which there was no escaping before her guardians left the table. Aunt Hortensia then retired for her Afternoon Rest, leaving Lily in the custody of Sennet, who was intent on improving her chess—well away from the windows.

"My dear young lady, the pawns make up half your army. You simply cannot hope to defeat your opponent without using them."

"Sacrificing them, you mean."

"Sacrifices must be made if you are to triumph. There is, alas, no such thing as a bloodless victory."

"But why should it be the pawns who are sacrificed? They don't get to decide. I think the king and his counsellors should lead the fighting. It would be much fairer."

Sennet sighed, and rubbed his temples again.

"Chess is a metaphor, my lady. One can only take a metaphor so far. After all, if chess were literal, the castles would not move. The game is a stylized version of reality, from which certain valuable lessons may be garnered."

"Such as that a queen can go anywhere?" Lily said wistfully.

Sennet sighed and pinched the bridge of his nose.

"A chess queen is a queen-consort. You will be—or, rather, *are*, though subject to a regency in your minority—a queen regnant, reigning in your own right. More analogous, in fact, to a chess king."

"Spending my whole life running away, one square at a time?" Lily cried in dismay.

"You persist in taking the game too literally. The king's movements are constrained only while the enemy is at large, which is the framework of the game. The twin objectives of the game, remember, are to protect your king, and to capture the opposing king, thus defeating them."

"Then why don't the two kings fight a duel? That would be much more efficient."

Sennet was pinching his whole head now, applying pressure to both temples at once. This was serious.

"Efficiency is not always best. The other pieces become involved because—to humanize them as you do for a moment—they know that if their king falls, their kingdom falls. No land will stand without its king. That is why the king *cannot* be taken. If the king is lost, all is lost."

"But…" Lily ventured, wondering if it was safe to push him further.

"Yes?" Sennet said, patient as ever.

"You said that the king is constrained only while the enemy is at large. We don't have an enemy, not since the War ended, so why—?"

She stopped, frightened by the expression on his face. Perhaps it had been tactless of her to bring up the War with one who had suffered through it.

Sennet was silent for a long time, his face showing uncertainty, sorrow, and, most unsettlingly of all, fear.

"My lady," he began at last, speaking quietly and with more than usual seriousness, "there is some knowledge which your tender age forbade we lay upon your shoulders. Your aunt—" He shook his head. "I have become less certain, of late, of where my duty lies, but Lady Hortensia—"

A click of heels sounded on the marble floor of the hall, and Sennet fell silent. Lily could have screamed. Of all the times!

The door swung open.

"It is time for your brewing lesson, Lily," Aunt Hortensia announced.

Sennet said no more, but bowed as they left the room. Lily brooded silently. So she was right! There *was* something they weren't telling her. Something important. Perhaps a little detour was in order, on her way out to the brewhouse…

⚜   ⚜   ⚜

Lily scowled out the brewhouse window at her aunt's retreating form. Brewing was her least favourite lesson—Holly was a magnet for mess—and Aunt Hortensia had managed to thwart her every chance to investigate the Hedge, without so much as turning a hair.

"Don't worry," Holly said comfortably as she put on the hideously unbecoming cap which kept her hair clean. "We're not doing anything gloppy today; we're just going to fumigate a barrel."

"It's not just that," Lily said, pulling off the loathed cap and matching apron and flinging them into a corner of the straw-strewn floor. "Something's going on, and no one will tell me what." She looked at him narrowly, but he wouldn't meet her eye. "Holly, you'll tell me, won't you?"

"What's going on," he began, and Lily's heart leapt, "is a brewing lesson. Here's the barrel—I'll just put the bung down here..."

She scowled at him.

"If you persist in making that face, you can expect to get wrinkles," he said, in a fair imitation of Aunt Hortensia.

Lily tried to hold the scowl, but it slipped, and she broke into giggles.

"That's better," Holly said. "You know I'd tell you everything, but I don't know anything. Not even my own name," he muttered, rummaging under the workbench for a thin iron rod.

This was true, Lily knew. He'd lost his memory in the War, and no one knew his real name. Aunt Hortensia had bestowed on him the name Holly, for, as she observed, they had to call him something, and Holly meant *Am I forgotten?* in the language of flowers.

"Couldn't you just let me slip away?" Lily wheedled.

"More than my job's worth," Holly said firmly. "Tear a strip off this," he added, handing her a roughly woven rag.

"What's the worst she could do? You can't be sent out through the Hedge."

"She could build a siege catapult and fire me over the top," Holly said.

"She wouldn't! She didn't when you set the kitchen on fire."

"Occupational hazard. Could have happened to anyone!"

"Or when you blew up the chicken coop..."

"Entirely the chickens' fault. How was I to know that—"

"...or when that arrow skewered her favourite hat to the portrait of Great-Grandmother..."

"You were the one who fired it," Holly retorted.

"Under your supervision," Lily countered.

"How could I know your aim was that bad? I didn't even know it was *possible* to—"

"Never mind that!" She tore the cloth with some vigour. "How am I supposed to do the right thing, when I don't know what's going on?"

"No use fretting over what you can't change," Holly said. "Cheer up. This'll be fun."

The barrel to be fumigated was on its side in the middle of the floor. Holly took the strip of fabric from her and laid it on the workbench, next to the iron rod and a large potato.

"What's the potato for?" she asked. "Didn't you have enough lunch?"

"The potato," said Holly grandly, "is indispensable. Now, then. Barrel, bung, brazier; pot, rod, rag; potato. Ready. Oh, no, wait. Forgot the most important bit. Flower of yellowstone."

"*Flower* of yellowstone?" Lily had seen mentions of yellowstone—or, to give it its full name, yellow burningstone—in covertly studied books of alchemy, siegecraft, and the like, but flowers? "Don't tell me there's a flower that smells like yellowstone, because I simply refuse to believe it."

Holly pulled a thin metal phial out of his apron pocket and popped the lid off. Lily picked the lid off the floor and straightened up, wrinkling her nose.

"It's called flower of yellowstone because it forms in little flowery shapes," Holly said. "Isn't it pretty?"

"If cauliflower is pretty," Lily said, peering into the phial.

She took an unwary breath and reared back, nose pinched, trying not to gag. The smell was like the rottenest egg you could imagine, but more so. Holly seemed strangely unaffected.

"Right, so the flowers go in the pot—not too much, we only need a little—and that goes on the brazier." He handed her the phial, still two-thirds full, and she hastily shoved on the lid. "Here, wrap the rag around one end of this rod, while I keep an eye on the melting."

Finding herself a hand short, Lily slipped the phial into the hanging pocket which was tied around her waist beneath the folds of her dress.

"All blobby on one end," Holly specified. "We need a spill, too. I'll hold the rod..."

Lily passed over the duly wrapped rod and rolled a piece of stray paper tightly into a spill.

Holly was hunched over the brazier. "It's ready! Light the spill and pass me the rod! Oh—here it is. Watch this..."

Lily moved closer, spill in one hand and nose firmly pinched with the other. The rag went from white to yellow as Holly rolled it around in the melted yellowstone. Lily lit the spill from the brazier and stood poised.

"Light 'er up!" Holly shouted, a mad joy dancing in his eyes.

Lily put the spill to the rag at arm's distance, and a nasty yellow-gray smoke started to ooze out.

"Potato!" Holly cried. "Quickly!"

She dashed around him and seized the potato. Holly carefully lowered the smoking rag end of the rod through the bung-hole of the waiting barrel. He took the potato and pushed it onto the other end of the rod, before lowering the whole strange assemblage until the potato was resting on the outside of the barrel.

"Oh, so *that's* what the potato's for," Lily said, enlightened.

"Brilliant, isn't it? Never fails." There was a sudden thunk, and the potato rolled off the barrel. "Oh dear..."

The rank discoloured smoke began to seep out of the barrel and fog the room. Lily coughed and gagged.

"Ouch!" The forgotten spill had burned to the end and singed her fingers. She dropped it to the floor, where it immediately set fire to a wisp of straw. "Holly! Fire!"

Holly turned from his hectic flapping at the smoking barrel. His eyes widened at the sight of the growing conflagration on the floor.

"Step away!"

She retreated, coughing, into the corner as he reached

through the smoke for a large clear glass bottle on the shelf.

"Holly," she croaked, "that's not wa—"

Pop! went the cork. *Whoomph!* went the brandy as Holly poured it out. *Pock!* went the bottle as the bottom blew out in a stream of fire. Holly hastily dropped the remains. The barrel carried on smoking. Lily carried on coughing. The fire carried on spreading across the floor, borne on streams of blue flame.

"Don't worry!" Holly called. "It's all under control!" He was seized with a paroxysm of coughing, and knocked against the brazier. "Yeowch!"

The little iron pot tumbled to the floor, spilling what was left of the melted yellowstone. The quantity of stinking yellowed smoke increased noticeably. Lily could see Holly dimly at the other end of the room, crashing about with the barrels. She pushed further into the corner as the flames licked closer, seizing the despised apron and pressing it to her face. She was aware of Holly waltzing about with a large barrel, but her eyes were fixed on the advancing flame. Then all disappeared with a hiss and a sizzle as a wave of small-beer washed across the floor.

Small-beer being as close to water as it is possible to come without actually being water, this did the trick. It also washed the tarry remnants of everything else on the floor up to and over her shoes. A yellow stain began to creep up her dress.

"Holly!"

"There you are," Holly said, beaming at her across the wreckage. "All under control. What did I tell you?"

The bung bumped against her sodden shoe. She picked it up, grimaced her way across the sticky floor, and corked the still-smoking barrel without a word.

"I blame the potato," Holly said thoughtfully, but Lily did not stay to argue the point.

She had trailed almost up to the stairless kitchen entrance

before she realized that she was loose in the castle grounds, unsupervised. She could skirt round the castle and investigate the Hedge. She could even go looking for Burdock.

She stopped to consider this, and a miasma of rotten egg billowed up from her dress. Lily pressed her lips together and went inside. The Hedge would have to wait.

She was just opening her mouth to call pitifully for Aunt Hortensia, when she heard raised voices in the drawing room. To hear Aunt Hortensia's voice raised was not so unusual as to excite comment, but the other voice was Sennet's. She'd *never* heard him raise his voice before, not even when Holly's pet frog had spawned a mass of tadpoles in his bath. She stared at the drawing room door in silent shock—until she heard her name.

"Lily needs to know," Sennet said.

"She is only a child," returned Aunt Hortensia, her voice high and imperious.

"She will be of age in a matter of days," Sennet said. "You can't hide the truth from her forever. You can't hide *her* forever."

Lily crept closer to the drawing room door and found it slightly ajar.

"Master Sennet," Aunt Hortensia replied, the ice tinkling around the edges of her voice, "have the goodness to remember that Princess Lily is under my care. I have always acted in the manner I consider most consistent with her well-being, and I see no reason to change that merely because she is to celebrate another birthday."

"My lady," Sennet said, unusually impassioned, "I have obeyed you as Regent, as duty decreed. But time is running out…"

Lily pressed closer to the gap.

"Enough," Aunt Hortensia snapped. "I will not hear another word. My poor late sister pleaded with what were practically her last words that I should keep her only child safe."

"Lily will never take her place as queen if she stays here," Sennet returned, his voice stronger now.

Lily's breath caught in her throat. *What? Why?*

"But she *will* be safe," Aunt Hortensia insisted. "The world is an uncertain place, as you ought to know."

"I do. But it must be faced, sooner or later—and in my opinion, better sooner. I want only what's best for Lily, as you do."

Aunt Hortensia sniffed. "Well!" She broke off, and sniffed again. "What on earth is that smell?"

Lily darted away, appearing innocently at the entrance to the hall as Aunt Hortensia swept through the drawing room door.

⚜   ⚜   ⚜

An hour later, Lily was nearly drowsy with delight. Aunt Hortensia might be controlling, but she certainly knew how to make a fuss of someone.

She'd drawn Lily a hot, scented bath and laid out her softest, warmest dress to change into; and now Lily was tucked into the most comfortable chair in the drawing room, with a stool at her feet and a rabbit-fur shawl over her knees. The remains of an afternoon tea of legendary proportions stood on the table nearby.

This last was partly a peace offering from Holly, and partly the result of his brief but lively interview with Aunt Hortensia. Whether he'd had the threat of a catapult hanging over him, Lily wasn't sure, but he had certainly been inspired to produce his best. There were the lightest of scones—with honey *and* jam—as well as little cakes, dainty sandwiches, and even a delicious miniature lemon tart. The tea trolley had positively groaned as Holly wheeled it in.

"Another cup, Lily?" Aunt Hortensia enquired.

"No, thank you, Aunt—I believe I have had an elegant sufficiency."

Aunt Hortensia inclined her head and carried Lily's empty cup back to the trolley. Lily sighed happily and wiggled her toes towards the bright crackle of the fire. This was almost worth the unpleasantness in the brewhouse. Almost.

Her aunt returned, carrying a large folio beautifully bound in lavender. Sennet bowed and excused himself to the library, removing the trolley as he left.

"I thought perhaps you might enjoy looking through some of my sketches," Aunt Hortensia said, carefully laying the folio on Lily's lap. "I believe there are one or two portraits of you as an infant, as well as other scenes of interest from the time."

"Oh, *yes*, thank you!" Lily said.

This was a privilege she had hitherto been denied, and one that strongly suggested increased openness on the part of her aunt. Perhaps Master Sennet had not spoken in vain.

Aunt Hortensia took a seat nearby, where the light was best for needlework.

Lily turned the page, and found her mother looking at her with a sweet smile. "Oh, wasn't she beautiful!"

"Indeed she was," Aunt Hortensia said, her voice unaccustomedly quivery. "I trust you shall grow up to be just like her. She was the sweetest, gentlest young lady imaginable."

Lily leafed on through the pages, laughing at the chubby beribboned ball she once had been, and looking with interest at the scenic depictions of the palace in Denton—overshadowed by the great persimmon tree in the town square—and the fortress of Roxburghe.

"Oh, and here's Candra! Only I don't see the Hedge."

"A scenic artist is always free to take liberties with the scene before them in the interests of composition," Aunt Hortensia said briskly. "I believe I have mentioned this to you in your drawing classes."

"Oh, yes," Lily said, and turned the page hastily. Candra had looked uncomfortably exposed. "Who's this?"

A rather oddly dressed man stood by a handcart with all manner of items hanging off it: teapots and trowels and what appeared to be lengths of lace.

Aunt Hortensia leaned over with a creak of stays. "That is the pedlar—such a picturesque fellow, I simply had to sketch him."

"Where did you meet him? Was he in Denton, or...?"

"Don't allow your sentences to trail off, Lily. Always know what you intend to say, and say it."

"In Denton or somewhere else?"

"Dear me, the fellow was everywhere. I believe he travelled throughout the country, peddling his wares. We encountered him several times, and your father seemed quite taken with him. *Not* a suitable friendship, I would have thought, although I must say the man was always very well-spoken and polite."

Aunt Hortensia returned to her embroidery and Lily leafed on. She stopped to gaze at a picture of her father—rather a stiff depiction, she thought—and noticed a corner of paper sticking out from between the layers which made up the mounted pages of the folio. Aunt Hortensia appeared intent on her embroidery, so Lily hazarded a gentle tug on the corner. The thick paper moved without tearing. She worked it free and laid it flat on the page before her.

It was a pencil sketch of a rather handsome man—if sharp, angular features were to your taste. He seemed to be regarding her with the faintest hint of disdain—it was something about his eyes. They had been tinted pale blue, the only colour in the entire sketch.

"Aunt Hortensia, who's this?"

The only reply was a horrified gasp. The next moment Aunt Hortensia was beside her, the sketch snatched up in her hand and her embroidery forgotten on the floor.

"Where did you find this?"

"It was tucked behind this picture of Father," Lily said nervously. "I'm sorry if I—are you all right, Aunt?"

Aunt Hortensia was trembling, and so white as to appear almost blue. She set her lips and tore the sketch in half, then in half again, and again, until she could tear no more. Then the pieces were flung on the fire, and Aunt Hortensia sank into the fireside chair across from Lily's to watch them burn.

"Who was that?" Lily asked in a small voice.

"That was your father's *worthless* older brother," Aunt Hortensia replied, her normally restrained voice filled with fury.

Evil Uncle Phelan! A shiver went through her despite the rabbit-fur shawl.

"Uncle Phelan, who—who killed Mother and Father before the loyalists fought back and killed him?"

There was a silence. Aunt Hortensia continued to stare into the fire.

"Aunt Hortensia?"

"Yes," she said finally. "That is what happened. Now you must put him right out of your mind and never think of him again."

⚜   ⚜   ⚜

Contrary to Aunt Hortensia's instructions, Lily thought about a great many things that night, as she waited for the creak of the floorboard outside her door. When her aunt looked in, Lily put on a convincing performance of The Sleeping Innocent, the covers pulled up to hide her darkest dress: a blue velvet which was only to be worn on very special occasions.

Well, this *was* a special occasion, Lily reasoned as her aunt left the room. More importantly, this was an occasion for not being seen.

She slipped out of bed, put on her matching shoes, and arranged a bolster in her bed, to be on the safe side. Creeping down the stairs with a guilty thrill, she was halfway to the front door when she heard the board creak again overhead.

Heart pounding, Lily took to the nearest shelter: the statue of Queen Magnolia as a young woman.

Aunt Hortensia came down the stairs, and Lily stopped breathing altogether. Her aunt didn't appear to be searching, however; she had on her warm winter pelisse, and as Lily watched, she crossed the hall and went out the front door. Aunt Hortensia sneaking out in the night? It didn't seem possible.

Still, there was no way Lily was going to follow her aunt out the front door—that was just asking for trouble. She would have to take the back way, through the kitchens and round by the kitchen garden. It wasn't much further this way; Burdock's cottage was to the south of the castle, just visible from the long windows of the ballroom.

Lily dashed through the vegetables, screened by the garden's wall, and crept across the grass, avoiding the crunchy gravel path despite the damp assailing her shoes. There was no sign of Aunt Hortensia, but there was, she could see, a light in Burdock's window. Perhaps he had taken a turn for the worse...

Now she could hear voices. She slid around the corner of the cottage and crouched, heart thudding, under the slightly open window.

"You *agreed*," Aunt Hortensia was saying fiercely.

"The situation has changed," a hoarse voice replied.

Lily realized with a little shock that it must be Burdock speaking. She'd never heard him say more than a word at a time before, and that word was usually "eh." And now here he was using whole sentences with polysyllabic words? Perhaps it was Master Sennet with a cold. But no, *that* was Sennet—saying that he was sure an agreement could be reached. Poor Master Sennet; he liked to think everything could be solved through diplomacy.

"I can't maintain the Hedge for much longer," Burdock was

saying.

"You *must*," Aunt Hortensia said.

Was that all this was about: a gardening dispute?

"I am growing weak faster than I had thought possible," Burdock said.

If Burdock was sick, why was Aunt Hortensia insisting he keep on with the garden work? He was a very good gardener, but it wasn't as though none of the castle residents knew how to prune or weed. Arcelian children learned to garden almost before they could walk. It was strangely unkind.

"I must speak to her," Burdock wheezed. "She's old enough to know."

Know what? *Know what?*

"I forbid it," Aunt Hortensia said. "Master Sennet, you will not cooperate with this madness."

"Yes, Lady Hortensia," Sennet sighed.

"Our sole purpose is to keep Lily safe," Aunt Hortensia went on. "No one must be allowed to endanger her—for whatever reason."

"Soon, there will be no safety anywhere," Burdock whispered.

"I do not wish to hear another word," Aunt Hortensia said firmly. "Master Sennet, kindly give me your arm."

Lily held her breath. The door creaked, and the gravel crunched as her guardians departed, keeping up a muttered debate as they moved away. Lily waited for them to move out of hearing before she dared move. There was no way she could get back to the castle before them, and following too close invited discovery. But there was one thing she could do...

Tingling all over with excitement, she got to her feet and cautiously picked her way to the cottage door. It creaked as she opened it, and she froze. There was no response, so she shook herself, slipped inside the door and pulled it closed behind her.

The cottage appeared to consist of one room, with a table and chair on one side and a funny sort of long box with curtains over it on the other side—like the beds she'd seen in fairy tales.

Then a hand pulled aside the curtain, and Lily gasped. It wasn't Burdock at all. It was an old man with a cloud of white hair, dressed in ragged green. A stranger.

Downhill from Here

"Lily!"

She backed towards the door. It was Burdock's voice, or the voice she'd thought was Burdock's, but...

"Don't be afraid, my lady," the old man said, pulling himself up in the bed, half out into the light.

He was very frail, whoever he was.

"Are you Burdock," Lily asked cautiously, "or...or...?"

Or who?

"Yes and no," he wheezed. "I have been acting the part of a gardener since you came here."

"You're very good at it, for someone who's only pretending," Lily said.

He gave a brief half-laugh, stopping on the brink of a cough.

"I am, in truth, a gardener," he said. "But my name is not Burdock. I assumed the name—and the face—at your aunt's insistence."

Lily blinked at him. What on *earth* had made Aunt Hortensia demand someone change their name and their appearance—no, how was that even *possible?* He didn't look anything like Burdock; it couldn't possibly be a disguise.

"My name is Woodward," he said, and a little colour and strength came into his face at the very mention of the name.

"Woodward the *wizard?*" Lily gaped at him. "From the stories?"

She'd seen illustrations, but he looked so much weedier in person that she hadn't noted the resemblance.

"From Arcelia," he said. "Your aunt forbade me to make myself known to you."

"But why? And what's happening to the Hedge?"

He sighed. "The Hedge—no, there's no time for that now. The daily rites, the rotation of crops, the yearly festivals—do you know why we do all these things?"

"For the good of the land," Lily said, "and ourselves, of course," she added dutifully.

"How are they for the good of the land?"

"Well, they're...good for it," Lily said lamely. "It's just what you do."

"Hortensia has a lot to answer for," the wizard muttered. He pulled himself up further in his bed, leaning against a sagging pillow. "The ceremonial gardens; the rites and observances of each day and week; the rhythm of the year; all these ensure the health of the land. The health of the land is the magic of Arcelia. The life of Arcelia."

Lily blinked, trying to take all this in.

"So the Hedge is browning because...?"

"Never mind the Hedge for now. What has she told you of Restoration Day?"

At least she could show him she knew something. "On the twenty-second of Grenian, every fiftieth year, the monarch stands on the balcony of the palace in Denton, sounds the Horn of Vale to summon the people, and then descends to the square to unlock the land with the Persimmon Key, thus restoring to each family their ancestral lands, regardless of loss or sale."

"Wearing the Lunula," Woodward added.

"Oh, yes."

How could she have forgotten the most beautiful of the three Requisites? She'd only ever seen a picture of it, but it was a sort of crescent, decorated with the phases of the moon—rather like a tiara except for being solid instead of lacy.

"And the next Restoration Day is?"

Lily opened her mouth and closed it again. "I don't know. No one's ever said."

Woodward sighed deeply. "This is the year. The Requisites—the Lunula, the Horn of Vale and the Persimmon Key—were taken away for safekeeping during the War. You must retrieve them before Restoration Day."

"But...today is the thirty-first of Budd!" Lily said in dismay. "Grenian starts tomorrow. That means Restoration Day is less than a month away!"

Woodward closed his eyes, apparently in some pain.

"Can't it be put off?" Lily asked. "I'm not nearly ready," she added, thinking of her wardrobe and its total unsuitability for a royal progress. If only Aunt Hortensia would let her dress like a proper grown-up lady, instead of a girl not even old enough to put up her hair!

Woodward propped himself up on one elbow.

"Restoration Day is the most important rite of all," he said with wheezing emphasis. "Do you know the Fate?" He sagged back into the bed.

"Of course," Lily said. She took up a suitable pose and recited the poem which Arcelian children had been taught since time out of mind.

> When the round of life is broken
>   with the breaking of the year;
> When the orphan and the widow
>   weep in darkness and in fear;
> When the kin of Vale have weakened
>   till they cannot bear the load;
> When the heartless masters beat them
>   to their knees under the goad;

When the people are divided
   from each other and the land;
When their holdings are abandoned
   into few and grasping hands;
When the land cannot lie fallow,
   but is stripped of all it bears;
When the dead cannot lie easy
   in the land that once was theirs;
When the poor man's debts shall drive him
   into thralldom for his bread;
And the people shall fall silent
   in the shadow of their dread;
Then, in hunger, crops shall dwindle
   under flood and slip and frost;
To a foreigner's dominion
   shall the land at last be lost.

"That is what will happen if Restoration Day does not," Woodward said, eyes closed and face pained. "The death of the magic of Arcelia."

"Oh," Lily said, sobered. She could not neglect her duty to her country... And of course, there would be dressmakers in Denton. She cheered up. "I'm sure I can manage it."

She could see herself already, clad in robes of silver and white, her head crowned with the elegant silver sweep of the Lunula. She stood on the balcony with her people gathered below, watching her with eager eyes as she lifted the jewelled horn to her lips. She took a deep breath, and realized that Woodward was speaking—had been speaking for some time, his breath a mere zephyr past the bed-hangings. She leaned closer.

"...ashamed to send you out so unprovided for, but I can see no other way. As the magic has waned, so have I. I may not survive the breaching of the Hedge."

"I thought you were immortal," Lily said, startled out of politeness.

"So did I…" He turned his eyes to her. "You must leave Candra, my lady. You must go through the Hedge."

"But why should that hurt you?"

"As you have noticed, it is dying. I have drained myself to maintain the illusion that protects you…and I wither. When the need for the Hedge ends, I can rest, and I do not know but that my rest may be forever."

"Then I won't go," Lily said. "Not if it's going to kill you."

"It will kill me if you don't," he said. "I and Arcelia both."

"Then I'll go now," Lily said, taking a step towards the door. He gazed at her, his faded eyes wet.

"I am sorry I could not protect you better. I was…overconfident. I did not realize…"

"That's all right," Lily said. "I've had quite enough of being protected." *More* than enough. Really, *why* Aunt Hortensia thought she shouldn't know—!

"Once you leave Candra, there will be no returning," he said. "Once you pass through the Hedge, Candra will be seen as it is, not as the overgrown ruin I have made it seem."

Lily frowned at him. From the way he was carrying on, anyone would think people wouldn't be glad to see her when she finally returned. After waiting for fifteen years!

"I do not wish to deceive you." He was whispering now. "Hortensia wished to keep you in ignorance, but you must know the truth before you…"

His voice was fading, and he beckoned her nearer. She stooped, but then straightened in a flash at the crunch of feet on the telltale gravel outside.

"…danger…"

He didn't have to tell her that. Lily had not lived fifteen years at Candra without recognizing her aunt's step when she heard it. She looked around, but there was nowhere to hide—and now no time. The door was flung open so violently that it hit the wall and swung back. Aunt Hortensia stood framed in the doorway, her eyes burning with cold fire.

"Lily, come away from him!"

"But—"

"Now!"

Aunt Hortensia seized Lily's arm and yanked her away, hustling her through the doorway with a hand on each shoulder.

Locking one of Lily's arms under hers, she turned back to the lighted room and addressed the wizard. "Stay away from her. I ought to have known better than to trust you again!"

She pulled the door shut with a light bang, and started back along the gravel path at a speed Lily struggled to match.

"I do not know what he may have told you," Aunt Hortensia said, "but I can assure you he is not to be trusted. He has broken his promise..."

"He's dying, Aunt Hortensia!"

"Nonsense," Aunt Hortensia sniffed. "Woodward is not human; he is not mortal."

"He said he thought he wasn't mortal, but he is."

"And you believed him? Be careful now; the stairs are a little slippery. Make sure you have both feet firmly on the step before you take another."

After five slow step-together, step-together, the thin rim of patience holding Lily's temper in finally cracked and gave way. She tore her arm away from her aunt and skipped lightly up the remaining steps, two at a time. Aunt Hortensia staggered against the wall, her face ghastly in the moonlight.

"Lily! Come back at once! No—stay where you are! Don't move!"

Lily stamped. "Stop telling me what to do! I'm nearly eighteen, I'm old enough to go up and down stairs by myself, and I'm old enough to play my part in Restoration Day!"

"You don't understand the dangers! You must trust me; have I not always done what was best for you?"

"I don't know," Lily said, astounded to find that this was true. She didn't know, not really.

"Have I ever allowed you to come to harm?" Aunt Hortensia demanded.

"N-no," Lily said. "But..." She was confused. There was too much to think over, and she hadn't had the time.

"But nothing," Aunt Hortensia said briskly. "Come along. You ought to have been asleep hours ago. We will discuss the penalty for your deceptiveness and disobedience tomorrow. I am more disappointed with your conduct than I can say."

Lily glowered silently all the way to her room, Aunt Hortensia ramrod straight at her side.

"You will stay in your room until further notice," Aunt Hortensia said, and closed the door.

Lily heard the scrape of metal on metal. *Surely not...* She rushed to the door and rattled at the handle in vain. By the time she stopped, she was panting.

Aunt Hortensia had locked her in. She was a prisoner in her own castle.

⚜ ⚜ ⚜

The first lavender light of dawn began to creep across the sky, far across the valley. Lily stood at the window, her breath coming short and fast. Today was the day of her destiny...

She had arrayed herself in a lacy afternoon-dress of shell pink, her matching satin dancing slippers and a heavy velvet cloak in the slightly deeper colour Aunt Hortensia called *faded rose.*

The cape's deep hood concealed the sort of chignon Aunt Hortensia didn't approve of for girls, as well as the dark shadows under Lily's eyes. She'd never been up all night before, and it both frightened and excited her.

Lily took a deep breath to steady herself and stepped out through the window onto the roof. A queen ought not to have to sneak out across the roofs like this, but there was nothing else for it. Aunt Hortensia would be guarding her like a hawk. The main thing was to be well away before she rose.

The sun began to rise over the eastern mountains, the first rays crossing the valley in a single step and gilding one side of the castle roofs. Lily paced serenely along the ridge of the main roof towards Scholars' Tower, her breath showing in little puffs against the shadows.

If memory served... She inched her way along to where a sturdy cast-iron pipe led down to the service wing. It took some less-than-elegant manoeuvring to get in a position where she could take hold of the pipe without losing her grip on the roof above, but it wasn't long before she stood firmly on the lower roof, shaking her skirts out and smoothing her ruffled dignity.

From here it would be a piece of cake. Roof ridge to gable-window roof, gable-window roof to gutter, gutter to the raised roof of the laundry, laundry roof to ground-floor roof, ground-floor roof to the top of the woodshed, and from there it was a mere hop down to the back courtyard.

Having carried out this programme, Lily gave herself a quick once-over and found no other damage than a bit of damp from the dew. Excellent. She heard Holly yodelling something cheerful to himself in the kitchen and decided it would be best if he didn't see her. Not that she doubted his loyalty, but he couldn't keep a secret to save himself, and Aunt Hortensia was terribly good at extracting the truth.

Hurrying from the courtyard into the adjoining kitchen garden, she skipped through the rows of stolid cabbages—which she would *never* eat again, she decided, unless they were sautéed with butter and caraway, the way Holly served them on special days—and out the door in the far wall. The castle parklands stretched out before her, gowned in silver dew. The sight took her breath away for a moment, and an unfamiliar pang assailed her. Then her ear caught a crunch of gravel, and she ducked back into the cover of the doorway.

Master Sennet was up early, and heading towards Woodward's cottage. Lily bit her lip. The longer she waited, the more likely she was to be discovered, and who knew how long Sennet would be? She could appeal to his loyalty, but it was impossible to be sure which way he would decide his duty fell. Perhaps she had better just go without seeing Woodward again. What more was there to be said? She darted past the ballroom windows, her cloak hem brushing the grass free from dew behind her.

Lily spared a moment for the morning rite in the ceremonial garden, alone there for the first time in her life. The serenity of the dewy morning seemed to fill her as she rose and glided away. She had picked out the place for her entry into the world the night before. She would depart from the eastern side of the castle grounds, which would save her having to walk around the outside of the Hedge before heading down the eastern flank of the mountain towards Denton, the capital. *Her* capital.

As she approached the Hedge, she could see that the brown tinge had deepened. It was only the edges that were dying, though; the heart of each shrub that made up the Hedge still showed strong dark green. Now that she looked at it in the growing light of day, it seemed sturdier than her imagination had rendered it last night. She had imagined herself passing through it like a ghost, the brown foliage crumbling away as she went. Nothing would pass through this like a ghost—not even a sword. Perhaps it was thinner further along…

It wasn't. She chose the brownest-looking area, crouched down to see where the trunks were, and positioned herself between them. This was it. She was going Out. She took a deep breath and walked into the Hedge. A twig poked her in the eye.

Lily recoiled, eye watering freely. She dabbed the offended eye with her lacy handkerchief. It must be possible to get through, because Woodward had said she had to. She certainly wasn't going to crawl under it. That was one area where she and Aunt Hortensia saw eye to eye: Ladies do not crawl on their bellies in the dirt.

Lily set her jaw. She wasn't going to take any nonsense from a string of shrubs! She put her head down and tried to part the branches with her arms, and this time the twig scratched her hand. She wrapped the handkerchief around it tenderly and scowled at the Hedge.

"I am your queen," she said, in a threatening undertone, narrowing her eyes beneath her hood. "You *will* allow me to pass." She stepped forward.

Hedges were no respecters of persons, evidently, for the springy growth rebounded against her with just as much vigour as before. She was tweaking her garments back into place when a quiet click sounded across the crisp stillness of the castle grounds.

Lily turned to see the cottage door opening, and in desperation she plunged into the Hedge, snapping off twigs, then little branches, forcing her way into the midst of it. One branch tugged down her hood. She turned her head to free the hood and another branch snagged her hair. This enraged her, and she began breaking branches in earnest, bending the larger ones back and forth until they gave way and stayed where she put them.

The darkness of the privet began to give way to the light of early morning. Lily plunged towards it, trampling branches and bending them back with no thought for aught but getting out of the Hedge. One last large branch would not break or bend, but forced her to squeeze herself painfully past it. She half-fell out into tall grass, finding to her relief that no one had witnessed her ordeal. Silence reigned behind her. Master Sennet must have been preoccupied. She took a deep breath to compose herself.

Lily felt a tug at her skirts and yanked them free with a snap and a tearing noise. *Oh dear.* She surveyed the rip. It would want mending, certainly, but now was not perhaps the time. Lace hid rips well, and the Hedge showed browner where she had gone through it—browner every time she looked, in fact.

One bold step towards the rising sun and she was half-choked by her cloak. Lily took the time to free it carefully from where it had snagged on the Hedge, velvet not being so easy to hide rips in as lace. She could almost see through the Hedge where she had fought her way through, and she began to feel guilty. She'd never mistreated a plant in her life, and now look what she'd done! The cloak dropped free, and she bit her lip.

She laid an awkward hand on the Hedge. "You did a good job, and I think you can stop now."

There was a creak, and the Hedge sagged slightly in front of her. She took a precautionary step backwards. Yes, the brown was definitely spreading—spreading as she watched. Was Woodward—?

It didn't bear thinking about. She had her quest to fulfil, and she'd better be about it before Aunt Hortensia unlocked her door and found the bolster in the bed again. Lily shook her skirts into order (hiding as much of the damage as possible) and started forth on the quest for her kingdom.

Her way lay at first through a meadow. It was remarkably overgrown considering that it was only the first day of spring—though to be fair, the winter had been mild—and there were flowers blooming here and there. Lily gave herself a little examination on the names and symbolic meanings of those she knew, and was pleased to award herself the very highest of marks. She even picked herself a posy of the more felicitous ones—spring crocus for youthful gladness and the pleasures of hope, snowdrops for consolation, and heartsease for thoughts—and tucked it in the sash of her dress. The ranunculus—*ingratitude*—she carefully ignored, and kept walking.

From her geography lessons, she knew that Candra was built atop a mountain in the Western Ranges. Denton was more or less at the foot of the mountain, on the floor of the valley which constituted the kingdom of Arcelia. This flat bit, or rather *plateau,* wouldn't go on for much longer, then. Which was just as well, as she had the horrible feeling that she might still be visible from the higher parts of the castle, and she might already have been missed. It occurred to her that Master Sennet had a telescope in his study, and she quickened her pace.

Or, rather, she tried to. As romantic as it seemed to be walking through a meadow of wildflowers, the grass was actually quite long, and quite hard to pass through. Walking fast seemed a recipe for tripping on tangled stems and taking a fall. Not queenly in the least.

To her relief, Lily soon reached the edge of the plateau. The ground—less overgrown now—dropped gently away before her feet, and the view—! The lower slopes of the mountain were thickly forested, the eastern mountains stood tall and proud, and the valley itself swam in a soft mist. It was *beautiful.* It was hers, and she loved it, and she was sure it loved her too. She was unsure of when or where her people would come to meet her, but happily, it was all downhill from here.

It was a beautiful morning, the sun was beaming down on the fresh, springy meadow, and Lily could not have kept her heart from soaring if she had wished to. She felt justified in thinking she was doing rather well, in fact. Aunt Hortensia might well be upset now, but when Lily returned at the head of a cheering crowd, dripping with Requisites and hailed as queen, well, Aunt Hortensia couldn't very well scold, could she? She might even curtsy, although Lily felt that this was probably a little too much to expect, however technically correct it might be.

Of course, it wouldn't all be cheering crowds and beautiful dresses and jewellery. There would be State Dinners and Diplomatic Conversation and Balls. There might even be more dashing dance partners than Master Sennet and Holly (who danced creakily and bouncily, respectively). Handsome young foreign princes, perhaps. Aunt Hortensia had touched upon the subject but lightly, deeming it not yet suited to Lily's tender years, but the novels in the library with the rose-patterned end-papers had a good deal to say on the subject, albeit, Lily considered, somewhat repetitively, and poorly illustrated.

Lily picked her way down the mountainside, imagining a bevy of smartly uniformed princes with indistinct watercolour features, hanging on her every word. It was a charming dream, until Lily tripped on a thick tussock and, nearly falling headlong, decided she had better pay a little more attention to her present situation.

It was at this point that she realized she was hungry. Not only that, but she had not had the foresight to bring any food with her. Aunt Hortensia was most severe upon the impropriety of Keeping Comestibles in One's Bedroom, and there was no way she could have raided the kitchens without Holly finding out. It would have been no good.

Lily sighed and drifted to a halt. Now she thought about it, she felt weak—terribly weak. Was this some dreadful effect of breaching the Hedge that Woodward hadn't warned her about? She sank down on a tussock. She was so tired, she could almost wish she were back in her bed at Candra, so soft, so comfortable—so long ago! In fact, she hadn't actually *slept* in her bed since the night after Burdock had disappeared. No wonder she was tired. She was out of sight of Candra. Perhaps she'd just have a little nap to refresh herself…

Lily lay down among the tussocks—which weren't as comfortable as they looked—and carefully arranged her cloak for the most becoming effect, just in case a passing peasant or shepherd should happen upon her. Remembering the princess who had slept for a hundred years, only to be wakened by a kiss, Lily carefully removed the posy from her sash. Clasping it in one hand, she put it to her nose—thus fending off any potential kisses—and fell asleep, breathing in the scent of snowdrops.

⚜   ⚜   ⚜

She was woken by a piercing scream.

Lily's eyes jolted open and she sat up, heart pounding. The sun was gone, the sky was dark, glowering with storm clouds, and the voice that had screamed was now laughing, crying, sobbing with joy. She turned, and there, tottering down the hill towards her, was Aunt Hortensia. Lily got to her feet, shook out her skirts and braced herself for the impact.

In but a moment Aunt Hortensia was upon her, shaking her, kissing her, clasping her to her bosom—or, at least, to her corset, which was rather unyielding—and showering her with tears and reproaches. It was all very uncomfortable.

"Aunt Hortensia—"

"How *could* you, Lily? You have no *idea* of the—"

"Aunt Hortensia, we're going to be caught in the rain," Lily said loudly.

This was, as she had hoped, enough to derail the scolding for now. Aunt Hortensia was a firm believer in the dreadful consequences of Getting Caught Out In The Rain. It began with a chill, and the next thing you knew it was double pneumonia and your loved ones were airing their mourning clothes and ordering black-edged notepaper.

"Come, we must go back at once," Aunt Hortensia said, taking firm hold of Lily's hand and starting uphill again.

"No," said Lily, planting her feet.

"Lily!"

"We'll never make it back to Candra before the rain," Lily pleaded. And neither of them were dressed for it.

Fear might have hastened Aunt Hortensia's steps downhill, but Lily was quite certain she wouldn't be able to outrun a rainstorm uphill. Neither would Lily, of course, and she didn't fancy getting soaked to the skin any more than her aunt did.

"We must get you home as soon as possible! In any case, there is no shelter to be had here."

"We could shelter in the Forest of Renwick," Lily said. "That would be a bit drier, at least." It was also further downhill and closer to Denton, but Lily had no intention of pointing this out.

Aunt Hortensia hesitated, the first time Lily could remember seeing her do so. There was a distant flash, which illuminated the lines around Aunt Hortensia's eyes, followed by a rumble of thunder. Lily looked away, embarrassed to have seen the fear in her aunt's eyes, and more embarrassed to have been the cause of it. There was another flash, another rumble.

"Aunt Hortensia, I think we'd better go into the forest."

"In a lightning storm? Supposing a tree is hit and falls on you? Or starts a forest fire?" Aunt Hortensia seemed to be having trouble breathing.

"It's more dangerous out here," Lily said. "Master Sennet says that lightning takes the shortest route to the ground—it hits whatever is highest. Which would be us," she added, in case her aunt had not taken the moral of the story.

There was another flash, nearer at hand, which seemed to make up Aunt Hortensia's mind for her. She took Lily's arm and hurried her downhill towards the forest.

The first drops of rain came pattering down as they reached the edge of the trees. Aunt Hortensia put an arm over Lily, in a patently useless attempt to shield her from the wet, and hurried her into the thicker parts of the forest, where they might reasonably expect to find a drier place to wait out the rain. The underbrush caught at their skirts and stockings, and Lily draped the tail of her cloak over one arm; it was easier that way. Aunt Hortensia, however, wouldn't lift her skirt hem to step over obstacles, which slowed them further.

The slower pace gave her aunt a chance to catch her breath, and having recovered it, she put it to good use. She spoke long and well of her shock at finding Lily gone; Lily's unbecoming underhandedness in defying the locked door ("and how you made good your infamous escape, I *dread* to consider,"); the promises she had made to her dearly departed sister (Lily's late lamented mother), practically on her *deathbed*, that she would care for and protect her sister's only child; the years, the sacrifices she had poured into ensuring that very safety; and returning by that path to the present, she once more went over the agonies of spirit she had undergone on finding all her efforts wasted.

She hinted darkly at being revived from a dead faint by Sennet with one of Holly's phials, which she could only *hope* contained sal volatile. (Certainly volatile, Holly had said.) She had resolved on setting out *instantly* to restore her erring niece to as much safety as could be provided for such a heedless, headstrong girl, and had left Sennet and Holly guarding the castle, anxiously awaiting the fugitive's safe return and pleading to be allowed to take part in the rescue themselves.

It was a dramatic and affecting tale, but Lily thought it prudent to make no reply; and if Aunt Hortensia chose to interpret her silence as docility, well, Lily was not going to tell her otherwise. Yet.

The forest of Renwick had a thick canopy, but water will descend, one way or another, and the rain was coming down steadily. Lily had had more than one dollop of cold water down the back of her neck, and was starting to wonder if going home to Candra and setting out better provisioned might be the more sensible course. This led her to think of Woodward, and wonder whether he had survived the Breaching of the Hedge—or the Wrath of Aunt Hortensia.

"Is Woodward…?" she asked, unwilling to state the question baldly, and unsure of how else to put it.

Aunt Hortensia sniffed. "Took himself off," she said, her voice quivering with wrath.

"What?"

"Naturally, it was my first suspicion upon finding your *shameful* deception repeated." (The bolster, Lily presumed.) "Imagine my horror when I discovered not only that you were not present, but that he, pledged to protect you, had absented himself! I had Sennet search the cottage in case he was, er, otherwise occupied—" (relieving himself, Lily judged by the pinker hue on Aunt Hortensia's cheek), "—but he had quitted the place entirely."

Lily's heart lurched. Surely, Woodward couldn't just cease to exist?

"Betaken himself to his eyrie, I shouldn't wonder." Aunt Hortensia sniffed, and stopped dead. "Lily, you have not encountered anyone, have you? Not met anyone by the way?"

"No, Aunt Hortensia."

"Not even in the distance?"

"I haven't seen a soul," Lily said, wondering why her aunt was making such heavy weather about this.

"I am most relieved to hear it."

Aunt Hortensia took two paces forward and then stopped again. Lily braced herself, wondering what she was to be interrogated about next.

"Lily, stay here, and don't move. Not an inch, do you hear me? And don't make a noise."

Lily waited, dripping, as her aunt moved away through the trees. Perhaps this was her opportunity to—

Aunt Hortensia reappeared, beckoning.

Opportunity lost. Lily reluctantly picked her way through the wet underbrush to where her aunt stood. It was a cave,

with a sort of tumble-down stone wall across the front giving
it the semblance of a room. Inside the cave, it was blessedly
dry, if rather cool. Lily shivered.

"Out of that wet cloak, this very moment," Aunt Hortensia
ordered, "and if you are not taken ill it will be a mercy, and
one I'm sure you don't deserve."

Lily complied, and was glad to find the cloak had absorbed
most of the rain. It was sodden; the rest of her clothes were
merely damp. Aunt Hortensia laid the cloak and her own wet
pelisse on a wide ledge at one side of the cave. The coverings
made it look even more like a bed, Lily thought, and she tried
to stifle the thought of her warm soft bed at home, along with
a yawn. She shivered again.

"Chilled," Aunt Hortensia chided. "As I thought. You
had better walk briskly up and down the room until you are
warmed through."

Privately, Lily felt that she had done quite enough walking
today, but there was no arguing with Aunt Hortensia. Except,
she thought gloomily as she paced up and down, there would
have to be, or there would be no quest for her; it would be
back up the hill to Candra, in disgrace until she was practically ninety. Arguing with Aunt Hortensia didn't bear thinking about, but she would have to. She shivered once more, and
paced faster.

Aunt Hortensia stood guard at the front of the cave, looking
out at the falling rain. If only a welcoming party would come
to the cave and carry her off in triumph to Denton, over-ruling
Aunt Hortensia completely! Mind you, they would have to
know that she had left Candra, and where she was... But, of
course! Woodward would tell them; that must be why he had
left Candra. That, and to avoid Aunt Hortensia.

At least, being here, she could tidy herself up and wait for
the welcoming party in some semblance of comfort. Just as
well Aunt Hortensia was guarding the entrance, really; she

would keep everyone at bay until Lily was ready to receive them. She could see it now: the dignitaries gathering around the cave—at a respectful distance, of course, no jostling—and finally Aunt Hortensia's mauve-clad figure stepping back into the darkness to give way to a dainty shell-pink form, appearing gracefully at the entrance with a shy wave. The dignitaries huzzahed, and threw their hats in the air.

"Lily, you will catch a chill standing about like that!"

Lily sighed and resumed her pacing. It was a lovely, heart-warming scene, and she replayed it several times in her mind, with extra emphasis given to the part where Aunt Hortensia stepped back into the shadows. Then her imagination moved onto the coronation ball, and she began to insert little half-steps in her pacing, with a twirl at the end to turn her back again.

"Lily, I trust I do not see you *dancing*, at a moment like this! Consider the trouble you have caused, and if that does not steady you, I shall indeed despair."

Lily sighed again, and stopped in the middle of the floor. Her stomach growled. Aunt Hortensia stiffened.

"Really, I can only hope my ears deceive me."

"I haven't had anything to eat since dinner yesterday," Lily said, half under her breath.

"And whose fault is that, I should like to know? Perhaps it will do you good to have an unseasonable fast day, to consider the duty you owe to your elders, and how far you have fallen from it."

Lily clamped her mouth shut, gritting her teeth against the words that wanted to come frothing out.

"Don't clench your jaw; it is most unladylike. And why do I not see you walking?"

Lily turned on her heel and paced very slowly towards the back of the cave, making the foulest faces she could contort her features into. There was the ghost of a sigh from the front of the cave.

"It is rather hard to tell in these conditions, but I expect it will be tea time by now."

Lily slumped. This was the final blow. Afternoon tea was her favourite meal of the day, and to think of it being served now, by the library fire, without a morsel in her stomach to comfort her! Even the simplest of teas would be a delight, even if it were no more than a plain scone with butter. Her stomach growled again.

"Lily! Stand up straight, for goodness' sake. Being in disgrace is no reason to slouch about as though you were some sort of low tavern wench."

Lily could bear no more.

"Aunt Hortensia, I'm going on a quest for the Restoration Requisites," she said, her ears seeming to cower away from her mouth's audacity. "I'm sorry I left without telling you, but you wouldn't listen."

"I trust I know better than—"

Lily ploughed on, casting aside caution along with Rule #5 ("a lady never interrupts"). "I am the queen of Arcelia, and my country needs me! I'm grown up now, and I know what I'm doing. I don't know why you don't trust Woodward, but I do—and I don't trust you!" There was no going back now. "You're so frightened because of what happened to Mother and Father that you're too scared to let me do anything. You want to keep me a baby forever. Well, you can't! I'm grown up now, and I'll do as I please!" She stamped. "And I'm going on my quest, whether you like it or not. Even if you think you can drag me back up to Candra, I'll run away again and again. Even if you lock me in! Because that's what you want, isn't it? To keep me a prisoner forever!"

She looked up through angry tears and saw her aunt totter backwards, a hand clasped to her bosom. A wave of guilt swept over her.

Lily rushed over, and in the dim grey light saw a blue tinge to her aunt's lips.

"Aunt Hortensia! I'm so sorry, I didn't mean to hurt you, I didn't mean..." She felt clumsier and more foolish by the moment. "You're not well. Let me help you to a seat."

The blue tinge faded, to Lily's great relief, but still Aunt Hortensia spoke not a word. Lily began to take fright, and in the coldness which followed the hot rush of words, she was not certain she could withstand any reply that came.

"Supposing you have a little lie-down. I'll make a cushion for your head." She bundled the cloak and pelisse together into a makeshift pillow. It was a little damp, but anything would be better than resting one's head on the cold stone.

Aunt Hortensia gave a faint gasp, and lay down, closing her eyes. Lily backed away. She couldn't leave her aunt like this; she *couldn't*. She would have to wait for her to recover, and then set out again. Lily sighed, and went to look out at the pouring rain. Regret set in, and she was guiltily aware that it was not unmixed with triumph. But she *had* to go, for Arcelia's sake. Aunt Hortensia must be made to understand.

"Aunt Hortensia," she said, her voice echoing against the walls of the cave, "I shall still go on my quest."

There was no response.

"I thought you ought to know," Lily said, in a smaller voice. She waited.

"Aunt Hortensia?"

She crept back into the cave. Aunt Hortensia was asleep already. The confrontation would have to wait.

❦   ❦   ❦

Lily woke with a squeak from a confused nightmare in which the Castle of Candra had turned into a dandelion and blown away. A moment's glance reminded her where she was, and reassured her that her noises had not woken Aunt Hortensia.

She was a solid mass of aches, she found as she prised herself off the floor, and numb in more than one place. Variegated green light filtered in through the cave mouth; the morning sun was shining through.

Lily got to her feet and dusted herself off. Strange that Aunt Hortensia had slept so long. Perhaps she would have to make early-tea noises to wake her. She coughed politely. Aunt Hortensia did not respond.

"Aunt Hortensia?"

Still nothing. Lily frowned, remembered her aunt's strictures on avoiding premature lines and wrinkles, and stopped. Aunt Hortensia wasn't usually a heavy sleeper. In fact, as Lily knew to her cost, a mere suspicious creak of a floorboard was usually enough to wake her and summon her forth to investigate. Stranger still, her aunt didn't seem to have moved at all during the night. Aunt Hortensia might conceivably be as disciplined in her sleep as in everything else, but she didn't have so much as a wrinkle in her skirts—not a fold out of place. It wasn't natural.

"Aunt Hortensia?" Lily enquired gently. "Aunt Hortensia!"

Not a twitch.

"Aunt Hortensia!" she shrieked, feeling a fool, and terrified, and half-wishing her aunt would suddenly start to scold her for being so unmannerly as to shout at her elders. Lily took her aunt by the shoulder and tried to shake her gently, but she was unmovable, as though part of the rock. Aunt Hortensia was dead! Lily caught her breath in a terrified sob, the dreadful weight of guilt already pressing her down. But wait! Was she imagining—? No, there was movement still: a slow and gentle rise and fall. Aunt Hortensia was—just barely—breathing.

Lily straightened up and leaned against the cave wall, sobbing with relief. The rough stone scratched her face; there was a pattern carved over the ledge. She leaned closer. It was some sort of plant, by the looks of it, only visible when the light struck it at just the right angle. Her finger traced the lines, and a memory awoke in her mind. Vervain.

The little rock-drawing was of a sprig of vervain, a scented plant much beloved of butterflies and—her heart lurched—symbolic of enchantment.

Recognition

Aunt Hortensia was in an enchanted sleep. It didn't seem real. It was too much like the story of the princess who slept a hundred years. Lily went pink at the thought of Aunt Hortensia waiting to be woken by her true love's kiss.

Perhaps I ought to fetch Master Sennet. Lily blushed again. Aunt Hortensia would never have hinted by so much as a breath—and nor would Master Sennet, of course—but Lily had eyes. She *would* fetch Master Sennet.

And tell him what? That Aunt Hortensia was in an enchanted sleep and he needed to come and kiss her? Lily went hot and cold all over just thinking about it. No, that wouldn't do at all. And, in any case, she didn't really *know* that Aunt Hortensia could be revived by a kiss. Or by anything.

She batted the thought away. She wasn't an expert on enchantments, and nor was Master Sennet. Of course! Woodward was a wizard; he would know all about these things. There was no point going back to Candra if he wasn't there. Much better to go on to Denton—she'd probably meet him on the way, guiding the welcoming party.

She felt better already. Woodward would sort it out. She bent down and kissed her aunt's cheek, waited long enough to see it made no difference, and left the cave. She was rather cold without her cloak, but she walked briskly, no one being there to forbid it, and soon warmed. The sun was shining, the

sky was blue, and she would have been enjoying herself if only
she didn't feel so painfully empty.

Denton was slightly further north than Candra, so she
veered to the left as she went downhill. She hopped over
a little stream, stepping from stone to stone, and followed it as
it trickled down the hill, heading, no doubt, for the great river
Parsifal, which would carry its waters to the Norward Sea.
She walked on and on, the terrain becoming ever less steep as
the day wore away.

The afternoon cooled, and Lily found no more patches of
sunlight falling through the forest canopy. She looked up, fearing another onslaught of rain, but the sky was as blue as ever.
Regardless of how far she had come (*miles* and *miles*, her legs
said), she was still in the shadow of the mountains, for the sun
was disappearing behind them long before it would actually
set. Of course, Candra, at the peak, would have sun for hours
yet. She shivered and went slowly on, trying not to think of
tea on the terrace, bathed in the golden late-afternoon sun.

⚜   ⚜   ⚜

Tea was indeed being served on the terrace, but not quite as
Lily had imagined it. The bursting of Candra's "bubble" of
magic had come as quite a shock to the occupants, but they
were doing their best to keep up standards. Holly had adapted
one of the braziers which were used on the terrace on cool
summer evenings, and the small copper kettle suspended over
it was just coming to the boil.

Holly unhooked the kettle and poured the water over the
leaves in the pot, the steam momentarily fogging up his glass
mask.

"I do wish you would put aside the protective wear, my dear
fellow," Sennet said, gloomily consulting his pocket watch. "It
is hardly appropriate dress for tea."

"Three minutes," said Holly, replacing the kettle on its hook
and removing his padded gauntlets. "You can't be too careful

when it comes to hot liquids. Now where did I put the what-sit?"

"The whatsit?" Sennet enquired.

"Thing like a hat—for the pot."

"Oh! The cosy. Quite so." Sennet fished it out from among the assortment of items pertaining to a Proper Tea, and the pot was soon decently clad. He checked his watch. "Two minutes." He looked at the three settings carefully arranged on the filigree table and sighed heavily. "I don't suppose you'd care to join me?"

"Not quite usual," Holly said. "I don't know what her ladyship would say." He lowered his bulk into one of the wicker chairs all the same. "Can't we do *something?*"

"The Lady Hortensia," said Sennet slowly and thoughtfully, "stands in place of a regent. It was agreed, fifteen years ago. It could be seen as somewhat irregular, appointing a regent not of royal blood, but..."

"Not much choice," Holly said.

"In any case, the arrangement could not be ratified but by a meeting of the Great Council, which was..." Sennet searched for the word with just the right shade of meaning.

"Impossible," said Holly bluntly. "Time?"

"Indeed. Er—one minute." He left his watch open on the table in front of him. "We are agreed, then, that the Lady Hortensia is, to all intents and purposes, regent on behalf of the Princess, that is to say, *Queen*, Lily, until such time..."

"Until she's eighteen, which is this Middweek. But neither of them is here to give orders."

"Yes, but in the absence of any commands from the queen—of age or not—we are honour bound to obey the regent. And," he said miserably, "she ordered us to stay here. Will you pour?"

They eyed the steaming pot askance. Never, in the entire fifteen years of Holly's memory, had anyone poured but the

Lady Hortensia.

"Um—you can," Holly said. "I'll lend you my gauntlets if you like."

"Very kind," said Sennet with the wraith of a smile, "but I believe I may be able to pour tea without them." He did so, they politely handed each other the sugar and milk, and so the ritual was observed.

"Mind you," said Holly, just as Sennet said, "Of course—"

"After you," said Sennet graciously.

"No, you first," Holly said. "I insist."

"I was merely going to remark on the additional difficulties inherent in our position, now that the magic by which the castle—er, household—was sustained has dissipated, and the immediate necessity for, ah, manual labour has presented itself."

"That's more or less what I was going to say," said Holly, "only not quite in those words."

"There is certainly a good deal to be accomplished," Sennet said meditatively, stroking his beard with one hand and raising his teacup with the other.

"Cleaning," said Holly, as one who speaks of long-forgotten horrors.

"Not to mention all that Burdock—which is to say, Woodward—was accustomed to do. Not only the gardening, but tending to the livestock, and perhaps a little fishing."

Holly brightened up at the mention of the fishing.

"Perhaps I could tickle up a trout for dinner tonight. The ladies might return at any time, you know. Baked with lemon…"

"Do you really think that they'll return before dinner?" Sennet looked at Holly, his eyes dark and sad and tired.

"Stands to reason," said Holly with a heartiness that rang a little hollow. "They probably got caught in that rainstorm yesterday afternoon, took shelter somewhere overnight and started back this morning."

"I suppose," said Sennet doubtfully. "I would have expected to see them back by now, if so."

"Always longer uphill than down," Holly said. "And the Lady Hortensia…" He coughed tactfully. "Not perhaps quite so young as she once was."

"My dear fellow!" Sennet protested. "She is hardly in her old age!"

"Of course not…"

"In her prime, I would have said."

"Um. Yes…"

There was a somewhat awkward silence.

"Perhaps," Holly suggested, "you could go up the tower and see if they're just outside?"

Sennet brightened a little. "Excellent idea. I shall do just as you suggest. Allow me."

He carefully reassembled the tea tray and Holly carried it away. Sennet hurried up Scholars' Tower, where he spent the rest of the afternoon hunched over his telescope, straining his eyes to the east.

⚜ ⚜ ⚜

One of the consequences of walking all day, Lily found, was that you hadn't the least desire to stay up late. Going to bed with the sun—something she had protested vigorously as a child in the nursery—now seemed ideal. If only there were a bed to go to! She was starting to feel weak in the legs.

She had, of course, gone without food before. Nobody ate on Pruning Day between dawn and dusk, but as Pruning Day was in the depths of winter this didn't work out to very long. And, in any case, Pruning Day was mostly spent in quiet reflection on what bad habit one might work at pruning from one's life in the coming year. A day *and* night without food, in early spring—while walking halfway across the country, no less—was another cup of tea altogether. She thought of a cup of tea, sweet and milky, and almost swooned.

Lily leaned on a nearby tree for support until her head cleared. Looking up, she saw the waters of the stream disappearing into a little river. The banks of moss cushioning the feet of the trees each side of the river looked so soft that she sank down with barely a thought of getting stains on her dress. A handful or two of watercress took the sharp edge off her hunger.

Her dress looked like a pink pearl on a bed of green velvet. A very pretty picture, if only someone were there to appreciate it. She began to imagine her quest in terms of paintings. The Princess in Attendance on Her Enchanted Aunt. A Pearl Beside the River. The Rapturous Return. The Princess—no, *Queen*—Finds the Horn of Vale.

That last gave her pause. She didn't actually know where to find said Horn, nor either of the other Requisites. But, of course! Naturally, it would be a ceremonial quest, not an actual search—that was why Woodward hadn't told her where to look. She would complete the descent to Denton, where she would be suitably welcomed; then the tour of her kingdom would begin, with the Requisites being ceremonially "found" at intervals along the way. This wasn't the sort of thing that would simply be left to chance.

Relieved of her anxieties, Lily was soon lulled to sleep by the soothing sound of the river. Water rushed through her dreams, and, in the deep of the night, she awoke to find that it was, once again, raining. She began to feel positively nostalgic for the enchanted cave.

There was only one thing for it. She was going to have to shelter in a tree. She had read of a princess in a fairy tale (well, she might have been a peasant, but she was bound to turn out to be a princess sooner or later) taking refuge in a tree. To be sure, her tree had been a spreading sort, with long low branches, and this forest tended more to the tall and straight, but she was sure she could find something that would do.

Lily took a cautious step and felt the cold rush of water in her shoe. Goodness! She must have rolled over in her sleep; she'd been lying much closer to the river than she thought. A step in the opposite direction gave her the wet slap of underbrush against her skirts. She heard something tear as she felt her way to a suitable tree and attempted to climb.

She soon decided that the princess (or peasant) of the fairy tale had been entirely revisionist in her story. Climbing a tree in skirts was problematic enough; climbing it in the dark when you, it, and the skirts were all wet was a feat born of desperation. Yet eventually, scraped, bruised, and triumphant, Lily was ensconced in the tree. She wrapped every possible limb around the branch on which she had settled, tied herself to it with her sash, and nursed her sore fingers. All in all, she felt, it could have been much worse.

⚜ ⚜ ⚜

How much worse was revealed by the first light of dawn reflecting off the muddy waters surging below, mere inches from Lily's dangling feet. The stream had burst its banks in the night, and she was trapped.

Lily sat and stared. Her lovely bed of moss had completely disappeared. She shivered. Of all the ways people could die, she felt drowning was *quite* the worst. She'd always stayed away from the fish ponds at home, and even the idea of a really deep bath was a little unnerving. What if you just—slipped…? She tightened her grip on the branch. Now was definitely not a good time to slip. She couldn't swim, and she was quite certain that a flooded stream was not the best place to try to learn.

Lily tried to look behind her, without relaxing her hold. The waters didn't reach too much further; she could still see underbrush not so far away. She untied the sash, and ever so carefully began to work her way around from branch to branch.

The dry ground was still too far to reach from this tree. Should she drop into the cold water? Who knew how deep it was, or how likely to sweep her away? Or should she try to climb from tree to tree?

She would have to break one of the first rules Aunt Hortensia had instilled in her as a child (after Young Ladies Do Not Talk With Their Mouths Full): Young Ladies Do Not Go Climbing About In Trees. Admittedly, she was already in a tree, but not swinging from branch to branch like some sort of ape in petticoats. She sighed.

Five minutes later, flushed with elation, Lily was letting herself down from another tree. She had done it! It might not have been terribly graceful or ladylike, true, but she had done it. Full of confidence, she started downhill along the edge of the floodwaters, and then remembered that she was still on the wrong side of the stream.

Her mind went back to Sennet's maps, spread out on the library table. There was no way to reach Denton without crossing either this little river, or the great river Parsifal on the valley floor. She would just have to walk back *up* the mountain until the river became narrow enough to cross. Lily could have wept, but, instead, she shook out her skirts, straightened her spine, and marched herself back uphill.

Some hours later, she was still heading uphill and upstream, and still on the wrong side of the river. She trudged along, nibbling on a handful of wild violets (in the language of plants, *love in idleness*—whatever that meant). It was another thing of which Aunt Hortensia did not approve: Young Ladies Eating Standing Up. ("We are not *bovines*, Lily.") Lily was guiltily aware of being *glad* Aunt Hortensia wasn't here.

At this point in her meditations, she heard a thump, and then a bump. She looked up and saw a funny little round boat bobbing about, tied to a partly submerged tree. Could this be the land-magic, providing for its monarch at last? She plunged towards it, knee-deep, and untied the rope. The jerk of the current nearly pulled her arm out of its socket, but she set her jaw and pulled right back.

This was a *sign*, and she was not going to let it get away! She towed it to the edge of the icy water, shivering, and climbed in. Seizing a nearby fallen branch, she shoved the land away. The branch was rotten, and a good third of its length fell off at once, but it did the job. The little boat spun out into the current.

Something tickled her wrist. She looked down, shrieked, and hurled the branch into the river. The woodlouse fell off her arm and scuttled about in the bottom of the boat. Lily yelped again and pulled her feet up onto the bench seat. The boat rocked wildly, and she put her feet back down, clutching at the sides. Woodlice might be part of the great interconnected networks of nature, but she would much rather they weren't directly connected with her. Insects didn't bother her; spiders she rather admired, but *nothing*, in her opinion, ought to have that many legs.

A shout rang out behind her. The boat spun around and showed her a man in the distance, waving, or shaking his fist. Perhaps he wanted to cross the river too. Well, it was too late now. She felt a little embarrassed at just leaving him there, but there was really nothing she could do.

The flooded stream was running fast, and while any rocks were well submerged, there was more than one tree fallen in the stream which—*ouch!*—the boat could bang against. The boat didn't seem to mind; it just spun around and started off again. Lily sucked her fingers, holding on tight with the other hand, and glowered.

They were moving frighteningly fast, and were soon out of the trees and slowing as the land flattened out. She must be nearly there! Scanning the horizon for any sign of Denton, Lily failed to see the large stump looming and was flung headlong into the filthy water. Flailing, she found her feet, caught her breath, and looked around for the boat. It was disappearing rapidly into the distance, borne on an expanse of churning water—Parsifal!

Her gaze followed the flow downstream to where it met a walled town. At last! The river curved around three sides of Denton, making it a natural fortress. Caught in the crook of Parsifal's elbow, as Sennet liked to say. Thankfully, no river stood between her and the open side of Denton, only this filthy floodwater.

But, wait, that wasn't right. The forest of Renwick was meant to come practically down to Parsifal's banks. Lily tripped over a stump and clutched at it to save herself. *A stump...*

She looked around. Nothing but stumps. The forest had been destroyed.

Lily stared at the devastation. This was no case of a few trees felled to make room for a house or garden. That was perfectly normal. No, this sort of clear-felling was reserved for the worst of circumstances, such as a tree disease that could be contained no other way. But, then, the trees would be burned...

Her face puckered. There was a nasty smell on the wind... like the time she'd forgotten to turn the compost for her First Garden as a little child, and it had gone all slimy.

It wasn't long till dusk. Better to get through this foul muck while she could see it. She pressed her lips together and ploughed on, her wet skirts constricting every step she took with their clinging embrace. She sometimes stumbled, and occasionally slid into an unforeseen dip which soaked her to the waist again, but the waters receded the closer she came to the city.

And the closer she came, the stronger the smell. There were piles of rubbish heaped up on the deforested stretch of land, twice or even three times her height. There were all sorts of refuse mixed in together, too: plant material decaying to slime instead of being composted; bones and meat scraps left to stink instead of being properly earthed. Broken odds and ends of brick and slate sat unchanging in the rotten mess, and she could even see bits of metal rusting away.

Lily began to feel quite ill. Denton had developed that epitome of foreign degeneracy—a *dump*. No wonder Woodward had said the land-magic was dwindling! She set her jaw. Things had obviously gone very much downhill in her absence, and as for Restoration Day, well, if there was anywhere in Arcelia that needed restoration, here it was.

Darkness threatened at the edge of the sky. Lily hurried. Denton was disappearing behind a stone wall—to complete the town's fortifications by closing off the western approach, she supposed. The wall, incomplete but with a great gate in the middle, ran alongside the North-South Road to where it met the river on each side. The road itself was unlike anything she had seen before, all grey and smooth like a millipede.

The gate was closed, but as Lily watched, a little door in the gate opened, and two people came out. People! Lily stumbled in her haste. One carried a large basket of clothes—a laundress, then. Following her was a tall fair man, whom Lily instantly identified as an Easterling. No Arcelian had that yellow fairness of hair, and very few were that tall. He wasn't dressed like a merchant, so what was his business here? He had the laundress by the arm, and her simple, round face was clearly distressed.

"Unhand her!"

The pair turned at Lily's clarion call.

"What?" the Easterling asked, in badly accented Arcelian.

"I said unhand her," Lily demanded. "My countrywomen are not to be thus…manhandled."

The Easterling snorted. "I'll handle her however I like, girl. Unless I see something better worth my time." He leered at her.

"I warn you," Lily said, revulsion and anger battling for control of her features, "if you don't step away this moment, it shall be you who suffers for it. My authority is not to be trifled with."

"Just who do you think you are?" the Easterling demanded.

Lily's chin rose. "I am Lily, daughter of Frederick, the son of Gauderic, the son of Roarke Meilyr, and I am Queen of Arcelia!"

There was a gasp from the laundress. The Easterling's jaw dropped and his grip loosened. The laundress wrenched herself free, seized her basket and fled down the northward road.

The Easterling was still staring at Lily.

"You are only a stranger in these parts," Lily said, "and perhaps do not know what constitutes decent behaviour. But I advise you to keep your hands to yourself in future, or you will face the consequences."

The Easterling was struggling to find words. Overcome, no doubt. "You—you are the little Lily? From long ago?"

"I haven't the least idea what you mean," Lily said. She considered switching the conversation to Easterling, in which she considered herself fluent, but decided the last thing she wanted was to make this odious man feel in any way at home. She turned away, but he was at her elbow in a moment.

"You must come in," he said, gesturing to the gate.

First of the would-be hangers-on? An escort was hardly necessary—she wasn't going to lose her way in the twenty paces it would take to reach the gate—but it didn't seem worth arguing the point. He hammered on the gate for her, which saved her knuckles at least.

«Open up,» the Easterling called in his own language. «There's a girl for the Magister.»

This was no way to announce a queen's arrival—and who was this Magister? A hatch in the gate opened and another Easterling face looked out. Was Denton entirely populated with Easterlings these days?

«He's away north, you know that,» the gate-guard said. «And so were you, a minute ago, after that girl. What happened—she tired of your ugly face already?»

«Never mind her,» the Easterling replied. «Open the gate.»

The little door in the gate opened, and Lily's escort waved her forward.

She did not budge.

"Open the gates. All the way." She caught a glimpse of an eye-roll as he turned to the guard.

«Go on,» he said. «It'll give you time to send for A-Division. They'll get cross if they're left out.»

The guard grunted and spat, but Lily heard running feet a moment later, and a creak as the gates began to open. As she waited, she shook out her skirts. They were torn and filthy, her face likely didn't look much better, and in the absence of her cloak, she had nothing to draw about her but her dignity. This was not how she'd imagined her entrance, but she was certainly not going to slink into the city like a beggar, even if she looked like one. At least it was getting dark; lower visibility meant few would see her until she'd had a chance to bathe, change, and enjoy a good night's rest.

The gates had opened almost to their full extent when she heard the tramping of boots and saw a double column of men appearing out of the shadows. Easterlings again! Presumably, this was the "A-Division". They were wearing slate-grey uniforms with black trim, and, she had to admit, they did look most impressive. This was more the sort of welcome she'd had in mind.

The Easterlings at the gates stood straighter and saluted as the double column came to a halt. The Easterling she'd met outside nodded in her direction, and received the barest flicker of a nod from the A-Division leader. Lily nodded regally to the gate guards and swept through the gates to join her guard of honour. To her surprise, they formed into a tight rectangle around her. To ensure her privacy? It seemed odd...

The A-Division were clearly the elite among the city's guards. Naturally, she would have preferred an escort of her countrymen, but there were periodic fashions for exotic bodyguards, and one must not appear ungrateful.

A balconied building loomed before them, towering even over the Easterlings. The palace!—though rather less ornate and beautiful than it appeared in Aunt Hortensia's drawing. A thrill of excitement ran through her. She wished she could see the Key Tree. It must be in the courtyard somewhere...

They ascended the wide stone outer stair and passed through the massive doors. Lily could hear the occasional scuttling of feet as people got out of the way. They crossed a large echoing hall paved in great squares of black and white marble, ascended two flights of stairs, and came to a halt outside a door, at which the leader knocked. Lily mentally *tsk*ed. One does not knock when announcing royalty. The door is simply opened and the presence is announced.

The door swung open.

"This is her," her escort announced.

He stepped aside, revealing a starkly furnished office. The last of the light came through the tall windows on the right— there was the balcony—and illuminated a large, unoccupied desk at the front of the room. Out of the shadows at the rear of the room hurried a small, nervous man, ink stains on one hand and papers in the other. An Arcelian, at last! His gaze seemed fixed on her filthy shoes, but it travelled up her muddied skirts and bodice in what Lily could only consider a most inappropriate manner. When his considering gaze reached her icy grey glare, he took an involuntary step backwards.

"Er, yes," he said. "Arrangements as specified. And send a runner after the Magister—he needs to know."

"I beg your pardon!" Lily snapped, but the bodyguard

closed ranks around her and marched away, and she had, perforce, to move with them.

What was going on here? And what, she demanded silently as they descended, was that *smell?* If that wasn't an uncleaned latrine, she was—

The detachment came to a halt, and the two in front stepped aside. At the same moment, she was given a violent shove and she staggered forward, falling heavily onto a cold stone floor. The door slammed closed behind her, and for the second time in her life, she was locked in.

Lily scrambled to her feet.

"How *dare* you!" she shouted at the door. "Don't you know who I am? Unlock this door!"

There was a faint echo of mocking laughter down the stone corridor. Lily threw herself at the solid door and hammered on it with both fists.

"Let me out!" There was no reply. "I will have you executed! Exiled! Tarred and feathered and tied backwards on an ox to be chased over the border! I shall never forget, and my vengeance shall be terrible!"

She stopped, her chest heaving. She was being ignored. Again. She seized the first thing which came to hand—the clay pot which sat in the corner—stepped back, and hurled it at the door. It burst into satisfying shards, and the latrine smell intensified. Oh, how *disgusting!*

Turning, she glared about the dimly lit room. Or, rather, the cell, for there was no doubting now that she was in the palace dungeons. There was nothing else to throw but a stuffed sack on the floor. The walls were of stone, with a fireplace built in opposite the door. To the left, the faint light gleamed on the iron bars which divided her cell from the space beyond. She rushed to them, seizing two and trying to force her way between them. It was all in vain, for they were closely set, one pressing into the outer edge of each of her cheekbones.

"Traitors! Tergiversators! Treacherous wretches of the most depraved variety!" she hurled into the darkness.

"Leaf and bud!" said a rough and unmistakably male voice from near her feet. "Will you keep it down?"

With a squeak, Lily flung herself away from the bars. A man! Not an Easterling, from his accent, but still! A *prisoner*, for who knew what vile offence, and practically close enough to touch! She backed away until her spine was pressing against the wall, thankful that the bars were so close together. Imagine if—no, she didn't want to get hysterical.

She slid down into a sitting position and tried to reassure herself. This was clearly all a dreadful misunderstanding, and, no doubt, those responsible would be suitably punished when the Magister returned. *Whenever that might be...*

She pushed the thought away. Her shoulders were sore where she'd been shoved, and her hands were skinned where they had struck the floor. A particular measurement of punishment would go to *that* fellow. How he dared! She had never been struck before, and the insult to her dignity rankled worse than the pain.

Exhaustion swept over her in a wave. She felt for the sack of straw which passed for a mattress, crawled onto it, and fell into sleep.

⚜   ⚜   ⚜

Pale light was reaching in when she woke, coming through a tiny barred window near the ceiling of the other cell. Its occupant was curled up in the darkest corner.

Lurking, she told herself, and shivered. Daylight was doing nothing for the charms of the cells. Now, she could see the heap of filthy straw in the other cell, the grime of the sack she was sitting on (which she hurriedly vacated), and the state of her clothes, which was frankly horrific.

The floor froze her thinly-covered feet in a moment, so she moved back onto the sack, eyeing it with disfavour. Look at that! Actual *grains* of dirt! On a mattress! That she'd *slept* on! One of them jumped, and Lily screamed.

There was a convulsion in the corner of the next cell, and a bleary voice shouted, "What? What is it?"

"*Fleas!*" Lily cried in horror, now standing pressed against the bars, as far from the verminous mattress as she could get.

"Is that all? Screaming that loud this early, someone should at least be cutting your leg off."

There was a rustle behind her, but Lily could only think about that mattress, destroying that mattress, getting fire somehow and destroying…

"There's one," said the voice, suddenly close by, and she felt a pinch on her leg.

She screamed again and fell away, turning as she went to see a grimy face staring through the bars at her.

"Got it," the face said with satisfaction, crushing something between two even grimier fingernails. "Got to keep on top of them or they'll eat you alive."

She stared at him. "You're a *dwarf.*"

He stared right back. "I know."

She flushed and looked away.

"So, what are you in for?" he said conversationally, almost as though they had been properly introduced.

Lily ignored him and went to the door. Still locked. She knocked, and followed up with an assertive "Open this door at once!"

"Ooh, wish I'd thought of that," jeered the dwarf. "I could have been out of here ages ago."

"Will you be quiet!"

"No use yelling for the gaoler," the dwarf said. "He'll be off making gruel. I hope."

Lily ignored him. A sound had caught her ears. Footsteps. Someone was coming!

"Open up!" she called. "At once, do you understand?"

There was a rattle of keys. At last!

The door to the other cell creaked open.

"Not *that* one!" she cried.

"Wossis?" asked a surprised voice.

Lily swept over to the bars. In the doorway of the neighbouring cell stood a gaoler, dressed in grubby layers against the chill. He had a pot of gruel in one hand and a broken-off spear in the other. The spear was pointed at the dwarf, who tipped the gruel into his bowl, apparently unbothered by the iron spike bobbing about in front of his face. Lily fixed the grubby gaoler with her gaze.

"I have no idea what *that* is," she said, not even caring if she was being rude. "*I* am Lily, Queen of Arcelia. Clearly, someone has made a terrible mistake. Fortunately, you are in a position to rectify it."

"Eh?"

"Kindly unlock the door of this cell at once!"

"Can't do that," the gaoler objected. "Not without direct permission from the Magister—or a chitty, of course."

"The Magister will be horrified to find I am here," she said. "He will want me released at once."

"Then why'd he put you in prison?" the gaoler asked. Clearly, he was not the shiniest trowel in the potting shed.

"He doesn't know I'm here. Someone made a mistake!"

"Can't want you released if he doesn't know you're here," the dwarf said, with his mouth full.

Lily fixed her most devastating glare upon him, and he grinned at her.

"No one, as far as I am aware, has asked you to contribute to the conversation," she hissed, and turned back just in time to see the door slamming shut behind the gaoler. "Now look what you've done!"

"Oh, right—sorry. Hey, gaoler," he called, "where's her gruel?"

"I wasn't told," a muffled voice on the other side of the door said. "Not my job, if I'm not told." His footsteps shuffled away.

The dwarf grimaced sympathetically. "Here. Have some of mine."

Lily looked down at the grubby hand proffering the little bowl of thin porridge through the bars. She hadn't eaten in a long time, but…

"No," she said. "Thank you, but I don't believe my standards have yet dropped so far." *Oh, please, let the Magister come back soon!*

"Bit of a fussy eater, are you?" the dwarf asked, taking a slurp straight from the bowl.

Lily looked away, shuddering. How coarse!

"That won't last."

"I'm sure the Magister will be along to correct this vile injustice in a moment," Lily said. "In any case, I'm not fussy about food, only *cleanliness*."

The dwarf snorted. "Seen yourself lately?"

"I am a victim of circumstances," Lily said, head held high. "Ouch! Something bit me!"

She rubbed the place through her skirts, and an itch immediately sprang up. She clenched her hand and pulled it away. Ladies did not scratch, *ever*. The dwarf was leaning back against the wall, laughing.

"You're disgusting," she hissed.

"You're pathetic," he replied, but there was no malice in his tone, only a sort of amused tolerance that Lily found extremely irritating. "Want me to teach you to catch fleas?"

"You stay away from me," Lily said, hastily removing herself from the vicinity of the bars.

The dwarf just laughed and carried on slurping his gruel with what seemed unnecessary noise.

"Really! Can't you use a spoon?"

"Yeah," he said, "I'm a magic dwarf who can conjure spoons

out of thin air. There are no spoons in prison, silly."

"Don't call me silly! It's *silly* not to have spoons."

"Prisoners can't have spoons in case they sharpen them into weapons."

"You can *sharpen* a *spoon?*"

"How would I know? No need outside prison, no spoon inside."

"I wouldn't know," Lily said. "*I* don't make a habit of spending time in prison."

"I've tried to kick the habit myself," the dwarf said, sniggering.

Lily welcomed the shuffling return of the gaoler with relief. She'd had *quite* enough of this, and her patience was at an end. Insulted, shoved about, forced to spend the night in a cell that reeked of—well, anyway, it *reeked*—and there were fleas, not to mention this impudent wretch, and the sooner she was out of here, the better. With some very specific herbal soap, in case any of those horrible fleas tried to come with her.

"Gaoler," she said commandingly, "I want to speak to you. Come and unlock this door at once! *This* door, mind you."

The dwarf snorted again and nearly choked on his gruel.

She heard the gaoler's footsteps coming closer. *Yes! At last!* A little hatch in her door slid open to reveal a little barred window.

"There's no gruel to be had, and no use—" he began.

"Never mind that," she said impatiently. "I want you to let me out of here. There has been some sort of misunderstanding, and you will get in trouble if you don't do what you can to fix it."

"Eh?" he said.

Lily controlled her rising anger. Shouting at this poor fool would do no good.

"I am not supposed to be here," she said, slowly and clearly. "You must unlock the door and let me out."

The gaoler began to tremble. "Can't. Not without the Magister's say-so. Or—"

"—a chitty." Lily sighed. "So you said. But the Magister will be angry when he finds you have kept me here. Can't you anticipate his orders—do what he wants before he says it?"

The man stared at her blankly. Lily quelled the urge to grab the bars and shake them.

"How soon will the Magister be back?"

"He's gone for days, they said. Up along the coast to Murdock."

Lily's heart sank. Murdock was at the foot of the eastern mountains, right across the valley.

"I heard they're after him with big news," the gaoler continued, "so maybe he'll be here tonight. Or early day after."

"But that's far too long!" Lily cried, dismayed at the thought of staying in this filthy hole an entire day and night to come. "Listen! I am not going to put up with this a moment longer. I am Lily, daughter and heir of Frederick, son of Gauderic, son of Roarke Meilyr, and I am the Queen of Arcelia! You *will* let me out, whether the Magister is here to approve or not!"

The man shook his head, face shadowed with fear.

"Leaf and *Bud!*" Lily exclaimed. Aunt Hortensia did not approve of such lively expressions for young ladies, but she was past caring. "If the Magister isn't here, how will he know if I'm on this side of the door or that?" she asked, pounding it with her fist.

"Magister's always watching," the gaoler whispered, beginning to tremble again.

"Then he *is* here!" Lily said, pressing forward with eagerness. In a moment, vindication! Followed no doubt by grovelling apologies, and the best of everything Denton had to offer.

"He's there," the gaoler said, his eyes slewing round. "Always watching."

"Out of the way!" Lily cried, almost pushing the gaoler away from the barred opening in her eagerness.

He stepped back, half-gesturing towards a picture on the wall which was lit by bluish light from a lantern. Lily's eyes fixed on it. A moment later the blood drained from her face, and she clutched the bars to keep from falling.

The portrait was a little older, the lines around the mouth more deeply grooved, but the sharp features were the same, as was the cold disdain in the eyes—the eyes that looked bluer than ever in the lantern's unnatural light.

It was Evil Uncle Phelan.

Chemistry

Lily sank to the floor. The cell swayed around her, and the world seemed to turn with it. Evil Uncle Phelan was *dead.* He had *died.* That's how the War had ended. He had killed—

Her history lurched vertiginously; all was rearranged, all fell into place. He had killed her parents, yes, but it was their deaths, not his, that ended the War. The light burned in her mind with a cauterizing brightness. Evil Uncle Phelan had *won* the War. Aunt Hortensia had *lied.* The one seemed as earth-shatteringly impossible as the other.

So this was what Aunt Hortensia had feared all these years. More and more made sense. Aunt Hortensia had saved her, yes, fled with her from the fortress where her parents had died. Aunt Hortensia had protected her. To the very last, Aunt Hortensia had tried to keep her safe—had tried even to keep her ignorant of the dangers that threatened her. The dangers, she realized, that Woodward must have been trying to warn her of when Aunt Hortensia had burst in. She felt cold, cold all over, cold right through, and she couldn't stop shaking.

"Put your head down," advised a voice, a long way away.

Automatically, she did as she was told, and the room slowly settled into place around her.

"Uncle Phelan," she said into her skirts. "Magister."

"Where've you been the last fifteen years, under a rock?"

"Candra," she said, and it seemed like another world.

"The ruin? At least make it believable."

"It was an illusion," she said wearily, each word plodding out like a prisoner chained to the one before. "Woodward set it up for my protection, framed by the Hedge."

"Sure he did. I'd say drop being Lily, and pretend you're a loony who thought she was a princess," the dwarf advised. "Act mad; drool a bit."

Lily got to her feet, went to the bars, and stared unblinkingly at the dwarf.

He drew in a hissing breath. "You *are* her. You, I mean. Not dead. Not till the Magister sees you, anyway. Those eyes! No getting round that. Weird way to choose a ruler, if you ask me—grey eyes. Random."

"Birth order is just as random," Lily retorted, a bit of warmth returning. Under sentence of death she might be, but she wasn't going to spend the rest of her life being criticized by this rude gaolbird. "And, in any case, I am the only child of the last monarch; therefore, I am *queen*."

"Magister doesn't see it that way."

"Why do you call him Magister, and not—King Phelan?" The words tasted rank in her mouth. "Or, more correctly, *Prince* Phelan?"

"You really have been under a rock. Kingdom's been abolished. No king, no royalty, none of the old stuff. He's against the lot."

"What do you mean, old stuff?" Lily enquired icily.

"You know. Festivals, garden things…how everything was done. All round the land and that. It's been banned."

Lily was no longer feeling giddy. Even her hunger had dropped away, and left her feeling light. No, she felt as though she *was* light, focussed through a glass to a point of burning precision.

"Do you mean to say," she said, her diction like cut glass, "that Evil Uncle Phelan has *abolished* the entire structure by which this land and its people live? How is that even *possible?"*

"Ban it. Punish those who break the ban. Easy."

"The people wouldn't stand for that. It's out of the question."

"Tell that to the Wolves."

"The wolves?" Her brow wrinkled.

"Easterlings. Magister's hired thugs."

"Oh—I saw them."

He snorted. "You saw maybe a handful of men. They're everywhere—garrisons across the country, Wolf Packs roaming about. The Easterland's emptied its prisons, I'd say, and they've all signed up as mercenaries."

"No! How could he...?" She stopped. A man who would kill his own brother would do anything.

"Dunno. You can ask him yourself soon enough."

Lily got to her feet, the energy of her anger coursing through her. "I have no intention of waiting to see him."

"What, you're going to ask to be let out again?"

She turned her back on him and scanned the door. It wasn't the sort that would lift off its hinges, and, in any case, there was nothing to use as a lever. Wall—solid. Fireplace—*chimney!* She put her head in and looked up. It was dark, but wide. Wide enough.

"Remember me to Phelan," she said loftily to the dwarf, and began to climb.

There was plenty of charcoal in the fireplace itself, but it had clearly been a long time since a fire had burned there. She wriggled upwards, coughing as she dislodged soot, and gasping occasionally when a particularly rough surface scraped her palms. Her nose caught the welcome scent of fresh air.

Elation sped her efforts, and she was moving upwards with remarkable speed when her head hit something very hard. She reached up to rub the bump, and felt an iron bar. It stretched from one side of the chimney to the other. She'd have to squeeze past on the other side—no. There was a second bar. Between them, they blocked the chimney fast. In desperation, Lily seized one in each hand and let her full weight hang from them. They didn't budge. There was no way past. No way out. She would have to go back.

The descent was even more painful than the ascent, her already scraped palms made raw by the roughness, and each downward movement needing to be checked before it became an uncontrolled fall. She was perhaps two thirds of the way down when a deposit of soot shifted under her hand; she slipped, grabbed, lost her grip, and slid downwards, hitting the hearth with a bone-jarring thud and spilling out onto the floor in a cloud of soot.

Lily sat up slowly, coughing, aching all over, her hands skinned and stinging. She was trapped. And what really hurt, more than the aches and scrapes or the lump on her head, was that she had walked into the trap. Walked in with head held high, thinking all would fall into place before her. Her eyes welled, and she blinked back the tears. She would not cry. Not in front of this jeering dwarf.

Despite her best efforts, one tear tipped over the edge of her lid and cleared a path through the grime and soot on her cheek.

"He's not stupid," the dwarf said. "You'd better drink something before you choke."

She looked up. He was holding out the gruel bowl through the bars. There was still a little left.

"Thank you," she croaked. She took the bowl, tried not to think about how he'd been drinking from the same bowl only minutes before, and took a sip. It was lumpy and tasteless, but at least it wet her throat.

"I'm Malin," he said. "Malin of Burnaby, obviously. Where else would a dwarf be from?"

"And what have you been imprisoned for?" Lily asked. "If

it isn't rude to ask. My education did not include prison etiquette."

He laughed. "I don't mind. I'm in for guerrilla warfare, inciting rebellion, and generally pissing the Magister off."

"Really?" Lily brightened. At least *someone* wasn't taking this lying down. But then, he was in prison. Her face fell again. "I'm surprised he hasn't executed you."

"He's working up to it. Maybe on Restoration Day, just in case anybody gets any ideas."

"Restoration Day...that's what I came for," Lily said.

He pursed his lips. "Don't like your chances. Valley's a mess, Magister's got control, and the whatsits—Requisites—haven't been seen since the War. Probably been destroyed, like the Key Tree. And you're in prison about to get your head chopped off."

The Key Tree was gone! So unless someone had taken a cutting for the next Key before Phelan destroyed it, Restoration Day was lost already. But Woodward had said the Requisites had been hidden, so perhaps there was still hope.

"So unless you can sound a missing horn with your lips and your lungs in two places, I can't see it happening," Malin summed up.

"Really! Must you be so—graphic?"

"Hey, I'm probably in for something worse."

"What could be worse than having your head cut off?" Lily asked, feeling the hysteria rise.

"Something slower."

Lily thought about this. He was probably right.

"I don't see why *you* should get special treatment," Lily said. "*I'm* the one who's a threat to his power."

Malin snorted. "You? Don't make me laugh; I'll crack a rib. What have you done, besides trotting up and handing yourself over?"

"It's not what I've done; it's who I am. And, anyway, what

have *you* done?"

"Who caused the stampede through Murdock Great Market which near as nothing trampled him flat?" Malin demanded. "Who stole the Wolves' quarter-pay for the whole southern district? Who sabotaged the machinery at the manufactory he was visiting, *while he was there?* I've done plenty, lady."

"The correct form of address is *my lady*," Lily said.

"Burnabaise don't use titles."

"You don't seem to be doing anything now," Lily said, ignoring this.

"Nothing I can do," Malin said, scowling. "Besides killing the fleas."

"Why don't you get rid of that nasty pile in the corner?"

"How?"

"I don't know...throw it out the window!" He glared at her. "Oh, of course. It's too high."

"Anything else obvious you'd like to point out?"

"Why not burn it?"

"That'd just make it stink worse. That's stable straw— soaked full of ox piss and cow-splat."

"Cow-*pat*," Lily corrected.

"I wish."

"What? Oh, how *disgusting*."

"Look on the bright side."

"Which is?"

"You won't have to smell it much longer."

"That remark was in the worst of taste," Lily snapped.

"Oh, come on. Cheer up. The way you look now, he might not even believe you're a princess."

"I am not a *princess*," Lily said. "I am *queen*."

"Don't tell him that."

Lily turned her back on him. Perhaps she was going to die, but she *refused* to be made a joke of. If only she didn't look such a mess! She felt in her pocket for a handkerchief. No, that was long gone. At least she had her toilette etui with her. The comb soon tidied her hair—left down to cover at least some of her reprehensible clothing—and the nail scissors and file did what they could for her ragged nails.

"You're facing death, and all you can think of is how you look?" Malin asked.

"If I must die, I will die with dignity, as befits a queen," Lily returned.

She bitterly regretted Aunt Hortensia's dictum that young ladies did not wear scent until they were eighteen; the tiny crystal perfume bottle that came with the set was still empty. What else could she do? She still had her hussif; perhaps she could mend some of the tears in her dress. She reached into the pocket again, and her fingers closed around something unfamiliar.

It was one of Holly's phials. Of course. She'd put it in her pocket during the brewing lesson, and then—well, been distracted, to put it charitably. Of all the things to carry into an already stinking cell! The smell of lant was bad enough, but adding this! Something stirred in the depths of her mind. Lant and yellow burningstone…burningstone and lant. Was it something she'd read? She closed her eyes and tried to conjure the page out of her memory. An old page, yellowed, with scratchy writing. Something to do with castle defences? Or attack. She forced herself to concentrate.

"If that's a magic escape potion," Malin's voice intruded, "I want some."

"Quiet! I'm trying to think."

"Try harder."

Lily screwed her eyes tight and willed the page to appear before her. It was singed…yes! That was it! Black powder! Fermented lant, burningstone and—charcoal.

Her eyes popped open.

"You're still here," Malin informed her.

She ignored him. "That stable straw—was it piled up like that when you arrived?"

"No, it was all over the floor. Why?"

"Did you notice a whitish crystalline deposit?"

"I noticed some dried up old piss, if that's what you mean."

"Good! Kindly put some in that bowl and pass it to me."

He blinked. "What?"

"Kindly put some in that bowl—"

"*My* bowl?"

"Yes."

"*No.*"

"But I need it!"

"Not going to happen. One, that's *my bowl*, and two, I'm not picking through that pile for anything."

"You handled it before."

"With my boots!"

"Don't be so…"

"Sensible?"

"Finicking!" Lily snapped. "You're not the lady here, after all."

"At least I have standards!"

"*You* have—! Fine!" Lily said. "Move the pile towards the bars *with your boots* and I'll do it myself. *I* won't be the one regretting it when I leave, and you get left behind."

"You're going to get out of here with some dried up piss? This I have to see."

He shovelled the pile across the cell to the bars. The smell billowed. Lily pressed her lips tightly together and tried to breathe as shallowly as possible. She took the tweezers out of the toilette set. It was a pity, but sacrifices had to be made.

"Oh—and I need the bowl."

"Not going to happen."

She didn't bother arguing. A piece of the shattered pot would do instead. The straw was eye-watering, but amply provided with the little crystals. By the time she'd gathered all she could find, Lily's back was aching, her eyes stung, and Malin had gone to lie down, apparently overcome by boredom. She used the rounded end of the phial to grind the crystals to a rough powder. It didn't look like much. But, then, she didn't know how much she would need. She selected a few choice pieces of charcoal and ground them into the same dish.

"What happens now?" Malin asked, back at the bars again. "You disappear in a puff of smelly smoke?"

"Something like that," Lily said. She couldn't resist crowing, just a little. "Fermented lant—"

"What?"

"The crystals."

"Oh, *right*. And here was me thinking it was just old piss."

"Which forms a salt: saltpetre. Which, when ground with charcoal and yellow burningstone," she popped the lid off and waved it airily under his nose, "produces black powder."

His eyes narrowed as his nose wrinkled. "You just happened to have burningstone in your *pocket?*"

"If you must know," Lily said, "it is used in brewing. My education has been very wide-ranging."

"Not wide-ranging enough," Malin said, with that irritating grin.

"I don't know what you mean," Lily said, carefully shaking the appropriate amount of burningstone into the greyish powder.

"You're going to grind that up with the other ingredients?"

"Yes," she said, phial poised to begin. "Why?"

"You hit black powder, what's going to happen?"

She paused and thought about this for a minute. He was right. It was too risky. The last thing she needed was to explode herself before Evil Uncle Phelan even got here. That would be worse than walking into his trap in the first place.

But—she looked at the pot shards. They were all too small, or the wrong shape, or—she shuddered—soiled. She was going to need that bowl.

She turned to Malin, a gracious smile on her face.

"I am sure," she said, "from the, er, nature of your crimes, that you are a loyal subject, and—"

"Nope."

"I beg your pardon?"

"I'm Burnabais. I've got no loyalty for Arcelia, or their kings. Or queens."

"But—" Lily stopped. Now was not the time. "You certainly don't want to see Phelan triumph, do you?"

"At least he's not trying to soil my bowl!"

"Would you refuse aid to his worst enemy?"

"I *am* his worst enemy, and how does it help me to filth up my bowl? They don't wash up in here, you know!"

"Could you live with knowing that you could have struck Phelan a terrible blow—even from your prison cell—and you didn't?"

He hesitated. Lily hastened to press her advantage.

"All I'm asking is to borrow the bowl…"

"*No.* But I'll tell you what. You use that powder somewhere it'll do me good, and I'll let you have my pot."

"Is it clean?"

"Of course it's not clean! What do you think I use it for, flower-arranging?"

"Then it isn't any good. Anyway," she pointed out, "it wouldn't go through the bars in one piece."

He glared at her. "This is blackmail."

"Not at all! This is diplomatic negotiation."

"Diplomats negotiate for somewhere to put their piss?"

"It's not *my*—" Lily began, and he laughed.

She hastened to change the subject. "I shall use the powder in the fireplace. The wall will be thinnest there."

He scowled at the fireplace. "Maybe. But that leaves me stuck in here."

"And?"

"Look, you can't do this without my help."

"Can't I? I could grind the burningstone on the floor."

"Wait!" said Malin. "Get me out and I can help you—get you to safety."

"Can you indeed?"

"I know my way around."

"My knowledge of the valley of Arcelia is encyclopaedic," Lily said haughtily.

"And fifteen years out of date."

She hesitated. He had a point. On the other hand, did she really want to be in his company any longer than she had to? But, then, who else could she be sure wasn't on Phelan's side?

"The wall is thicker in the middle," she said slowly, "which decreases the likelihood of a successful breach. I'm not sure the benefits are a sufficient trade-off for the risk. I shall have to think about it."

"Think fast. The Magister's on his way. And think about this: How are you going to light it?"

Lily tried to conceal her dismay. She hadn't even thought of that.

"I'll hit it with the metal phial," she said, jutting her chin. "You said that would work."

"*Maybe.* And even if it does, you'll still be Queen Lily the Left-Handed."

"I'd rather lose my hand than my head," she snapped back.

"I have a flint," he said. "Put the powder where we can both get at the hole, and I'll light it."

Lily bit her lip. Would the wall breach there? She carefully laid down the phial and went to look.

"Take it or leave it," Malin said. "We both leave our cells, or we both stay."

"Actually," said Lily, "it's only one cell. The bars and your door are more recent additions."

"Bit of a...been in a lot of cells, have you?"

"Connoisseur. And no. But I have studied defensive architecture, a subject which is sometimes regrettably necessary for a royal lady to know."

"So are we staying or going? Not that I think it'll work."

"If it's not going to work, why are you making such a fuss about where the hole goes?"

"I'm not giving up my bowl for nothing. A mad crazy half-chance," he added bitterly, "but not nothing."

Lily considered. There was no way out of the cell at present but through the door, and that was locked. Even if the gaoler did eventually return and unlock it, she wouldn't be able to overcome him single-handed and then escape through an unfamiliar building filled with who knew how many Easterling mercenaries. Nor did she want to take the risk of blowing her hand off. And Evil Uncle Phelan drew closer every hour...

"Very well," she said, and he grinned. "But if it fails to breach the wall because it's so thick, I hope you will feel suitably chagrined when Evil Uncle Phelan executes me, *and the last hope of Arcelia is lost.*"

"I wouldn't know chagrined if it bit me on the face," Malin said sunnily.

"Kindly cease babbling and hand me the bowl."

He hesitated. "Sure the pot won't do?"

"Not unless you want to pour the contents on the floor, wipe it out, and then smash it," Lily said.

"I'm going to regret this. No, I *am* regretting it," he grumbled, but he handed her the bowl all the same.

He heaved a deep sigh as she tweezered the flowers of burningstone out of the grey powder and into the bottom of the bowl.

"No execution for me," Malin said, glooming through the

bars. "Either this works, or I starve to death, because I am *never* eating out of that bowl again." There was a moment of silence, broken only by the tapping of the phial in the bowl. He heaved another sigh. "It was a good bowl, that."

"Land's sake, have you nothing better to do than stand around eulogizing the bowl?"

"Nope."

"Then take this nail file and start removing some of the mortar for the hole."

"All this talk of black powder, and now you want me to tunnel out with a nail file?"

"Unless," Lily said, restraining the urge to roll her eyes, "you want to light the powder while holding it in place with the other hand, you had best make some space to pack it into."

Malin took the file without another word, and began scraping at the mortar between the blocks.

"Maybe we *could* tunnel out," he said after a while. "This stuff's really crumbly."

"It's new," Lily said. "Dating from the time of the alterations, I should say. And as Aunt Hortensia observes, they don't make things like they used to."

Silence fell again, marked only by the scratch of the file and the soft tapping of the phial.

"It's the old stuff further in. Looks like we'll need the powder after all." He groaned dramatically. "I'm going to miss having hands. And a face."

"Why don't you light it from a distance? I imagine waxed thread would do quite nicely."

"You have some?"

"Of course. A lady always has her sewing materials to hand."

They worked steadily into the evening, the only interruption occurring when the gaoler arrived with the evening gruel and found no bowl to put it in. Malin explained that he had "lost it," and the gaoler retired, mumbling to himself about requisition forms.

It was well into the middle of the night before they finally finished their preparations, working by the dim light filtering through from the street. The greyish powder had been carefully—*very* carefully—packed into the spaces Malin had cleared around the stone block, and Lily's waxed thread was unreeled across the floor. Malin stood ready with his flint.

"I'm surprised that wasn't confiscated," Lily said.

"Do I look stupid enough to set fire to a cell while I'm locked in it?" he asked, then grimaced. "Don't answer that." He took a deep breath. "Here goes nothing!"

Lily hunkered down in the far corner and put her hands over her ears.

Malin struck a spark on the first try. It leapt to the thread and crawled across the floor with agonizing slowness. The powder caught, and then Lily could see nothing but the power of the flame cutting through the billowing smoke like a sword. It was a fast burn, and the last of the flame was still leaving an after-image on her stinging eyes when Malin plunged into the cloud of acrid smoke.

"Wait for me!"

The smoke thinned and Lily's heart dropped. The wall still stood.

Malin applied his weight to the blackened block. Stone grated against stone.

Lily flung herself at the wall. The block gave, grated again, stuck, and then, under their desperate assault, gave way altogether, crashing onto the cobbles outside with a crack that echoed down the empty street.

Malin squeezed past the last bar by the wall and through the hole, slithering rapidly out of sight. Lily scrambled after him, became briefly stuck in the far-from-smooth hole, and was unceremoniously yanked through to the street. The next moment she was up on her feet and dashing away, Malin keeping pace beside her. Shouts resounded behind them—mostly of "Fire!"

Elation flooded through her. Not only had her plan worked, but she was free, and she was running—the next best thing to dancing. She went to duck down a side street and was hauled back.

"Let go of me!"

"This way!" he hissed.

"But that'll take us to the river!"

"Only way out!"

"But I can't swim!"

"What?"

"I. Can't. Swim."

Even in the darkness, Lily could see he was rolling his eyes.

"Why did I ever agree to—?"

"Because you wanted to live!"

He glared at her. "Fine. We go out by the edge of the wall. Don't blame me if we get killed."

"*You* said you could get us—"

"And no more talking!"

With a vengeful glare, she pulled her arm free from his hand and set off in the direction indicated. He soon overtook her, and she decided to follow his lead. For now. He'd promised to take her somewhere safe, and she might as well let him. She just hoped he knew what he was doing. The commotion behind them was growing, and it would not be long before their escape was discovered. Chemical lanterns exposed them to the risk of discovery at every corner. To be seen would be fatal.

Malin seemed to be in his element, darting this way and that, indicating a turn with an economical move of his hand, some-times diving down alleyways she hadn't even seen were there. Sometimes, he'd raise a hand and come to a stop, and she had, perforce, to stop to avoid cannoning into him. It was better than being dragged about by the arm, but he still had much to learn about how one behaved to a queen.

They came to a halt again, in the shadows near a brightly lit street which ran alongside the new wall. It wasn't quite complete here, but a guard stood alert in the gap. The news must have travelled fast.

Malin stood still for a few moments, and then turned, pushing past Lily. "Don't move."

She wasn't intending to. With a big armed Easterling standing so close, his eyes searching the darkness in a way that made her flesh crawl every time they passed over the shadows in which she stood—no. She wasn't going to move. She was, for the first time, thankful that her clothing was no longer the pristine shell pink it had been when she left Candra. Filthy she might be, but at least she wasn't glowing in the dark.

Lily felt a movement beside her arm and started.

"Calm down," Malin muttered. "And get ready to run."

Her heart hammered. This was madness. They would never make it past that man. He would see them, and then it would be—

There was a crash down the street, and the Easterling shot away like he'd been fired from a bow. Malin dashed across the street, with Lily close behind. They threw themselves over the wall-works and passed out of Denton into the rank-smelling darkness beyond.

❦   ❦   ❦

The morning was still crisp around the edges when the Magister's large white riding ox swung in at the gates. The guard flushed, saluted, and hurried to open the gates and get out of the way. Anything to get away from that cool, appraising gaze.

Wolves hastily saluted and scattered as he descended to the cell. They re-formed into little muttering groups in time to watch the night-duty officer following his master's steps. The man was clearly trying to ignore the quiet asides of «Wouldn't like to be in his shoes,» and other such comments.

The officer found the Magister examining the evidence.

"Sir!"

"It appears that the explosive was produced in this very cell," the Magister said reflectively. "Under your very nose, as it were."

"The gaoler doesn't do his rounds after the evening meal," the officer said apologetically. "It wasn't thought necessary."

"How often are the cells cleaned out?"

"Er—cleaned, sir?"

"You are familiar with the term."

The officer flushed. "Well, yes, sir, but it wasn't thought necessary to—"

"Lant, you notice," Phelan said, indicating the pile of soiled straw. "Charcoal in the fireplace. Everything laid on but the yellow burningstone."

"I'll have it cleaned out at once."

"And when you have finished airing it out, perhaps you could attend to the hole in the wall," Phelan said.

The officer writhed. "Of course, sir."

"And have all prisoners searched in future."

"Yessir!" Anxious to redeem himself, he went further. "There was a disturbance at the wall-works shortly after the explosion, sir. No one seen, but—"

"Yes. Indicative."

Encouraged by this, he went on. "I've had patrols out searching ever since. Whichever way she went, we'll find her."

"A great deal of activity, in fact, with little thought behind it."

"Sir?"

"Whom did she speak to?"

"Day-shift, sir," the night-duty officer said, pleased to be able to shift some of the responsibility.

"And the gaoler?"

"Well, yes, probably."

"Find them. I want to know what they know."

"Of course, sir. You want to find out where she's going."

"No. I want to find out where she came from."

"Very good, sir." He took a step to the door and whistled. The gaoler came shuffling down the passage. "And the dwarf?"

Phelan waved a hand irritably. "Send to Burnaby for him. Every rat goes back to its hole."

"Very good, sir."

The gaoler appeared, his clothes rustling gently as he shook. "M-Magister?"

"The girl who was in this cell. Tell me about her."

The gaoler continued to shake, his eyes wide with fear.

"What did she look like? What did she say?"

"Terrible things," the gaoler muttered.

"Terrible things will happen to you if you don't speak up," the night-duty officer said, anxious to restore a little of his lost prestige.

The gaoler emitted a faint moan.

"I believe you have some orders to fulfil," Phelan said to the officer. His voice was quiet, as always, but the man flinched, saluted hastily and made his escape.

"No one is going to punish you for telling the truth," Phelan said. "Just make your report."

There was a convulsion in the rustling layers: the gaoler pulling himself together. "Didn't hear much. She complained a lot."

The corner of Phelan's mouth quirked slightly.

"Wanted to see you," the gaoler continued. "Saw your picture and was took poorly, seemingly."

The mouth quirked further before flattening out again. "What else did she say?"

The gaoler began to quiver again. "She said—she said—" His voice dropped to a mumble. "Said she was queen, she did."

"Did you notice her eyes?"

The quivering intensified. "No," the gaoler whispered.

"So you *did*."

The gaoler hunched as though to withstand a blow.

"Now, listen carefully, gaoler. Did she say anything about where she had been before?"

The gaoler nodded feverishly, glad to get off the subject of eyes. "That runt asked her. Candra, she said."

The Magister's eyes narrowed. "Candra? You're sure?"

"Yes! Cos the runt said no, it was a ruin, and she said it wasn't a ruin, it was a nillusion."

Phelan stood still for a moment, processing this.

The night-duty officer reappeared in the doorway. "Sir! The men are assembled and ready to make their report."

"Never mind that now. Get all the men that can be spared ready to march on Candra in one hour."

"The castle of Candra? But that's—"

"Every rat goes back to its hole," Phelan repeated, and strode out of the cell.

The officer hurried after him, and the gaoler sagged gently against the wall, wiping the sweat from his face with one grubby sleeve.

⚜ ⚜ ⚜

Lily woke in a ditch, the fetid mud slowly oozing past her face. Her head throbbed, her legs ached, and everything in between felt sick. After taking temporary shelter in the dump—she shuddered at the memory—they had run for the rest of the night, first heading south, following the line of river and road;

and then veering west to avoid the notice of a roading crew. It had the quality of a nightmare: dark figures moving in the unnatural light, as the reek of scorched vegetation rose from the steaming substance they spread.

"Pourstone," Malin had said, and that was all.

Not till she'd been floundering with exhaustion had Malin finally taken pity on her and stopped, and by then she'd been beyond objecting to her accommodation. Lily pushed herself stiffly up out of the mud.

"Afternoon," said a voice nearby.

She craned her neck around to see the dwarf, apparently at his ease, further down the ditch.

"Good afternoon," she responded, with cold courtesy.

His clothes did not show the dirt nearly so much, she noted, and somehow he had managed to keep his face out of the mud.

She sighed. "I need a bath and a complete change of clothing."

"Got a magic potion in your pocket for that, have you?"

"Your mockery is exceedingly inappropriate," Lily said, taking her comb out and trying to work it through her hair. "Particularly considering that you owe your present liberty to the contents of my pockets."

He flushed. "I'm paying for it, aren't I? It'll be dark soon. We can get going again."

"How far south are we at present?"

"Not far past where Percy bends east," he said, using the river's familiar nickname.

"Rich farmland," Lily observed, eyeing the dark soil which made up the sides of the ditch she sat in.

"Lattie-land, these days."

"Lattie-land?"

"This is where the first latties were. They're all latties round here now."

"Is lattie a dwarf term?" Lily enquired.

"Dwarf? Not likely! Short for some fancy word the high-ups use. Most people call them latties."

"Yes, but what *is* a lattie? You're not *explaining* it at all."

"A lattie is...eh, you'll see."

Lily rose painfully to her feet. "Then perhaps we had better be going."

Malin had a quick look round then hopped out of the ditch. "Come on, then."

She looked up at him. "Well?"

"Well what?"

"Aren't you going to help me out of this ditch?"

"Your arms and legs painted on?" he asked, but he extended a muddy hand and hauled her out. "Can you manage to walk, or do you need me to carry you?"

Lily shook her arm free of his grasp. "I am perfectly able to walk, thank you."

"Good," Malin said, setting off along the edge of the ditch. "Because you probably weigh about as much as I do, and even I get tired."

Lily went bright pink. She was glad he couldn't see her face. What did one even *say* to a person who was so totally lost to all sense of decorum? Thankfully, he did not expand on the subject, but just kept jogging along the margin between the ditch and the surrounding fields.

Casting about for a change of subject, Lily seized on the fields as the only available material. She had nothing to say about ditches.

"What large fields," she ventured. He just grunted, so she carried on. (A lady always carried the burden of conversation when others were devoid of small talk, Aunt Hortensia said.) "Is it some sort of communal arrangement?"

This time, he snorted. "Communal! It's a lattie."

"You keep saying that," Lily said, failing to keep the irritation out of her voice, "but you don't say what that means!"

He waved an arm. "See these fields?"

"Indeed," she said, casting an eye over the expanses of turned soil. "If you recall, it was I who raised the subject."

"You see how even the rows are?"

"Yes. They must have very adept ploughmen."

He snorted again. "Ploughmen nothing! It's a machine that does it—like a dozen ploughs in a row. Takes a fair few oxen to pull it, too."

"How clever," Lily said, imagining this super-plough cruising across the land, coming down to the ditch where they walked, and then... "But how does it turn?"

"See for yourself," he said, waving an arm.

Lily peered through the gathering darkness at a large triangle of unploughed land. "What's this for?"

"Nothing. It's waste. Not ploughed, not planted, not cared for."

"Left fallow, you mean?"

"Left fallow every year, while the rest of the field gets no break at all."

"How does that work?" Lily's brow furrowed, until she remembered her aunt's strictures on wrinkles and smoothed it again.

"It doesn't. The crops get poorer every year."

"Then why do they do it?"

"Because the machine needs them to," he said sourly.

"How silly," Lily said. "Cooperation is all very well, but if it isn't in the land's interests—"

"This isn't cooperation," Malin snapped. "The machine needs fewer workers, which means fewer people to pay, which means more profit for the man who owns all these fields."

"But this can't all be—"

"Can't it? You get in good with the Magister, there's no end to what you can do."

"But, surely," Lily reasoned, "the land needs a certain number of people for planting and weeding and harvesting and so on, even if one person owns it? Ploughing's only one part of it, after all. With all the different crops—"

"There are no different crops. One machine plants, another drags up the weeds, another harvests the crop. It wouldn't work if you had different crops in the same field, so they don't. A fraction of the labour, and a fraction of the cost. Especially if you use thralls."

"Thralls?"

Lily had heard of thralls, but only in books. They were like slaves who belonged to a piece of land, so even if the person they worked for died, they wouldn't be free.

"What do you mean, thralls?" she demanded.

"I don't want to talk about it," he snapped, and sped up.

Then you shouldn't have brought it up, Lily retorted silently.

If he was going to speed up every time she spoke, she'd never be able to keep up, longer legs or not. He kept up the pace as the darkness deepened, and she was reduced to following him by sound alone. As she passed the unseen fields, she mulled over what Malin had told her. It seemed very foolish, particularly given the poor results, and, really, it was quite like that bit in the Fate:

> *When the people are divided*
>   *from each other and the land;*
> *When their holdings are abandoned*
>   *into few and grasping hands;*
> *When the land cannot lie fallow*
>   *but is stripped of all it bears...*

You would think they would know better, Lily thought, and turned her concentration to not tripping on the rough ground. After about an hour, the rhythm of Malin's footfalls slowed, and Lily, thankful for the slower pace, eased up too.

"Quiet," he muttered.

"I haven't said a word in *hours*," she hissed back.

"There's an inn up ahead," he said, still in an undertone. "We'll keep our distance."

"An inn?" Visions of hot baths and warm soft beds with down covers danced before Lily's eyes. And food! *Hot* food! "Ooh, let's go there!"

"Are you mad? Do you know what day it is?"

"No," she said absently, mind still on the enticing prospect of cleanliness, warmth and rest.

"It's the fifth today. Wolves get their quarter-pay."

"Did you say the *fifth*? The fifth of Grenian?"

"Yep. The place will be full of—"

"Do you mean to tell me," Lily demanded, "that I spent my eighteenth birthday, the most important day of my life to date, the day on which I came of age, *lying in a muddy ditch?*"

There was a muffled giggle from the darkness before her. "Sorry. It's just—" Further peals of muffled laughter suggested that he was more entertained than sorry.

"If you think," she hissed venomously, "that I am going to go trailing around after you in the mud when I could be celebrating my birthday with a bath, a hot dinner, and a decent night's sleep, like I deserve after all I've been through, you are very much mistaken!"

She tried to sweep past him, but a hand came out of the darkness and latched around her arm.

"If you think," said Malin, and there was no trace of a laugh in his voice now, "that you can walk into an inn full of Wolves spending three months' pay on hard drink, and walk out alive again, *you* are very much mistaken."

Lily hesitated. On the one hand, the comforts she deserved. On the other hand—duty. As the last hope of Arcelia, she had a duty to run no unnecessary risks with her royal person. She hissed with frustration.

"It's not *fair*," she said in what was meant to be a private undertone.

"Life isn't fair," he returned, letting go of her arm. "Wish I could have slept through my eighteenth birthday."

Her determination never to speak to the wretch again fought a losing battle against her curiosity.

"Why? What could possibly be worse than lying in a ditch like—like some sort of dead thing?"

"Being flogged in prison and *wishing* you were dead in a ditch," he said.

"Goodness! Have you spent a lot of time in prison, then?" There was a note of trepidation in her voice. What, really, did she know of this fellow she was trusting with her safety?

"Of course not," he said, sounding offended. "I hardly ever get caught. This isn't my first escape, you know."

"I beg your pardon," she said, formal again. "I simply hadn't realized you'd been in prison back then, too."

"Back then? That was six weeks ago!"

"What? You're—you're *eighteen?*"

"I'm a bit weather-beaten, all right?" he said defensively. "We don't all sit around on silk cushions drinking cream, you know. Come on. Can't stand here all night."

"I don't sit on—!"

Lily hastened after him before she could lose the sound of his footfalls, silently fulminating. He might have his tricks for getting the last word, but he would learn that she was not to be trifled with. Drinking cream indeed!

They kept going all night, running, then walking, then trudging as the long hours took their toll. The first glimmer of dawn in the sky revealed a sea of darkness ahead of them: the forest of Burnaby. Malin picked up the pace.

"Hurry up," he said over his shoulder. "We won't get there before full day at this rate."

Lily set her teeth and tried to limp faster. Her dancing slippers were practically worn through, and he wanted her to hurry up? It was *miles* to go yet, there was no way they would get there before daylight anyway, and why, oh why wasn't there somewhere safe that was closer?

A Place of Safety

She just needed to close her eyes for a moment…

Lily stumbled and fell. Malin hoisted her up again, and she found herself leaning on him like a crutch as she hobbled through the trees. They staggered out into a clearing dominated by a small sturdy house. People came pouring out, and she forced herself to stand upright and muster what dignity she had in her rags to meet them.

The first to reach Malin was a little boy of perhaps ten, who leapt upon him with cries of joy. He was rapidly followed by a girl a few years older. They drew back and stared at Lily.

"Who is this?" the girl whispered to Malin.

He turned to Lily. "This is my sister Daisy and my brother Kern." He coughed awkwardly. "This is…"

"I am Lily, Queen of Arcelia," Lily said, and had the satisfaction of watching their eyes widen.

A moment later, they turned away, all three of them looking back towards the house. Lily's gaze followed. There in the doorway stood a sturdy young woman, arms crossed and eyes unfriendly.

"And this is my sister Pasque," Malin said with a sort of desperate cheerfulness. And then, "She's our guest, Pasque."

Pasque gave him a look that promised Words with him afterwards, and stood back to let them enter, face set.

"Daisy," she said, "put down some cloths. I don't want the

floor dirtied."

Lily flushed as she went in. How rude! She might be filthy, but she was still queen, and anyone ought to be proud to have her under their roof. Particularly a humble roof like this: the door opened straight into the main room, which evidently served as kitchen, dining room and sitting room all in one.

"What a charming home," she said, looking about her.

"Thank you," Pasque said tonelessly. "Kern, Malin, fetch water for washing. Daisy, see to the breakfast. I need to run an errand."

Kern and Malin picked up buckets and left, followed by Pasque. Daisy began slicing bread to toast over the kitchen fire, and breaking eggs into a cast iron pan. Lily sank into a haze, half asleep, but distantly aware of what was going on around her. She washed her face and hands in a proffered bucket of surprisingly warm water, sat down on one of the low chairs, and stared at the plate of fried eggs and toast that appeared in front of her.

"Might I have a knife and fork?" she managed at last.

Malin rolled his eyes and Kern snorted. Daisy clipped them both around the ear simultaneously with a skill born of long practice, and brought the cutlery. It was not what Lily had been used to, but it would do. Pasque returned and began toasting some more bread without looking at anyone.

"The Council wants to see you," she said. "This evening."

Malin jumped up. "Pasque, how could you?"

Taking his sister's arm with one hand and his plate of food with the other, he towed her through the door to the other part of the house. It was not, it turned out, a very effective barrier to sound.

"You couldn't even give her a day?" he demanded.

"She doesn't belong here, Malin," Pasque hissed back furiously. "You had no business bringing her here."

"She saved my life! I promised I'd get her somewhere safe."

"There is nowhere safe! Bringing her here *makes* it not safe!"

Lily cut her remaining egg and toast into smaller and smaller pieces, eating one morsel at a time. Being a witness to a family quarrel—about oneself!—was bad enough, but to have nothing to pretend to occupy oneself with would be infinitely worse.

Daisy coughed ostentatiously. The voices on the other side of the door sank to whispers, the toast dwindled into crumbs, and Lily, sagging against the wall, fell asleep.

⚜ ⚜ ⚜

Holly banged a pot down on the stove, his normally open face bunched in a deep frown. Slice it any way you liked, they should've been back by now. If it wasn't for Lady Hortensia's orders, he'd have gone out looking for them days ago. He would've done it anyway, but he didn't like to leave Sennet alone. And Sennet was always for Doing His Duty, even if his judgement was against it. Orders were orders.

But they should have been back by now! Exasperated, he clapped the lid on the pot with a clang. His thoughts had been going in circles for days. He practically had a rut in his brain. Maybe he should go, brave all Lady Hortensia's wrath. He shivered at the thought, his mind's eye conjuring only too vividly an image of that lady in a state of displeasure. Maybe he—

He stood still, listening intently. Was that Sennet *running?* And down stairs, at that! Holly's heart lifted with a bound and he swung out of the kitchen to meet Sennet with a beam.

Sennet staggered down the last few stairs, clutching at the balustrade. His face was grey and drawn, covered with a sheen of sweat. Holly's heart dropped so far he could feel the punch in his gut as it landed.

"Master Sennet—you're ill!"

Sennet forced himself upright. "Phelan," he said, his voice hoarse with gasping.

A parade of goosebumps did a death-march down Holly's spine. Phelan!

"He's coming here," Sennet said tonelessly, "with a large force."

Holly drew a long shuddering breath.

"Lily..."

"No. Phelan himself, and all those men, for an old man and a cook? Think, man!"

Holly thought, and his heart, resilient as always, bounced back up. "He thinks she's here..."

"Yes," Sennet said, a soldierly glint in his eye.

"He's bound to find out..."

"Eventually."

"You're going to buy her time," Holly said admiringly.

"I am. As much as my life or death can buy." Sennet straightened up, and Holly could see the old war-time Sennet shining through. "I will think none the worse of you if you elect to leave before Phelan arrives. Or, rather, I will think very much the worse of you, but I will not stop you leaving."

"Leave?" Holly said indignantly. "When there's so much to be done? I can finally try out all my booby-traps without her ladyship calling for my head!"

He turned away, plans already forming. A hand on his shoulder arrested him.

"It is no light choice," Sennet cautioned. "Once they arrive, there will be no leaving for us. Never again."

Holly, momentarily sobered, looked thoughtfully at the older man. Then he straightened up, clapped his hand on Sennet's shoulder, and nodded firmly.

"For our Queen," he said.

"For our Queen."

⚜   ⚜   ⚜

A hand shook Lily awake, none too gently.

"Time to go," Malin said. "The Council will be sitting soon."

"What?" She sat up, consternation brushing away the last of her sleep. "I can't go like this!"

"Why not?"

"I will not be meeting with any Council until I have had a bath and a change of clothes."

"You can't just—"

"Watch me." She set her jaw.

Malin glared at her. "There aren't any clothes here big enough for you, all right? So—"

"What about the museum?" Daisy said, distracting attention from Lily's flaming cheeks. "It's got big-people clothes."

"We don't have time!"

"We'll go to the museum at once," Lily said firmly. "Kindly lead the way, Daisy."

Malin followed, arguing all the way. Lily paid him no heed. She was the queen; the Council would wait for her.

The museum turned out to be a one-roomed building, run-down and in sore need of dusting. Boxes and chests lined the walls, with a couple of dim glass cases taking pride of place. Lily was drawn straight to the one in the far corner where a dull gleam of gold caught the light.

It was a full length court gown; cloth of gold woven in a pattern of flowers. It was the sort of gown that would make a queen of a scullery-maid; on her, it would be breathtaking.

"Perfect," she said, her aching feet forgotten.

Carefully opening the case, she lifted the gown off its frame and draped it over Daisy's proffered arm. There was a shimmer of gold as the gown moved. Lily caught her breath in horror. Gold dust was sifting onto the floor at Daisy's feet. She snatched up the gown again in disbelief. She could see Daisy's horrified face through the netting left behind as the gold fell to dust and drifted away.

"You are not wearing that to the Council," Malin said. "We

have standards."

Lily controlled herself with an effort.

"It can't be helped," she said reassuringly to Daisy, who looked about to cry. "I'm sure there's something else here."

"Anything," said Malin, "as long as it's quick!"

The other glass case contained a suit of armour.

"That would work," said Malin.

"It's for a *man*," said Lily.

Each box and chest was opened and looked through, its contents considered in turn.

Malin started thumping the door frame. "Come on!"

"I do think we'd better hurry," Daisy said anxiously. "We shouldn't keep the Council waiting."

"I have no wish to be unpunctual," Lily said, "but I am sure it would be no compliment to the dignity of the Council, or myself, for me to appear unwashed and in rags."

"Perhaps I'd better go and run the bath," Daisy said, and slipped out, avoiding Malin's eye.

Lily kept looking, ever more frantically. There had to be something here!

"You already looked in that one," Malin growled.

Lily straightened up and surveyed the clothing strewn around the room. There was nothing—*nothing*—here that was suitable for a royal lady to wear on a formal occasion. Her face threatened to crumple and she turned to face a dark corner. *A lady does not show her emotions in public,* Aunt Hortensia's voice echoed in her mind. Lily fought her face under control and turned to survey the scene.

"You're wasting time," Malin said. "If you're a queen, you're a queen. Why does it matter what you wear?"

"Appearances are important," Lily said, and swallowed hard.

"It's who you are that matters, not what you look like."

"Appearances are like a promise. The person has to keep

that promise, but it—it helps people know what to expect."

"Expect how?"

"For example," Lily said, feeling more in control of herself again, "when people look at you, they don't expect you to know anything about clothes."

Malin looked down at his rough, travel-worn clothes. "At least I know quality when I see it."

"*Quality?*" Lily said incredulously.

"*My* clothes don't fall apart after five minutes."

Lily blushed, pulled her rags straight and turned back to the boxes.

"You know the Council is headed by the two oldest dwarves in Burnaby, right?" Malin asked.

"Of course I know. What of it?"

"They're going to die of old age before you finish finding something to wear, that's what. Move aside."

Lily stepped out of the way as Malin bulled his way through the boxes, grabbing an item here, an item there, and burrowing for a remembered piece that had been buried. In under a minute, he presented her with a messy heap of clothing.

"Here."

There was a split skirt made of some dark grey woollen material, a white linen shirt, a thick warm cloak of dark blue, and a complicated arrangement of two pieces of blackened leather held together with straps and buckles.

"Oh—and these." He added a pair of boots and a bowl-like helmet.

"A *helmet?*"

"Better safe than sorry."

"And my feet are not that big."

"I'll loan you a pair of socks."

Her instinctive disgust reached her face before she could capture it.

"Clean, all right?" he said defensively. "You'll have to keep your own for the rest—this isn't that kind of museum."

"The rest?" Lily asked, and instantly wished she hadn't.

"Drawers and that," Malin said. "Come on."

Lily considered the pile of clothing—so *practical*—and then what was left of her shell-pink dress. She shivered. Wool was warmer...but it was all so *plain!* Perhaps she could have the pink dress mended. She bit her lip.

"Come *on!*"

"I don't know..."

Malin rolled his eyes. "You know your drawers are show-ing?"

One horrified glance at the place indicated was enough to make up her mind. She flung the dark cloak around herself and hurried for the door.

⚜   ⚜   ⚜

Lily walked through the darkened woods, feeling herself again. She was clean at last, and the clothes, she had to admit, fit quite well. The leather thing turned out to be a cuirass, a sort of leather bodice. Armour, really, though it didn't look it. And the helmet looked almost like a crown as it rested on her clean damp hair.

The only problem on her horizon was the dark cloud strid-ing beside her. Malin was nearly hoarse from all his shout-ing through the bathroom door, going on about how time was wasting and the Council would be waiting for them, and no one kept the Council waiting, until Lily was sick of the sound of his voice. And, then, after all that, he had refused to have a bath or change himself. He stalked along next to her in a mood as filthy as his clothing.

"I suppose it's too much," he said, "to ask you not to say anything stupid?"

"I have been taking lessons in elocution and diplomacy since I was a child of six," Lily said with some asperity.

"Too bad you skipped the lessons on sense," he retorted, but before Lily could think of a suitably stinging reply, they arrived.

The Council clearing was crowded with dwarves. They filled the space and spilled back into the trees on all sides. Pulling back as Lily approached, they watched her with curiosity, excitement, or suspicion.

The centre of the clearing proved to be a firepit, full of branches burned to glowing coals. The two Elders sat close to its warmth, watching her approach. The man was so old he looked papery, and the Burnabaise beside him seemed almost translucent. Lily wondered how old they were, and then castigated herself for the impertinence.

"Introduce us, Malin," said the old man, his voice as papery as his appearance.

"Betony Old-Woman; Waite Old-Man," Malin said.

These were the ceremonial titles of the Elders, Lily knew, but it sounded strange and a little rude, all the same.

"And...?"

"You know who she is," Malin said.

"We know who she claims to be," Old-Man corrected him snappishly.

"I am Lily, daughter of Frederick, son of Gauderic, son of Roarke Meilyr," Lily said, and there was a murmuring in the trees. "I am the Queen of Arcelia—and of Burnaby." She heard a muffled moan from Malin and plunged on nevertheless. "I have returned to claim the place that is mine by right."

"This isn't that place," Old-Man said bluntly.

Lily wavered, opened her mouth and closed it again.

"Now, don't be harsh to the poor girl," Old-Woman said, and her voice was surprisingly strong, coming out of such a small and delicate body. "She has enough troubles without you shouting at her."

"Troubles which she's brought here!"

"Why *are* you here, dear?" Old-Woman asked, and Lily couldn't bring herself to resent the informality of the address, so warm and kind was her tone.

"I—it's—I'm…" Lily started, and realized she was babbling. She stopped, took a deep breath, and began again. "Restoration Day is coming. I mean to see that it takes place as custom dictates, and to destroy the corrupting influence of the traitor Phelan."

"But Phelan isn't here," Old-Woman said.

"Yet!" put in Old-Man.

Lily frowned. Why were they so surprised to see her?

"I expect the support of all my subjects," she said. There was an indrawn breath, and silence. "I am here in particular because Malin brought me here, in payment for his freedom."

Beside her, Malin dropped his face into his hands with a groan.

"We can't help you," Old-Man said flatly.

"But you don't understand!"

"*You* don't understand," Old-Woman said, and there was a steel to her voice that had not been there before. "We sent our fighters to support your father in the War, and how few returned! But the Magister does not forget, nor does he forgive. We are penned up in our lands like cattle; those who leave are subjected to forced labour, or sold as thralls. Your problems may be grievous, but we have our own. We cannot help you."

"But maybe *she* can help *us*," Old-Man said, and there was something in the way he looked at her that she did not like.

"Exactly!" said Malin, taking his head out of his hands. "She's the only one who can rally the Arcelians against the Magister. She has position—what d'you callit—?" He waved a hand at Lily.

"Legitimacy," Lily said.

"She's the head of the axe that'll chop him down," Malin continued enthusiastically. "We provide the haft—and the heft—to put behind her. No more Phelan. Think of it!"

"Or," said Old-Man. "Or…"

"Or what?" Malin asked.

Lily's head was reeling. Was Malin suggesting she should head an army of dwarves against Phelan? Was that what *she* was suggesting? She was only certain that she needed help. She tried to follow the conversation.

"Or we face up to reality!" Old-Man snapped. "What chance do we have against Phelan's Wolves? Try to think with your head once in a while instead of your muscles. We can't fight them."

"*I* fight them," Malin said.

A vein bulged in Old-Man's forehead. "And you keep getting caught!"

"At least I'm doing something, not just sitting in an armchair and complaining about how things aren't like the old days," Malin growled.

"*You* are half our problem," Old-Man said. "And you could well be half the solution, you criminal oaf."

"I'm no oaf!"

"You're a stink in Phelan's nose!" Old-Man shouted. "Who knows how good we could have it if you weren't upsetting him all the time!"

Malin stood speechless. The crowd was listening, eager for the drop of every word.

"You're nothing but trouble," Old Man went on, "and she's worse! This is all your fault! I say we hand the pair of them over to the Magister and enjoy a little peace at last!"

It was out. The crowd broke into tumult, voices raised, for and against, and each one trying to be heard over all the rest. Old-Woman, visibly distressed, tried to calm them, but no one paid her the slightest bit of attention. Lily saw her wriggle on her chair, and wondered if she were trying to climb down. Then her hand reappeared from the sheepskins padding the wooden chair, with a small bundle clutched in it. This she hurled into the glowing embers, and a column of green fire shot up. Even Malin took an involuntary step backwards, and Old-Woman seized her moment.

"The idea is grotesque," she said. "The Council is not in agreement."

There was a moment more of hush, and then the furore broke out again. Lily watched, helpless, as the debate over her fate roiled around her. Someone grabbed her arm and she squealed and pulled away. Malin spun away from his heated argument and a gleaming hatchet blossomed in his hand. Silence fell. Lily trembled.

"You do not draw steel in the Council," Old-Woman said, in a whisper that could be heard all over the clearing.

"But you do barter the life of a fellow dwarf?" Malin asked, holding her gaze. He was shaking too.

Old-Woman looked away, the firelight glinting off a tear on her cheek.

"The Council is not in agreement," she whispered.

"Which leaves it to every Burnabais to decide for himself," Old-Man said with satisfaction. "And I think the feeling of the meeting is clear."

Lily looked around. There were fewer dwarves in the clearing, she was sure of it. Perhaps they had melted away, wanting no part of what would follow. She took a step closer to Malin. A circle of bolder dwarves was forming, closing in on the pair of them. Malin shifted, looked each in the eye, and shifted again. Some would not meet his eye, some met it brazenly, but Lily noticed one whose eyes dropped only for a moment before catching Malin's gaze again. A silent agreement. Of what?

Her question was answered almost at once. The circle tightened, and Malin charged his unspoken ally, knocking him to the ground. The circle was broken, and Malin was out. Lily dashed at the gap, sailing over the fallen dwarf with a graceful leap. A hand snatched at her cloak, but she pulled away. The split skirt gave her all the stride she could desire, and her longer legs gave her the edge. She plunged out of the clearing and away, hard on Malin's heels.

⚜   ⚜   ⚜

"Report," Sennet said. He eased his aching joints into a library chair and wrapped his hands round a mug of soup, which was all the dinner they had time for that evening.

Holly put down his own mug and took a deep breath. "Eastern lawn mined; particular attention to the approaches to the ceremonial garden. Booby-traps arranged. Storm shutters locked in place on the lower two floors."

"Provisions?"

"Water supply secure so long as we hold the ground floor. Potatoes, cabbages, and rabbits stashed all over, though the rabbits are prone to relocating themselves."

"Indeed," said Sennet.

He lifted the lantern which gave the dim room its only light and directed its beams into a corner. The scratching sound resolved itself into two small rabbits nibbling on a cabbage. It was one of a row of stolid cabbages which extended all along the wall of shelving. They twitched their noses at him, and carried on nibbling.

"Just how many cabbages do we have?" he asked, sitting back and taking another sip of soup.

"Lost count," Holly said. "Going on for two hundred, I think."

Sennet choked.

"Not all for us," Holly reassured him. "There's the rabbits, obviously, and the cows are penned in the ballroom. I'll need some for defensive purposes, too."

"Defensive purposes?" Sennet croaked.

"I can do things with cabbage which your granny never dreamed of," Holly said with a trace of pride. "Oh, and there's this. Just in case they somehow disarm us..." He handed Sennet a sealed cachet of thin paper. "Swallow this and you won't be answering any questions, never mind how loud they ask."

Sennet looked at him with eyebrows raised, and then took it, tucking the little packet between the frayed layers of his collar. "Suddenly, I find myself thankful I have survived your cooking all these years."

Holly coughed. "Yes, well...if you don't need me just now, I have some things to cook up in the hall."

"What sort of things?"

Holly hesitated. "Let's just say I wouldn't want to be the first to open the front door. Oh, and avoid naked flames."

"On which note," Sennet said, his head thrown back and his eyes narrowing, "can you smell smoke?"

⚜   ⚜   ⚜

Lily ran, the cold night air tearing at her lungs and the trees whipping at her face. Her eyes strained to keep Malin in sight. He moved fast, ducking and dodging, but he kept his hatchet in hand, and it caught what little light there was. She was gaining on him...

He whirled, and the hatchet passed only inches from her cuirass. Lily fell back with a yelp.

"You! Why are you following me?"

"What did you think I was going to do, stand there and wait to be bartered off to Phelan?"

"Seems more your style."

Lily hissed with frustration. "You promised me you'd take me somewhere safe, and you haven't!"

"Maybe it would have been safe if you hadn't gone throwing your weight around!"

"I'm the—"

"Shh!"

"Don't you shh me!"

"They're behind us." He turned, breaking into a run.

Lily followed close until he came to a stop, listening intently.

"Lost them." He was breathing heavily, his hand flexing on the hatchet's haft.

"As I was saying, I am the queen, and I have every right to demand the support of my subjects!"

"Subjects? Listen, Burnaby—"

There was a crash from the underbrush nearby. Lily froze.

"Burnaby is not subject to Arcelia," Malin hissed. "We go our own way."

"It doesn't seem to be doing you much good," Lily breathed back, trying not to be distracted from the sounds of the search around them.

"Keep your voice down."

The searchers were moving away, it sounded like, but still— too close.

Lily simmered. "Burnaby is too small to function as a nation without Arcelia's protection."

"You call this protection?"

"This is Phelan's doing—not mine! Of course Burnaby shouldn't be taken advantage of. But supposing I—changed things."

"You aren't in a position to change things."

"If I screamed," Lily whispered demurely, "that would change a few things, wouldn't it?"

"You'd be captured too."

"What have I got to lose?"

"What have you got to gain?"

"If you take me somewhere safe—"

"Where's safe?"

"Home," Lily decided, a pang rippling through her. "If you take me to Candra, I will reconsider the position of Burnaby."

"In the kingdom you don't have! And if I don't?"

"I'll scream. After all, if I'm going to be executed, I don't see why you should get away free, after you promised you'd help me!"

Malin groaned, a low, subterranean growl. "I should have taken a vow of silence."

Lily smiled in the darkness. "I'll take that as agreement to my terms."

"This is blackmail, you know."

"Not at all. This is practical diplomacy," Lily said serenely.

Malin uttered a hollow laugh. "This way."

"This way, *my lady*," Lily corrected.

"I told you, Burnabaise don't use titles." He pushed away.

They heard no more of their pursuers, but Malin insisted they ford the river rather than risk one of the bridges. The water was waist-deep, and, to Lily's puzzlement, faintly warm. She only knew of one warm river in the valley, and surely...

"This isn't Parsifal, is it?" she asked.

"Course it is."

"But it's so small!"

"You should see Percy where he springs between the Burning Hills," Malin said. "Narrow enough to step over and hot enough to cook in."

"You've been to Parsifal's spring?" Lily asked, amazed and more than a little envious.

"I've been everywhere, pretty much."

It was clear he was not in the mood for conversation. Lily concentrated on trying to walk quietly in her wet, steaming skirts.

An hour or two later, they were out of the trees and under a sky scattered with frozen stars. Lily studied the constellations. There were the Burning Hills, sparkling echoes of their name-sakes to the south, and there was the Rabbit, jumping over the Leaf and Bud until the world's end. At least the stars hadn't changed.

Lily pulled the cloak tighter around her, thankful for its thickness despite the drab colour. And, after all, who would see it? She would have to keep a low profile on the way back to Candra, lest Phelan's Wolves find her. She sighed. So much for being the cynosure of all eyes.

All eyes had been on her in the Council clearing, but she had not enjoyed the experience. Perhaps Malin was right; Burnaby wasn't really part of Arcelia. Arcelians, she was sure, would never have so much as *considered* selling her to Phelan to gain favour. Except...Phelan was Arcelian, wasn't he? And there were some who had followed him in the late War, and not her father, their rightful king. She shivered and huddled closer into the cloak. Perhaps staying out of sight was best, and not just for fear of running into Wolves.

They were out of Burnaby now, and into the gently rolling lands of Arcelia proper. They crested a low hill, and she could see for miles. It was beautiful, but she could not help wondering where, under that cold sky, the cold heart of her uncle slept. If he ever slept. Or had a heart.

"Come on!" Malin said. "The sooner we get there, the sooner I can get back to tormenting Phelan."

"Wouldn't it be more prudent to lie low for a while?"

"Where? *I* can't go home."

"I'm sorry," Lily said. "I didn't think they'd turn against you." *Or me.*

"Yeah, well, can't be helped," Malin said gruffly. "Do we have to hang around here all night?"

"It's just—so beautiful," Lily said, a catch in her voice. "The way the moonlight lies on the folds of the hills, swathed in the darkness of the trees..."

"Very poetic. Can we go now?"

"The beauty of the first light of dawn as it bathes the lofty peak in gold..."

"Too poetic. Dawn isn't for hours."

"Candra is always the first to see the dawn," Lily said proudly. "Bathed in the rising and the setting sun; that's why its name means *luminous*."

"That isn't dawn," Malin said. "It's fire."

Lily stared, her pupils dilating until the bright burning point was all she could see.

"No!"

And she was running, stumbling, falling down the hill, everything forgotten but the need to reach her stricken home. She scrambled back onto her feet and found herself swinging round, Malin's weight at the end of her arm.

"Stop! Think!"

"Master Sennet," she said, her voice betraying the tears she would not permit to fall. "Holly!"

"There's nothing you can do," Malin said urgently. "Except steer clear of the one place in the valley Phelan's likely to be."

"They were all I had left," she mourned.

"Yeah, well. Looks like neither of us is going home now."

Lily struggled to gain mastery of herself, choking her sobs down.

"Where to now?" Malin asked.

"I—I *can't*," Lily began.

She felt the tears welling up again and stopped. She had to know. Setting her face towards that dreadful light, she forced her feet to march on.

"Stop!"

Lily shook her head and kept going. Malin's footsteps followed her down the hill and she sped up. She was running nearly as fast as she could when she was hit from behind and came crashing to the ground with all the wind knocked out of her. She tried to kick away the weight pinning her legs down.

"Wolves!" Malin hissed at her, and she went limp with terror.

In the silence, she could hear them marching, close at hand. Malin crawled up beside her. "Stay still. Keep down."

She lifted her head far enough that she could see the starlight winking on the steel they carried. It was a column of men, marching towards Burnaby. Lily and Malin watched them march away in silence.

"Your family…"

"Will be safer without me," Malin said, bitterness tainting his words.

Lily sat up, nursing fresh pains where the cuirass had dug into her. "You tackled me. You *dared* to lay hands upon—"

"I asked nicely, which you can bet the Wolves wouldn't have. So where are we going now?"

She got to her feet, turning away from Candra so she didn't have to see that dreadful light. The curved end of the valley lay before her in the moonlight—Burnaby, most of it, but the foothills leading up to the eastern mountains were true Arcelia. Her eye followed the hills as they tumbled up towards the white peaks of the mountains.

"Of course…" she breathed.

"Of course what?"

"Woodward's eyrie! It's up on Mount Wardell—that one there, next to the Whitelaw."

The Whitelaw was the highest mountain in Arcelia, capped with snow year-round.

"I know which one Wardell is!"

"He disappeared from Candra; he *must* be there. And who better to—to advise than Woodward?"

She had almost said "to take over." Being queen wasn't supposed to be like this. Woodward would sort things out, and she could get on with preparations for Restoration Day like she was supposed to.

"Mount Wardell," she said firmly, and after one last lingering look at the halo of destruction surrounding her childhood home, she turned away and started slowly east.

⚜   ⚜   ⚜

Holly wiped a smut of falling ash from his sweaty brow. Who'd have thought that dried privet could burn so well? Even here, behind the sturdy castle walls, the heat was intense.

"Breach!" Sennet's voice echoed down the stone staircase.

"Already?" Holly galloped up the stairs, heart pounding.

"They're breaking down the Hedge as it burns," Sennet said, peering around the edge of the window-blind, "and running through."

"They'll be scorched," Holly said.

"They are certainly moving with alacrity," Sennet said dryly. "Prepare to repulse—"

A gargling scream came from the grounds outside.

Sennet's lips crooked. "It would appear that your little surprises are having quite an effect."

Holly blushed with pleasure.

"Just as I thought," Sennet went on. "They're targeting the ceremonial garden."

Further screams and shouts echoed off the castle walls.

"Or, rather, attempting to." He flashed a wicked grin at Holly.

Holly had a look for himself. "They're retreating already? That was easy!"

"A mere preliminary sortie," Sennet said. "Testing our defences."

"And finding them sound," Holly said proudly.

"Mm. Though if I am not very much mistaken, Phelan will be mapping the traps that have been set off. He'll know where it will be safe to send troops through. We had better be prepared."

⚜   ⚜   ⚜

Malin insisted they stay off the road, deserted as it was. Not that Lily minded. The pourstone road made her skin crawl, the way it lay in an unbroken line across the land like an endless millipede. An endless, dead millipede. No—worse than that, because this had never been alive. Even a dead millipede would have more life in it than that, as a thousand forms of life worked in it to restore it to the soil.

The soil itself was alive in Arcelia. The land was alive. Alive, but with these scars of unlife marked out across it. Lily set her jaw and looked fixedly in the opposite direction. Here was a hill, taller than the others, with the blocky remains of a great building atop it.

"Wait a moment!"

"What is it now?" Malin snapped.

"It must be!" Lily said, heart soaring. "The fortress of Roxburghe!"

He looked at the tumbled stones, black against the hillside. "Yeah. Ruins. Come on before I catch my death of standing around waiting for the Wolves to catch up."

"Don't you see? *That* is the place of safety! It must be *meant*," she said breathlessly, starting up the slope at a painful run.

"Meant my—" He broke off. "We're not going there. It's a waste of time!"

She turned on him. "I am queen of this realm, and *no one* tells me where to go. I am going to the fortress. You may do as you wish."

She started climbing again, and was soon aware that he was at her shoulder.

"I did say you could go," she pointed out.

"I promised I'd get to you a place of safety," he growled.

"I thank you for your faithful service," Lily replied, in her best queenly manner.

"This isn't service!" he snapped. "This is me doing what I said I'd do. I'm just making a point. This place isn't safe; it's a ruin."

"That's what you said about Candra," Lily said, unable to keep a thrill of excitement out of her voice.

"You aren't thinking...you are, aren't you? What have I done? Stuck with a madwoman who's hell-bent on getting herself killed. I was safer back in the prison," he groused. "At least then I knew I had a few weeks to live."

"Oh, stop complaining," Lily said, momentarily forgetting her blisters as she scrambled up the hill towards the looming ruin. "It will all be over soon and you will be handsomely rewarded."

"I don't want a reward," he muttered. "I want to not die."

The crumbling walls reared above them as they neared the ruin. Lily caught her breath in wonderment and began to run. Malin started to run after her and then gave it up.

"Better hope there's no Wolves camping out in there," he called up.

Lily stopped, poised on the outer edge of the curtain wall. She took a deep breath and plunged across.

Malin caught up with her standing in what had once been the inner keep, the very centre of the fortress. Blackened, scattered blocks of stone loomed against the lightening sky, showing where the walls had once stood, proud and high. Nothing now stood higher than Lily, straight as a tower in the midst of her ruins, her face frozen in a mask of rigid control.

"Sorry," he said. "I did tell you."

She made no reply.

"Best get going. Sun's coming up."

Lily took a deep breath. "Do you smell that?"

"I haven't had a bath in months, all right?"

"No—rosemary."

He sniffed. "No. Yes. You probably stood on it."

"Rosemary for remembrance," she said. "Someone remembers."

"Or it's just growing. Can we go now?"

She walked past him to the edge of the wall and stopped again, stooping to touch something barely visible.

"Harebells—for grief."

He gave up and watched her clamber about the ruins. She came back with a little posy in her hand.

"It's a grave-garden," she said. "Or a memorial garden. For my parents. Each plant is here, only…spread out. Maybe because of—of how they died."

"Or to hide it," he offered.

"Why would you hide a memorial garden? That defeats the whole point."

"I told you," he said, starting down the hill. "It's illegal. Not just for royalty, for anyone."

Lily drew breath in a disapproving hiss. "How can he *do* that to people? He *must* be stopped."

"We'll be lucky if *we* don't get stopped," Malin said. "It's practically broad daylight."

"It is not. But we can go now."

"Finally! Wardell?"

"Wardell."

He broke into a run, bounding across the terrain which was becoming more visible by the minute as day dawned in the valley of Arcelia. Lily followed, trying not to slip and fall, the precious posy tucked into her waistband. Someone remembered. It was too soon to give up hoping yet.

⚜   ⚜   ⚜

Holly lurched out of his chair, woken by Sennet's quick double stamp—a signal they had borrowed from the castle rabbits, which now infiltrated every room.

"What is it?"

"White flag," Sennet muttered, peering out into the bright daylight.

"He can't surrender," Holly pointed out muzzily. "He's sieging us."

"Parley party," Sennet said. "Keep a look out at the rear, will you? I don't trust this."

Holly nodded and jogged away to his post. The little detachment of Wolves came to a halt in easy view.

"Parley!" the leading officer shouted up. "We bring an offer from the Magister."

"I'm listening," Sennet replied.

"The offer is addressed to the young lady. You will call her forth that we may speak with her."

"Set her up in the window like a target, you mean," Sennet said indignantly. "What kind of doddering fool do you take me for?"

"It is important that we speak with her," the Wolf officer repeated. "A second will not do."

"If a second will do for Prince Phelan, a second will do for the queen," Sennet countered. "Does he expect she will come and go at the bidding of a mere salaried flunky?"

The Wolf officer bristled. "I am no flunky! I command all the troops in these divisions!"

"And I command the garrison of Candra," Sennet replied. "It appears we are perfectly matched for a parley. Do continue."

The Wolf officer barely hesitated; he knew his part.

"I am authorized by the Magister to extend the following offer to the young woman."

Sennet bristled at this disrespectful description, but kept silent.

"If she will surrender herself into his custody, neither she nor her supporters shall be harmed."

"That's it?" Sennet asked. "Complete surrender—surrender of her person to imprisonment, her castle to occupation, and her cause to its utter ruin—in return for a paltry promise of no personal injury?"

"It is the best offer she will get," the officer shouted back. "Tell her that! The monarchist cause was defeated fifteen years ago. There is nothing left to fight for. This is a most generous offer, extended by the Magister merely to save himself the little trouble it would take to destroy you all. Remember that. To burn this castle down would be the work of minutes."

"I doubt he will take such a step," Sennet called back, "considering the mistake it led to last time."

"This is the only offer of mercy she will receive," the Wolf barked. "Tell her that!"

"Such a momentous decision will require much consideration and consultation with advisers," Sennet temporized. "Days will be required."

"She has until tonight."

Hidden Worth

The moonlight glinted on the patches of snow and ice on the sides of Mount Wardell, casting shadows around the two figures toiling up the slope. Lily was, by this point, only too thankful for the sturdy boots and the second pair of socks. She only wished split skirts came with split petticoats. Flannel ones, for preference.

"It shouldn't be—much further," she gasped.

"That's the third time you've said that." Malin, annoyingly, was not out of breath at all. "So much for book-learning."

"And you know exactly where it is, do you?"

"Hereabouts," Malin said vaguely.

"Are you sure we haven't wandered onto the Whitelaw by mistake?"

"No, I've been here before, sure of it."

"What, and you haven't been to the Whitelaw? I thought you'd been everywhere!"

"Nothing up there to see. No Wolves to annoy. What's the point?"

Lily stopped and straightened her aching back. "Is that it there? That dark bit?"

Malin squinted. "Could be. That, or a crevasse which will swallow you whole. After you."

She shot him a Look.

"Fine," he said. "I'll scout around. Try not to do anything

stupid."

A moment later, he waved her on, and she slipped and slid across the icy slope to join him. Woodward's porch was surprisingly warm, considering it was made of ice. Or perhaps it was just the shelter from the wind it afforded that gave her that impression.

"Knock," she said, looking at the grand doors gleaming faintly before her.

"And have my knuckles freeze to the door? No, thanks. Anyway, it's open." Wrapping an arm in his grubby cloak, he shoved at the door, which swung back on invisible hinges with a faint hiss.

The room within lay in complete darkness except for a pool of moonlight on the floor by the window.

"Woodward?" Lily called cautiously.

There was a faint echo, no more.

"Hullo!" Malin bawled, causing Lily to jump violently. "No, must be out. Or deaf. Is that a pile of blankets I see there? Just what I always wanted. See you in the morning."

"You're just going to go to sleep?"

Malin looked up, already wrapping himself in two blankets at once.

"What else? Calling's no good. Can't see anything. Might as well get some sleep."

"But...what if there are Wolves around here somewhere?" she asked lamely.

"They practically never come up here. No one to harass."

"What about Woodward?"

"And they don't believe in wizards."

"Are you sure it's safe?"

"Would I wrap myself up like a hot potato if I wasn't?"

"It's hardly proper," Lily demurred. "Sleeping in someone's house when you haven't been invited..."

"Fine. You stay awake all night again. I'm going to sleep."

"Where will I sleep?"

"Anywhere you like, as long as you shut up," he mumbled into his blankets.

"I can't sleep in here! Not with—" she could feel the heat flooding up her face "—with you."

The only answer was a snore.

Shivering, she crept across the floor, gathered an armful of blankets and crept away. There had to be another room here somewhere! After banging her nose and then her elbow walking into walls, she found a door and made herself a warm little nest just inside it.

Better than a ditch, she reminded herself as she tried to find a comfortable position, but a feather bed it wasn't. How long had it been since she'd last slept in a bed? While trying to decide whether to count the nights or the times she'd been asleep, she dropped off.

⚜   ⚜   ⚜

They were ready and waiting when the parley party returned.

"Were there that many of them before?" Holly muttered as the Wolves tramped across the pockmarked eastern lawn.

"No. But, this time, they've come for prisoners or a fight," Sennet murmured. "Against the code of warfare for a parley party to start hostilities, of course, but I doubt that will stop them. *We* shall not breach the parley unless they do so first. In any case, the longer we can keep them talking, the longer she has. We are fighting for hours and minutes now." He straightened his clothes, fingering the collar for a moment. "Keep observation to the rear unless I call."

"Two stamps for alarm?" Holly asked as he left the room.

"And seven for war," Sennet said gravely.

He kept them waiting as long as he could without their tempers boiling over.

"Well?" barked the Wolf commander. "Where is she?"

"I *do* apologize for keeping you waiting," Sennet began in slow and measured tones. "Lateness may not be a breach of the code of parley, but, as I am well aware, it is most certainly a breach of good manners, and, as I say, I do apologize."

"Never mind that! Where is she?"

"Oh, that's very good of you, very good indeed. I can't tell you how glad I am that simple courtesy is not quite lost even under such, ah, circumstances as these."

The commander looked up at him irritably. "Where is she?"

"Ah, yes, of course. Well, yes. Not entirely unrelated to my unpardonable lateness, really, as a matter of fact. These few hours didn't, in the final analysis, constitute quite enough time to make such a decision, you know, being as it is such a, well, such a momentous decision, if you know what I mean…"

The Wolf commander interrupted, trying to shout him down, but Sennet maundered on with such oblivious determination that the Easterling gave up, before the attempt robbed him of his dignity.

"—affecting not only *her* in a very—a very personal way, but also, and I think this is very important to her, affecting the wellbeing of her dependents, and, indeed, that of all her people individually and—and as a whole."

Sennet stopped. He could hear the commander's teeth grinding.

"She's had all day," the commander growled. "That's it. Either she walks out those doors or the assault starts. Right now."

"Oh, I say, that's a bit much. I mean, the code of warfare doesn't allow…"

Sennet tailed off as the Wolves, on a signal from their commander, began to wind their crossbows. The commander looked up at him with the first hint of a smile as the Wolves placed their bolts and raised the bows.

Sennet straightened up. "Very well." He lifted his chin, and prepared his legs to drop him to the floor at a moment's notice. "You may tell Prince Phelan that the queen will not be accepting his terms."

To Sennet's surprise, the commander waved his men to lower their weapons, though not, he noted, unwind them. The commander moved a few steps closer, not marching, but in a casual saunter. Sennet stiffened. So far, the exchange had proceeded just as he had expected—but not this. For the first time, he felt unprepared.

"And you?" the commander enquired, his voice just loud enough to hear. "What will you accept?"

Sennet's mind spun. So that's what this was. An attempt to corrupt the captain of the garrison into betraying his queen.

"She is young and inexperienced," the commander went on persuasively. "There could be great benefits for an older, wiser head who might consider the situation in a more prudent light."

Sennet could see why Phelan had made this man commander. His mastery of Arcelian was exemplary, and his performance as spokesman of the parley party a triumph—he doubted even Phelan could do so well.

The idea of capitulating was impossible, of course; not merely physically impossible, in that they could not surrender a queen who wasn't there, but impossible for a man of honour. But should he pretend to be swayed? He might be able to buy more time, but deception was dangerous. One could very easily end up deceiving oneself.

He chewed his lip, considering, and the commander, evidently taking this as a good sign, nodded and smiled encouragingly. A grimace of distaste appeared on Sennet's face before he could stop himself. Well, that decided that, then. His acting skills weren't up to it, and it was with relief that he cast deception aside and finally said what he thought.

"If you're looking for a traitor," he bellowed, hoping his

voice would carry clear across to Phelan, "you're looking in the wrong camp! I am no traitor, and my loyalty lies in no man's purse. Which is more than can be said for—"

At this point his legs remembered their duty, and he flopped to the floor. His "—you!" was drowned out by the thwack of bolts into the walls and ceiling, followed by the tingle of shattered glass as the remains of the window fell to the floor.

Moments later, seven quick thuds reverberated through the castle. Seven stamps. War.

⚜   ⚜   ⚜

The morning sun was high in the sky, the ice house a-dazzle with a thousand tiny sparkling points of light, when Lily's scream tore across the silence.

Malin dashed through the doorway, hatchet in hand and blanket trailing, and fell over Lily. Her horrified gaze remained fixed on the low bed across the room. Just visible under a pile of dark brown blankets was the cold, bluish face of Woodward the wizard.

"That's not good." Malin put his hatchet away and shook off the blanket's tangling embrace. "Think he's dead?"

"I—I've never seen a dead person," Lily whispered.

"Lucky." Malin stooped over the still face. "He's pretty cold." He listened. "Can you stop that chattering for a minute?"

Lily clamped a hand over her mouth to stifle the rattle of her teeth. Woodward wasn't the only one who was cold.

"He's not breathing."

"How can he be dead? He's like—like the land itself! How will we survive without him? How will the land survive?"

"Too many questions before breakfast. We're not dead yet—that's something." He pulled the covers back.

"Malin!"

"What? He's not going to feel it. Stop talking, will you?" He put his head on one side and rested it on Woodward's chest.

Lily's jaw dropped. She hitched it up, glared at him, pulled herself out of her blankets and shook herself out. She was formulating a stinging lecture on the importance of showing respect for the dead, with side notes on showing respect for the royal living, when a broad grin spread across Malin's face.

Lily stared at him.

"His heart is beating," Malin said, straightening up. "He's not dead. He's just—I don't know, dormant or something."

"Like a root in the winter soil?"

"Something like that. Better keep him well mulched." Malin pulled the covers back up, tucking them in carefully.

Emotions poured over each other, faster than Lily could react to them. Disapproval of Malin's informality. Relief that Woodward wasn't dead. And, finally, the worry of what she was meant to do now.

"Can't we wake him up—just to ask him a question or two?"

"Answer questions? He's not even *breathing*."

"But—but—what am I supposed to do now? How could he do this to me?"

"Right. He's halfway dead, but *you've* got problems."

"He can't have meant this to happen. He wouldn't just send me off without trying to help me."

"He doesn't look up to much," Malin said.

"He managed to get himself here," Lily pointed out.

"Without us or Wolves spotting him along the way?"

"I think he can just…stop being somewhere and start being somewhere else," Lily said. "Like he did in the garden, with the dandelion."

"So why here?" Malin asked.

"Perhaps…oh! That must be it! He knew I'd be looking for him, so he came here as a sign."

"Of what?"

"A sign," Lily said impressively, "that *this is where the Restoration Requisites are hidden.* It must be! Where else would it make sense to hide them, but in the wizard's own home? You said yourself the Wolves practically never come up here."

"Maybe."

"That was why he spent his last effort bringing himself here—to act as a signpost for me in my quest. Oh, *dear* Woodward!"

"So if they're here, how come the Wolves haven't found them?"

"Because they are hidden. Obviously."

Half an hour later, the small suite of rooms had been thoroughly searched. Even Woodward's blankets had been sifted through.

"They're better hidden than I thought," Lily admitted.

She paced once again through the main room, its window gazing onto the valley below. A lazy plume of smoke curled up from the forest at the foot of the mountain. She came to a stop at the room's one piece of decoration: a plaque inlaid with a pattern of coriander leaves, set into the floor.

Why coriander? Dandelions would make more sense, being Woodward's emblem. Dandelions meant *rustic oracle* in the language of flowers. Coriander meant…she searched her memory. *Hidden worth.* She gasped.

Malin looked up from his nest of blankets. "What?"

"This plaque," Lily said, kneeling down to look for the catch, "depicts coriander. Coriander means *hidden worth.*"

The plaque shot upwards and Lily shot backwards. Recovering herself quickly, she had the satisfaction of seeing Malin completely taken aback.

Hastily, she wrapped her cloak over her hands to protect them from the ice. Malin came closer for a better look as she carefully lifted the plaque off its pedestal and set it down. Together, they peered into the pedestal. A small wooden box rested within. Scarcely daring to breathe, Lily reached down and picked it up. Something moved within as she raised it to the light. She drew a deep and tremulous breath. This was the moment of her destiny. Secretly, she was rather glad Malin was here to see it. It might teach him a thing or two!

"Shouldn't it be—" Malin started.

"Shh!" She lifted the lid off with a graceful flourish.

The box contained two glass marbles.

"—bigger?" Malin finished.

Lily stared in silence at the two little balls rolling about in the bottom of the box, her face frozen. There was a hissing sound beside her, then a gulp, and then Malin threw back his head and roared with laughter. Suffused with rage, Lily hurled the box at the wall. It crashed into splinters, and the marbles rolled across the floor. She stared out the window, humiliated, infuriated, enraged. How could Woodward do such a thing to her? How could he be so...so disloyal? And what was she to do now?

Malin hiccupped to a stop. "Sorry, but—the look on your face!" he choked.

She ignored him. Behind the flaming anger, a cold despair was growing. Denton, Burnaby, Roxburghe, Woodward... every source of help and comfort proved empty, and, now, to be mocked like this! The cold sank into her feet, her hands, and crept its aching way through her body. Behind her, Malin began picking up the pieces of the box.

"Not much left but tinder," he said. "I'm impressed. Didn't know you had it in you!"

A picture of Aunt Hortensia's disapproving face hovered before Lily's stinging eyes. All she had left was herself, and her belief in herself as queen. To have behaved in such an unqueenly manner!

"You're not such a cold fish as you make out," Malin said. "You should throw things more often; people might like you more." He appeared at her shoulder, proffering the remains of the box. "Toothpick?" And he was off again, in a full, rich, body-shaking laugh. This was too much.

"Our world is doomed to end," she hissed at him, "and all you can do is laugh?"

The paroxysm subsided. "Never say die. We've made it this far, after all."

We? Lily swept away to the other side of the room, ostensibly to check on Woodward.

"No use losing your sense of humour," Malin called after her. "He must have meant something by it."

Lily turned on him. "How can you possibly think this was his intent? It—it's a *joke!*"

"Who could have pulled a switch with all that fancy coriander stuff going on?" he asked reasonably. "Anyway, none of the Restoration Day stuff would fit in there, would it?"

This was undeniably true. Wearily, she returned to look at the coriander plaque. Malin gathered up the marbles from the corners of the room to which they had rolled.

"Have a look. See if it means anything to you."

Lily looked down at the two glass spheres as they rested on his palm.

"No, nothing. Now, if they'd been flowers—! But what could two marbles possibly mean?"

"They didn't roll anywhere interesting," Malin contributed.

"One orange, one blue," Lily murmured.

Malin perked up. "What was that?"

"The marbles. One's blue and the other's orange."

"No—you said one orange, one blue."

"It's the same thing."

Malin rolled the marbles around until they swapped places on his hand, staring intently at them the whole time.

"What is it?" Lily asked impatiently. "What difference does it make which way round they are?"

"You can't see through the back of his head," Malin muttered.

"*What?*"

"And never upside down," he added.

"I *demand* that you tell me what you mean," Lily said.

He looked up and shook his head in mock disapproval.

"Or I'll throw something else at the wall," she added.

He grinned. "Could be nothing, but I know a man who has eyes like this. One orange, one blue, reading from left to right."

"Who is he? Where is he? Maybe he—"

"No idea where he is now. Could be anywhere. He's a pedlar, goes all over."

A pedlar...

"With a handcart," Lily said. "Teapots and lace..."

"You know him?"

"My father did," Lily said sadly. *Wait.* "My *father* did!"

Their eyes met.

"Malin," Lily said, "I *must* find that pedlar!"

❧ ❧ ❧

Holly and Sennet had kept watch all night, but the main assault force did not move in until day broke. Each kept watch from one side of the shattered window as the Wolves spread out across the grounds. This time, the Easterlings were carrying makeshift battering rams: trees freshly hacked down and stripped of their branches. This time, they had a plan.

"As I thought, Phelan was taking notes," Sennet murmured, watching the movements to the northeast. "Although his cartographic skills do not seem equal to mine."

The booby-traps were still doing sterling service, and the pockmarked "safe routes" of pre-exploded traps seemed eager to snare the unwary with a wrenched ankle or a tangling fall.

"Are they taking that one round to the ballroom?" Holly asked anxiously, as a ram-carrying party moved into his field of vision to the southeast.

"It makes sense," Sennet conceded. "The long windows are practically doors, and if they get a foothold there, they could use it as an internal stronghold…" He seized his quiver. "We had better be waiting for them."

"I think we'd better not," Holly said, and giggled.

Sennet looked up at him sharply. "You think this is funny?"

"No, it's just…it turns out a steady diet of cabbage is having unintended effects. Er, potentially toxic effects."

"The cows are sickening?"

"No, they don't seem bothered. But it's probably not safe for a person to go in there. Definitely not with any kind of flame. Or anything that could make a spark, if it comes to that."

"Such as the nails on hobnailed boots?" Sennet enquired.

"Exactly so," Holly agreed.

They listened as the distant thuds sped up. Holly opened his mouth to speak, but Sennet hushed him. They listened in silence as the thuds became a crash, a crack, and, finally, a hiss and a roar.

Holly almost jigged in place. "Oh, I wish I could go see!"

"Steady, soldier. There's a battle ahead of us."

"Of course," Holly said penitently, and then began to laugh.

The Wolves were trying to retreat, their hair smoking and their clothes afire in places. Occasional cows stampeded past, knocking them down, and the harried Wolves were past remembering where their safe routes were.

"They're pulling back past the Hedge," Sennet reported from his vantage point on the other side of the window-frame. He carefully manoeuvred his telescope into position, focussed it, and began to laugh.

"Have a look," he gurgled, and collapsed in his chair where he gave full vent to his mirth.

Holly put his eye to the telescope and squinted thoughtfully at a scene of argument and dissent.

"That'll teach him to hire mercenaries," Sennet said exultantly.

"I don't understand," Holly said, frowning at the telescope.

"What you see before you, my dear fellow, is, if I mistake not, a pay dispute. Having, no doubt, been told that they were mostly there for show, and possibly that the castle was held by a girl and an old woman, no more, they find the reality to be somewhat different, and are probably demanding danger money."

"Out of Phelan?" Holly said dubiously. "You'd think they'd know him better than that by now."

"I doubt they will get much out of him," Sennet admitted, "but it all buys us time. Buys *her* time."

⚜   ⚜   ⚜

Lily had two grazed hands and a scraped leg by the time they reached the tree-line, so eager was she to be on the way to solving this mystery Woodward had left for her. Malin jogged tolerantly along behind her, waiting every time she fell but never, she noticed, offering to help her up. Considering the possible meanings of this, she tripped over a tree root and fell again.

"Where are you even hurrying to?" Malin asked.

Lily shook the leaf mould off her skirts. "We're going to find the pedlar!"

"Where?"

"We will ask around," she said loftily.

"That'll end well. *Hello, we're on the run from the authorities and we'd like some information.*"

There was a whistle and a thunk. Lily whirled, to see an arrow quivering in a tree trunk at the height of Malin's head. Malin himself was nowhere to be seen.

"Take cover, you idiot!" said the injured tree.

She turned instead to see where the arrow had come from. A big, broad-faced fellow stood waist-deep in the underbrush, carefully nocking another arrow.

"Who're you?" he asked, his voice slow and suspicious.

"I am Lily, the Queen of Arcelia," Lily answered, leaving out her lineage for brevity's sake. The tree groaned behind her.

The man looked even more suspicious, but at least he wasn't firing again. "They said you was dead. You don't look dead."

There was a rustle in the underbrush behind him, and a diminutive old woman looked out.

"What's all this noi—?" she began, and caught sight of Lily. Her mouth stayed open, forming an O which matched the roundness of her eyes.

"Leaf and bud, it's dead Queen Celandine," she gasped, and then her eyes narrowed. "No, it ain't, though... You must be Princess Lily."

Lily inclined her head.

"The name's Violet," the old woman said, bobbing a curtsey that made her momentarily disappear beneath the brush. "Gran Vi's what I'm mostly called. And this here's my grandboy, Roley. Make a bow, Roley."

As he did so, she spotted the bow and arrows he was trying to hide behind his back, and, the next moment, her sharp eyes alighted on the arrow in the tree.

"Roley, you never! You did!"

She hauled him down by his sleeve and gave him a clip around the ear. He stood rubbing it and looking deeply embarrassed.

"I'm that ashamed!" Gran Vi said.

"That's quite all right," Lily said graciously. "The arrow went nowhere near me."

"...warning shot..." mumbled the big man.

"Nowhere near *you*," the pierced tree said sourly. "*Quite* all right!"

"Who's that, then?" Gran Vi demanded.

Malin stepped out from behind the tree. "Malin of Burnaby." His gaze dared her to make anything of it.

"I've heard of you. Travelling with the princess, are you? How'd that happen?"

"I wish I knew," he muttered.

"I'm afraid we haven't much to offer, m'lady, what with one thing and another—"

"Just passing through," Malin said hastily.

"—but I'd be pleased to offer you a cup of tea, if you'd be willing to accept."

A cup of tea!

"I would be *delighted*," Lily said.

"Just a minute," said Malin, and beckoned her aside.

"Do excuse us for a moment," said Lily, and followed him. "What is it?"

"These people have nothing," Malin said in an undertone. "You can't just swan in and take what little they have!"

"I *am* what little they have." Lily's voice vibrated with passion. "And I will not take that from them!"

Just how little they had was soon borne in on her as they entered the broad clearing in which their home had, until recently, stood. Faint smoke was still rising from the remains of a cottage. Personal belongings, uprooted plants and the occasional aimless chicken were scattered across the rest of the space.

"Pardon the mess," Gran Vi said dryly. "We had a few callers last night."

"Wolves?" Malin asked.

"Who else?"

Lily looked at the wreckage, frozen. Was this what they had done to Candra?

"W-why did they do this? Why?"

"Intimidation," Malin growled.

Gran Vi coughed meaningfully. "That, and we ain't exactly been following all these fool laws they have these days."

"You mean—" Lily began.

"We keep to the old ways," the old woman said. "Maybe we need to hide it a bit better. Seems like there's Wolf Packs coming through every five minutes these days. Must be I'm getting old."

Lily was dumbfounded. "You've gone through this before?"

"Must be—what, three times now?"

Roley nodded solemnly.

"And you haven't caved," Malin said admiringly.

"I'm too old to change," Gran Vi said, hobbling over to the fire and poking it up. "And I'll be darned if I start letting some upstart snip of a blue-eyed back-stabber tell me how to live. Pardon my language, I'm sure." She turned to Lily. "I forgot he was your uncle."

"Oh, please," said Lily earnestly, "I wouldn't *dream* of moderating your language."

Their eyes met and the old woman cackled. "I'm sure I can think of a few more things to call him if I put my mind to it."

A rustle in the trees had them all turning their heads, as a dark woman in a plain dress emerged into the clearing. She stopped dead and stared at Lily.

"Here's Marigold," Gran Vi said, "just in time for a cuppa. This is the Princess Lily, Marigold, as everyone thought was dead all these years!"

The woman unfroze and moved forward. "Queen Lily, surely," she said, her voice hesitant and low.

Lily inclined her head graciously. "Quite right."

"And what brings you to these parts, my lady?" she asked, taking the heavy kettle from Gran Vi and pouring a stream of steaming water into the waiting teapot.

"Bless me if I didn't forget to ask," Gran Vi said.

"We're—" Malin began.

"No need to discuss such things over tea," Lily said firmly, ignoring the look in Malin's eye. The social graces must be observed, even sitting on a fallen tree trunk, drinking tea from a chipped earthenware mug. "Do tell us about yourself, dear Violet."

"There's no use calling me that these days, it's been that long. I've been Gran for more'n thirty years, and Mam another thirty before that, and not a soul has called me Violet since my dear husband passed on twenty or more years ago."

"I'm so sorry," Lily murmured.

"Can't complain. He was seventy-two, and it's a woman's lot in life to outlive her man, more often than not."

There was a hastily muffled sound from where Marigold was pouring tea. Lily tactfully kept her eyes averted.

"You'd be thinking I'm an old woman now, and you'd be right," Gran Violet went on. "Going on sixty-five years it must be since Geric—that's my husband—came to join me on this land. I've lived here all my life. Born in this very house. A year or two after we wed, along came Eddi—just the one, same as my parents just had me."

Lily's confusion must have caught the old woman's eye. "Oh, Marigold's not my daughter, though she's been as good to me as any daughter could be."

Marigold smiled briefly. "Kind of you, Mam."

"Rubbish," said Gran vigorously. "A good wife to my son and a good mother to my grandsons, and that's all a woman can ask, never mind pothering round after an old woman like me. This land'll be yours when I'm gone, and none more deserving of it. Where was I?"

"Your son Eddi," Lily prompted.

"Oh, yes. Well, he grew up, and wed Marigold here, and then along came Deni and Roley, four years apart, and the seasons rolled along, as they do. And then there was the War."

An indefinable stiffness seemed to fall on her listeners. Lily sipped her scalding tea, eyes lowered.

"Fifteen years ago. Geric was five years buried. He never saw the War, and I'm thankful for that. Eddi wasn't so young as he had been, going on for fifty, but he went off to fight all the same. Insisted. Said Phelan had to be defeated, come what may. It'd be a quick war, he said, and no point waiting around; now or never. P'raps he wanted to keep an eye on Deni—dead set on going, *he* was. They get it in them at that age, got to go off adventuring or some sort." She fell silent, gazing back down the years.

"How old was he?" Lily asked gently, hoping to prompt more of her recollections, but not daring to ask the question that buzzed in her head.

"Twenty," Marigold said huskily. "Just had his birthday, three weeks before he left." She turned back to the fire and stirred vigorously.

"And that was that," Gran said. "Eddi was right; it was a quick war—especially for him. Lost in the first week. Untrained land-men up against professional soldiers. Word came through eventually, but we'd guessed long before."

"And—and Deni?"

"Word never came," Marigold said shortly.

"I'm so sorry," Lily said, her eyes prickling. "It's terrible, not knowing." She couldn't imagine what that must be like, stretching out year after year.

"Not your fault," Gran Vi said reasonably, dashing at the corners of her eyes. "You weren't but a baby. It's that…ooh, I could strangle him with my bare hands."

"Indirectly, that's what brings us here," Lily said, setting down her empty mug.

"To invite me to Denton to strangle the Magister? Let me pack my nightie and I can leave in five minutes," Gran Vi said, cracking a smile.

"Gran, you didn't ought to talk like that," Roley said reprovingly.

"Pardon an old woman's anger," she said, "but that man! Life on the land's hard enough, but it has its rewards. And then he comes along, like—like one of them nasty flowers that grows out the side of a tree and sucks away its life till it withers and dies. I don't hold with killing as a rule," she said simply, "but if it's him or the land that's got to die, I'd much rather it was him."

"Hear hear," said Malin.

Lily felt in her pocket for the two marbles and held them out where all could see.

"Do you know anyone with eyes like these?"

"Pedlar," Gran Vi said immediately. "Only feller I've ever seen with eyes that don't match."

"Seen him lately?" Malin asked.

She sucked her teeth. "Not these—two summers, would it be, Mari?"

"Three," Marigold said.

"When the storm blew that old oak down," Roley volunteered.

"So it was, so it was. Three summers now."

Lily bit her lip. "Do you think he's—"

"Dead?" Marigold finished. "He was no friend to Phelan."

"Could be he retired," Gran Vi said encouragingly. "He wasn't so young as he once was, and pedlaring's a hard job. Or maybe he just gave up on the hills. Or set up shop somewhere out of the weather."

Lily sighed. Another dead end. He could be anywhere— or nowhere!—and Restoration Day was less than two weeks away.

"He brung us news from Corrie," Roley said lugubriously.

"That's a point. Corrie might have news of him," Gran Vi said, snapping her fingers.

"Who is Corrie?" Lily asked, interest stirring again.

"She was engaged to our Deni," Marigold said.

"Coreopsis, her proper name is, but none'll call her that. She's at the Leaf and Bud inn, down over."

Malin nodded. "I heard he was round the inns a lot."

"And not just for the custom," Gran Vi said dryly. "Still, if you've a fancy, you could head that way. Corrie'd be sure to make you welcome, and we'd be much obliged if you'd carry our greetings with you. It's a good day's walk," she explained, "and we don't get down there much these days."

"And with good reason," Marigold muttered.

"Why is that?" Lily asked.

"The Leaf and Bud's in Dunlop," Marigold said. Lily recognized the name: a large village at the foot of the eastern mountains, some way north.

Malin scowled. "Wolf Pack garrison."

❖   ❖   ❖

"The front door is starting to crack," Sennet said, his voice calm and his head cocked to receive every sign from below.

Holly stepped back from the window where he had been harrying the ramming-party with his arrows and listened for a moment.

"Better brace," he advised, wedging himself into a corner.

The blast rippled through the whole building; and in Scholars' Tower, a gentle shower of plaster dust sifted down like icing sugar.

"Ten minutes till we're wide open," Holly said, dusting himself off. He might be soon to die, but he jolly well wasn't going to go to his death looking like a fairy cake.

"Right. I'll take over at the window and pick them off as they regroup," Sennet said, "and you start phase two downstairs. Try to avoid being seen, if at all possible—we don't want them getting an idea of our numbers."

Holly nodded and exchanged his bow and quiver for the little bundles he'd prepared earlier, slipping out the door and down the stairs into the dimness of the shuttered floors below.

The front door—or, rather, the hole where the front door had been—showed no signs of life, so he arranged some small and snappy surprises for the first wave of invaders and shooed away the rabbits who showed an unhealthy interest in them. He did not have to wait long. Whether propelled by fear of Phelan or greed for some promised reward, the Wolves surged back with a will.

Holly slid from Observation Point #1 to Observation Point #2, where he was better cloaked by the darkness. From this vantage point, he saw the Wolves set off his little snappers, which did a great deal to restore them to what Sennet had called their "previous state of nervous apprehension."

As more Wolves poured in, they split into two main forces and branched left and right from the hall. Holly frowned. Whatever Phelan was paying these people, he wasn't getting his money's worth. You took a group of mindless thugs and gave them weapons, and all of a sudden they thought they were an army. But they had no idea of what it took to be a soldier.

How was he going to deal with two separate forces of Wolves without getting caught by either—or, worse, getting pincered between them? Wait, though…

His mind sparkled, and a new plan was born. It was risky, but the payoff was too great not to try it. He only hoped he lived long enough to tell someone about it.

There was a sudden movement in the darkness, a cry, a little thud…then pandemonium. Holly, his eyes long attuned to the darkness, could see what they could not; the darting movements all around them, which they were firing at wildly, were the castle rabbits—a veritable mêlée of them. Holly made a mental note to commemorate these unwitting defenders of Candra in the event of his survival, and moved on. He wished he had kept his earplugs; the Wolves did not have good aim, and a wounded rabbit was not the sort to crawl away and die quietly. The sound was ear-piercing, unnerving…effective.

Holly waited. The officer managed to restore order, in time, and roundly castigated his men for wasting their ammunition on rabbits when there were clearly greater threats about them. From now on, he ordered, they were to verify floor-level targets before firing. Holly pieced the meaning together from his small store of Easterling, and rejoiced. By dint of suitable noises, he drew them on to his chosen location, right in the middle of the castle.

His ears caught the sound of the Wolves approaching from the other direction; he needed to be quick. He fumbled the precious white metal arrangement from his pocket, checked his escape route, and closed his eyes. They were nearly upon him, from both sides. He started the reaction and, eyes still closed, skidded the precious bundle out into the middle of the room. He clapped a hand over his eyes. It all depended on the timing…

The Wolves picked up the movement; he'd expected that. Obedient to their officer's command, they all stared, trying to identify it—and then it went off, burning with a brilliant white light Holly could detect even through his hand. A full-scale panic took hold. The Wolves fired blindly; the double doors on the other side of the hall opened, and the officer in command of the second detachment slumped to the floor, a bolt in his leg. His men were not slow to respond to the attack.

Staying low, Holly crept back up the service stair. His work here was done. It was only delaying the inevitable, but every minute they gained was a little victory of its own.

⚜   ⚜   ⚜

Gran Vi insisted her guests stay the night, it being Fallowday, the traditional day of rest. Roley managed to scavenge enough for a temporary shelter, which kept off the fine rain that fell all through the night.

By the time they said their farewells, it was raining heavily. Roley set them on the path north—they had to keep to the hills as long as possible, Malin insisted—after which, they would descend nearly due west to Dunlop, at the foot of the hills. When Lily asked how they would know when to turn west, Roley turned grave and silent.

All he would say was, "you'll know," and, soon after, he left them.

Lily understood what he meant when they came to the edge of the trees. A wasteland lay ahead of them: a desolated, desecrated hillside. Not only had every tree been hacked down, but even all the smaller plants that had flourished under their canopy. Anything big enough to be profitable had been dragged away, and the rest left to rot. Lily stared, and struggled to believe.

"How could they? How could anyone be so foolish? This isn't coppicing—nothing will grow back from this. There's nothing left for next year, or—" She stopped, and stared in silence for a moment. "He must be mad."

It had never before occurred to her how much of the trouble of going downhill was spared by the trees holding the hillside in place as you descended. With the root systems rotting below and the rain turning everything above to mud, it was all too easy to slip, slide and fall. Her cloak was soon a motley of dark blue wool and reddish earth, sodden with the constant rain.

The low cloud would make excellent cover for their approach, Malin said, but Lily found herself wishing for a more waterproof cover as she squelched along. And perhaps also a chance to have her clothes washed, as she'd spent last Launderday climbing up Mount Wardell.

It was nearing dusk when they finally approached the outskirts of the town. Lily waited, wrapped in her cloak in the shelter of a rotting tree stump, bracken pulled over her by Malin to make her disappear. He'd insisted on having a surreptitious look around, so she was left here cogitating on the evidence to hand thus far.

Dunlop was no longer the large village she knew from her geography lessons. It had recently been added to, with rows of flimsy little dwellings, all alike, and big, boxy buildings with chimneys. This couldn't be ordinary population growth; it had to be an influx of people from the surrounding country-side, and she suspected it hadn't been entirely voluntary. An-other problem for Restoration Day to put right. The big boxes must be the manufactories Malin had mentioned. She made a face at them. Even the Denton dungeon wasn't that ugly.

They didn't look all that new, and they weren't aging well. The one new thing in the town was the grey wall going up around it, like the wall cutting off Denton. From this distance, it resembled a millipede curling around the town, and she shuddered, fervently hoping there was nothing so crawly in the bracken around her. The queen and the land might be bound by indissoluble ties, but she drew the line at millipedes, with their scaly backs, and their long fringe of legs brushing—

There was a rustle in the underbrush close by and Lily leapt to her feet with a shriek.

Story and Song

"What did I tell you about not moving?" Malin scolded, for it was he. "No one'll spot you if you don't *move!*"

"I thought you were a millipede," Lily said, trying to sound dignified.

"Right. Don't tell me; I don't want to know."

"What did you find out?" she enquired. Anything to change the subject.

"The Leaf and Bud's this side of town—other side of the wall-works, though. Not the closest inn to the barracks, so we should be all right."

Lily extricated herself from the bracken. "What do they need a wall for if they have a garrison?"

"Tolls. Dunlop's a trade hub in these parts. They'll tax everyone coming in or out. That'll pay for the garrison and then some."

"But what will they do when people can't afford to pay the tolls?"

"Raise the tolls on whoever's left, probably. Keep quiet."

Lily wanted to shout, "This is my kingdom! Stop telling me what to do!" but that would be improper, and, in any case, he was right about the need for silence, so she contented herself with a haughty glare and swept away, her cloak dragging bits of broken bracken behind her.

She also reluctantly accepted the need for a subtle approach, rather than a proper entrance through the front door. As Malin said, just because Corrie was loyal, it didn't mean her patrons were. They waited under the dripping eaves of an outbuilding in the cobbled yard until a door opened and a woman fitting Roley's description stepped out, her "crinkly hair" now scattered with silver.

"Corrie!" Malin called quietly.

The woman's head turned.

"Who's there?" she called sharply. "Show yourself!"

Lily stepped forward and dropped the hood from her head. Corrie stared at her, unspeaking, and finally drew in a long, satisfied breath.

"So you're not dead, then, after all," she said, and a smile slowly spread across her face.

It was not a simple, guileless smile like Roley's. Though unmistakably a happy smile, it portended a number of pointy and unpleasant things for those of Phelan's ilk who stood against her. Cheerful as she doubtless was, Lily sensed this was not a woman to cross and turn your back on.

"But that wasn't your voice I heard calling."

Malin came around the edge of the building. "Malin of Burnaby. We've just come from Gran Vi."

"A long-dead princess in company with a twice-dead hero, come down the mountain to bring me greetings," she said. "They sing of you, Malin, when they can scrape together the coin to get drunk, and they think the ears aren't listening. And they pay for it, too. Lost a week's wages for singing myself, once. Lucky to get away with so little, seeing as I was sober."

Malin grinned. "I owe you."

"Is there somewhere in your inn we could talk?" Lily asked.

"Privately," Malin added.

Corrie's face darkened. "It isn't my inn any more. It's Jaimes's inn."

"Who's Jaimes?" Lily enquired.

Corrie snorted. "A mangy cur that fancies himself running with the Wolves."

"Corrie!" shouted a harsh and scratchy voice from within. "Where y' got to?"

This was followed by words that made Lily's ears burn, even though she was uncertain of the meaning of most of them, and quite certain the rest were being incorrectly used.

"Cowshed!" hissed Corrie and flung herself back up the steps and through the door.

Lily and Malin fled back to their hiding place, waiting to be sure of no prying eyes before they ventured out in search of Corrie's chosen rendezvous. There was a distinct earthiness of smell around more than one of the outbuildings, but only one of them mooed.

"Oh, how *sweet*," Lily said.

The sole occupant of the cowshed was a large red cow with short horns and a mild eye. Lily hastened to find her a wisp of hay, which the cow lipped up with dignity.

"Do you want to feed her?" she asked Malin.

"No."

"Don't you like cows?"

"The last time I was this close to a cow, it broke three of my ribs with one kick," Malin said sourly. "So, no, I don't like cows."

"Well, I'm sure this cow won't kick you," Lily said, feeding the cow another wisp of hay. "She's lovely." The cow gazed at her adoringly. "I wonder what her name is."

Malin snorted. So did the cow, but much louder. Malin edged closer to the door.

"Think what you're missing," Lily said, gently stroking the cow's face as it lipped a piece of hay out of the bale she sat on.

"More broken ribs. You have no idea how painful that is."

Though not uncomfortable with cows herself, Lily was sensitive to the discomfort of others. She rose and coaxed the cow to follow her to the other side of the shed. Seeing the horns and great round feet pointing elsewhere, Malin relaxed.

"I broke my arm when I was eight," Lily said reflectively, scratching the broad forehead before her.

"At least with a broken arm you can still breathe," Malin said. And then, "How?"

"I fell off the roof of the back scullery."

"*You* were on the *roof?*"

"I'd never seen Aunt Hortensia so scared. She didn't even scold," Lily said quietly. "I didn't think she'd ever let me out of doors again." The cow butted her hand gently and she resumed scratching. "It's probably just as well she never found out I was on my way down from the third floor roof when I fell."

Malin was leaning back against the wall, shaking with silent laughter. He recovered himself. "And you were a good girl and never did it again?"

"Oh, no. I never went on the roof again—until it was the only way out."

"You have hidden depths," Malin said admiringly. "Even if you are a bit—" He froze.

"What?"

"Someone's coming."

❧   ❧   ❧

Sennet leapt up the familiar stairs to his rooms three at a time, his empty quiver bouncing on his back. Bolts clattered off the stone walls behind him as the Wolves fired into the darkness. He hurled himself through the door. Holly slammed it shut behind him and leaned on it.

"The second floor is overrun," Sennet panted. "Time for a barricade."

He put his shoulder to the oak bookcase which stood closest to the door. Holly hauled at it from the other side.

"Easier if the books were out," Holly puffed.

"No time," Sennet replied, but the sound of hobnailed boots on the stairs gave them the last bit of energy they needed.

The bookcase slid in front of the door, and was soon joined by Sennet's desk. The door rattled and thumped. A book fell off the top shelf, and Holly shoved it back amongst its fellows.

"Our last stand," Sennet mused. "Only fifteen years late!"

"Pity we're out of weapons," Holly muttered. "Not much of a last stand. What's a soldier without weapons?"

Sennet lifted his head. "An excellent point."

"What is?"

"A soldier without weapons," Sennet said commandingly, "is merely the castle cook. You saw the fire, you saw the troops, you were afraid of the fighting. Naturally, you fled to the tower. Imagine your horror when your hiding place became the focus of the siege."

"Are you suggesting," Holly said indignantly, "that I should leave you to die at the eleventh hour, just to save my own miserable hide? Anyway, why can't you be the cook?"

"Because Phelan knows me," Sennet said. "We have scores to settle. He will see to it that I do not leave Candra alive."

"I don't like it," Holly said with a grimace. "It's—disloyal."

"Your first loyalty is to the queen," Sennet reminded him sternly. "And—and perhaps, if you survive, you could tell the Lady Hortensia of what passed here."

Holly's face contorted in thought.

"There is little time left to decide," Sennet warned. "I could simply order you."

Holly made a face. "You can't order me. I'm just a cook."

"Good man."

"I'll go snivel in the corner, then, shall I?"

Sennet's hand came out and arrested his departure. They looked into each other's eyes for a moment.

"Lady Hortensia," Sennet said. "Don't forget."

Holly nodded and went to curl up in the corner, a fleeting smile on his face. Behind him, Sennet took down the book Holly had so hastily reshelved, and put it back in its right place.

⚜   ⚜   ⚜

Lily shrank into the shadows as the door opened. All she could see was the lantern, which blinded her to the newcomer's identity.

"Sorry it took so long to get away," Corrie said, and Lily relaxed. "I've brought some food in case you're hungry." She closed the door, hung the lantern on the wall and expertly shouldered aside the inquisitive head of the cow. "Not for you, Flossie!"

"What a pretty name," Lily exclaimed. "I was wondering."

"Does she kick?" asked Malin, watching the shifting hooves closely.

"Only Jaimes," Corrie said with a wicked smile. "So we won't be disturbed."

She hooked an empty bucket with one foot and pulled it under the lantern to serve as a table, laying out three small tankards, a wedge of cheese and a hill of bread rolls.

"My goodness," said Lily, "what a lot of bread!"

"Not as much as it looks," Corrie replied. "They mill the goodness out, so it takes at least twice as much to fill you."

"How silly," Lily said, inspecting the white roll Corrie proffered. It did look very fine and delicate, to be sure, but brown bread was what she had been raised on, and you couldn't fool Aunt Hortensia into thinking anything better.

"Don't even start me on what they've done with the beer," Corrie added, scowling fearsomely.

"What have they done to the beer?" Malin asked innocently, a troublemaking glint in his eye.

"First, they started bringing in this mass-produced stuff— as though machines would know how to make good beer!—

and insisting it be offered in every inn alongside our own, whether our customers wanted it or not. And why they would want it when it wasn't much cheaper and tasted of—well," she said, glancing at Lily and visibly restraining herself, "you can guess what it tasted like. So there wasn't much call for it, except among the desperate sort who found it'd get them drunk quicker and cheaper than proper drink—for it's strong enough stuff—and we never used to have many of *them* at the Leaf and Bud. Well, the stuff wasn't selling, as I say, so then they started to tax us for brewing and serving our own—tax by barrel *and* by serve, if you can believe—and every year the tax went up, two or three times some years. At the same time, everyone's getting poorer, for the crops aren't so good as they were at first, and these new manufactories aren't too free with their pay, either."

She sighed. "You can't blame people for buying bad drink if it's the only thing they can afford when they meet their friends of an evening. The crops kept getting poorer, and what there was was all going to the big 'factory. I couldn't get the grain to make a decent brew without half-crippling myself with the debt."

Lily and Malin ate and listened in sympathetic silence, sure of where this tale was going but willing it to end otherwise.

"Then, five years back, they brought in the law that made it an offence to sell any drink but theirs. For customer safety, they said! When everyone knows that it's their brews that go wrong for want of proper attention. Just a few years back, a young fellow died, and how many damaged, all because they'd made a mistake at the manufactory and the stuff was completely toxic."

Corrie shook her head sadly. "But what do you expect? They may have someone who knows brewing involved, but the people who make the decisions don't know and don't listen. I've even heard the workers aren't allowed to taste it, so how would they know if it's poison?"

She sat back and stretched her tense shoulders. "Well, you can see how it all worked out. Deep in debt and banned from brewing—eventually, I had to sell the Leaf and Bud to Jaimes. For a fraction of its true worth, I might add, but he'd scared off any other bidders and it wasn't as though it was a good time to get into the business. So that was that. I didn't want to leave the place, and you wouldn't get me into one of those manufactories if you carried me in stone-cold dead. So now I'm the barmaid, with cleaning thrown in. And milkmaid, of course, because Jaimes won't go near Flossie, but he still wants the milk. But where are my manners? You must want a drink."

She got up and scuffled in the corner. Lily looked at Malin apprehensively. He winced and shrugged. Lily steeled herself as Corrie returned with a very small barrel under her arm. Whatever happened, a queen was gracious...

"The last of the Ginger Tickle," Corrie said proudly. "Managed to keep brewing it a bit longer than the real beer. It's a proper family drink."

"Thank you," said Lily, hiding her relief.

Corrie poured out, set down the barrel, nudged Flossie away from it, and raised her tankard.

"To the Queen," she said, and she and Malin drank (Lily knowing that it wasn't polite to drink a toast to yourself).

Then Lily rose, tankard in hand.

"Restoration Day," she said gravely, and they drank to that. The Ginger Tickle was light, sparkling, and just sweet enough to balance the ginger's fire.

"If it ever comes again," Corrie said, with a sigh.

"It will," Lily said, in her best approximation of Aunt Hortensia's I Do Not Want To Hear Any Discussion voice.

"Freedom," said Malin.

That toast emptied the little tankards, so Corrie refilled them and then leaned back against the now peacefully cudding cow.

"What brings you to the Leaf and Bud? Not just bringing greetings from friends, I'm sure."

"We're looking for the pedlar," Lily said. "The one with mismatched eyes."

Corrie frowned and shook her head. "He's not been here in years—two or three at least."

"Do you know where we might find him?" Lily asked, clinging to hope.

"Haven't heard, sorry—and most gossip passes through the taproom sooner or later. But I'll keep an ear out. What do you want him for?"

"Well, Woodward—no, Restoration—Candra... Perhaps I had better just tell you the story from the start."

Lily plunged in. She could not have asked for a better audience. Corrie was absorbed in the story, soaking it up like a sponge.

"Oh, that'll make a fine song," she said when Lily's account had wound to the present day. "I'll have it in verse by morning—parts of it, anyway—and if they aren't humming the tune down at the wall-works by the time three days are out, it won't be my fault."

"The wall-workers? You reckon?" Malin said dubiously. "They're in Phelan's pay."

"It's a miserable life. Locked up in dormitories, separated from their families, long hours, lousy pay. You two are the first scrap of real hope we've had these fifteen years. A piece of golden good news after fifteen years of bad? The tale wouldn't even have to be well told to run like fire. And speaking of tales...that cave, where your aunt is—"

"Yes?" Lily said eagerly.

"I've heard a tale about it. Years ago now, before the War, but I thought of it as soon as you mentioned the enchantment."

"Does the tale say how to break it?"

"It's a young couple in the tale," Corrie said, settling herself

comfortably against Flossie's side. "Running from the lad's
father, who doesn't approve of them wedding. Young feller
lets his girl have the bed, sleeps in the mouth of the cave to
protect her, all very innocent and romantic. In the morning,
finds he can't wake her."

"So he lies down beside her or starves to death watching
over her, I suppose," Malin said. "Romantic sorts are usually
impractical idiots."

Confronted with four cold female eyes (and even the cow
did not look impressed), he put up his hands in mock surrender and fell silent.

"No," said Corrie. "Not this one. When he realized he
couldn't rouse her, he built a stone wall across the mouth of
the cave—to keep out intruders—and set off to find the answer
of how to wake his beloved. He roamed across the length and
breadth of the land. Some say he even went over the mountains into the East, and visited the Westwynn in his search for
knowledge."

This caught even Malin's attention.

"At last, he found the answer he'd been looking for, though
whether it came from an ancient book, an ancient tale, or an
ancient wizard, I do not know. In order to free his beloved
from her sleep, he would have to sprinkle her with the water
that flowed between the Burning Hills."

Malin drew in his breath appreciatively.

"A perilous journey," Corrie went on, "but his love drove
him on, and he looked, at last, on the source of Parsifal, where
he springs burning clean from between the Burning Hills.
He filled his little bottle with the water and hurried straight
back to the cave. The entrance was overgrown, but he tore the
branches down with his bare hands, so desperate was he, and
pulled the stone wall to pieces at his feet, just wide enough
that he could slip in. There she lay, just as he had left her.
Hands trembling, he uncorked the bottle."

By this time, Lily was trembling with the tension too. She pulled her knees up to her chin and hugged them fiercely.

"He sprinkled the water over her, just as he had been told; and just as he had been told, she woke. But just as he was about to clasp her in his arms, her eyes fell on his face. She cried out in terror, and, breaking free, she fled the cave. Heartbroken, he threw himself down on the enchanted bed and lost his sorrows in oblivion.

"As for his beloved, she hid in the forest for many days before she dared to venture out. And when at last she did, it came to her that many years had passed since the night she had lain down in the cave, and that the man she had fled in terror was not, as she had supposed, her love's father, but her love himself. Wracked with guilt, she found her way back to the cave, and found him there asleep where she had lain. But alas! She did not know how he had woken her.

"Like her love before her, she covered the land with her footsteps, asking all she met if they knew the secret. But though all knew of her love and his long search, none knew the answer, for, in hurrying to her side, he had not paused to tell a soul of his joyful secret.

"Time went on, and she grew old, and she could no longer walk so far in searching for the answer to her quest. So, at last, with slow and sorrowful steps, she went her way back to the cave, to see her lost love again. She meant to be with him to the end, to lie herself down in the crook of his arm and sleep there at his side until the Rabbit finally ate the Leaf and Bud."

Lily felt for her handkerchief, remembered she didn't have one, and surreptitiously dabbed at her eyes with her sleeve.

"But as she bent over him, she gave him one last kiss—and he awoke. Springing from the bed, he seized her hand and led her out of that dark enchanted place, into the sunshine of a fair spring day. And so they lived out the last of their years, in perfect understanding and perfect content."

Lily heaved a huge sigh. "It's a beautiful story, and just what I needed to know. But…"

"Good luck getting through Burnaby," Malin finished.

"It's unusual, as stories go," Corrie said. "Generally, they don't so much tell us what to do as give us a clue and make us work it out for ourselves."

Lily frowned thoughtfully. "A clue. That's what we need from this pedlar. He didn't leave any hidden messages with you, did he?"

Corrie laughed heartily. "All he left besides his wares was that nonsense rhyme of his—The Lanky Lad."

"I know that one," Malin said.

"It's a popular drinking song," Corrie said. "There's that *deeply drank did he* bit. And it doesn't make much difference if you get the words mixed up."

Malin inflated his chest and began to sing in a rough baritone, waving his tankard in time with the words.

> The lanky lad unlocked the door
>   To set the flowers free;
> His mouth to trumpet's other end
>   And deeply drank, did he.

Corrie continued, her voice warm and low.

> The moon is rising in the north,
>   A sign for all to see;
> For none can buy the pedlar's wares
>   Save he whom it must be.

"I heard it was *she* whom it must be," Malin said.

"I've heard that," Corrie agreed. "Everyone has their version. Gives them something to argue about."

Lily sighed. It really was nonsense. They would have to find the pedlar himself and get the message from him in person.

"This rain," Malin said, jerking a thumb at the door, "does it ever stop?"

"Spring rains," Corrie said apologetically. "They're worse than they used to be, I'm sure of it. We've always had heavy rains here at the foot of the mountains, but it's getting more extreme."

"I don't think it's just here, either," Lily said. "Parsifal was flooded where he meets the Renwick stream, and that had burst its banks."

"The point is," said Malin, "it's hosing down. Reckon we could stay here safely overnight?"

"It's leaving in the morning that would be dangerous," Corrie said. "I come out at dawn to milk Flossie, so I could let—" She broke off and dived for the lantern, blowing it out with one hastily-gulped breath. "Out!"

Instinctively, they moved towards the door, Lily finding her passage blocked by a warm hairy wall of cow. The rumbling behind the rain grew louder, there was a wet, heavy smack as the shed jerked on its foundations, and the wall behind Lily collapsed.

She went down with a scream, the mud sucking at her clothes and dragging her down into the cold, heaving mass. Something sharp stabbed at her leg. She recoiled, and hit something warm and moving: Flossie the cow, struggling to rise. Lily clung to Flossie's side, kicking with all the might her buried legs could muster.

There was a loud sucking noise as Flossie rose to her feet, pulling Lily free. Lily tried to follow as the cow shambled out of the half-collapsed shed, but the cow's legs were far better suited for walking in knee-deep mud. She floundered towards the door. Malin was shouting; she collided with him, and he stopped.

In the distance, she could hear shouts of "Slip!" and the corncrake voice of Jaimes assuring his patrons that the slip had not reached the inn itself; there was no need to leave. The next moment, a strong arm reached through the doorway and hauled Lily out.

"Wolves!" Corrie cried. "Run!" She gave them a shove in the right direction.

Lily ran as though in a nightmare: darkness, shouting, danger close behind, and her legs barely able to move. The mud-soaked folds of her cloak and skirts clung to her legs, wrapping around her as though the earth itself were trying to swallow her whole. And the next moment, she was falling...

Lily gave only the shortest of shrieks before the dark, cold water engulfed her. She flailed, surfaced, coughed, choked, and tried to refill her lungs.

Malin grabbed her arm. "Shh! And stop thrashing," he added, "you'll draw the Wolves."

Lily's feet touched bottom, the water lapping at her chin. A few breaths calmed her, but the chill of the water soon had her juddering with cold.

"Wh-where are we?" she whispered piteously, mentally kicking herself for sounding so pathetic.

"Trench for the wall foundations," Malin said. "Should've remembered it came this far round."

Lily's only reply was the chattering of her teeth. At least the rain was easing at last.

There was a ripple in the water, and suddenly Malin was close behind her, his shoulder touching her back, his head at her shoulder. She pulled away. The impudence!

"Huddling's the only way to stay warm," he explained.

"It's not appropriate," Lily said, her face feeling hot enough to warm the whole ditch and everything in it. "Why are you suddenly as tall as me?" she asked, desperate to change the subject.

"You know what they say; everyone's the same height in water and earth," Malin said. The full moon emerged from behind the clouds and showed him her baffled face. "Floating or buried."

"Oh, I see. I'm not floating."

"No? Too bad—I was hoping you'd finally learned to swim." He looked up at the moon. "Of all the times."

"Good—we can see where we're going," Lily said through her chattering teeth.

"And everyone will be able to see us going there," Malin retorted. "We'll just have to risk it. You'll catch your death of *appropriate* cold otherwise." He began to move down the ditch.

"You can't catch a cold from being cold," Lily said, following with slow, exaggerated strides through the water. Aunt Hortensia had taught her this in her lessons on Household Physic.

"No, but you can catch being dead from being cold," Malin said. "You get so cold you stop shivering; maybe you even think you're warm. You get sleepy, you go to sleep, and that's it. You never wake up."

Lily was feeling a little sleepy, but as she was still shivering violently, she figured she was probably all right.

"Think warm thoughts," Malin advised. "It helps."

"Warm thoughts?"

"Hot dinner by a roaring fire, steaming hot bath, warm dry socks, rabbit-skin slippers...you get the idea."

Lily thought of winter tea in the library: glowing logs in the fireplace—so hot Aunt Hortensia would have a little decorative screen placed to protect her complexion from the heat—piping hot tea, scones fresh from the oven with the butter melting over them, almost too hot to eat...

It didn't seem real. Not only not real here—no one had an imagination that strong—but not real ever, as though it belonged in a story, or, at the very least, had happened to someone else. But she felt warmer; she wasn't even shivering any more. She looked back in memory at the plump little white-clad figure at her tea, wrapped in a cosy knitted rabbit-fur shawl. Was that her? Perhaps this was what having a sister was like: someone like you and yet unlike.

She was interrupted in these dreamlike wonderings when she collided with Malin, who had stopped in front of what appeared to be a blank wall of mud. He turned to glare at her, but his expression changed to one of alarm when he saw her face.

Lily stood peacefully, like a marble statue of herself unaccountably erected in a flooded ditch, while several Malins seemed to swarm around her, working on the muddy ditch wall, climbing out, climbing back in again, messing about with ropes and talking to her while peering earnestly into her face, though she couldn't make out their words, or why they were so excitable. It was all right, she wanted to tell them. She wasn't even cold any more. She just couldn't find the words, so she smiled muzzily instead.

She didn't remember how she got out of the ditch, but she retained a vague memory of walking somnambulistically through a dark and pathless forest, alone but for two hands on her shoulders, pushing and guiding her. It was not until later that she realized the hands must have been Malin's, so entirely disembodied did they seem.

The first thing she was fully aware of was the pain in her arms and legs. She found herself sitting on the ground with a small fire practically at her feet, her cuirass and boots beside her. Her legs under her skirt were burning. Her skirt was smoking, and Malin rubbed at the burning skin on her arm.

"No," she said, trying to pull her arm away. "Hurts."

"Good! You're not dead, then," Malin replied, and turned his attention to her other arm.

"Skirt burning," she objected.

He checked. "That's not smoke; it's steam."

She glowered at him. He sat so close she could feel the warmth of his skin through their shirts. It came to her that she must be cold. She was shivering.

"Shivering! Finally!" said Malin, and dropped her arm,

turning back to the fire to build it up.

The pain receded to Lily's hands and feet, but the rest of her was still achingly tired. Her head drooped down on her knees, and then jerked up again as Malin clapped two pieces of firewood together.

"No sleeping," he barked.

"But I'm *tired*."

"Better safe than sorry."

"I order you to let me sleep!"

"You can't tell me what to do."

"But I'm the queen!"

"Then I'm succeeding."

Lily frowned. Her mind didn't seem to be working as fast as usual. "Seceding?"

"Whatever. I'm Burnabais; I don't have to follow an Arcelian queen."

"But you *are*," Lily pointed out. "And not your Council." She thought about this. "Although I can't say I blame you in the latter case."

Malin scowled. "Fine. I'm a rebel all round. I'm just helping you because I want Phelan gone and you're the best chance I've got to make that happen."

"How is it *helping* me to keep me awake? After the day I've had! Days, in fact."

"You fall asleep before you thaw out, you might never wake up. Lucky Phelan."

"But I *need* to sleep," she wailed softly, almost weeping with self-pity.

"Later. When you're warm and dry again."

"I am warm and dry," she objected.

"Your teeth are chattering, your clothes are soggy, and you only just thawed out your head," he replied briskly. "I'm taking no chances."

Her head drooped, and he smacked the pieces of wood together again.

"Next time, I'll bang them on your helmet."

"You wouldn't dare!"

"Of course I would. Wouldn't think twice."

She set her chin defiantly on her knees and glared at him. "There are more—more civilized ways of keeping someone awake. If you insist on torturing them."

"Quieter than this?" Malin asked, waving the wood. "Because the fire is risky enough without sending out a signal to the Wolves."

"Civilized conversation," Lily murmured. "If you have to."

"So talk."

"About what? And why me?"

"Because if I talk, you'll just go to sleep."

"Maybe you should consider taking lessons," Lily giggled.

Malin glared. "Talk. About—I don't know, slips."

"Slips," Lily said blearily. "Fine. If you want a lecture, I'll deliver one."

She launched into a declamatory style borrowed from Aunt Hortensia at her most pompous, in which every consonant was precisely pronounced, every vowel fully rounded.

"Slips are characterized by a sudden and major movement of the topsoil, not infrequently associated with heavy rainfall and insufficient anchor-planting—or catastrophic loss of vegetable life, both above and below the soil."

"Lack of vegetables causes slips?" Malin asked sceptically. "Sounds like a threat to make you eat your cabbage."

"Cabbage is perfectly palatable when lightly sautéed in butter with toasted caraway seeds," Lily corrected him. "And, in any case, it's rude to interrupt. Where was I?"

"Vegetable catastrophe."

"Oh, yes. In addition to these primary causes, the likelihood of slips can be exacerbated by the phase of the moon."

Malin sat up, a piece of firewood forgotten in his hand. "You're pulling my leg."

"I assure you," Lily said with hauteur, "I have not the least desire to associate myself with your leg in any way. The principle is the same as the pull of the moon drawing the water up in tides at certain times."

"Yeah, but this is *land*. Dirt."

"Which is saturated in water," Lily pointed out.

"Mm. How are you feeling?"

Lily took stock. "Exhausted."

"Cold? Damp?"

She shook her head. "Can I go to sleep now?"

He nodded, and she sagged backwards, asleep before he had even finished banking the fire.

⚜   ⚜   ⚜

The first light over the eastern mountains crept through the tower window and gently brushed the battered barricade with gold. The crashing of the ram took on a definitely splintery note. Holly peeked through his fingers as Sennet straightened his academic robes, tweaked the collar, and braced himself.

Seconds later, the barricade fell. Wolves clambered through the breach, scanned the room, and overpowered Sennet in moments—moments that were, admittedly, full of the sounds of steel and swearing. Three of the Wolves bled freely as they kicked and dragged Sennet and Holly down to the hall.

"She's not there, sir," the captain said. "We've checked thoroughly. But we do have these two prisoners."

Phelan's blue eyes glittered as he looked them over. Sennet stood soldier-straight despite the painful grip on his arms; Holly cowered, practically suspended from the Wolf holding the scruff of his neck.

"Sennet. Loser again, I see. And this—person?"

Sennet flicked Holly a dismissive glance. "Castle cook. A good cook, but the oaf is useless at everything else."

Holly bit his lip and glowered.

"So where is she?"

Sennet remained silent. Phelan nodded to a Wolf, who gave Sennet a powerful backhanded blow across the face. Holly winced.

"Where is she?"

Sennet stared straight ahead, blood trickling from his lip.

With the smallest of gestures, Phelan restrained the Wolf who moved to strike again. He stared at Sennet thoughtfully.

"Every man has his breaking point. It would only be a matter of time before I found yours. But..." His lips quirked, and he moved closer. "Why waste time on your breaking point, when I already know your weak point? You may be prepared to sacrifice your life—but what about his?"

Before Holly could blink, Phelan had a dagger at his eye. Holly gave up on the idea of blinking. He'd hate to miss his own death, after all. His eye began to water.

"Well? You were never one to rush things. Would you like time to decide? Very well. Ten."

Sennet began to look uncomfortable.

"Nine. Eight."

A sweat broke out on his brow.

"Seven. Six."

Holly's eye was streaming now. He just hoped Phelan had a steady hand.

"Five. Four."

Sennet seemed to shrivel as Phelan looked at him, to grow old in that moment. He became an old man huddled in his robe, grasping fitfully at the collar with nervous fingers.

"Three. Two."

Holly's burning lungs reminded him he had not breathed in some time. Might as well, he decided, while he still could. He tried to breathe in without moving, causing a strangled sort of grunt. Phelan's gaze flicked to him for a moment, and, in that moment, Sennet's hand went to his mouth.

"One." Phelan drew back his arm to strike, and Sennet shuddered, crumpled, and fell.

Phelan stopped, his arm curled around like a snake coiled to strike. Holly broke loose from the Wolf's grip and fell to his knees at Sennet's side, tears now pouring freely from both eyes. He took up Sennet's wrist and felt for a pulse.

"He's dead!"

"An old trick," Phelan said.

He kicked Holly aside and grasped Sennet's neck in one hand. There was silence. Then he stood, and dropped Sennet's limp body to the floor. Holly winced as Sennet's head bounced off the marble.

"Dead indeed," Phelan said. "I didn't think he'd have the courage."

"Shall we kill this one, sir?" one of the Wolves asked, clearly eager to show willing.

"Will it make the dead man speak?" Phelan asked, and the man flushed, trying to recede into the crowd and away from that piercing eye. Phelan turned to Holly, a teary mess on the floor. "You don't know where she is?"

Holly shook his head vigorously. "She left days ago! I'll tell you all I know!" He began counting on his fingers. "It was...it was..."

"She left. Did she come back?"

"No."

"Does she know anyone to whom she might turn?"

Holly thought about this.

"No one who isn't dead," he said eventually. That earned him a small lift of the thin lips.

"If she finds you, you will inform me immediately. I shall see to it that you are well rewarded."

Holly ducked his head.

Phelan turned to his officers. "Third detachment, secure

and garrison the castle. First and second detachments, back to Denton with me." He turned to look at Holly again. "Why are you still here?"

Holly hastily slung Sennet's body over his shoulder and staggered to the broken remains of the front door. He had only one thought in his mind: to put as many miles of Arcelia between himself and Phelan as possible.

⚜   ⚜   ⚜

Lily pushed herself awkwardly into a sitting position, blinking against the daylight. Her clothes, thick with mud, had dried like board around her.

"Come on," Malin said, bashing his clothes with a fist until the dust powdered out. "We've been here too long."

"I am not going *anywhere* until I have had a bath and a chance to launder my clothes," Lily said firmly. "I can hear a stream not far off."

"It's not even Launderday!"

"I am a queen," she said haughtily. "I see no reason why I should appear to my people in the guise of a clod of dirt."

He followed as she worked her way stiffly down to the stream.

"No knowing how long it'll take to find him," Malin said. "No time to lose!"

"Stop fussing," she said. "And stop following me!"

"I wish I could."

"The essence of a bath is *privacy*," Lily said. "Go away!"

"What if someone else stumbles on you?"

"Very well—stay in earshot, then."

"I wasn't going to *look*," Malin said. "You'll be sorry if a Wolf jumps out and I have to come running from half a mile away."

Lily hesitated.

"That's a chance I will have to take," she said at last. At the edge of the pool formed by a gentle eddy of the stream, she turned and looked back. "Further!"

Muttering, he crashed off into the underbrush. "Better?"

Lily squinted. There was no sign of him. "Yes."

She scrubbed and rinsed her clothes first, and then laid them on the bank to dry in a patch of sun. Shivering, she slipped back in to wash herself—and froze. She could hear whistling.

"Malin?"

The whistling stopped. "What?"

Oh, the *relief.* "Do you mind? Bathrooms are not generally fitted with minstrel's galleries."

He laughed. "It's that catchy drinking song! Can't get it out of my head."

The chill of the stream did not make for languid bathing. Lily hastily climbed out and dressed in her still-damp clothes.

"You can come back now," she called, and Malin reappeared. "Now it's your turn."

"What? No! We've wasted enough time already!"

"I refuse to travel onward with such a grimy companion."

He glared at her. She steeled her gaze to hold his. Finally, he scowled, and started pulling off his boots. Lily hastily withdrew before any more of his clothing could be removed in her presence. She marched up and down, blushing vigorously and humming to take her mind off it.

"Quiet in the gallery!" Malin called, and she realized what she was humming.

"Well, you put it in my head," she snapped back.

A moment later, a voice rose in song, putting words to her tune. Apparently, Malin was, like Holly, fond of singing in the bath. Lily blushed again. At least Holly could only be heard when the wind was the right way, and, even then, Aunt Hortensia would hustle her off the terrace and indoors before any further embarrassment could ensue.

> The moon is rising in the north,
>> A sign for all to see;
> For none can buy the pedlar's wares

Save she whom it must be.

The last line was muffled; apparently Malin was resuming his clothing. In a moment more, he appeared, marginally cleaner, jerkin over one arm and wet shirt clinging to his chest. Lily looked away and hurriedly tried to think of something to talk about.

"Where shall we ask after the—?" She stopped. "Can you hear that?"

There was a high-pitched squeal, just on the edge of hearing.

Malin cocked his head. "Injured rabbit, sounds like."

"Isn't it afraid of attracting a predator?"

"I'd say it's past that," Malin said. "Might even hope for one. Move cautiously," he added, checking Lily's impetuous stride in the animal's direction. "And no more baths!"

It was a rabbit, crawling across the forest floor with the dull shaft of a Wolf's crossbow bolt protruding from its side.

Malin's hatchet flashed. The squealing stopped.

"Thank you," Lily said, blinking away tears. "What kind of person shoots an animal and doesn't bother to go after it?"

"Wolves," said Malin succinctly.

He removed the bolt as cleanly as possible, and they buried the sorry little thing where it lay on the forest floor.

"How long ago do you think it was wounded?" she asked, certain she wouldn't like the answer, but working up a steam of righteous anger all the same.

Malin didn't answer. In fact, he didn't appear to be listening.

"How—" she began impatiently, but he put a hand on her arm without moving his head.

"Shh. Less than a day. Keep your voice down."

Lily frowned and listened till she heard it too. Away in the distance, there were crackles of movement. They were not the only ones in this neck of the woods.

"Wolves?" she breathed.

He shook his head, almost imperceptibly. "Too few. One, maybe two."

Very slowly and cautiously, he moved towards the hint of sound, each step carefully considered before he placed his foot. Lily followed, making sure her feet fell in precisely the same places Malin's had. It was a frustratingly slow and unexciting way to move about; the only excitement came when the sounds ahead ceased.

"Gone?' Lily asked under her breath.

"Staying still," Malin replied, barely audible. "Didn't recede."

Had their cautious approach been heard? It seemed not, for they reached a clearing where a young woman sat, unaware of their presence. Lily was certain they had made no sound, but the young woman started looking nervously about her all the same, and seeing she was not alone, her face blanched in terror and she fled before either could say a word.

"Oh," said Lily.

"Mm," agreed Malin, taking a cautious look around before sidling into the clearing. Lily perched on the recently vacated rock in the middle.

"Oh, I see!" she said. "Look—there, there, there, and there."

Malin circled the clearing, looking at the little plants poking through the leaf litter.

"Secret ceremonial garden," he concluded at last.

"Memorial garden," Lily corrected. "No water element."

"Don't they usually have cypress, rosemary...?"

"That would be too obvious here. But look—cudweed."

"Cudweed?"

"It means *everlasting remembrance.* Just think of the devotion that's been put into this, the never-failing remembrance of a loved one that defies even—"

"How does cudweed *mean* anything?"

"The language of flowers. Don't you know—?"

He rolled his eyes. "Flowers don't talk. Even *you* should know that."

"But you can send messages with them."

"Really? What's the flower for *run away?*"

Lily thought for a moment. "Pennyroyal."

"Are you making that up?"

"No. Well, it's *flee away*, but that's more or less the same."

Malin came to a sudden halt, staring at his feet.

"What is it?" Lily asked with trepidation.

"I think I know who it's for."

She came to his side and he pointed down at two circles of glass nestling at the base of the cudweed.

"Broken bottles?" Lily said, puzzled.

There was something familiar about them...

One orange, one blue.

The Horn of Vale

"Oh, *no!* Not him!" Lily sat down on the stone seat and sobbed, her face buried in her skirts.

"You're crying," said Malin, his tone suggesting he'd just spotted a mythical creature.

"It's a memorial garden," her muffled voice returned. "It is perfectly acceptable for a lady to shed tears in a memorial garden."

"You cry because of where you are, not for actually being upset?"

"A lady should always be in full control of her emotions," Lily recited.

"That's the stupidest thing I ever heard," Malin said.

Lily's head snapped up, her eyes full of tears and anger.

"You know nothing about it! You have no idea what it's like to be royal! Everyone else might fall apart, but I have to be strong!"

Malin rolled his eyes. "I'm strong. Doesn't mean I have to pretend not to care."

"I'm crying now—" and indeed she was, "—isn't that enough for you? That poor man! What must Phelan have done to him?"

"It might not have been Phelan," Malin said reasonably. "He wasn't young, and his liver hadn't had the easiest time of it."

"What do you mean?"

"He drank too much. That's how he came to be a pedlar, I heard. Used to be a captain or something in the army, but he wasn't dependable."

"And he never conquered his weakness? That's almost more tragic," Lily said, and sobbed some more.

"Not the easiest person to cheer up, are you?"

"We are in a memorial garden," Lily said, wiping her eyes. "Cheerfulness would be entirely inappropriate."

Malin sighed. "Don't you ever want to do something inappropriate? Run, laugh, cry when you feel like it?"

Marry for love. The thought popped unbidden into Lily's mind and she pushed it away.

"The *appropriate* thing to do in a memorial garden is to remember the loved one lost," she said firmly.

"Who I barely knew, you never met, and neither of us loved," Malin retorted.

"He was my father's friend," Lily said. "We should do *something.*"

"Fine. We'll sing a song in his memory."

"Very well," Lily said. "What song shall we—no."

He grinned.

"No!" she protested. "You can't sing a drinking song in a memorial garden! It's entirely inappropriate!"

"I can't think of anything more appropriate," Malin said. "It was his song, and he was a deep drinker, after all."

Lily had just brought herself to the point of opening her mouth to join in—one would not want to show disrespect, after all—when a thought struck her. *His mouth to trumpet's other end, and deeply drank, did he.*

Malin broke off. "You're not singing!"

She turned to him. "His mouth to trumpet's other end, and deeply drank, did he!"

"So if you know the words, why aren't you singing?"

"It's a riddle—he's talking about drinking from a horn. A

horn, Malin!"

"So?"

"The Horn of Vale! It has to be!"

"Why does it have to be?"

"He was my father's friend. He went everywhere. No one would have suspected him," Lily said feverishly. "It must be! My father gave him the Requisites for safekeeping; he must have done. And then the pedlar wheeled his cart away..."

She could see it in her mind's eye, Aunt Hortensia's sketch come to life. "And hid them. And then he composed the song, and spread it around, in the hope my father would one day return to find them—that's the "he whom it must be" bit. And then maybe he changed it to "she" when he knew my father was...gone, and it would be me."

"We're not far from Holbrook," Malin said thoughtfully.

Lily frowned. What had that to do with her discovery?

"The inn at Holbrook is called the Ox and Trumpet," he explained.

She smiled dazzlingly, and with cheerful heart and drying tears, began to sing.

⚜   ⚜   ⚜

Night was falling when Holly laid his burden down under the trees of Renwick. He laid Sennet's body out, straightening his crumpled robes and picking bits of twig out of his hair. Over one shoulder was not the most dignified way to travel, and he was glad, in a way, that Sennet hadn't been there for it.

Holly stretched his aching back, scuffled in his pockets and drew out a small, very thick glass bottle with a thick encrustation of wax over the tiny cork. Taking a deep breath, he broke the wax and worked out the cork. Then, with one swift movement, he put the bottle to Sennet's slack lips and upturned it. Shaking out the last drop, he recorked it, returned it to his pocket and started to chew on his knuckles.

It was a risk. A dreadful risk. He hadn't been able to test it—much. On the other hand, what was there to lose? And if he failed, who would know? He started on another knuckle, and faced the truth squarely. It wasn't what would happen if he was wrong that worried him. It was what would happen if he was right.

By the time it happened, he had almost given up hoping—or fearing. He sat, staring into darkness, a half chewed knuckle in his mouth, and the short, sharp choking noise made him leap half out of his skin. Hastily, he rolled Sennet over, and made a face as his friend's stomach violently ejected everything that had been put in it.

"Who's that?" an acid-rasped voice croaked out.

"It's just me. Holly." He wiped Sennet's mouth with a corner of his apron and helped him to sit up and put his back against a tree. "You'll feel right as rain in a minute or two."

"Dark…" Sennet mumbled, his head lolling.

"Night-time, not your eyes," Holly reassured him. "We're in the forest of Renwick, if that helps."

There was a long silence, then Sennet lifted his head. Holly could see his eyes glittering in the darkness.

"Insubordination!" Sennet said.

Holly sighed. "I was afraid you'd take it like that."

"Deception!"

"How else could I get you out?"

"I was entrusted with the castle's defence!" Sennet snapped. "I should not have left! And you! Such a web of deception! Against a superior officer!"

Holly glowered at him. "I appeal to the queen. If she'd rather have you dead than alive, then I'll be a good boy and cut your head off myself!"

Sennet snorted.

"I didn't tell *you* any lies!" Holly said virtuously. "I said it would kill you, and it did—at least till I gave you the antidote.

So then I was the commanding officer."

"You should not have abandoned your post," Sennet said, but Holly could tell he was caving.

"A tactical withdrawal to facilitate a new phase of guerrilla insurgency," Holly rattled off, and hoped Sennet would swallow it.

"I don't suppose even you know what that means," Sennet said dryly.

"It means we go looking for the queen and woe to anyone who tries to stop us," Holly said happily.

"Mm. Very well," Sennet said. And then, "Eurgh. Ugh. What did you put in that stuff?"

Holly reviewed the list of ingredients. "Um...cinnamon?"

"What I am tasting," Sennet said coldly, "is *not* cinnamon."

"No?"

"I take it further inquiry would be inadvisable."

"You'll probably sleep better if we just leave it at *cinnamon*," Holly said. "And you'll need a lot of it. Sleep, that is."

"Not until I've had a full report. What exactly took place while I was, er, dead?"

⚜   ⚜   ⚜

The messenger stood to attention. He'd been warned there were stormclouds gathering in the Magister's office, and his news was not as good as he would have liked. Best foot forward, and don't make a mistake...

Vetch, the Magister's private secretary, took up pen and paper, ready to put every word of the report on record.

A sheen of sweat covered the messenger's brow. The Magister was sitting at his big desk—had it made from the tree in the palace square, some said—going through papers. Hadn't even looked up. The messenger focussed his efforts on not wobbling.

Finally, the Magister lifted his head. "Report."

Vetch poised his pen.

"On arrival, we discovered evidence of a considerable disturbance among the dwarves, sir—"

"Violent?"

"So-so. Nothing serious. But they seem very divided, sir."

"Divided..." Phelan mused, seeming not displeased.

"There were a good number present who were only too pleased to oblige us with information."

"But they were not forthcoming with the prisoner."

"No, sir. They attempted to capture him the night before we arrived, but he escaped."

Phelan's brow darkened.

"In company with the girl, sir."

Phelan sat back in his chair. "Indeed." After a few moments of silence which weighed heavily on the messenger's nerves, he smiled. "Two birds with one stone, then."

"Sir?"

"You are dismissed."

The messenger left, hasty with relief. Behind him, the Magister was giving out instructions.

"Patrols to be stepped up across the valley. The moment either of them shows their face, I want to hear about it."

⚜   ⚜   ⚜

"I don't like it," Malin groused.

They were sitting in a thicket of trees some way down the road from the Ox and Trumpet, waiting for passers-by to leave the way clear.

"You don't have to like it," Lily said. "You just have to do it. We don't have anything to use as a blindfold, so I'll just have to keep my eyes closed."

"It's an insult to the dignity of Burnabaise everywhere," Malin continued.

"It's a disguise, that's all! Would you rather we just walked in and introduced ourselves?"

"It would make for a livelier evening."

"We don't want lively! A discreet entrance, a prompt trans-action of the evening's business, and an equally discreet exit; that's what we want."

"Since when do queens make discreet entrances?"

"Since the War, when the loyalties of certain elements of the population became less...certain."

"Like Burnaby's, you mean?"

Lily sighed.

"Look, let's not beat about the bush," Malin said. "I'm not helping you round half the country out of loyalty, all right? I'm doing it for the same reason I did all the rest: I want Phelan gone, and you're my best way to do it."

"Oh, I see," Lily said. "I thought you were helping me, but, no, you're just trying to use me."

"I'm not—!" He sighed. "All right, I am, but you'd do the same for your people, wouldn't you?"

"Your people do not appear to appreciate your efforts," Lily said tactfully.

"Some, maybe. They're sheltered from the worst of it. But I've never heard a thralled dwarf complain I was making trouble."

"The thralls will be freed—and recompensed," Lily reminded him.

"Only if you somehow get rid of Phelan," Malin said. "I'm a realist. I know I'm probably going to get killed doing this, and I want to be sure it'll be worth it."

She looked him in the eye. "I give you my word, there will be justice for the thralls, Arcelian and Burnabaise alike."

"Justice isn't enough," he said bluntly. "I want freedom."

"Of course they'll be free!"

"Not just for the thralls—for all of us. We'll never really be free as long as Arcelia rules over us—doesn't matter if it's you or your uncle."

A sharp pang went through Lily at being thus lumped in with her worst enemy, but she bit her feelings back and tried to be diplomatic.

"Burnaby is too small to survive as an independent country," she said, and waited to see how he would take it.

His mouth twisted, but he held back whatever it was he was going to say. Clearly, she was not the only one who had to wrestle with her feelings.

"Maybe," he said at last. "But freedom of some sort we've got to have. Not being treated like children, with people making decisions for us and not telling us anything."

This was a new light, and one in which Lily found herself suddenly in sympathy with Burnaby.

"Autonomy," she said.

"What?"

"It means that you stay part of Arcelia, but you make your own decisions," Lily said.

"Yeah—that. Autonomy for Burnaby. Those are my terms."

Lily considered. The details would need to be argued out later, but the primary thing was to displace the usurper, and for that she needed Malin's help.

"All right," she said. "I give you my word."

"Shake?"

"As long as you don't spit on your hand," Lily said warily.

"If you insist."

He gave her hand one firm shake and then pulled a large handkerchief out of his pocket.

"*You* have a handkerchief?" Lily asked.

"What? They're useful—bandage, sling, bag, garrotte…"

"Blowing your nose?" Lily suggested.

"How much use is a cloth covered in snot? Turn around."

"Why?"

"So I can tie this over your eyes." He did so, deftly and firmly, leaving her ears unmuffled. "Now, aren't you glad I didn't blow my nose on it?"

She was, but refused to say so. He took her left hand, put it on his right shoulder, and led her out of the bushes.

"Careful," he muttered, "the pourstone's a bit cracked along here."

"It cracks?" Lily said, surprised. "It looks so...indestructible."

"Looks can be deceiving," he said. "Look at me. I look like a *servant*."

"Try to remember to talk like one," Lily said. He snorted in reply.

The cracking road proved to be less of an obstacle than Lily had feared. Her ears brought her the sounds of voices, pouring liquid, and the odd snatch of song. Then her nose told her they were standing outside the inn, an inn with a quite passable cook...

"Ready?" Malin muttered.

"Yes."

They went in through the inn's wide open door.

"Oh! This way to the private parlour, ma'am," said a girlish voice, and Malin towed her down the hall and to the left. She felt for a seat and sat down as gracefully as she could. "Your servant can go into the public bar," the maid added, "it's just through—"

"He is my eyes. He will stay with me," Lily said, in her most autocratic tone.

She could hear a buzz of conversation from the public bar; clearly, their arrival had not gone unnoticed.

"Er—very good, ma'am."

The maid's voice reminded Lily of salted butter, though she had no idea why.

"Kindly inform the innkeeper that Lady Persicaria is waiting in the parlour," she said. Persicaria meant *restoration*—and, hopefully, the innkeeper would take the hint.

"Yes ma'am."

The door closed.

"We're being watched," Malin muttered in an undertone. "Looking round from the public."

"Clotbur," Lily said, ignoring the indignant start Malin gave, "look around and describe the room to me."

"Red velvet upholstery," Malin growled. "Fluffy wallpaper."

"Flocked," Lily corrected. "Of what colour?"

"Sort of dirty cream. Furniture's walnut, by the looks of it. Couple of pictures on the walls. One's the Magister; one's... some sort of dead woman in a boat."

"The Dreaming Duchess," Lily said. "A classic tale of this region."

The Duke's ship, so it was said, had been lost at sea, and the Duchess had taken to spending hours lying in a small boat at the riverside, listening to the water running past the hull. Perhaps she thought it would bring news of her lost love. Years rolled on and her hair turned grey, the colour faded from her clothes, and still she lay there with the face of a young woman, dreaming of her beloved.

One day, the servants found the boat was gone, and the Duchess with it. Tales began to be told of a small boat drifting out to sea, carrying the form of a sleeping woman—the Dreaming Duchess, it was said, endlessly searching for her lost love.

It was bad luck to see the Dreaming Duchess, though Lily had never seen why. After all, what harm could a sleeping woman do? Aunt Hortensia had merely tutted about superstition and changed the subject.

"Go on," she instructed Malin.

"The carpet's a sort of washed-out red. Expensive-looking, though. And there's an oak bar at the far end, with a bunch of silver tankards and that. Some sort of drinking horn thing.

Looks big."

A horn! Lily bit her lip. There was no way she could have said it so carelessly, as Malin did. She was about to ask for details when she heard a heavy tread come down the hall and the door opened again.

"Lady Persicaria?" a voice like rich gravy asked.

Why this association of voices with food? Was it the delicious smells wafting about the inn, or not being able to see?

"Indeed," Lily said, and heard the door close. "I should like some refreshment, Master—?"

"Beech is the name, ma'am. Can I press you to a spiced currant cordial on this cold night?"

"That would be entirely acceptable," Lily said graciously. "And perhaps a mug of cider for my servitor."

"Of course, ma'am. I'll have those poured immediately. A silver cup, of course, for your cordial, ma'am."

"I don't care for silver," Lily said. "Clotbur tells me you have a drinking horn here—I will have my drink in that."

"Er..." said Beech.

"Is there a problem?" Lily asked.

"Well, you see, ma'am," Beech said, speaking a good deal lower, "that's rather a particular horn—one of a kind, as you might say. It was left to me by a late friend of mine, and he made me promise to save it for a very particular guest."

"This friend of yours," Lily said. "What were his eyes like?"

Beech hesitated.

"And the guest's eyes," Lily murmured, "what of them?"

"L-lady Persicaria—"

"Of the house of Angrec," Lily said, "if you take my meaning."

He was old enough, she judged, to know sufficient of the language of flowers for that. Angrec meant *royalty*.

"I trust," Lily said in a louder voice, "you do not wish me to remove this blindfold."

"Oh! No! No, ma'am, there's no call for that at all," Beech said hastily. "I'll just get that horn for you—and the cider, of course." He hastened across the room and banged on the bar. "Sage! A half of cider and bring me a jug of the spiced cordial—the best, mind you."

"Yes, Pa," a creamy voice called back.

"And dinner," Malin muttered to Lily. "Don't forget."

Beech returned to her side. "Perhaps you would care to, er, to, er, examine the horn while your drink is prepared, my l—ma'am?"

"Indeed." Lily put out her hand, and the horn was put into it. It was surprisingly light for so large a thing.

"I wouldn't stay here any longer than you need, m'lady," Beech murmured. "Not every family round here is loyal. Too many depend on Wolves for trade, if you take my drift. I wish I could give you a bed for the night, but I fancy you might be safer elsewhere."

Lily tugged the blindfold down slightly so she could take a peek at the horn. It was beautifully carved with intricate scrolls and festoons of many plants, and the mouthpiece had been covered with a decorative pommel which turned it into a drinking horn.

"*His mouth to trumpet's other end...*" she murmured.

"Have we got time for some dinner?" Malin asked in an undertone.

"As long as you're well away before closing, you should be all right," Beech said.

"Pa?"

Sage's voice sounded closer at hand than Lily had expected, and her head automatically whipped round. The blindfold slipped.

"Half of cider and the best currant. Also, Darnel wants a glass of the..."

Her voice trailed away as she saw Lily's eyes. Frozen with

horror, Lily gazed past her into the eyes of the man leaning round the corner of the bar.

He recovered his composure first. "Well! Magister will be interested, won't he?"

"I'll not have guests threatened in my house, Darnel," Beech said stoutly.

"That's no guest, that's—"

Lily heard no more, as Malin seized her hand and pulled. Through the door, down the hall—past the public bar which was already in a clamour—and out through the open door. They made a beeline for the nearest cover: a tongue of forest that seemed far too far away.

They reached it in safety, but its haven was illusory. It was a mere fringe of trees, on the other side of which was a field, and beyond that a timber yard. The wet earth clung to her feet, but she stumbled on. They pelted through the piles of timber, Lily desperately clutching the horn in her free hand, and came to a sudden stop as their feet pounded on decking.

"River!" Lily gasped.

"I can see that! Swim!"

"I can't!"

Malin groaned, and Lily tried desperately to think of a way out. The river was steep-sided and deep—it would have to be, for timber to be loaded here. There was no way she could wade across. On both sides, the timber yard's fence came down to the water's edge. And judging from the shouts coming from the road, there was no going back and trying to find another way.

The moon came out—Malin groaned again—revealing steps which went right down into the water. Lily darted down them. Perhaps, if she hunched down, they wouldn't see her...

"A boat!" Malin said beside her. It was tied up under the decking, little more than a rough canoe.

"That would take us downstream," Lily said, hope blossoming. "Away from the road!"

"Stealing another boat? Anyway, there's only room for one."

Lily flushed, and wished she hadn't told him about the "magic" boat in the Renwick stream.

"Better to lie low here till the hunt dies away," Malin muttered. "You'd be seen downstream, anyway."

The thought flashed into Lily's mind like a bolt of lightning.

"Not me," she breathed. "The Dreaming Duchess."

Heedless of Malin's whispered protests, she clambered into the boat and untied it.

"Not like that!" Malin said. "Here, let me."

A moment later, she was floating free. Malin slipped into the water after her, staying close by in the shadow of the hull. Lily carefully arranged her skirts—concealing the horn—and lay back in what turned out to be the unpleasantly damp bottom of the boat.

Hands folded, eyes closed, the Dreaming Duchess sailed silently and swiftly down the river in the moonlight.

⚜   ⚜   ⚜

Lily sat under the trees in the dappled midday sun, staring down at the horn in her lap. The leaves above her rustled in the breeze and a new shaft of sunlight bathed the horn, giving it a glow like a jar of warm honey.

"The Horn of Vale," Lily sighed, and put her head on one side to admire it better.

An explosive snort from Malin broke her reverie.

"What's so funny?" she demanded.

"That young fellow last night," Malin said, choking with laughter.

"Was that who shrieked?"

"One look and he was off like a streak of lightning," Malin gurgled. "So white he practically glowed in the dark."

Lily couldn't prevent a giggle escaping her lips. "I wish I'd seen it!"

Malin wiped a tear from the corner of his eye. "Happy times. So, where do we hit next?"

Lily frowned. "I've been trying to figure out the rest of the riddle," she began.

"No, you haven't; you've been mooning over that horn," Malin said. "Give it here."

"No!" She tucked it protectively under a fold of her cloak. "It is mine to guard and care for. And I *have* been thinking about the riddle."

"So what does it mean?"

"We already know what the second and fourth couplets mean—the horn, and the one who is to come. The third couplet obviously refers to the Lunula—the moon element, you see. Though what it means by rising in the north, I don't know."

"Just nonsense, I'd say. The moon rises in the east, he knew that."

"Maybe something to do with the Norward Sea?"

Malin groaned. "I hope not. The last thing I need is to tow you out to sea."

"At least you can swim. Anyway, that means the first couplet must refer to the Persimmon Key."

Malin recited:

> The lanky lad unlocked the door
>   To set the flowers free.

"Exactly," Lily said. "In fact," she added, with a surge of excitement, "that's what the lanky bit means—land, key. Lanky."

"So what does that mean?"

"I don't know," she confessed, and relapsed into silence.

"We can't sit here all day," Malin said eventually. "Restoration Day is coming, whether you know what the riddle means or not."

"Don't rush me!" She stared into the distance, her lips moving. "Unlocked the door...flowers free. There aren't any notable doors in Arcelia..."

"Not that I ever saw or heard of. Gates, yes. Doors, no."

"I suppose it could be a gate..." Lily said, "but, no, if he'd meant gate he would have said so. The significant part is the flowers. I think."

"You *think?*"

"Well, the Key is the part of Restoration Day most closely associated with the land, isn't it? The people are summoned by the *Horn,* the monarch wears the *Lunula,* and the land is unlocked by the *Key.*"

"So...?"

"So," Lily said, pleased to find that everything was fitting nicely into her new theory, "the Horn we found in an inn, a place where the people gather. So the Key—"

"—will be found where the land gathers?"

"Don't be silly. The Key has to be kept out of the earth until Restoration Day. *But,* when you consider the land element, and the pedlar's mention of flowers, it suggests a place where the land grows flowers. And, if I am not mistaken," Lily said triumphantly, "we are *not* a thousand miles away from a village famed throughout Arcelia for its flower-growing."

"Blosse? I always thought that was named after the month."

"It's all falling into place," Lily said. "You know, I wouldn't be surprised if the land was somehow *leading* us. We always seem to be in just the right place."

"A cowshed in a slip?"

She ignored him. "And that boat last night, right where we needed it, and bringing us ashore so conveniently."

"Boats are always convenient for you, aren't they?"

Lily had the grace to blush. "Let's be going."

She scrambled eagerly to her feet. The Horn of Vale fell to the ground, and she seized it with a cry, turning it over anxiously to be certain it was unharmed.

"You're going to want a string on that, to wear it," was Malin's only comment. "Or you'll lose it."

⚜   ⚜   ⚜

"So, this language of flowers," Malin said, as they wended their way towards the village of Blosse. "Is there a flower for everything?"

"I don't think so...and it's not all flowers; some are trees or fruit or even vegetables."

"Vegetables?"

"Cucumber for *criticism* and cabbage for *gain*."

"So you could read a message into your dinner?"

Lily giggled. "I suppose you could."

"Does Lily have a meaning?"

"*Majesty*," Lily said immediately. "Well, that's the Imperial Lily. White lilies mean *purity* and *sweetness*—"

Malin snorted.

"—and arum lilies mean *beauty* and *purity* and *resurrection*. They're my favourite."

"Arum lilies—that's those white ones with the yellow stick down the middle, right?"

"Yes," Lily said, pleased to find he knew something about a subject so dear to her.

"They're poisonous," Malin said.

"What?"

"You eat some of that, your lips start burning, your tongue swells up, your throat swells up, and then—"

"I have never," Lily said coldly, "considered *eating* an arum lily."

"Just as well," Malin said.

They walked on in silence for some time.

"What about Lily of the Valley?" he asked at last.

"*Return of happiness.*"

"That fits."

"Do you really think so?"

Travelling single-file as they were, she was glad he couldn't see the pinkness of her cheeks.

"You coming back has made a lot of people happy. Even me," Malin said. "Sort of. Even if I die tomorrow."

"Gum Cistus," said Lily, without thinking.

"Eh?"

"It means *I shall die tomorrow*," she explained.

"There's a *flower* for that?"

"Really and truly," Lily said.

"Really and truly," Malin replied, "I don't plan on dying tomorrow. Or today, if it comes to that."

"I'm glad to hear it."

They fell into silence again.

"So if you're a lily of some sort, what am I?"

Lily bit back the urge to say *loam*, and substituted "Hmm..." so he'd know she was thinking about it.

"Camomile," she said at last.

"Camomile," he said, voice dripping with disgust. "That muck old folk drink to settle their stomachs, when tea has got to be too much for them?" He stalked on.

"You're offended," Lily said, stating the obvious. "I'm sorry, I wasn't thinking of the medicinal aspect."

His back did not unbend.

"And I certainly wasn't thinking of the sweet smell," she said acidly.

He snorted. "What's it mean, then?"

"*Energy in adversity.*"

"For camomile?" He sounded dubious, to say the least.

"Because camomile pulls itself together when you tread on it," she explained. "So the harsher it's treated, the stronger it gets."

"The stronger it gets," Malin echoed thoughtfully. He lapsed into silence for several moments. "Thanks."

There was still some tension in the air when he spoke again. "How about one for the Magister?"

"Oh, that's easy!" Lily said with a laugh. "Lettuce—*cold-hearted.*"

"We could send him a bunch of lettuce with one of those die-tomorrow flowers," Malin joked.

"Gum Cistus? But that means *I* shall die tomorrow."

"Well, what's the flower for *you* shall die tomorrow?"

Lily frowned thoughtfully. "I don't think there is one."

"What fool kind of language is that?"

"I think we must be getting close," Lily said, changing the subject before she said something she'd regret. "Look at all these little fire-daisy plants. I suppose it's the time of year for it. And this field, too...and that one. How strange. Aunt Hortensia always said that fire-daisies should be planted in between rows of other plants, to keep off the insects. Are they waiting for a late planting?"

"No," Malin said, not looking up. "This is all they grow now."

"What?"

"They dry the flowers, grind them up and sell them to the latties. Who mix the powder with water and spray it on their crops."

"How silly," Lily said. "Why not just plant the fire-daisies directly into the lattie fields?"

"Because," said Malin, "like I said before, it's all set up for one kind of plant per field. If they put the daisies in between the rows the machines would get them all messed up together."

Lily thought about this. "It seems a lot of trouble to go to."

"Someone's coming," Malin said.

A tall, thin figure was making its way towards them, down

the path between the fields.

"Watch what you say," Malin warned. "And don't call me Clotbur, or I promise you there will be trouble."

Lily watched the figure approach. "He's very lanky, isn't he?" she said, and gasped. "Malin! Do you think fifteen years ago he would have been a *lad?*"

"Maybe," Malin muttered. "I bet he didn't have that creepy moustache back then."

Lily opened her mouth to censure his rudeness, and then shut it again. Now that she could see it clearly, it was only too obviously an unfortunate choice of facial hair. It crawled across the man's upper lip like a millipede.

"Be careful what you say," Malin repeated. "You don't know who you can trust."

"I'm sure the pedlar wouldn't have entrusted the Persimmon Key to anyone who was not perfectly worthy of the trust," Lily said, full of confidence. She smiled warmly as the lanky man drew up.

"Visiting Blosse?" he asked. "Perhaps I can be of service."

"*Just* what I was hoping for," Lily said, and pushed back her hood. "I am Lily, your queen."

The man's eyes opened wide, as did his mouth, but he recovered quickly and made a passable bow. "Basil of Blosse, at your service, m'lady."

"And this is Malin of Burnaby," Lily continued.

The two males eyed each other for a moment, and contented themselves with curt nods.

"To what great good fortune do we owe your presence among us?" Basil asked Lily, ushering her along the path towards the village. "Do come this way, my lady."

Malin stumped along behind.

"We come seeking a key," Lily said. "*The* Key, in fact. You see, we found the horn, hidden as a drinking horn, so now we—" She stopped. She was babbling. *So tired...* She drew a breath.

"Perhaps you would prefer to speak of the matter after a rest, m'lady? And, of course, some refreshment."

The idea was enticing, but she didn't want to waste a moment.

"I'd better tell you," Lily said, "and then perhaps you can institute inquiries on my behalf while I take my repose."

"Excellently considered," Basil murmured.

"Are you at all familiar with a song that begins: *The lanky lad unlocked the door?*" Lily asked.

Basil's eyebrows rose. It was clear he had not been expecting this.

"We believe it to be a coded message," Lily said, "which has already directed us to the finding of the Horn of Vale."

She waved it by way of proof, and was pleased to see that it caught the man's full attention. Indeed, he could hardly tear his eyes off it.

"The decoding of the song has now brought us to Blosse," she continued. "The reference to flowers in the second line, you see; and Blosse being known for its flower gardens; and the Persimmon Key being inextricably linked with the land or soil element."

"I *see*," Basil said. "We are entirely at your disposal. I trust you will allow me to act as your guide in these matters while you are with us. Ah, and here we are in the village. Allow me to make you known."

Blosse was not, after all, such a very large village. A short alleyway brought them out into the small cobbled square, at the centre of which was the village well. Lily seated herself at the highest point on the stone surround that she could find, without risking falling into the well if she fell asleep. She nodded to Basil to proceed.

He struck a pose and filled his lungs. "People of Blosse!" he proclaimed, and heads turned.

His voice was undeniably smooth, even at great volume. Perhaps, Lily thought sleepily, he might be persuaded to act as Denton town crier—or, better yet, as palace butler. Imagine that voice announcing guests at a ball, the way he was now announcing her. Even Aunt Hortensia could not fail to be pleased.

A crowd formed faster than Lily had anticipated. Malin shifted uneasily and came to stand near the bottom of the well's stone steps. Basil's magnificent voice rolled on, though he never got around to mentioning the Horn of Vale, Lily noticed. Finally, he rolled to a halt. Even in her dozy state, Lily could feel the uneasiness from the crowd. One man gave it voice.

"We don't want another war!" There was a murmur of agreement. "Not with Magister, not with nobody."

"There is no question of war," Basil said smoothly. "Merely a matter of—shall we say, collecting lost property? If a passing young lady chooses to consult the people of Blosse on a gardening-related matter, surely that is no concern of the Magister's."

"He's trying to have it both ways," Malin muttered out the side of his mouth to Lily.

It was clear to her that the crowd were not supportive—fearful would be the word she would use—but Basil seemed positively enthusiastic, and she had no doubt of him being able to persuade anyone to anything, given time enough. She only wished he had remembered her wish to retire and rest while all this was taking place. Her jaw was nearly aching with the effort not to yawn.

An old man tapped his way out of the crowd, leaning on his stick, and Lily perked up. Here, surely, was someone who would remember all the history of Blosse and everything that had ever happened in it.

"I'm the oldest gardener in these parts," he said, his voice creaking with age, "and let me tell you, that young whipper-snapper of a pedlar never left anything in Blosse that wasn't paid for, excepting that drat-stupid song of his. Nothing for you here, and things being what they are, you'll excuse us if we'd rather you moved along and looked elsewhere."

Lily's heart sank, but Basil turned to her, a reassuring smile twisting up the corners of his long thin moustache.

"Don't, by any means, be discouraged, my lady. I can assure you I will forward enquiries with the utmost energy. And, now, perhaps you would care to remove to my own humble residence for some refreshment?"

Lily got to her feet, mouth dry, stomach empty and legs aching. Food! Drink! Sleep! She allowed him to lead her away from the crowd, down a cool, shady alley and towards a fine-looking stone house.

"Beat it, you!" came a mutter behind her, and Lily came to a stop.

Even as a mutter, Basil's voice was distinctive. But who—? She turned, and saw Malin glaring at him. Surely not...

"I beg your pardon," she said, "I must have misheard. I could almost fancy you were refusing to extend your hospitality to my companion."

Basil tried to usher her through the doorway, but she would not budge, and he was forced to speak. "My lady, it is hardly fitting for a young lady in your position to be seen consorting with a *dwarf*."

"He has saved my life on more than one occasion," Lily said. "I would not be here without him."

"Certainly, some recompense for his services would be considered a kind gesture on your part," Basil said, his voice soothing. "Doubtless that was his motivation in attaching himself to you. But you are among your own people now—he can go back to his, and we can all move on."

For one moment, Lily wondered if he was right. She needed

her people's support, and Malin would want to look after his family; he should be rewarded for all he had done for her.

"You don't want him getting above his station," Basil hissed, and the distortion cast by his words fell away. This wasn't some opportunistic money-grubber they were talking about; it was *Malin*. Opportunistic, perhaps, but...

"His station," Lily snapped, "is at my side."

"I am not proposing to leave you unattended," Basil said hastily. "Not at all. I shall be always at your side, for whatever need. I flatter myself I am of more use than this—runt."

"You do flatter yourself," Lily said coldly. "He is a man of action; you appear to be made of nothing but words."

"You seem very *attached*," Basil sneered, his moustache echoing the disdainful curl of his lip. "Very fond. Such a high value you place on him! I find myself wondering..."

A knife flashed in Basil's hand. Malin hurled himself towards them, hatchet drawn, and was brought up short by Basil's blade against his neck.

"*How* high do you value him? Above that horn you carry?"

Rise and Fall

Lily stared at Basil, her face white and her eyes blazing with pure loathing.

"Make your decision," Basil said coldly. "I have no intention of standing here all day."

It was no use calling for help—it was only too plain that the people of Blosse did not wish to get involved in any clash of loyalties. She could not risk creating a diversion; it would be a gamble on Malin's life. To hand over the Horn of Vale, the treasure of her ancestors and an integral part of the rite of Restoration Day was unthinkable. But to stand by and watch as Malin was—no. Unbearable.

But perhaps he was only bluffing. Murder was a serious offence, after all. Perhaps gentle words would persuade him...

She met Basil's gaze. It was cold and hard, and she could not understand how she had taken him for a helpful, loyal friend, even for a moment. If ever a man had pure self-interest written on his face, this was he. Her eye fell, and met Malin's. He didn't look afraid, or even angry. He just looked.

Lily made her decision. With an inward wrench she was sure she would feel to her dying day, she held out the Horn of Vale.

Basil smiled, and Lily wondered how she hadn't seen that his smiles never reached his eyes. His knife withdrew from Malin's neck, just enough to allow Malin to slide away, not far enough to risk any sudden action.

"A pleasure to have dealt with you," Basil murmured, still smiling.

Lily backed down the street as Malin circled cautiously around Basil, neither taking their eyes off him for a moment. At the end of the little street, they stopped, still looking back.

"Shall I put my hatchet through his head?" Malin asked under his breath.

"No!"

"He's a traitor."

"Yes, but…the Horn is for the people," Lily said unhappily. "How can I call my people with a horn stained with Arcelian blood?"

How could she call her people without the Horn? Somehow, she would have to get it back.

Once out of sight, they turned and ran, out of Blosse, through the fields, and into the welcome cover of the woods. Even then, it was some time before Lily was prepared to listen to her aching legs and stop to rest. Malin twirled a leaf into a cone and scooped some water from a passing rivulet.

"Here."

"Thank you." She sipped. It was cool as it trickled down her burning throat.

"You didn't have to do that," Malin said.

Lily sighed. "Yes, I did."

"Regretting it?"

"No! It's just—what am I going to do now? How can Restoration Day proceed without the Horn of Vale?"

"Perhaps there's a spare," Malin suggested.

"A *spare?*"

"Well, Vale had two horns."

Lily frowned. "Who needs two horns?"

"I don't know; they just grow that way." Following Lily's bemused look, he continued. "On oxen. Vale was an ox."

"What?"

"You didn't know? I thought everyone—"

"But...but Vale...ploughed up the Valley of Arcelia, and..."

"You know the story, then? I always wondered how he did it. Head down? Head on one side?"

"*Vale* was an *ox*? How do you know?"

"Every Burnabais kid grows up on Vale stories," Malin said. "Besides, it's called the Horn of Vale, isn't it?"

"Yes, but that's like the Sword of Roarke," Lily said lamely. She thought for a minute. "Burnaby has lots of stories about Vale?"

"Yep."

"A shared mythology is an element of shared nationhood," Lily murmured.

"Well, it's the same valley," Malin conceded. "But we're not subjects, all right? Not subject to anyone."

"The question is moot, unless we get the Horn back."

"Maybe we sneak back tonight, break into the place?" Malin suggested.

"I suppose," Lily said drearily. "What other hope have we got?"

"Might as well get comfortable, then," Malin said, and proceeded to form himself a soft depression in the underbrush to lounge in. Halfway through his scuffling, he stopped. "You thought long and hard before you handed it over, didn't you?"

"Well, I..."

"I'm not offended," he said. "Pays to think. Just wondering what made you decide the way you did."

"It was—it was who he wanted me to be."

"Eh?"

"Someone who takes loyalty for granted."

"Like you did in Burnaby?"

Lily thought back, and blushed. "I may have expected a loyalty I did not find, but I have *never* repaid loyalty by casually discarding someone when they're no longer required."

"Right."

"The nerve of that man!" Lily fulminated. "Imagining that I'd cut you off at his word, when all he'd done was talk about what he was going to do! And for all I know, if I'd gone with him, I'd have found a knife in my ribs before long."

"Not him," Malin said. "I know the type. Fancies himself a leader but doesn't like to get his hands dirty. No, I reckon he had his eye on a softer way to power."

"A softer way?" Lily asked, bemused.

Malin waggled his eyebrows. Lily's jaw dropped open.

"Eugh! How could he—how could he possibly think—? That's *disgusting!*"

"So marrying a commoner is beneath you?"

"Commoners are one thing," Lily declared, "but he's probably twice my age!"

"Princesses marry worse, from what I hear," Malin said. *"Old* men."

"Well, maybe once upon a time," Lily said. "For the good of the nation. But not any more, and," she added, before Malin could say any more, "definitely not hypocritical, xenophobic, two-faced *creeps* with moustaches like millipedes."

Malin chuckled appreciatively.

"Not quite the handsome prince of your dreams, eh?"

Lily blushed, then flushed, with embarrassment and horror respectively.

"If I thought I'd be married off to a man like that, I'd throw myself into Parsifal."

"You can't swim."

"That's the point."

"Not even—what was it you said? For the good of the nation?"

"I've been thinking about that," Lily said. "The land and the monarch are bound up together, so it seems to me that if the monarch's life is blighted by a dreadful marriage, it'll be bad for the land, too."

"Something in that," he agreed.

"So it is part of my duty to Arcelia to marry wisely."

"You're thinking about getting married already?"

"A monarch owes it to the nation to raise a good successor before they die, and monarchs...don't always live very long. It's best not to leave it too late."

"There's more to marriage than producing heirs," Malin growled.

"Of course there is. But it's something I have to bear in mind."

Malin grunted and scuffled himself deeper into his den.

"Eighteen's not that early," Lily said after a while. "Deni was engaged to Corrie when he was only twenty."

"I suppose." He stopped suddenly. "You don't think Pasque's going to want to get married any time soon, do you?"

"I don't know. She didn't exactly make me her confidante."

He scowled. "She'd better not."

"Marry? Why not—too *young?*"

"No—Burnabaise are more mature than big people at any age."

Lily repressed a snort of disbelief.

"One," Malin said, "Jarret is nowhere near good enough for her, and two, this is no kind of a world to bring little ones into."

"We are going to change that. The second bit, anyway. Who is Jarret?"

Malin's face twisted. "He's the Burnaby version of Millipede. He'd be the first to agree with selling you off to Phelan—me too, probably, if he thought Pasque wouldn't get to hear of it."

"So you're exercising a veto?"

"Eh?"

"Like with royalty. When a member of the royal family is

to marry, lots of people have a say, but only the monarch has the right to say no. Well, and the person getting married, obviously. One can't always choose the person one wishes, but one can always say no to everyone else."

"Hang on," said Malin. "You are the monarch, right? So you're both the, er, veto people."

"Yes, that makes it harder."

"Harder? I'd have thought that'd make it a whole lot easier."

"Easier to marry," said Lily, "but harder to be certain one is making the right decision, without the monarch to confirm it. I mean, what if I'm blinded by—by my feelings?"

"Real love doesn't blind you; it makes everything painfully clear," Malin said, a bitter note in his voice.

Lily desperately wanted to know how he knew this, but as she was trying to find a way to ask which wouldn't reveal her level of interest in the answer, he hissed, "Get off the path!"

She did so, and was rewarded shortly thereafter by seeing Basil—or, as she now thought of him, Millipede—riding a trim ox rapidly northwards down the forest path. She watched him go.

"He's looking for us," she breathed.

"He's not looking at all," Malin murmured back. "I'd say he's heading to Murdock."

"To betray us?" Lily asked, panic clutching at her heart.

"No…plenty of places closer if that was his plan. He won't want to get involved with the Magister—he'd have to explain why he let us go, for a start. I'd say he's taking the horn to sell to the dealers. At that pace, he'll be there on Martday, just in time for Murdock Great Market."

"And we," Lily declared, stepping out with wilted hope reviving in her heart, "will be right behind him."

"Just one thing," Malin said, getting up and shaking off the dead leaves.

"What?"

"Murdock's a major garrison—second only to Denton. The place will be crawling with Wolves."

⚜   ⚜   ⚜

Phelan stared down at the map on his desk.

"The Ox and Trumpet," he said, the tip of his paper knife resting on the precise point on the map.

"Yes, sir," the Wolf officer said. "With the dwarf, still. Word is she stole a decorative drinking horn."

"A horn?" Phelan questioned, his head snapping up.

"Yes, sir."

"You searched the area? Asked for sightings?"

"Yes, sir. No sign of her. There was a boat missing from the timber yard, but we found it washed up further down the river towards Blosse. Could have worked loose."

"Any sightings of the boat in between?"

The Wolf shuffled his feet. "Yes and no, sir…"

"It's one or the other, captain."

"Plenty of embarrassment and no hard facts. All we got was an old woman yammering about some ghost story of a lady in a boat."

"The Dreaming Duchess," Phelan murmured. "Clever of her."

"So it was her in the boat, then?"

"Of course it was!" Phelan snapped. "Ghost stories are all nonsense."

"Speaking of nonsense, sir…"

"Well?"

"It reminds me, the local informant—Darnel, his name is—said the girl mentioned that nonsense song. From the pedlar we had our suspicions of."

Phelan sat in silence so long the Wolf wondered if he'd been forgotten.

"Sir?" he began tentatively.

"I want a transcript of that song on my desk in five minutes," Phelan instructed Vetch, who nodded and immediately began scratching away on a second piece of paper.

"You are familiar with the words, I see," Phelan remarked. "You have heard them at a public house, perhaps?"

Vetch gave a little nod.

Phelan watched him until the sheet was handed over. "I trust you exercise moderation. I would not like indiscretion to rob me of your services."

"I'm v-very careful, sir," Vetch said, going pale.

"Good." Phelan scanned the sheet. "Captain, I want you to put all my Arcelian operatives in that quadrant on alert."

"It'd be finding a needle in a haystack, sir!"

"A simple task, captain, providing one has a lodestone."

"Sir?"

"If she is using this—drivel—to guide her," Phelan said, flicking the paper dismissively, "there is no need to waste effort in searching for her. We'll use this to bring her to us."

"A trap, sir?"

"A trap."

⚜   ⚜   ⚜

Lily was surprised at how easy it was to get into Murdock. Malin insisted they walk a few yards apart so as not to jog the memory of anyone looking for a young woman and a dwarf travelling together. Both kept their hoods well up. As they drew closer, they simply merged into the stream of people heading towards the city gates, all of whom, she noted, were focussed on their own business and paying no attention to any-one else.

Once through the gate, having been loosely surveyed by a bored guard's gaze, only the jostling crowd kept Lily from stopping in wonder. Where Denton was a dingy grey, Mur-dock was full of colour. Little booths lined the walls each side of the broad streets; handcarts plied their trades through the streams of people like boats in a river; building materials surely not of Arcelian origin distinguished the buildings and proclaimed the owners' taste and wealth to the teeming crowds.

And the crowds! Looking about to be sure she hadn't lost Malin, Lily saw not only Arcelians but Easterlings out of Wolf uniform, and occasional Burnabaise. There were even people whose origin she could not guess at. One caught her staring and she hurriedly looked away, pressing up through the crowds to keep closer to Malin.

They followed the broad street which led through the city, the crowds ever more pressing as the smaller streets to each side fed further people into the throng. In her efforts to avoid being separated from Malin altogether, Lily found herself right behind him as the crowd jostled her about.

Scents and sounds swam around her head: the songs of unknown birds, spiciness from a passing handcart, huckster's cries (largely unintelligible to the uninitiated), and the wholesome breath of fresh timber from the wagon lumbering down the street, its elderly ox-team seemingly oblivious to the crowds around them.

And then she heard someone singing, somewhere in the crowd. It was a catchy, cheerful, almost cheeky, little tune. She couldn't quite hear the words, and she pushed closer. A phrase or two was all it took, and her blood ran hot and cold all at the same time. Heedless of appearances, she put a hand on Malin's shoulder. He half turned and shrugged it off, with a warning look.

"Listen!" she hissed. "Twice-dead hero and long-dead queen!"

He listened, his eyes widened, and he frowned. "She works quickly!"

There was an *oof* and an *ow* which didn't go with the tune—

someone taking exception to the song, it appeared. There was a ripple in the crowd and the voice took up again somewhere else, with a hint of a snigger. Another voice began to hum along.

"Keep close," Malin muttered. "We're nearly there."

The pressure of the crowd was easing, and Lily could see there was an open area up ahead, but she was completely unprepared for what came next.

They were at one corner of a vast square, large enough to hold Candra and its whole park, she guessed. Every inch seemed full of shops, stalls, merchants, buyers and merchandise. Three sides of the square were made up of huge, long buildings; warehouses perhaps, or shops—some of those nearby had swathes of fabric displayed from their little balconies. The fourth side was more open, but Lily could see masts and sails, and cargo hoists. The salty, tangy, fishy smell of the harbour drifted across the square, elbowing aside the myriad other scents—some nice, some not—that cloyed the market.

Malin pressed on, and Lily darted after him. She'd never seen so many people in her life, and she loved it! They passed stalls hawking foods, fine fabrics and perfumes, and Lily was well on her way to falling in love with Murdock Great Market when they emerged into the livestock section.

"Was this where you caused the—?"

"Shh!"

Of course. Silly of her. Lily sniffed, and her face puckered. This was *not* the smell of a healthy manure-pile. The pens were packed with animals—sheep, poultry, calves—all looking listless, dispirited and ill. Lily's excitement ebbed. There was something wrong here. She squeezed aside to make room for a cart pulled by a weary, tottering ox. Malin was squeezed up next to her.

"Why are all the oxen so old?" she asked.

"Bobby calves go for meat," he replied. "Costs too much to feed them till they're grown."

"But—what's going to happen when the old oxen die?" Lily objected.

"People rich enough to raise them will name their own price," Malin said, "and the poor will go without."

The cart finally passed and the crowds closed up in its wake. Lily was starting to feel sick—it was as though the very air was rotting—and was much relieved when Malin turned a corner and led her away from the livestock area. The air gradually cleared.

They were heading to the very centre of the square, where a great fountain continuously poured from above the height of the highest stall. A useful landmark, Lily guessed. But when they reached its lower bowl—practically large enough for a small lake—Malin stopped. Lily sidled up to him and realized he was filling his water bottle, as were others around him.

"Where are we going?" she murmured.

"Jewellers first," he replied, "then on to Antique Alley if we don't fi—"

He was shoved aside by a large man with a bucket to fill.

"Beat it, runt! 'Fore someone teaches you not to get in a man's way."

Lily's mouth opened in outrage, her lungs filled, and her mind was marshalling phrases when Malin said, "Leave it," very low, beside her.

She forced her mouth closed and turned away. The man was filling his bucket as though nothing had happened. He didn't even look at her as she strode away.

Catching up to stride at Malin's side, she hissed, "How can you just—?"

"What do you want me to do?" Malin said, in the leaden tone of tightly-controlled anger. "Talk back? Fight? Get arrested? Kill everyone in the market who stands against me?"

He was right. There was nothing she could do that wouldn't make it worse for him. She found she was grinding her teeth and forced herself to stop.

"You shouldn't have to—it shouldn't be like this!"

He flashed her a quick look and an unexpected grin. "Every little thing matters to you, doesn't it?"

She felt flattered until he added, "No sense of proportion."

"It's the principle of the thing," she said righteously.

"In times like this, one principle's all you can hope for. Pick one."

One principle? How could she pick just one? Truth? Justice? Freedom? Fairness? Right? She thought a little longer.

"The problem isn't too many principles," she said, "the problem is that one principle has a whole range of applications."

"This way," said Malin, and they passed between the two biggest Easterlings Lily had ever seen. They weren't in Wolf uniform, she noted, but they were most definitely armed.

"Jeweller's row," Malin said, by way of explanation. "Take a side. Find me if you see it."

"Mm," said Lily, already entranced by the fine examples of the jeweller's craft, laid out on drapings of velvet at each stall.

Each little shop had its own guard, she noted. Some had two, outnumbering the sole merchant making sales and wheedling customers. It made sense—if a thief got away from you in this crowd, you'd never find him again. She passed slowly down the row, cloak pulled close around her and hood covering most of her face.

She was only halfway down the row when Malin popped up beside her.

"Well? Nothing the other side."

"They're beautiful," Lily murmured, pacing on.

"Never mind that! Anything like—what we're looking for?"

"N-no. Oh, look—torcs!"

Malin scowled. "Move on."

She reached the end of the row, then stopped in the intersection. "Is it some kind of fashion? Torcs are symbolic of servitude—why would anyone want to wear one?"

Malin's scowl blackened. "They don't. But some find they can't feed their families on manufactory wages, so they sell their children as thralls. Owners put them in torcs. Some do it with Burnabais bonded labourers. Like collared pets," he added, his voice like a poisoned whiplash.

"Selling their children?" Lily repeated incredulously. "Who would do such a thing?"

"Parents who want their children to eat," Malin said, "even if it costs them their freedom."

> *When the poor man's debts shall drive him*
> *into thralldom for his bread...*

"And the Burnabaise are sold into bonded labour to pay for debts," Malin continued. "Even fictional ones. Officially fixed-term, but there's ways of keeping people under, if you want to. Treating bonded labour like thralls isn't lawful, but they're Burnabaise, so who's going to stop it?"

"I will stop it," Lily vowed, shaking with rage.

Malin managed half a smile. "You and your principles. Come on."

Fired with renewed purpose, Lily moved down the second row so fast she had to wait for Malin to catch up at the end, where two more impassive giants stood.

"Nothing?" Malin asked. "Right. Left here, then."

Here there were fewer guards, though still more than in most parts of the market. In place of velvet were rich brocades and faded tapestries; instead of artfully displayed single pieces, there were piles of this, that and the other, all old, worn, and carefully balanced to make the most of the space. Occasional glass cases displayed the tiniest treasures.

"Antique Alley?" Lily asked.

"Yep."

"It makes sense, having all the same sort of stall grouped together. And always in the same place?"

"Of course. Never find anything, otherwise."

"It's hard enough to find anything as it is," Lily said under her breath as they separated, each to one side of Antique Alley. It wasn't as hard as it looked, she soon found. The antique stalls were cluttered, but the clutter was carefully arranged so that every item was visible, if not exactly *displayed*.

There were quite a few furniture-sellers—antique furniture, naturally. Some items had her family crest on them. There was a little dressing-table seat which looked suspiciously like Aunt Hortensia's—from the sack of Candra? She couldn't pass it by. Crouching down by it, as inconspicuously as possible, she checked for the little dent on the inside of the leg. It wasn't there. She closed her eyes in relief.

"Charming little seat, isn't it?" a voice boomed above her.

Lily gasped and recoiled, eyes popping open. Now it was the boomer's turn to recoil with a gasp, his big frame tottering back on his short legs like a wardrobe in an earthquake. Her hood had fallen back; her face and eyes were visible to all.

Silence fell—at least in Antique Alley, though the roar of the market continued elsewhere—as everyone stared at Lily. She hoped she looked all right, and tried not to think about when she'd last done her hair.

She straightened, and waited for the reaction. The furniture man scuffled in his waistcoat pocket for an old coin and held it in his palm, looking at her, at it, and at her again. Malin bounded up and took in the situation at a glance.

"Oh, dung it."

The furniture man coughed. "My name is Jasper, head of the Guild of Antiquities in the time of the late King Frederick. Might I remark on the resemblance...?"

"My name is Lily, daughter of Frederick, son of Gauderic, son of Roarke Meilyr, Queen of Arcelia," Lily said gravely, and Jasper bowed. "I am pleased to meet you, Guild-Master Jasper. May I introduce my travelling companion, Malin of Burnaby."

"So you—I mean, the song—land's sake, what a day this is turning into," Jasper said, mopping his brow. "Do take a seat, my lady."

Lily seated herself in a rose velvet armchair, which seemed to please him. A frown crossed his beaming face.

"I'm afraid a good deal of my inventory may be rightfully yours," he said. "I, er..."

"I am not so much concerned with furniture as with a horn," Lily said, which seemed to ease him a little. "*The* Horn, if you take my meaning—I see you do—which has been adapted to appear as a drinking horn."

Jasper nodded. "It's quite an easy adaptation. Usually, a pommel is all it takes."

"Have you seen it?" Malin asked.

"No," Jasper confessed, "but I'll put the word around the guildsmen. If it's here, it'll be in your hands within the hour."

"Oh, *thank you*," Lily said, with such a wealth of warmth in her tone that Jasper went quite pink.

He turned to his assistant and muttered vigorously for a minute. The youth darted off.

"Well, now," Jasper said, rubbing his hands together. "While we wait..." He turned to Malin. "I take it you weren't planning any of your usual, er, festivities, long-dead hero?"

Malin went bright red and muttered something unintelligible.

"Twice-dead," said a younger man, one of the guards from two stalls down. "*She's* the long-dead one."

"Oh yes, of course." Jasper beamed. "Well, it seems to me some sort of celebration is in order. Our long-lost lady is returned to us! Long live the Queen, and down with—er, well, quite!"

The younger men of Antique Alley gave a cheer and surged forward, picking up the chair in which Lily sat and hoisting it to their shoulders. She gave a shriek of surprise.

"Malin!"

"Right behind you!" he called desperately as the chair-bearing party moved off. "Not sure this is a good idea," he said to Jasper, rolling alongside. "The Magister—"

"Haven't had a sniff of him in weeks," Jasper said happily. "Don't worry!"

"What about the Wolf garrison?" Malin snapped. "Have they suddenly disappeared?"

"Well, between you and me and the cobblestones, dear, er, fellow," Jasper said in what passed for a confidential tone over the cheering of the chair-party, "I hear there's been a bit of a falling-out there, over certain unpaid monies. I don't say they're on strike, exactly, but you know how it is with mercenaries. The moment the money stops flowing, the loyalty dries up."

"Finally, some good news," Malin said. "Hope it's true," he added quietly, but Jasper did not seem to hear.

They were out of the antiques area now and heading through the streets of stalls selling furnishing fabric, clothing and cloth.

Lily held on tight, smiled, and occasionally ventured a wave to the cheering crowds which gathered about her path. She fizzed with excitement. This was worth all the hardships she had endured! This was the heart of what it was to be queen, surrounded by the love of her people!

When her bearers turned a corner (cutlers) she caught sight of the tide of people surging after her and smiled radiantly at them all. Malin seized the chance to move up alongside her.

"Wolves might not be a factor," he called up to her. "Still, be careful!"

She nodded her understanding. If the Wolves were out of the picture, this could well be her chance to make a change, to strike a blow (figurative, of course; she didn't want violence) that would tip the scales in her favour. Murdock was of prime strategic importance to Arcelia.

Before they had gone halfway around the circuit of the market, Lily's excitement was beginning to be eroded by queasiness. The chair rocked with the movement of the bearers—all the more so each time a fresh bearer took a tiring man's place—and she was only too thankful she'd chosen a chair with arms. She only hoped the crowds couldn't see the whiteness of her knuckles.

But then there was a shout from behind her and she turned to see a group of older men—the men of Antique Alley, by their dress—pressing through the crowd to her side, one man distinguished by the way the others made a path for him. He waved a hand at her, and in it—yes! The Horn of Vale was found.

Her queasiness entirely forgotten, Lily took the Horn with a press of his hand, and raised it in the air. A louder cheer went up. She was pleased to find the antiques man had replaced her rough plant-string with a tooled leather strap, which she made immediate use of. The last thing she wanted was to drop it under the feet of a crowd like this! She smiled, waved and continued on her triumphal progress.

By the time they had gone halfway round the square, it seemed every person in the city was surging around her chair, shouting, cheering and seeking royal patronage for their goods.

There were merchants, both Arcelian and foreign, waving samples and calling up to her; shoppers trying to get close enough for a good look without losing their bags or baskets; grubby, skinny children cavorting with the excitement. And then Lily saw a rather showily-dressed youth slip his hand into the basket of a short, stout woman being jostled near the edge of the crowd. His hand came out, drawing something silvery.

Lily extended her arm with pointing finger, and her voice gave a clarion call: "Stop thief!"

Everything stopped. Everyone looked. The youth tried to wriggle away, but the walls of people had turned hostile around him. He stood there, a pathetic hangdog figure in his fashionable clothes, a fish dangling from one hand. The stout woman looked in her basket.

"That's my fish!" she cried. She snatched it from his unresisting hand and slapped him in the face with it before dropping it back in her basket.

The crowd roared with appreciative laughter; the woman flushed a little and tried not to smile. The youth, face still not red enough to drown out the fish mark, made another bid for freedom, but was collared by a couple of stevedores.

"Do you have anything to say for yourself?" Lily asked sternly.

"I'm hungry," the boy muttered.

Lily softened. "It is hard to be hungry," she acknowledged, and gave a rueful smile. "I haven't eaten all day."

The air around her suddenly sprouted with foodstuffs. She accepted a large loaf with a gracious smile, and placed it on her lap.

"But it is still wrong to take from others without their consent—particularly while one still has property to dispose of."

"I've got nothing but what I stand up in," the youth said.

"Which cost a pretty penny, if I am not mistaken," Lily returned with equanimity. "I am sure somewhere in this market there are traders who will trade you simpler clothes and coin for the items you now wear."

There was an enthusiastic shout from behind, and Lily caught one or two figures jumping up and down in the corner of her eye.

"Wear second-hand clothes?" the youth said, a hint of disdain marring his face.

"You were prepared to eat second-hand fish," Lily pointed out. She waited for the laughter to die down before adding, "and if second hand clothing is good enough for me, it is *certainly* good enough for you."

The crowd cheered.

"Shall we put him in the pillory, my lady?" one of the stevedores asked.

"To what end?" Lily enquired.

"Well, um, you know, so people can, er, reckernize him, and…"

"Laugh at him," his mate supplied.

"Yeah! And throw—er, er…"

"Food and stuff," his mate helpfully suggested.

Lily considered this. "He has already been recognized, laughed at, and assaulted with a fish. I'm not sure the pillory has anything more to offer."

"What do we do with 'im then?"

Lily looked the boy in the eye. "Are you prepared to work for a living?"

"Yeah! As long as it's—I mean, I don't want to shovel dung…" He caught the narrowing of Lily's eyes. "But anything's better than the pillory, right?"

"Indeed. Well, there is your answer, gentlemen. Give him a job."

The silence that followed was so intense Lily could hear the creaking of the ships across the great square.

"No offers? If you refuse to give him honest employment, you must share in the blame of his dishonest employment."

More creaks.

"No?" Lily asked. "Not even dung-shovelling? Beggars can't be choosers."

"I'm not a beggar!" the youth protested.

"No—beggars are honest with themselves and with others."

He subsided. Lily surveyed the crowd with a disappointed gaze.

Jasper stepped forward, waving his hands in a vaguely placatory manner. "Perhaps if we knew his skills, if any?"

"I'm good with my hands," the youth said, to snorts in the crowd. "Quick. Delicate."

A man in plain but clearly expensive clothes manoeuvred his way to the front, and made a little bow to Lily.

"Such skills could be put to good use in my weaving sheds," he said, surveying the blushing youth. "Although I like my employees to be dressed with less show and more quality, but I'm sure that can be arranged." The master weaver turned to Lily. "If you speak for him, my lady."

Lily looked at the boy. "What is your name?"

"Keelie, my lady. Please! I won't put a foot wrong—or a finger. I promise!"

Lily held his eye for a moment, then nodded. She turned to the master weaver.

"If he reoffends, he must make the loss good. And if he cannot, he must be given into bonded labour until his debt is paid."

The master weaver nodded his agreement. Lily tore the loaf on her lap into rough thirds and tossed one down to Keelie. He caught it expertly and grinned with relief. The weaver ushered Keelie away and the chair-party resumed their progress amid the cheering.

Lily found Malin battling through the crowd and caught his eye. He grinned at her, and she tossed his share of the bread down to him, eating little shreds of her piece in between smiling and waving as her chair rocked along.

So far so good, Lily told herself as her chair turned towards the great fountain at the centre of the square. Popular support and no move from the Wolves. And she knew where her next meal was coming from, which was a novelty these days. But she needed to know what to say to her people now. They were looking to her for leadership, for guidance. She must not fail them.

Her bearers lowered the chair at the foot of the fountain, allowing her to step off onto the wide rim of the lower bowl. She thanked them courteously and prepared to address the crowd, which filled the open space around the fountain thicker every moment. She waited for her breathing to return to normal before attempting to speak.

The secret of successful elocution, Aunt Hortensia always said, was perfect control of the vocal apparatus—and that included breathing. In the meantime, she simply showered smiles.

A disturbance in the crowd turned into Malin, making his way to the front with some difficulty. The people were packed in tight, and they were not used to making room for dwarves. Reaching the front, he hopped up easily onto the lower bowl and stood there, at barely arm's reach from Lily, surveying the crowd with watchful eyes.

Firmly putting aside any thought of what she or her clothes looked like, Lily summoned all the joy and excitement of the past hour and prepared to speak. She straightened her skirts with a little shake and filled her lungs.

"People of Murdock!" The buzz died. "Arcelians, Burnabaise, and travellers from many lands!" (Cheers.) "I thank you for the warmth of your welcome. I believe some of you have heard the recent song of our exploits—" (further cheers, and an attempt to break into song which was soon suppressed) "—which I can assure you is all too true. Malin, as you can see, is still with me."

She gestured to Malin, who didn't seem overly pleased. There was a half-hearted cheer from the crowd, lukewarm at best.

Lily pressed on. "I am especially glad to receive such a warm welcome in Murdock, a city of such great importance to our nation." (*Much* more enthusiastic cheers.) "Indeed, having now seen it, I am inclined to call it the greatest city of Arcelia." (Biggest cheer yet.) "Although, to be fair, I didn't see Denton under the most propitious conditions." (Laughter, with a few boos.)

"I have seen many distressing things in my travels around Arcelia," she continued, and the crowd sobered down a bit. "Things which I intend to see changed." (Subdued cheers.) "I have seen people dispossessed of their land." (Shouts of agreement.) "I have seen families and their elderly persecuted with violence and struggling to keep a roof over their heads. Good, decent families, who work hard and mind their own business." (More shouts of agreement.)

Lily felt the surge of power that comes to every orator who sways a crowd. "I have seen intimidation, violence and fear!"

The crowd was at fever pitch. Part of Lily knew it was time to wind up, to point to the future and end on a high note—but she didn't want this moment to end. She cast about for more examples.

"I have seen oxen struggling with loads they have grown too old to bear, and the calves that should have grown to replace them herded thin and pitiful into filthy, disease-ridden pens!"

The moment had passed; the crowd was off the boil. Few seemed moved by her words. Lily reached for the most startling defacement of them all.

"I have seen tracts of forest laid waste and destroyed, while the timber grown rich in our soils is shipped away, never to return. This must stop!" she cried against the outbursts of ugly shouts, before realizing she could see great piles of logs from where she stood.

This was big business in Murdock, and, from the sounds of it, people were not happy at the idea of seeing it disappear. She was losing them. She went on, hurriedly, forgetting to pace her words and sounding uncertain and nervous as a result.

"The degradation of our land in the name of efficiency and profit is not worth even the highest price we may receive for it!"

She stopped. The worst had happened. The crowd were not only turning against her; they had turned against each other. The tight packing of the fountain yard meant people couldn't necessarily get at their opponents, but people were shouting, red in the face; there was shoving and jostling everywhere, and more than one punch had already been thrown.

"Stop!" Lily called, with all the force she could project, and a slightly quieter moment followed. "I will not have war on my—"

Malin crashed into her, knocking her backwards into the icy water.

Good Men and True

"We really should have a sit-down," puffed Holly as he helped Sennet downhill through the trees. "I need one, even if you don't."

"I can walk unaided if necessary," Sennet said, taking a firm stand on his dignity, if not his feet.

"No, you can't," Holly said, propping his friend up against a tree. "Leaf and bud! Stop being so stubborn and have a rest."

"The queen may have need of us!" Sennet said, staggering from one tree to the next.

"Need or not, we're not much use like this."

Holly straightened up and winced, stretching his over-used shoulder. Nearly three days already, and they'd barely got further than half a day's walk.

"What are we going to do," he asked, "collapse on her enemies?"

"There's nowhere defensible to rest anyway," Sennet said. "So the point is immaterial."

"And what's that?" Holly said, pointing. The late afternoon sun lit up grey stone in the distance. "Looks like a cave to me."

"Unlikely."

"No harm in looking, is there?" Holly said, putting a shoulder under Sennet's and starting off again. "There! It *is* a cave."

"Possibly someone lives there," Sennet said. "We shouldn't impose…"

"If they have food," Holly said firmly, "I am jolly well going to impose till I'm blue in the face. And so are you. You can't expect to get over being dead on an empty stomach."

He hastened his pace, until Sennet was forced to plead for a mitigation of speed. The sun's rays illuminated the interior of the cave as they approached. Holly looked, and stopped dead.

"Lady Hortensia!" Sennet cried, and then clapped a hand over his mouth. "I shouldn't wake her. Dear me. I was carried away…"

"The Lady Hortensia," said Holly speculatively, propping Sennet against the wall, "is not, as a rule, a heavy sleeper." As he had discovered to his cost, in his rather pranksome youth. "And I've never known her asleep at tea time before."

"It's tea time?" Sennet asked. "How do you know?"

"Cook's internal clock. Never out." He tiptoed closer.

"Holly, I'm not sure you should—" Sennet began, and then jumped as Holly gave a single loud clap, only inches from the lady's ear. "Holly! Lady Hortensia, I do apol—"

He broke off. She had not moved.

"Oh, no," he said. "No!" And to Holly's intense distress, he dropped to his knees at her feet and wept.

"Um. Perhaps I…"

Holly looked around for something to do. He scurried outside for a moment and returned with a small bunch of scented flowers.

"Vervain," he said, for something to say, and tucked the posy into Lady Hortensia's hands, folding them respectfully across her chest. Then he stood back, and frowned. "Hang on." He took her hand again.

"Holly!" Sennet was making valiant attempts to regain his composure.

"She's still warm."

"What?" Hope dawned on Sennet's wet face.

Holly felt her wrist. "And she still has a pulse."

"What!" Sennet was up on his feet this time. "Breathing—is she—?"

"No," Holly said, frowning thoughtfully. "Strangest thing I've ever—no, wait, there it is. Breathing. Just."

Sennet was scrutinizing every detail of Lady Hortensia's appearance. "Lily's cloak! So they were together…"

"Not recently," Holly said, looking about the dusty cave for signs of life. "No signs of a struggle outside, though. Just heaps of vervain."

"*Vervain*," Sennet said, one long finger held up for emphasis.

"Enchantment?" Holly said doubtfully. "I mean, I know there are stories, but…"

"Holly," Sennet said, quivering gently with excitement, "have you any more of that, er, cinnamon mixture about you?"

"No," Holly said, full of regret. "I could probably find most of the ingredients out here though, given enough time."

"Cinnamon? In these woods?" Sennet sank back onto the ground, looking weaker than ever.

"Well, the cinnamon's not what you might call an active ingredient," Holly said. "It's more for disguising the flavour than anything."

"In which task," Sennet said, fixing Holly with a stern eye, "it failed completely."

"Sorry," Holly said. "I'll just go and—have a look round, shall I?"

"Please. I shall stay and guard the Lady Hortensia."

Holly nodded and made for the mouth of the cave.

"Oh—Holly!"

"Yes?"

"Is there anything I can do to help?" Sennet asked humbly.

Holly thought for a moment. "We'll need a good fire. And land's sake, get some rest!"

⚜   ⚜   ⚜

Lily pulled herself upright, away from the shock of the cold water, and stared dizzily at the long arrow that had landed on top of her, its stone tip splintered. She picked it up.

The next moment, Malin was up on his feet and dragging her towards the other side of the basin, putting the fountain's bulk between her and whoever had fired that arrow. Lily staggered to her feet, skirts swirling through the water. Others sprang into the basin, and, in moments, the water around her was frothing with struggling, fighting people.

A yell from Malin cut into her confusion. He was struggling with a knife-wielding man, and blood flowed freely from a long gash in his arm. Everything faded to iron-grey tones, but for the red of the blood dyeing Malin's shirt red and pinking the frothing water of the bowl.

Lily leapt forward, arrow in hand. It was a long arrow, and very springy. She delivered a stinging welt to the face of Malin's opponent, who howled and dropped his knife to clutch at his face.

"This way!" Malin shouted.

Side by side, they surged towards the far edge of the basin, Malin whirling his hatchet in an arc no one wished to intersect, and Lily's arrow delivering a stinging rebuke to anyone who tried to hold her back. They were nearly there when an ominous creak sounded, in time with a quiver beneath her feet. A violent crack, and the lower basin collapsed.

It was not far off the ground—at the very centre, it rested on the ground—and the sudden drop of a foot or two (or even three) was nothing compared to the chaos of large quantities of rapidly moving water filled with large numbers of fighting people.

Lily fought her way back onto her feet, and the water shoved her into a stone block. She fell again, and the water swept her away, depositing her on the cobbles. She sloshed back up, looking for Malin. He was gone.

Panic rising, she caught sight of a familiar arm flailing out from under the water beneath a man with a face like a long-dead weasel. Lily ran forward, half falling as her wet skirts clung to each other and to her. Weasel-face saw her coming, and swung at her with a knife, but her arrow outreached him. She noted with satisfaction the red mark spring up on his face as he fell backwards. She reached down, grabbed Malin's jerkin and pulled. He rose, sputtering.

Lily shook him. "Don't you ever do that to me again!"

"What?"

They glared at each other.

"There she is!" a voice trumpeted.

Their heads snapped around in the direction of this cry.

It was Jasper, with a little clump of fellow antique dealers. "Over here! This way!"

Malin rolled his eyes, but they darted through the wreckage towards the little group.

"Mind not drawing attention to her like that?" Malin asked as the antique band closed around them. They were armed with an assortment of elderly sticks, swords and daggers.

"Terribly sorry," Jasper said. "Didn't think. Anyway, we thought you might like to, er, retire from the scene. This way!"

Even once they'd barged and battled their way out of the fountain yard, the avenues and alleys were full of angry, armed people looking for a fight. The entire marketplace, it appeared, was in chaos. Stalls were knocked over or otherwise damaged, goods were scattered all over, and a significant number of people were taking the general disorder as an invitation to loot.

Lily tried to stop when she saw this, but the antiques men hurried her on.

"This is happening because of me," she said. "I have to put it right!"

"There's more gone wrong here than you can put right," Malin said. "Riot's not your fault. Well, not all your fault."

"Really," Jasper puffed, "I don't wish to sound unwelcoming, but I do think the best thing you could do for Murdock at this stage is to, er, well, to leave."

"Best thing you can do for yourself, too," Malin said.

They zigzagged across the great market square, heading towards the harbour, but forced to go out of their way, at times, when it was blocked by downed stalls, overturned carts, or a particularly violent knot of crowd. The great triangular log stacks loomed higher and higher as they approached.

"Wharf gate—between the Stacks," Jasper panted as he ran. "With commotion—might not be guarded."

A shout went up from behind. Jasper, at Lily's side, took a quick look and went pale.

"Wolves!" he shouted, sounding more than a little panicky.

Malin looked round. "Gate's too far. Up and over, quick!" He led the way, scrambling up the log pile.

It was harder than it looked, Lily found. While it looked something like a staircase, the "steps" were round and each as high as her waist. It was a tough climb, especially fully dressed in sopping wet clothes. Every moment, she expected another arrow to fly past her head, or, worse, into her back. She climbed faster, accepting hands wherever offered and forsaking prudent footing for speed.

Twice she slipped on loose bark, and was saved from smashing her chin into the log pile only by a quick grab from a fellow climber. It was on the second of these occasions, as she swung near the top of the stack on the end of a helpful arm, that she discovered why the Wolves weren't firing arrows at her. They were climbing up after her. This was motivation enough to scramble the rest of the way in record time.

The little band gathered at the summit, closely huddled.

"Shall we pull out the pins, send a log down?" one of the younger men asked, hefting the chains that bound the great stack to the ground.

"Are you mad?" cried Malin, knocking them out of his hands. "This stack starts falling apart and you'll kill us all!"

"And goodness knows how many others," Lily added, shuddering at the thought of the swathe of destruction just one of these massive logs could cut through the crowded marketplace. As she looked, the great fountain slowly toppled over with a crash that echoed around the square.

"And I thought I'd caused chaos," Malin muttered.

"Run for it, my lady," Jasper cried, waving his old sword with a distinctly swashbuckling air. "We'll hold them off as long as we can!" There was a cheer from his colleagues, who seemed to be strangely enjoying themselves.

"Don't get hurt," Lily begged, as they took up heroic poses atop the woodpile.

"Come on!" Malin said. "Backwards, or you'll break your neck."

It was definitely faster than going up, Lily thought as her boots thumped down onto the cobbles. They looked up: Jasper and his companions appeared to be surrendering, but were somehow still managing to slow the Wolves' progress as they did so. Lily and Malin spun around; the wharf area was half deserted, and the few people present seemed intent on minding their own business, come what may.

Lily risked a second look up. The Wolves were descending with speed. Malin grabbed her hand and started to run towards the curving prows of the two ships in the nearest berth. Lily matched him stride for stride. At the last moment, she realized he was aiming not for a ship, but the water between. She tried to pull back, but he had too much momentum and too strong a grip. She had barely enough time for a gulp of air before the dark waters closed over her head.

The water was every bit as foul as it smelled, full of the dregs of Murdock and the inedible parts of fish. Lily surfaced, took a gasp of air, and was pulled under again by Malin. When she surfaced again, they were under the wharf. She clutched at a nearby post to keep herself afloat. Her hands were slimy, and a strand of what she could only *hope* was seaweed was plastered to her face. She opened her mouth to tell Malin exactly what she thought of his high-handed dealings, but booted feet sounded on the planks above them. She froze. A little of the foul water slopped into her mouth and she closed it again, trying not to spit too loudly.

«I don't see them,» she heard an Easterling say.

«I heard in the tavern a song that says she cannot swim,» another voice volunteered.

«What about the runt?»

«Maybe she pulled him down with her,» he replied, laughing.

«Or they could be under the wharf,» the first voice said, and the scrape of steel filled the air.

Malin took a deep breath, and Lily took the hint. The next moment, a blade appeared between the planks of the wharf, and she was under. This time, she was prepared for the foulness of the water, and determined not to open her mouth the tiniest bit.

Time wore on, and they were still under the water, and her lungs began to burn. She would not notice—she would not! Little red stars appeared and began to dance before her eyes, and finally, finally, they surfaced. Lily drew in a deep breath of what passed for fresh air in Murdock harbour, and was unceremoniously pulled under again.

This time, they were moving, Malin towing her along. Twice more they rose briefly, and then sank. The third time, she knew what to expect and drew in the largest breath she had ever taken in her life. Which was as well, because this time they went deeper and stayed under longer than ever before, and she was once more seeing stars by the time they broke the surface.

She filled her drained lungs, but Malin did not pull her under again. Once she had collected a few more breaths, Lily could see why. They were squeezed up against the stern of a ship, the one place they could not be seen from the wharf. And given the shape of the ship, they couldn't be seen from its deck, either. So long as they were not spotted from the neighbouring vessel, they were safe. For now.

Footsteps rang on the deck above, and Lily drew a deep breath, ready to be pulled under again. The owner of the footsteps began to whistle. Lily caught Malin's eye. It was that catchy little tune which was rapidly becoming so familiar: the song of the long-dead queen and the twice-dead hero.

Malin looked dubious, but Lily was too certain to hesitate. Lifting a hand from the water, she knocked twice on the wood of the hull. The whistler didn't miss a beat, but, a moment later, the end of a knotted rope hit the water beside her.

Malin put a restraining hand on her arm, his face clouded with suspicion.

"We don't have a choice," she said, and seized the rope.

She was clear of the water in moments, and being helped over the taffrail by a strong arm. She sat in a wet wobbly heap on the deck.

"Thank you," she said, and, the next moment, Malin hopped over the rail to stand beside her.

"I think it would be wise if you were to lower your profile, dwarf," their rescuer said, his voice low and unhurried. He was not as tall as she had first taken him for, but very lean, and very well dressed for a sailor.

"I like to know where I stand," Malin said, and the man smiled.

"You stand on the deck of the ship *Scintilla*," he said. "I myself am the captain of this vessel, Mezerion by name. My crew you see there dicing in the bow."

There were two of them, one an Easterling and one more

foreign yet, and both big enough to dwarf the prow of the ship.

"And, now, perhaps you would care to go below?" He opened the hatch invitingly, and Lily stepped forward.

"I'll go first," Malin said, and did so, looking carefully about before he went down the ladder. Lily blushed at his rudeness.

"All safe," he reported a moment later, and Lily followed, glad of the privacy afforded by her split skirt. She found herself standing in a tiny wood-panelled corridor.

"You will find a washstand and an embroidered robe in the cabin behind the ladder," Mezerion said, "should you wish to change out of your wet things, my lady. I regret, dwarf, that I have nothing in your size."

"I'm fine," Malin growled.

Lily was already in the little jewel-box of a cabin, door closed, and stripping off her wet things. The robe was indeed fit for a queen. She carried the sad soggy heap of clothing out at arm's length. The hatch had been propped open, but Mezerion was gone. She heard him calling resonantly overhead.

"Did you catch that?" Malin asked in an undertone.

"Not a language I know, I'm afraid," Lily whispered. Running feet sounded on the deck above them. "Which is probably a good thing."

"How is ignorance a good thing?"

There was a thump of rope at each end of the vessel.

"If he were speaking to the Wolves, he'd use Arcelian or Easterling. That wasn't either, so he was probably speaking to his crew."

A sound of scrubbing came from overhead.

"Right. Explains the running," Malin said. And then, "*You* speak Easterling?"

"I would have thought *you* would—wouldn't it be useful?"

"I only know the rude bits," Malin said.

"Really!" Lily said, scandalized.

"They're the only bits I get to hear."

"I don't know as much as I thought," Lily admitted, "and definitely not the rude bits. Aunt Hortensia taught me—in case I had to marry an Easterling prince."

"Had to—" Malin began, then froze.

There were voices above.

"Where are you going?" That heavy Eastern accent had to be a Wolf.

Lily pressed herself against the wall.

"I told you this was a bad idea," Malin breathed beside her. "Trusting our lives to a stranger, in a dead-end trap!"

Lily did not answer. She was listening.

"...so, having completed my business," Mezerion was saying overhead, "I depart."

"What do you have on board?" the Wolf demanded. "We must search."

Lily stiffened. Malin drew a hissing breath.

"I carry the richest of luxury items," Mezerion was saying. "Delicate goods, easily damaged. Expensive."

"Pull back in and my men will come aboard," the Wolf said.

Lily quivered.

"And have their dirty paws rifling through my fine goods?" Mezerion demanded. "I think not."

Malin put a hand on Lily's shoulder, and she seized it, the tension wringing at her vitals.

"I have my orders," the Wolf said harshly.

"And I mine," Mezerion returned smoothly. "Orders from the rich and powerful of many lands, for the very best merchandise the world's markets have to offer. Do you expect me to present them with soiled goods? To lose their custom and bankrupt myself for the satisfaction of your men? Of course," he added slyly, "if you were to guarantee payment for any and all merchandise soiled or damaged by the search...but no," he continued, "we both know the Magister is not the one to pay for luxuries, damaged or not. Certainly, your men could not afford to recompense me out of what they are paid—or not paid," he hinted delicately.

Silence from the Wolf on the wharf. Mezerion pressed on.

"Really, it is insupportable! Not only do I pay the outrageous taxes demanded on my goods, and the ever-increasing charges for docking and wharfage, but, now, mark you, I am practically accused of being a smuggler!"

"It's not a smuggling matter, captain," the Wolf said quickly. "We are searching for a dwarf and a girl, calls herself princess."

"Dwarves I have heard of," Mezerion said, "but now someone is selling princesses? If I had known, I would have stopped by their stall." He laughed.

"Fugitives from justice," the Wolf went on, not laughing. "Last seen jumping into the harbour near here."

"Jumping into the harbour?" Mezerion asked incredulously. "Strange behaviour for a princess, wouldn't you say? But, really, do you think I would permit one who is covered in the slime and stink of these waters to enter my craft? Think of the water stains on my silks! The damp in my spices!"

The Wolf sighed so heavily Lily could hear it, pressed against the boards below.

"I even have my crew remove the dust of the stevedores' feet before we sail," Mezerion went on in full dramatic mode. And then, aside, in Easterling, «Karyu, you have missed a spot. Do it again and buff dry. And then the oilseed polish once we are under way.» His voice resounded as he returned to his declamatory style. "And yet, you believe I would haul two lumps of harbour muck into my jewel box of a vessel and— what? Dry them with my silks and scent them with my spices and perfumes? I—"

"All right!" the Wolf said. "You finished loading before they came this way?"

"And when was that?" Mezerion parried.

"Just now—with all the shouting."

"There has been so much shouting today. Which shouting?"

"Just now!"

"But of course we had finished loading, that is why we were preparing to sail. Until you demanded we stop…"

"Then get going!"

"One moment." He switched back into Easterling. «Karyu, you have finished cleaning the dust? Very well. All is prepared. Let us make sail.»

Lily could hear the Wolf stamping away on the wharf, shouting orders in Easterling to his men, followed by one very distinct phrase that made Malin snort.

"What did he say?" she asked. "Not the orders about the search—after that."

"Um…hard to translate. Not a compliment to the captain's manliness, put it that way."

There came the sound of water bubbling against the hull. They were moving.

"He's a very good actor," Lily said, a touch defensively.

"I don't like the way he looks at you," Malin growled. "Eyeing you up like that."

"The merchant's eye for a prospective customer, that's all," Lily returned.

"You'd buy his…frou-frou?" Malin asked with clear disdain.

"For goodness' sake, keep your voice down! You know how thin these planks are."

"Wolves won't hear."

"*He* will. Anyway, just because something's luxurious doesn't mean it has no use. I think my mother bought her wedding silks from him," she added dreamily.

"Your *mother*? You sure it's the same man?"

"Oh, yes."

"He doesn't look that old to me," Malin said suspiciously.

"He dyes his hair and moustache, didn't you notice?"

Malin snorted again. "Do I look like a hairdresser?"

The mental image gave Lily a fit of the giggles.

Once she had subsided, Malin returned to the fray. "Old enough to be your father or not, I don't like him. Or trust him."

"He hasn't failed us yet," Lily pointed out.

"Yet," Malin echoed ominously. "I know loyalty when I see it and I don't see it."

"He's a foreigner; why would he be loyal to me?" Lily asked. "He's a merchant, motivated by profit—call it self-interest, if you like—and he has the sense to know it's in his interest to help me."

"Or sail right up Parsifal and sell you to Phelan."

"I'm sure he wouldn't!" Lily said. But the seed of doubt remained, and in the silence, grew.

⚜   ⚜   ⚜

It could not have been as long a wait as it seemed, down under the deck of the *Scintilla*. When Mezerion appeared at the hatch, he was a dark silhouette against the early evening sky.

"It should now be possible for you to come on deck, providing you keep a low profile," he said courteously.

"A low profile?" Lily questioned.

"Don't stand up and wave," Malin said.

He went briskly up the ladder, and Lily slowly clambered after him. It was a beautiful evening, with the low sun sparkling on the gentle waves. The crew were continuing their game in the prow, fortified by something in a bottle.

"Please, have a seat," Mezerion said, gesturing to two large coils of rope amidships. "More comfortable than it appears, I assure you."

Lily tested this statement and found it correct. Malin flopped down next to her, and she uttered a cry of dismay.

"Malin! Your arm!"

Malin gave it a half-hearted look. "Eh—it'll be all right."

"After being washed in Murdock harbour? I doubt it."

Malin sagged further into his coil of rope, closing his eyes, and Lily realized he was even more tired than she. Had he stayed awake, keeping watch last night?

As the arm in question was lying on the top of the rope coil abutting hers, Lily took the liberty of gingerly parting the slashed edges of the shirt and peering at the wound beneath. She gasped.

"That bad?" Malin asked, eyes opening.

"Malin, this needs stitches."

"Don't worry; I've got a spare shirt."

"Not the shirt, your arm!"

Malin looked at it. "Bother."

"Might I have some hot water and a cloth?" Lily asked the captain.

He snapped his fingers at the crew, and a steaming bowl duly appeared, along with a clean, if well-worn, rag. Lily washed her hands, then soaked the cloth in the hot water, and paused.

"Malin, I think you need to, er…"

"Remove your shirt," Mezerion said, to her relief.

"What? No!"

"I don't want to accidentally sew your shirt into it," she explained.

"Wait—*you're* going to sew it up?"

"Is there anyone else on this vessel with fifteen years of daily needlework behind them?"

Mezerion and the crew shook their heads, solemn faces belying laughing eyes.

"Fifteen years? You're having me on."

"Not at all," Lily said crisply. "Aunt Hortensia believes in starting young ladies on needlework as soon as they're old enough not to try swallowing the thimble."

"Magnificent," Mezerion said, looking admiringly at Lily. "I have seen some of the work that royal ladies produce. Exqui-site! I tell you, my friend, you are in the hands of an expert."

Malin sighed. "Fine," he said, with undisguised resigna-tion. "Just don't get all worked up."

As though *she* would get worked up about... She blushed.

Malin loosened the shirt, hunched forward, grabbed the shirt at the scruff of his neck, and pulled. Mezerion closed his eyes with a pained look, from which Lily gathered that she was not the only one who found this an unorthodox method of removing a shirt.

"You should nev—" Mezerion began, and was interrupted by Lily's gasp of shock.

Malin's back was a mass of scar tissue, lines overlying lines, criss-crossing and disappearing into each other.

"Malin!" Lily cried in horror.

"I *knew* you would get—"

"What—when?" Lily stammered, aware she was both inter-rupting and staring, but not able to help herself.

"Stop fussing, will you?" Malin said defensively. "When the Wolves caught me the second time, they were still a bit hacked off about me getting away the first time. So..." He waved a hand in the general direction of his back.

"I never knew..." Lily said, eyes starting to well.

"Why would you?" Malin said uncomfortably. "I don't run around half naked, and, anyway, it healed before—before I met you."

"One would not think such a thing, to see you move," Me-zerion offered politely.

"Glad to hear it," Malin said, "seeing how much stretching I had to do to stop it healing stiff."

Mezerion's face showed the first genuine surprise Lily had seen on it.

"You mean to say you *exercised* your open wounds?" he asked incredulously. "It must have taken months to heal!"

"Not really," Malin said. "I heal quickly, and I wasn't doing much else with my time." He grinned.

Mezerion was shaking his head slowly from side to side. "Unbelievable. Not to say," he hastened to add, as Malin's expression changed, "that I do not believe you. The evidence speaks for itself. But such a feat! Such determination! I wonder the song does not speak of it."

Malin flushed. "I don't take off my shirt every time I meet someone new."

"Perhaps you should," Mezerion hinted with a wicked grin.

Malin flushed deeper red. "Arm," he said, waving it. "Remember?"

"Well, hold still, then!" Lily said, and set to work with the water and cloth, glad to have the subject changed. Malin's back looked bad enough healed; what it had looked like fresh, she—no, she didn't want to think about it.

"The pain," Mezerion said thoughtfully, "must have been considerable. And ongoing."

"Not as bad as the ongoing pain of being half-crippled," Malin said, in that end-of-discussion voice.

Lily rinsed the cloth in the bowl, and Malin examined his wound.

"Oo, is that a tendon?"

Lily turned back to see him wiggling the fingers of one hand to make the presumed tendon move, while poking at it with the other hand.

"Malin! Get your fingers out of there!" She slapped away his hand. "And stop wriggling. It's bound to get infected if you keep poking at it."

"When else am I going to get a chance to see under my skin?" he protested.

"Hopefully, never," Lily snapped. "Hold still."

She cleaned the wound again and frowned at it. Malin lay back with a put-upon sigh and closed his eyes.

"Truly remarkable, this one," Mezerion said lightly. "Imprisoned, wounded, and condemned to die, he nonetheless goes to considerable *pains* to ensure his movements are not hampered in the life he is condemned to lose."

"Paid off, though," Malin said without opening his eyes.

"Just as I always said," Lily said smugly. "He's an optimist."

"I am not!"

"Your actions say otherwise," Lily said, and fished in her hussif for a needle and thread. "Captain, might I borrow a flame for a moment?"

"A flame? Ah yes, of course. Do excuse me for some moments."

He went below. Lily returned her attention to the wound.

"I'm still worried it won't be clean enough," she said.

"It'll be fine," Malin said, in the dragging voice of one half asleep.

Lily thought a moment, then rose and went forward to where the crew diced. She smiled her most winning smile and marshalled her Easterling, since that appeared to be the common language of the vessel.

«Might I possibly have a little—?»

She got no further, for they very nearly knocked over the bottle and each other in their haste to find her a clean cup. One beaming crewman filled the tiny porcelain cup, then the other presented it to her as though his great flat hand were a silver tray.

She took it with a smile, and tested it with a tiny sip. Half the droplet turned into fumes in her mouth, thoroughly fumigating every crevice in her head, and the other half, she was sure, left scorch marks all down her throat. A tear came to her eyes and she blinked it away.

«Excellent,» she croaked politely. «Thank you, it's just what I wanted.»

Holding the little cup at a safe distance, she walked back

across the deck to Malin, who was now deeply asleep. Bemused, the two crewmen followed.

Lily carefully stooped down at Malin's side, then poured the contents straight onto his wound. Malin leapt up with a roar, the crewmen gurgled appreciatively, and Mezerion came out of the hatch like he'd been catapulted, dagger drawn.

"What the jumping rabbit was that?" Malin demanded, settling his hatchet back in its holster.

One of the crewmen rumbled a word Lily didn't quite catch, and Mezerion relaxed and returned below.

"Some of that," Lily explained, and the crewman with the bottle waved it by way of illustration.

"Why? Why would you do that?"

"To clean the wound, of course. Come, now, you can't tell me you've never felt worse than that."

"Not," said Malin pointedly, "in my sleep."

"I am sorry about that," Lily said, "but if I'd told you what I planned, you wouldn't have let me."

"You're right I wouldn't."

"So it's all for the best," Lily said, and smiled at him.

The crewman with the bottle laughed and said something which sounded suspiciously like «Women!»

Malin sank back down into his rope coil. "Well, don't do it again," he muttered.

"Of course not."

Mezerion emerged from the hatch, carrying a lamp, and some more of the clean worn linen. He lit the lamp from the mast light and carefully carried it across the deck to Lily.

"A flame, princess, and fresh linen for bandages. Also some silvered silk, as I fear your own threads may be damaged."

"Oh, thank you," said Lily. "How kind."

"We must keep you in good condition," he said with a glint of a smile.

She sterilized her scissors and a fine, sharp needle in the

little lamp flame, then threaded the needle with a single pass. Taking a deep breath, she turned to Malin, who appeared to be asleep again.

"Malin? I'm going to start stitching now."

"Thanks for the warning," he said, sitting upright in a single bolt.

Lily considered the wound. "I think I'm going to need someone to hold the edges together while I stitch. Perhaps—?"

She looked at Mezerion, who spread his hands gracefully.

"Alas, I must confess I have not the stomach for such work," he said. "But I am sure Tomaz—" He looked to the bigger crewman, who rose.

"I can do it!" Malin said. "I've got a spare hand. Just keep that bottle away from me."

Tomaz roared with laughter as he sat down again. The crew understood Arcelian, then, even if they didn't speak it.

Once Malin's hand was sufficiently clean, Lily showed him what she wanted done, and Mezerion decided to take a walk to the stern for a little fresh air.

"Now, just relax your arm," Lily said, needle poised over it.

"Easy for you to say," Malin grumbled. "How relaxed would you be if I was about to start stitching you up?"

"Not very," Lily admitted, "but, then, I've seen your stitching." This got a guffaw from the prow.

"What's wrong with my stitching?" Malin demanded hotly.

"Nothing," Lily replied, "really, it's just...more utilitarian than delicate, that's all. Now relax!" The arm obediently went limp.

"Delicacy, the woman's touch!" Mezerion rhapsodized from the stern of the vessel.

Malin opened his mouth to reply, but shut it again when the woman's touch stabbed into his arm. He made no sound as Lily's needle darted in and out, but he never took his eyes off it, moving his hand in perfect concert with hers as she worked her way down the arm.

Tomaz and his mate came to observe, Tomaz carefully holding the bottle behind his back in case Malin should spot it—but he never looked up.

«There is no knot,» Tomaz said, pointing to the top end of the work. «It will come undone.»

«No, it won't,» said Lily, and had to turn back to Arcelian. "Anyway, knots rub and work loose."

"You will never see a knot on a lady's embroidery," Mezerion agreed. "Unless it is a decorative knot. But, otherwise, never. Not even on the back."

Lily reached the end of the gash and wove the thread between the stitches and the skin. A quick snip and the needle rethreaded, and the tail at the top was likewise tucked neatly under the criss-cross of stitches. The crew aahed appreciatively.

"Finished?" Mezerion asked, and strolled back.

Malin performed a series of checks on the range of movement in the arm.

Mezerion bent over for a closer look. "Herringbone? An excellent choice, if I may say so, my lady. Both practical and appealing to the eye." He winked at Malin. "You look very dashing, my friend. You should wear stitches always."

"Not bad," Malin said, admiring the effect. "Thanks."

"You're welcome. I should put a bandage on it," Lily said.

"And we should dine," Mezerion added. "It grows late."

The crew evidently interpreted this as an order, for they left off admiring Malin's arm (and back) and went off about their duties. Mezerion remained to watch Lily expertly wrapping a neat tight bandage around Malin's arm.

"You're good at this," Malin said, apparently unable to keep the surprise out of his voice.

"Aunt Hortensia says every lady should be able to tend to the basic physicking of her household," Lily said, "in times of peace—or war."

"A great lady," Mezerion murmured. "And now, perhaps—dinner?"

As the evening wore on and the darkness grew, Lily found herself greatly conflicted. On the one hand, Malin's rough manners did not show him at his best in such elegant company. All very well when crawling about in muddy ditches, but here!

On the other hand, Mezerion's manners, though as courtly as ever, made her feel more than a little uncomfortable by the time he had finished his fourth—or was it fifth?—glass of blue liqueur, and she was glad not to be alone on this ship with these strangers.

The crew had put their own bottle aside hours ago, safely tucked in a coil of rope, and they were now humming quietly to themselves in the darkness, one in the rigging and another sprawled along the rail.

A stifled yawn provided the excuse she needed to retire, the captain insisting that she should retain the use of the one cabin. It was a fine, still night; he would be perfectly comfortable on deck with his men.

She bade them all a polite good night, took the offered lantern, and went below. The cabin was fitted with a box-bed rather like the one in Woodward's cottage, only more ornate. The mattress was stuffed with down, she was sure, and she had barely time to sink into its soft embrace before she fell asleep.

But in the deep darkness of the night, she woke, heart thudding. There was someone else in the room.

High and Dry

Lily sat up, veins coursing with terror.

A harsh whisper came through the darkness. "Lily!"

"Malin? What are you doing here?" she hissed, her relief rapidly overtaken by outrage. "This is entirely inappropriate!"

There was a creak as Malin sat down on the side of the bed. "I told you he couldn't be trusted. He's taking us to Denton."

"How do you know?"

"He said so."

"Don't be silly! If he were going to betray us, he wouldn't tell you, would he?"

"He's drunk," Malin said bluntly.

"It still doesn't make sense. He would've handed us over to the Wolves in Murdock, wouldn't he?"

"Not if he wanted to get the credit, he wouldn't. Motivated by self-interest, you said, remember?"

Lily was silent. She wanted it not to be true, but there was nothing to stand against it.

"What do we do?" she whispered at last. "Do you think you can get away? You're a strong swimmer."

"Without you? What's the point? No one's going to take *me* for a long-dead queen who has every right to boot out the Magister."

Lily felt that confusing muddle of emotions again: pleased not to be discarded as a burden, but disappointed in herself

for being, once more, the reason for someone else being im-
perilled. If only she had learned to swim, they wouldn't have
been in such danger fleeing the Ox and Trumpet. One could
not depend on convenient boats forever.

"We're too far out, anyway," Malin added.

"We'll have to get closer to shore if he's planning to sail up
Parsifal," Lily said. "We'll just wait until there's enough of a
wind to sail the ship further in, and…"

"He'll have us in chains by then," Malin said. "He's no fool.
We'll have to risk it first chance we get—say, tomorrow night."

"But what will we do till then?"

"Pretend we don't suspect," Malin said. "And you'll learn
to swim."

Lily started to protest, and then gave up. He was right.
There was no way around it.

"All we need now," Malin muttered, "is some excuse for getting in the water…"

"It *is* Launderday tomorrow," Lily said.

"You make your usual fuss about that, then," said Malin,
and slipped away.

⚜   ⚜   ⚜

Mezerion was a little red around the eyes the next morning—
Lily could sympathize, as she had not slept at all well after the
interruption—and made no objection to the laundering plan.
He even suggested that—while they were becalmed—she
might try learning to swim, for her own safety while at sea.

This almost disarmed her suspicions, until she saw the subtle gesture with which he bid his crew follow them. So they
were under guard, and Mezerion did not fear her learning to
swim. Hardly cheering.

The water wasn't too bad, all things considered. It wasn't
night, the sea was neither rank nor freezing, and she was looking forward to being properly clean for the first time in a week.
It was just that there was so much of it; water in all directions

with nothing solid within reach but Malin. Every time she started to go under, there was Malin's hand lifting her chin out of the water.

"Look," he said for the nineteenth time, only slightly less patiently than the first, "you're more likely to drown in your bath than you are out here. I'm right here, the lads are just over there—" they gave a wave before attempting to wrestle each other under, "—and even Mezerion might risk getting wet if you were in danger."

Lily took a deep quivering breath and looked at him woefully.

"If you can float, you can swim," Malin said. "You just need to move while you float."

«Bunny paddle!» Tomaz cried enthusiastically, promptly disappearing beneath the waves as Karyu leapfrogged over him. He bobbed to the surface and set off in hot pursuit.

"My face keeps going in the water," Lily said crossly. "I can't concentrate on paddling if I can't breathe!"

It seemed like it should be so simple—everyone else did it with the greatest of ease. But, somehow, it didn't work out that way, not when *she* tried, and the knowledge that it should have been easy made her that much more cross that it wasn't.

"Look, I'll *hold* your head up," Malin said. "Then you can just paddle."

This seemed to work. Malin wasn't quite towing her, but she had to paddle to stay with him.

"My lady, you advance!" came a lazy call from above. «Tomaz, you frisk like a mermaid!»

«Ugliest mermaid I've ever s—» Karyu shouted before being interrupted by a faceful of seawater splashed up by Tomaz's unmaidenly fist.

Lily smiled wanly, and realized that Malin was no longer holding up her chin.

"Hey!" She stopped and floated.

"Why'd you stop?" Malin asked.

"Why did you?"

"Because you didn't need me any more. You just thought you did."

"You could have warned me!"

"Then you wouldn't have let me."

"You're quite right I wouldn't have!" Lily snapped, aware this exchange had something familiar about it, but unable to stop herself.

"There you are, then. All for the best." He grinned at her.

"Why, you treacherous, two-faced tergiversator!" Lily fumed, trying not to smile, without success. "That's it! I'm getting out."

She swam to the rope ladder hanging from the stern and had barely set foot on its rungs when she heard a whoop behind her. She turned just in time to see Malin execute a nose-diving roll before popping to the surface again.

"You did it!" he crowed. "Without thinking! Oh, you should always do things when you're angry; you're so much better at them then."

"Hmpf!"

He swam after her, and she moved as fast as she could up the ladder, accepting Mezerion's assistance to climb over the rail at the top.

"To be fair," Mezerion said, handing her a towel for her hair, "it was less painful than the trick you played him."

Malin, still with that irritating grin, hauled himself over the rail and dropped into a wet heap on the deck.

Lily's lips twitched. "I suppose so. Truce, Malin?"

Malin propped himself up on his elbows. "Truce?"

"A cessation of fighting," Lily informed him.

"Were we fighting?" he asked, with a wide-eyed, innocent look she found very suspicious.

"Would you like me to check your arm?" Lily enquired

coldly. "I'd hate to think of something in the seawater dirtying it again. I'm sure Tomaz will lend me—"

"No, no!" Malin said, scrabbling into a defensive position. "Truce, definitely."

Lily smiled. "Good."

Mezerion stood looking from one to the other. "You two are very much alike, you know? Iron souls."

"Yeah," said Malin, stretched out on the deck again. "I'm hard on me and she's hard on me. That's what we have in common. That, and jail time. That's enough to put the iron in anyone's soul."

"Come now," Mezerion said softly, lounging against the rail. "If half of what I hear is true, your life was not much easier before you met her."

Malin considered this. "Being in an explosion, that's new."

"A once-in-a-lifetime experience for anyone," Mezerion agreed.

"It better be."

"But, consider, she is being hard on herself merely by trying to keep up with you. She is not accustomed to lack of sleep, to continual physical exertion, to uncertainty over when she will next eat. You come to this ordeal in strength, and she in weakness, and yet she exerts herself to keep pace with you."

By the end of this speech, Malin was sitting up staring at Lily, who was staring at her lap and making much play with the towel and her hair in an attempt to cover up her blushing face.

"Worth a thought, perhaps," said Mezerion, and strolled away to the side rail. «Enjoy your sea bathing, children!» he called to his crew. «With this breeze, we shall sail away without you.»

"You wouldn't!" Lily said, almost sure he was joking.

"They know at least two are required to sail this vessel. Two who know just what they are doing," he added.

Was it a warning?

❦   ❦   ❦

Phelan listened in silence to the Murdock runner's report.

"Disappointing," he said at last. "I had expected the people to have realized their good fortune in being quit of the monarchy. Particularly in Murdock. And as for the actions of the Murdock garrison…"

The runner trembled.

Phelan turned to Vetch. "Send an urgent runner to Murdock." The secretary's pen scuttered over the paper. "Inform the garrison commander that I will be arriving shortly." He turned back to the runner. "You are to return by the coast road. It's longer, but I want all the outposts on high alert when she comes ashore."

"You think she's at sea, sir?" the runner asked.

"Given that the last sighting of her was at a harbour full of ships, the deduction is not a complex one," Phelan said dryly. "Start as soon as you've had the specified rest period. That will be at dawn, if I am not mistaken. No doubt I will see you starting as I depart."

The runner saluted and took his leave, keeping his face carefully neutral. Having the Magister's personal eye on his timekeeping was bad enough; he didn't need his company as well. He made his way to the couriers' rest hall, promising himself that all the Magister would see of him tomorrow was his dust.

❦   ❦   ❦

The day passed in elaborate courtesies on Mezerion's part—he seemed to enjoy playing the host—careful replies from Lily, and mostly silence from Malin.

In the late afternoon, Lily played chess with the captain, and found him a skilled opponent. She forgot her usual scruples, fought back with everything she had, and defeated him.

By dinnertime, she was becoming impatient, but she forced herself to continue being charming. Never had she been more glad of Aunt Hortensia's endless training in Elegant Conversation. Mezerion evidently did not suspect, for he helped himself liberally to his blue liqueur, and actually fell asleep while Lily was still on deck.

She went to the far rail and stood gazing out into the darkness towards where her land must lie.

"On good Arcelian land," she said softly, "there must be good Arcelian hearts, loyal and brave. If only we could reach them!" Every fibre of her being strained towards the invisible shore. "If only we could get closer…"

She tailed off, and turned, casting a quick glance at Mezerion in the dim light of the mast lantern. She whisked across the deck to where Malin stood brooding.

"It's a clear night," she said. "The Rabbit is clearly visible over the Leaf and Bud. And there's the Ox in the south."

"A nice night for star-gazing, then," Malin said sourly.

"A nice night for navigating by the stars," she corrected him. She turned to Karyu, who was reclining on the rail, and before Malin could stop her, she asked, «Will you help us sail closer to shore?»

Karyu shook his head vigorously and rattled off a string of Easterling in an undertone that she could not catch. Lily let her puzzlement show, and he sighed deeply.

"Captain," he said in an undertone. "Very angry."

He proceeded to demonstrate by means of miming just what form this anger would take—including, if he were to be believed, keel-hauling, sharks, and what might have been his liver, depending on how accurate his knowledge of anatomy was. Tomaz, lying on the boom of the furled sail, propped himself up on one elbow and listened. Karyu rounded his speech off with a comical sad face.

Lily took his hand, and allowed a tear or two to fall. «Karyu, he is going to sell me to my uncle, who killed my father and my mother and will kill me too!»

Now Karyu shed a tear or two, but, again, he prodded his liver and cast a meaningful glance in the direction of the snoring captain.

"He's drunk," Malin said. "He'll never know."

«He will know we helped, for we are awake,» Karyu said, looking at Tomaz, who was letting himself down and drawing closer.

"I could hit you both round the head with the back of my hatchet, if you like," Malin offered.

To Lily's horror, the crewmen seemed to be giving this proposal their serious consideration.

«Why not pretend to be…» She didn't know the word. «Like the captain. Wear some like perfume and pour the rest of the bottle over the side.»

The crewmen beamed and nodded vigorously.

«Very good idea,» Tomaz said. «Much better than hatchet.»

«A pity to pour it over the side,» Karyu sighed, and caught Tomaz's eye with a wink.

«Do not worry,» Tomaz said, patting Lily's hand comfortingly. «We will make it very convincing.»

"You still have to swim," Malin reminded her. "They won't run the ship aground just so you can hop off."

"Aren't there any wharves?"

"Any wharf big enough for a ship like this is going to be guarded by Wolves," Malin said. "Get ready to swim."

The crew soon had the *Scintilla* wafting gently across the waves in near-complete silence, only the creaking of the rigging and the breaking of waves on the hull disturbing the peace of the night. The gentle breeze, it appeared, was in their favour.

Lily stood at the rail, gripping it hard with both hands and trying not to think about drowning.

There was a brief muttered debate between the crew, and the sails were hauled in. The *Scintilla* slowed, until the only movement was the slow rocking of the waves. Lily tried to steel herself. Malin let himself over the side on the knotted rope that had fished them out of Murdock harbour, and, moments later, a tug on the rope announced that it was her turn.

"Head up and breathings full," Karyu advised her, helping her over the rail.

"Big breathings," Tomaz agreed, lending her a hand until he was bent double over the rail.

Lily could not repress the gasp that sprang to her lips as she sank into the water. Malin's arm was there to support her before she sank under it, mercifully, and she tried not to panic.

"Big breathings," came a whisper from the deck.

Lily struggled to obey, but managed to take in enough air to whisper back her thanks. Neck stiff, arms rigid, but still somehow floating, she kicked her legs feebly and was surprised to find she moved.

Slowly, they moved away from the *Scintilla*'s side. The long journey back to her land had begun.

⚜   ⚜   ⚜

"Not sure this'll work," Holly said, gazing doubtfully into the murky depths of the little glass bottle.

Sennet sighed and rubbed his temples. "I'm not sure we have any alternatives, my dear fellow. She must have been here since the day she left Candra, so, clearly, time alone will not resolve the issue. We cannot leave her here unprotected; nor can we long delay our journey to aid the queen. We must do *something*."

"I just don't want to get your hopes up," Holly said. "Cinnamon isn't the only thing I've had to leave out, and the whole process has been a bit, um, improvised."

"I understand," Sennet said. "Whatever happens, I know you have done your best."

"Right. Well." Holly considered the unmoving form. "Can you, er, open her mouth a bit?"

Sennet cautiously touched Lady Hortensia's face and eased her jaw down. Holly trickled a little of the liquid into the corner of her mouth, and, then, after a moment's thought, poured in the rest. Sennet carefully eased her jaw back into place.

They waited in hushed anticipation, barely breathing themselves. Finally, Holly broke the silence with a windy groan.

"No good. I told you so!" He threw himself down against the wall and scowled at the floor.

Sennet sagged.

They sat in silence while a beam of sunlight inched across the floor. Then Sennet sighed, raised himself stiffly to his feet, and dusted himself down.

"I'm afraid," he began, and stopped to clear his throat. "I'm afraid that we must leave her. No matter our, er, personal feelings, the queen must and shall have our aid. No matter the cost."

Holly lumbered to his feet and clapped a hand on Sennet's shoulder. "I'm sorry. I know you…" He tailed off. He couldn't quite put it into words, and anyway, Sennet knew what it was he knew.

"Thank you." Sennet heaved a sigh. "If I might have a moment to, ah, say my farewells?"

"Of course," Holly said hastily. He definitely didn't want to be witness to anyone's heart-wringing moments. "I'll be—outside. Obviously."

He made his escape. Out in the sunshine, he stood among the vervain and shed a sentimental tear. While he had no memory of his life before Candra, he was certain there must have been a young woman in it. A heart as big and squashy as his couldn't stay in a bachelor's ribcage forever. A distant murmur made him realize he was still in earshot, and he slid further into the shade of the trees.

It occurred to him, as he leaned against an obliging tree, that he was now Outside the Hedge, in a world which also contained women. Women his own age, women with laughing eyes, women who were, in point of fact, not all Lady Hortensia. Not that he had anything against Lady Hortensia, fine figure of a woman et cetera, but he wouldn't—his mind shrank back from the mere thought—he wouldn't like to swap places with Sennet, and that was a fact. A formidable woman, he reflected. And that voice!

The next moment, he leapt away from the obliging tree, rigid in every limb, as though a bolt of lightning had gone through him. Imaginative he might be, but no one could have imagined that voice so clearly, so resonantly, so…loudly. Almost against his will, his eyes dragged his body round to face the mouth of the cave. His feet were rooted to the spot, his throat so dry all he could manage was a papery croak. His eyes bulged.

There in the mouth of the cave stood Sennet, his weakness forgotten as he helped the Lady Hortensia step out into the sunlight.

"I have," she was saying, "the most dreadful taste in my mouth. Holly! Be so good as to fetch some mint."

The command bypassed his numbed brain and moved his feet towards the sound of water. Water. Damp. Mint. As he moved, his mind began to clear. Had Sennet…? He wouldn't! But what would she…

Unbidden, his mind began to depict the scene, and he firmly erased it. If Sennet had been caught kissing the Lady Hortensia, that was entirely their business, and he was going to keep as far out of it as humanly possible. He just wouldn't like to be in Sennet's shoes, that was all.

He found the mint, nipped off the choicest leaves, and started back, a broad grin on his cheerful face.

⚜   ⚜   ⚜

Lily spat out a last mouthful of seawater and crawled further up the stony beach of the little cove, every muscle screaming its protest. Beside her, Malin hauled himself to his feet.

"Someone's coming," he said. "Get ready to run."

Lily groaned. "I couldn't run to save myself."

But she clambered to her feet, nonetheless, and tried ineffectively to shake out her sodden skirts. Everything clung to her; it was like trying to walk in a full-body bandage.

"Oh, my dear!"

Lily looked up. A tall, elegant woman stood at the top of the little cliff that backed the cove, her long white dress fluttering in the wind. The early morning sun was so bright as it reflected off her clothes, Lily almost found her hard to look at. But she was so...so *clean*, Lily realized, moving towards the woman without even thinking.

"You must come up and rest yourself at the house," the woman said.

Malin put a warning hand on Lily's arm, which she hardly noticed.

"And your friend, too, of course," the woman added. "Senvy, run along up to the house. Have my maid draw a hot bath, and see the guest quarters are prepared." The boy at her side darted away obediently.

A hot bath! Lily staggered up the steps cut into the cliff, and the woman took her arm at the top.

"Laurel, my lady, and may I assure you that I and mine are entirely at your service. Ah, here's Senvy. Take the, ah, the queen's friend to the dwarf quarters, Senvy. See he's provided for."

Laurel kept up a flow of light inconsequential chatter all the way to the large white house—mercifully not far—but Lily found it hard to focus on that or anything. She was fighting back tears; everyone was being so nice, and she was so tired...

The bath was so deep she was almost afraid of falling asleep and drowning in it, but it was hot, and scented, and soothed her aches. An elaborate linen nightgown was laid out on the end of the large soft bed. When had she last slept in a proper nightgown? The last thing she saw before her eyes closed was a maid bearing away her wet and dirty clothes.

Lily did not know how long she slept, but the first thing she saw on waking was her clothes, clean and dry and folded on a chair. She stared at them, bewildered, and then at the room around her, until memory flowed back. Mezerion...swimming... And now this! She was almost in tears at the comfort of knowing that such loyalty was still to be found.

There was a tap at the door, and Lily composed herself. "Come in."

Laurel appeared around the door. "I see you're awake at last, my lady. I hope you've had a pleasant sleep. You must be starving! Now, you're not to get up until you're absolutely ready."

She clapped her hands, and two maids appeared, one bearing a soft, fluffy bedjacket and the other an elegant breakfast tray. There was a dainty silver teapot; a delicate cup and saucer; an ingenious little toast rack; and plenty of butter and jam. Altogether, everything was just as a real lady's breakfast tray ought to be; the sort of thing Aunt Hortensia would bring up as a treat when Lily was recuperating.

The maids poured tea and departed, but Laurel stayed, moving restlessly about the room and providing more of the elegant small talk which Lily now realized she had been missing. After all, she hadn't been in the company of a lady since...well, not since the cave, now she thought about it, and as for elegant small talk, she'd heard none since she'd left Candra.

At the thought of Aunt Hortensia and her childhood home, both now lost to her, she put down her teacup and dabbed at her eyes. Laurel was immediately all attention.

"You're distressed! Here, take my handkerchief—no, I insist!—and tell me all about it."

Such a flow of womanly sympathy was just what Lily had been longing for, and she poured out the whole story: Restoration Day, the quest, Uncle Phelan, Malin, Burnaby, the slip, the river, the riot, the Horn, the—well, she didn't know what to call Mezerion, but *pirate* was the word that sprang to mind— and the enduring puzzle of the pedlar's song.

"And you actually swam ashore?" Laurel asked incredulously. "My dear! How you managed! But that's just like men—never ones to put themselves out for your convenience, but only too happy for you to go out of your way." She shook her head. "But now you're back with us, we can see about what to do."

Lily lay back on the fat down pillows with a sigh of relief. Now she looked back at it, she was rather impressed with how well she had come through everything. Now, at last, she was to have her reward for enduring so much for so long; she was to be treated like a queen, and have her burdens shared.

"I'm afraid I can't offer you a suitable change of attire," Laurel was saying. "My clothes wouldn't come close to a proper fit—" she was quite tall for an Arcelian woman, "—and, naturally, I wouldn't dream of offering you the servants' clothes! But I've had your clothes laundered, and the least little mend here and there, so I hope you won't be too offended if I can't offer you more."

"Not at all," Lily said. "You've been only too kind as it is."

"Nothing of the sort," Laurel demurred. "Now, if you'd care to dress, there's a swinging chair out on the verandah that looks out over the gardens—terribly restful, and just the thing when you need to take things gently."

"Well, I can't stay resting forever," Lily said regretfully. "Restoration Day, you know. Time is pressing."

"Now, don't you worry a bit about that. I remember only too well how often that pedlar came through this way, and I've an old friend who may very well be able to help us with that riddle of his. In strictest confidence, of course. There's no reason at all why you shouldn't rest while other heads take up the burden for a while."

This was, Lily had to admit, only too true, and, besides, it would do her good to build up her strength after all the drains on her energy there had been of late.

"I'll just leave you to dress," Laurel said, moving to the door, "and send my maid to help you with your hair in a minute. She'll show you out to the verandah while I write a little note to my friend."

Lily swung her legs over the side of the bed. "Oh! I meant to ask—how is Malin?"

Laurel laughed. "Oh, he's fine. I don't imagine we'll be seeing much of him, though. You know how it is when these dwarves meet up; they have a thousand things to talk about and forget all about the rest of us!"

⚪ ⚪ ⚪

Lily let the maid usher her out to the verandah and settle her in the big, gently swinging chair. She snuggled into the fluffiest of fine woollen shawls, and enjoyed the scent drifting off the banks of narcissi in the tastefully laid out garden.

"Psst!"

Lily slowly turned her head. Malin was looking around the corner of the house.

He beckoned vigorously. "Come on!"

"Why?"

"Why? *Why?*" Malin looked about to pop. "How about your uncle's taken over the country, Restoration Day is only days away, and we still have two parts of a pedlar's riddle to solve!"

"Laurel's taking care of that," Lily said. "She has a friend who knows about that sort of thing."

"You *told* her?"

"Why not? She's a loyal Arcelian; why should I keep secrets from her?"

Malin edged closer.

"She could be in league with the Magister for all you know."

"But then she would have taken us prisoner on sight," Lily pointed out. "And not been so nice."

"All right," Malin conceded, "so maybe she's trying to keep in good with both sides. You still shouldn't trust her."

"Why not?" Lily demanded. "I don't see why you're so against her."

"Because she has thralls, that's why," Malin snapped. "Burnabais thralls."

Lily sobered. To think that such a charming woman—! But she didn't seem to be very politically aware, however dainty her interior decor. Perhaps she didn't understand. It was all too easy for fashionable ladies to be swept along by the tide of what was socially acceptable, and not stop to think.

"I'll speak to her about it," Lily said firmly.

"*Speak* to her?"

"Yes. And that will be quite tricky enough," Lily said defensively. "I don't think you realize the delicacy of the situation. We are guests in her home; to criticize her, to point out where she may not even realize she is going wrong—it's no easy task."

"Which is why we should leave now," Malin said, planting himself in front of her.

"Leave now?" Lily repeated, startled. "But why? It's Fallowday, and, anyway, we can't go anywhere until we know where to go, and we won't know where to go until we solve the rest of the riddle song."

"So let's discuss it on the way," Malin said impatiently.

"I don't see why we can't have help from others," Lily said, setting her jaw.

Malin set his, and they stared at each other in silence for a moment.

"That's what it is!" Lily cried. "You're jealous! You don't want anyone else to get the credit for helping me—not even my own people!"

"Rubbish! You're just taken in by the way she's rolled you up in cotton wool!"

"She treats me like a queen," Lily said, leaning forward to press the point. "Which comes as a refreshing change, I might add!"

"So honesty's not good enough for you any more?" Malin said, a dangerous light in his eyes. "Fine. You stay to be babied by the nice lady and her poor slaves. I'm going."

"Going where?" Lily asked, stung.

"Going to carry on the fight you've given up," Malin growled.

"I haven't given up," Lily said. "I keep telling you! I'm just gathering my strength while others work on the problem. Some people," she added pointedly, "like to think before they act."

"If this is you thinking, I don't think much of it. She's rotten and you're a fool to trust her, Lily."

And while Lily's outrage was still struggling for words, he turned on his heel and walked away.

❧ ❧ ❧

It was a journey such as Holly hoped he would never have to make again: downhill in the rain with one recently deceased companion and one recently enchanted, and neither of them steady on their feet.

Sennet insisted on giving an arm to Lady Hortensia, but he himself needed an arm as often as not, so Holly found himself fluttering back and forth from one to the other like an over-wrought hen, covering, he thought ruefully, about twice as much ground as needed.

He insisted on stopping beside the stream for a rest at tea time, and even managed to gather a few edibles for a semblance of a meal. As he scooped up some water in curled leaves by way of liquid refreshment, he heard voices downstream. All three froze. Easterling voices. The curled leaves floated away from Holly's numb fingers.

"Go," Lady Hortensia said, in the softest voice he'd ever heard her use.

"No!" Sennet said. "I will not leave you again!"

"I cannot hope to outdistance them in this condition," Lady Hortensia said. "You must go!"

"I am not leaving you," Sennet said. "And, in any case, I'm slow myself."

Holly hovered uncertainly. Should they all stay together? Should he go, or stand and fight?

Lady Hortensia turned the full force of her gaze on him. "Go!"

He went, hurling himself away through the trees, not looking back, not even when he heard the Wolves' shouts of triumph as they spotted their weakened prey. He ran on, until he had completely lost his breath and left the sound of voices far behind.

Sennet and the Lady Hortensia were taken. There was nothing he could do for them now but hope. Hope, and carry out his mission: find Lily and give her whatever help he could.

⚜   ⚜   ⚜

Lily did her best to relax and enjoy herself for the rest of the day, but it was no good; her peace was shattered. The past held the bitterness of her argument with Malin; the future held the nerve-wracking task of talking to Laurel about the matter of thralls. After all, she had promised Malin she would bring the subject up, and no matter what unkind or hurtful things he had subsequently said or done, she had said she would do it and that was that.

Even the luxuries were losing their savour. Nothing was quite as enjoyable once you were clean, warm, and well fed (not to mention well rested) as it was when you dreamed of it, cold, wet, and hungry.

She dressed for dinner in one of Laurel's robes, taken up for the occasion by the deft-fingered maid, and went to the delightful little dining room with all the eager anticipation of one attending her own execution.

The elegance of the dinner and its accoutrements did little to dispel the dread, but her hostess was uniformly charming, and she began to have hopes of turning the conversation onto the necessary subject without injuring the graces of discourse. After all, there was no need to be direct.

"Where is your little friend?" Laurel asked. "My staff say they haven't seen him all day. I thought perhaps he had gone out to the fields with the others for the day, but it appears not. Have you seen him?"

"Yes, I—" Well, this was awkward. How to tell one's hostess that her guest had fled in the belief that she was a two-faced traitress? "I saw him this morning, and I'm afraid we...had a disagreement. I think he's left."

"Oh no," Laurel said sympathetically. "How dreadful for you—and how unkind of him to leave like that! I must send a couple of my men out to find him." She murmured to a waiting attendant, who went out. "Now, don't you worry." She flashed a warm smile across the table. "He'll come back and apologize, and everything will be just lovely again."

Lily privately felt that this delightful vision of the future did not reflect a very accurate assessment of Malin's character, but she forbore to comment. Laurel had turned the subject to shopping, and this, she realized, was her chance to say what must be said.

"Speaking of Murdock Great Market," she said, "I was fortunate enough to browse the jewellers' stalls there, and I was

more than a little surprised to find torcs among their wares.
Would you believe," she said, lifting her eyes from her plate
and hoping to find some look in Laurel's that would prove this
all wrong, "that there are those in this day and age who keep
thralls? Like collared pets. Really, it is most distasteful, and I
need hardly add that such arrangements would not be looked
upon with favour following the restoration of the monarchy.
Indeed, I feel I must make it a priority of my reign to eradicate
such iniquitous practices."

"Indeed, my lady?" Laurel said, and she turned the conversation away with practised ease.

Lily could not feel that this was an entirely satisfactory response, but at least she had kept her promise to Malin and
made her point. Over-made it, perhaps, but her feelings had
carried her away.

The dessert had just been served—a spiced fruit pudding
with plenty of cream—when one of Laurel's many staff slid
deferentially through the door and handed a note to his employer.

"Do excuse me, my lady," Laurel said. "I must just see to
this."

Lily waved her consent, and concentrated on her pudding.

"Oh! How delightful," Laurel cried, and tucked the note
firmly away in her dress. "It's a note from my friend—the one
who knows about the pedlar, you know—and what do you
think? He's gone and solved the riddle for us."

Lily put her spoon down, dessert forgotten. Solved already!

"Part of it, that is," Laurel said. "He's working on the rest,
but he didn't want to keep you in suspense a moment longer
than he needed. You were quite right about *flower* being the
significant part, you clever girl. But he says it means *flour*—as
in bread, you know—and the place to look is in an old mill not
far from here, where the pedlar sometimes camped out."

Well! That would show Malin. Except he wouldn't be there

to see it. Lily tried to brush the little pang away.

"How wonderful!" she said warmly. "Do you think we might go now—this evening?"

"Just what I was going to suggest," Laurel said. "But…"

"Of course, I'll need to change," Lily said tactfully. "My own clothes are quite suitable for an evening ramble."

To her surprise, she felt more comfortable once she was back in her old clothes, the split skirt buttoned up and the cuirass buckles fastened. It was a good thing the split skirt had an adjustable waist, she brooded, considering how much weight she'd lost running herself ragged over the last couple of weeks. Though she was likely to put it all back on if she stayed at Laurel's table much longer.

Lily realized with a shock that it was less than a week now till Restoration Day. Where had the time gone? Less than a week, and so much still to accomplish! Including, she reminded herself sternly, figuring out how she was going to foil Evil Uncle Phelan. But that could wait. With the Persimmon Key so close at hand, there was no time for distractions.

She reached for her cloak, and then paused. Should she take the Horn of Vale? There was no need for it, as such, but she didn't feel comfortable letting it out of her sight. Being parted from it once was enough. She hesitated a moment longer, and then tied the cord through one of the straps on her cuirass. The Horn hung just below her hip, where the cloak would conceal it from view. Quickly, she clasped the cloak about her throat and slipped out of the room.

Seeing Laurel and her men gathered on the verandah gave her a faint misgiving. So many men to accompany them—were they expecting danger? Perhaps she should have left the Horn…

But there was no help for it now. They descended the stairs and started on their way. Laurel seemed less inclined to talk than she had been, and the party soon fell into silence. Lily walked, and thought.

The night was dark and cloudy, the way lit only by the lanterns the men carried. They paced down the road solemnly. Like a cortege, Lily thought, and she shivered.

She wished Malin were here to talk to. There was no one quite like Malin for dismissing eerie thoughts. He was so earthy, so real. A pang assailed her. Where Malin was earthy, Laurel was…artificial. Like a cut flower languishing in a vase without thought of the earth it once sprang from.

Lily shook herself. She must get rid of these hysterical imaginings. Corteges and cut flowers! There was nothing wrong with Laurel; nothing wrong with her for staying in Laurel's home. Malin just didn't understand the social differences; that was the problem. She'd moved into his world of inns and muddy ditches, but he couldn't make the move into her world of elegant manners and dressing for dinner.

Lily sighed, and looked up. Laurel's men were marching along each side of her, with two lantern-bearers at the front. It was just like—

Her blood ran cold. It was just like the "bodyguard" of Wolves who had taken her to the prison cell in Denton. She stole a look at Laurel, who caught her eye and smiled. It was a cold, predatory smile.

Lily's heart thrummed. She steadied herself. There was absolutely no reason to suppose…but it was no good. She *knew*, without the slightest shred of proof, that she was walking into a trap. And there was no way out.

Close Behind

By the time the old mill's bulk loomed dark against the sky before them, Lily was nearly as taut as a bowstring. She had walked a path of dread, despair, and self-castigation, but the sight of journey's end swept all away. Every nerve must now be focussed on finding a chance and taking it, or her quest, her life and her land would all perish together.

They halted before the wide wooden doors which would once have seen ox wagons unloading grain and loading flour in dusty sacks.

"It's not locked," Laurel said. "After you, of course, my lady."

Was she even trying to pretend now? It didn't matter, either way. There was no way out; the men with lanterns formed an aisle to the doors as two of them swung one open. The mill's dark mouth exhaled a breath of musty air.

Lily walked slowly forward. Perhaps, in the darkness within, she would be able to elude them... But two of them stepped in on either side of her, lifting their lanterns high so she could see, a travesty of the search they had supposedly come for.

The mill was abandoned, but not empty. The great stones still sat in their place, old half-filled sacks and dusty mess littering the corners of the open room. Shadows abounded. The ceiling, if ceiling there was, was lost in the darkness above.

Lily took a dragging step forward and Laurel laughed, a bright, brittle sound. As though on a signal—*of course it was a signal*, Lily's mind raged—Wolves stepped out from behind the bulk of the millstones and out of the dark corners.

Wolves before her, Laurel's men behind and beside her—there was nowhere to go but up. The Wolves began a slow saunter forward, closing the circle. Lily cast up her eyes, hoping against all reason for a rope to be dangling from the rafters. There wasn't one.

Her eyes kept moving up, and caught a glint in the darkness. A glint, and a patch of paleness. The Wolves took another step; their circle tightened, then closed, the millstones now at their back. Lily strained her eyes, only partially accustomed to the darkness as they were, and caught a cheeky grin in the shadows. Malin!

Malin, perched on a rafter with…a floury old sack. A flashback to one of Holly's baking disasters told her exactly what he planned, and she poised herself. The Wolves were three strides away now, closing in slowly with taunting smiles and insolent assurance in every step. A sprinkling of flour drifted down through the lantern light, and Lily moved.

With a greater, faster force than any tantrum had ever bestowed on her, she snatched the lantern from the man on her right and hurled it to the floor at the Wolves' feet, dropping to one knee as she did so.

The tall Easterlings took an involuntary step back, but one was not enough. The lantern smashed, the falling cloud of flour caught and, with a *whumph* which shook the rafters, it blossomed into a fireball over Lily's head.

She spun around and flung herself towards the door, through a maelstrom of shouting, confusion and burning hair. Malin was at the doorway by the time she reached it, and they raced through side by side.

A hand closed about Lily's wrist and jerked her painfully

back. She swung about and saw Laurel, face twisted with fury. Now was no time for diplomacy, Lily decided, and with one smooth movement, she brought her free arm around and slapped Laurel sharply in the face. A momentary loss of grip was all she needed, and she pulled herself away and fled into the darkness, nursing her stinging hand.

A quick plunge across the stream that fed the mill wheel, and they were away, pounding across fields and into the welcoming darkness of the forest once again.

Lily stopped at last, doubled over and gasping. Silence fell as Malin stopped and waited for her to get her breath back. She braced herself. Some things had to be said, and it would be easier to say them now, in the darkness, than to wait and try to say them later.

"Malin," she said, her voice hoarse and strange in her own ears.

"Ready to go?"

"Wait." She took another difficult breath. "I'm sorry." She did not try to soften the statement with any tasteful profusions of regret. "I'm sorry I didn't believe you, and I'm sorry for what I said, and I'm sorry I ever trusted that two-faced, soft-talking, treacherous…"

"It's all right," Malin muttered, closer at hand than she had realized.

"It *isn't*." Lily swallowed a sob.

"It will be. Come on." He took her hand, put it on his shoulder, and led her away through the trees. "Just like old times. You, me, explosions…" He sniffed. "Can you smell toast?"

She started to laugh, each breath scraping her already raw throat afresh.

"Don't get hysterical on me," Malin said. "Not far now and we can lie up for a while, both sleep at once."

"And then we've got it all to do again," Lily lamented.

There was a silence.

"Don't tell me you left the Horn behind."

"No! No, of course not," Lily said, overlooking how nearly she had. "It's right here."

"Well, that's something," Malin said. "One down, two to go. Here we are."

From the feel of it, their resting place was a mossy hollow between the spreading roots of some large tree. It was, perhaps, a trifle damp, and not really large enough for stretching out, but Lily was in no mood for fussing. They sat side by side with their backs to the trunk, but protected as she was by her cuirass, Lily still couldn't find a comfortable position.

"Beetle down your neck?" Malin asked at last.

"I just—can't get comfortable," Lily said. "My back doesn't feel right. Or my neck. Something..."

"Here," Malin said, "try this," and he put his arm around her.

She was about to pull away—this was hardly appropriate—when she realized how much more comfortable she was. His arm was in just the right place to rest her heavy head. Well, why not? Aunt Hortensia was not here to disapprove, after all.

"Thank you," she said.

"You're welcome," he replied, his voice right in her ear.

She frowned. "Malin, are we floating?"

"No, why? You feeling funny?"

"It's just—your head is at the same height as mine, and it didn't use to be."

He chuckled. "Burnabaise have long backs. Your height's in your legs—you shrink when you sit down."

"Oh..." She was getting sleepy, her head rolling gently towards him. "I told her, Malin...I told her it wouldn't be tolerated. Most distasteful, I said."

"What is?"

"Torcs and thralls," Lily murmured.

"You told her?" He sounded surprised. "Thanks. I mean, it won't make a blind bit of difference, but thanks."

"You're welcome." Lily's mouth formed the words automatically.

He sniffed. "Phew. Smells like you got a bit singed back there."

She was barely conscious now, his voice bouncing down a dark tunnel to where she lay. "Mm?"

"Lily, I love you, but you stink."

He sighed heavily and settled down to sleep, but Lily lay awake, her head on his shoulder and her burning face hidden by the night.

Lily, I love you.

⚜   ⚜   ⚜

The next day dawned on them breakfasting on foraged shoots and berries, while brooding over the two unsolved couplets of the pedlar's riddle song.

The warm delight of the night's declaration had contracted to a glowing core behind her cuirass, but Lily made no mention of it. Even if she were certain he'd known she was awake and meant her to hear it, she would still have no idea what to say—what she ought to say, or, more perilous yet, what she would like to say. To her relief, he didn't raise the subject again, and they focussed on trying to solve the riddle.

Lily recited:

> The lanky lad unlocked the door
> To set the flowers free.

"Not Blosse, not the mill," Malin said.

"If it was Blosse, no one knew; and if it was the mill…well, that would be a ridiculous coincidence."

"So where does that leave us?"

Lily sighed. "I don't know. Where did the pedlar go?"

"Everywhere. Villages, towns, hamlets, inns—lots of inns—people living up in the hills like Gran Vi...anywhere there's people. And all the bits in between."

Lily groaned. "Let's try the other bit."

> The moon is rising in the north,
>   A sign for all to see;
> For none can buy the pedlar's wares
>   Save he whom it must be.

"That last couplet isn't a clue *to* anything," she said. "It's just a...a marker. The other three couplets are for the three Requisites."

"We've been over this before."

"Maybe this time we'll notice something new," Lily said. "The moon is rising in the north..."

"Except it doesn't," Malin said. "It rises in the east, same as the sun."

"Not the actual moon. You're so *literal.* He means the Lunula."

"Which is rising in the north?"

"For all to see," Lily said, and sighed. Then she gasped.

"You've got it?"

"No—but, Malin, Evil Uncle Phelan must know where we are. I mean, more or less. He must be the friend Laurel was in contact with, which means..." She stopped, feeling sick down to the soles of her feet.

"Which means he knows about the song," Malin said.

Lily buried her face in her hands. "Oh, I wish I had never laid eyes on that woman!"

"Can't be helped. Come on. If the Magister's closing in, the sooner we solve this and get gone the better."

"One at an inn for the people, one...not a mill, but... Oh, this is impossible! Why couldn't he leave them all at inns?"

"How do we know he didn't?"

"Because Laurel—no, that's not right. Because..." Lily stopped and thought. "I don't know. I suppose I just assumed, after I had that Blosse idea, that each piece would be in a different place, sort of symbolic of the thing itself."

"Could be. Could be not."

"So the moon in the north, that could be an inn somewhere in the north of Arcelia?" Lily asked. "If only Arcelia's coastline wasn't so long!"

"Hang on," Malin said. "What does this Lunula look like?"

"It's sort of crescenty," Lily said, "with the phases of the moon on it."

Malin jumped to his feet. "The Last Quarter. It's on the coast road, not far west of Murdock."

"That's quite a long way," Lily said, biting her lip anxiously.

"Then we'd best get moving—before the Magister figures it out."

"Let's," Lily agreed, shaking the dead leaves out of her cloak. "And see if we can't figure out the other one on the way there. The thin boy."

Malin stopped dead. "What did you say?"

"The lanky lad, I mean."

"No, but what did you say?"

"The, um, thin boy," Lily said, blushing.

"The Thin Man," Malin said. "Sign of a skeleton. It's inland a ways, southeast, but we could be there some time tonight, if we keep moving. Then it's northeast to the Last Quarter."

"And then," Lily said, setting her jaw, "to Denton."

⚜   ⚜   ⚜

Lily lay on her stomach and looked down at the Thin Man, a huddle of roofs and a black and white smudge of a sign in the dim dawn light.

"Dangerous," Malin said. "Nowhere to hide."

The Thin Man was in stone country, a harsh northern region where a long-ago sea had left sandstone and limestone

aplenty; a land of thin soil, thinner vegetation, and—alas!—
practically no trees. Even lying flat on the little plateau which
overlooked the inn, Lily felt exposed. There was no covert approach, no sneaking in, nowhere to hide.

She sighed. "And for all we know, Evil Uncle Phelan could
be right on our heels."

"On our heels if we're lucky," Malin muttered. "Already
here if we're not."

Lily surveyed the ground again. Nothing had changed.
"We'll stand out like drowned flies in cream if we try to creep
down the hill and approach the inn from behind."

"What choice do we have?"

"We can scramble down this side of the plateau instead and
approach by road, like legitimate travellers."

"Just walk up to the front door? That's mad!"

"If Uncle Phelan *is* here, it's the last thing he'll expect," Lily
countered.

"Right, because it's *mad.*"

"Where's your sense of adventure?" she teased.

"*My* sense of—? All right! It's mad and crazy and we'll
probably get killed, but we might as well live while we're alive,
right?"

They wriggled back from the plateau edge and began the
descent, aiming to meet the road around a bend from the inn.

"At least the road is deserted at this time of day," Lily offered.

"Not for much longer. Listen. We get in, we get the key, we
get out, all right? No sitting down and ordering breakfast."

"Of course not," Lily said.

"And no calling me Clotbur."

They approached the Thin Man separately, for the sake of
appearances. The chalky dust on the cracked pourstone road
was white in the early light, but one point was whiter yet. Lily
looked closer. A little white flower had forced its way through

the cracks in the pourstone and was blooming there. It was spring, after all.

Lily walked on, smiling. Even the skeleton sign hanging over Malin's head didn't dampen her glow. And there was a warm light in the inn windows. Someone, at least, was awake and waiting for visitors. She just had to hope it wasn't her uncle or his men.

They drew into the shadow of the inn. The great front door was closed. Lily bit her lip nervously as Malin jangled the waiting bell. Who would answer? What would she say? There was silence within, and then the sound of footsteps approaching from a distance.

"I forgot to tell you," Malin hissed. "People say Belladonna, the innkeeper here, is mute."

"What?" How was she supposed to have a persuasive conversation with someone who couldn't talk?

The footsteps stopped on the other side of the door. Lily tensed. There came the sound of bolts drawing back, and the door opened. A bony woman in a plain black dress stood before them, assessing them with a practised eye. Judging from the bunch of keys hanging at her waist, this was the lady of the house.

"I—I'm..." Lily stopped, automatically obeying the woman's hushing finger to her lips.

She pushed her hood back. The light was dim, but it was enough. The innkeeper gasped, her eyes filling with fear. The next moment, she stepped outside the door and pulled it closed behind her. Her shaking hands fumbled with the long black keys, until she worked one free and handed it to Lily. It was surprisingly light and warm, for something that looked like any old iron key.

Belladonna gave her a nervous smile as she pulled the hood back up to shadow Lily's face. Then, taking her by the shoulders, she turned her around and gave her a firm push. The message was clear. She would do her duty as regards the Key, but Lily was not welcome here.

Lily knew it was prudent to leave anyway, but, all the same, she was hurt. She walked away stiffly, not looking back as the great door opened and closed behind her.

"That was easier than I expected," Malin muttered from some distance behind her. "Northeast from here. We'll turn off the road once we're—"

A shout erupted from the dusty yard behind the inn. «It's them!»

The Thin Man's outbuildings were suddenly bristling with Wolves, pouring out of every door. Lily slipped the Key down the front of her cuirass and ran. A window slammed open in the inn behind her, and a hard, clear voice called orders over the din.

"Magister," Malin spat as he pounded along the stony road beside her.

It took all Lily's self-control not to turn around and look. A confrontation was inevitable, she supposed, but not now! Not like this! She concentrated on running. They had a good head start, and they had both had plenty of practice in running the last few weeks, but these were Phelan's own troops, under his own eye.

A quick gesture from Malin guided her sideways, off the road and into a honeycomb of stone passages and standing stones, like a forest sculpted by water, wind, and time. It was the sort of place highwaymen might well choose to frequent; the ideal place for an ambush.

Lily could almost hope they would run into some bandits; it would at least provide a diversion, and if there was one thing they needed now, with such single-minded pursuers hard on their heels, it was a diversion.

"This way," Malin said.

They ducked down another channel, scrambled across a

gully, and ran on. She could still hear the shouts of the Wolves marshalling behind them.

"Lily," Malin puffed, "promise me you'll free the thralls. Even without me."

"Yes," Lily said, "but—"

Her lungs were burning. Now was not the time to question how she could possibly succeed without him, or where exactly he thought he was going, in this, her hour of need. They broke out into a more open area and sped up. Ahead, Lily could hear the rushing of water. A river! Perhaps they could escape that way. The rivers this far north flowed not into Parsifal, but to the coast—the coast where stood the Last Quarter. Hope gave her renewed energy, and she sped on.

Malin risked a quick look behind him.

"They're catching up," he panted. "Make for that gap."

Lily veered accordingly. The sandstone loomed up ahead, walls which narrowed rapidly into a passageway barely wide enough for one. A bottleneck.

Malin pushed her into the stone passage, its walls resounding with the roar of the river.

"Go!"

His hatchet was out and in his hand; no need to ask what he had planned.

"Malin—no!"

"Go!"

With a sob, she turned and ran. The river—she must make for the river. She slipped and fell, the gritty stone searing the skin off her hands. Ladylike deportment forgotten, she scrambled to her feet and ran on.

Before she was halfway across the ground between the bottleneck and the river, she realized why the water was so loud: the river became a waterfall. She dashed down to the edge, but there was no way to climb down.

She turned upstream, sobbing for breath. She *had* to get

away. There could be no thought of anything else. Malin was paying too high a price for her freedom for her to lose it. Gritting her teeth, she forced her numbing legs to carry her up the rough slope. She had nearly reached the rise which formed her horizon when a Wolf rose up in her path and, behind him, another.

The river—no. Too wide to cross, and too rocky and swift to survive, so close to the waterfall. She turned back, running along the edge of the water's course, scanning for a chance to cross. If only the rocks were not so far apart! She reached the head of the waterfall and looked over. The rising mist formed a rainbow in the rising sun.

"Lily!"

She froze. That voice...

Slowly, she straightened up and turned. A loose half-circle of Wolves surrounded her, alert, waiting. She might, perhaps, break through a gap, but they would catch her within two breaths. Futile.

The Wolves drew back on either side to leave a space. She tensed to run, and then compelled herself to wait. Someone was coming. The original of the drawing in Aunt Hortensia's sketchbook; the original of the painting that the Denton gaoler so feared. Evil Uncle Phelan was walking—no, *strolling*—across the stony ground towards her.

Even in that moment, her senses, tightened to the highest pitch, saw Malin lying limp on the ground, and a Wolf busy lashing his arms and legs together with rope.

Then he can't be dead, said the indomitable voice within.

Phelan passed through the gap the Wolves had made for him, and they closed ranks behind him. He stopped and looked thoughtfully at her.

"Remarkable," he said. "And where is your aunt?"

Lily held her silence, thankful that Aunt Hortensia, at least, had escaped Phelan's attention.

"It was Hortensia that hid you, was it not? There was a discrepancy in the body count at the time. But not," he stared at her thoughtfully, "in your case. I wonder whose it was. Not that it matters. A pity we couldn't check the eyes."

Lily fervently hoped this had been one of Woodward's illusions.

"Children all look much the same," Phelan continued. "A pity they don't stay that way. You have quite a look of your mother now. Is that what Hortensia depended on? Send her out with her mother's looks and the grey eyes, and watch the world fall at her feet? She should have known better. The world has moved on—the state has moved on."

Lily said nothing.

"The resemblance makes it difficult. The eyes could be got over—but not the face. But for that, you could live out your days a blind madwoman, with delusions of grandeur. A figure of derision." His eyes flicked over her. "You already appear a beggar."

Hearing these cold calculations of violence chilled her, but the remembrance of the parents she'd barely known—barely known because of *him*—turned the ice in her blood to iron.

"All so you could call yourself king?" she asked.

His face darkened. "Kings belong in fairy tales. Superstitious foolery. I govern. Therefore, governor, or magister. Not king."

"Or prince?"

"Not any more. That's history."

The anger was starting to rise from its old haunt within her, and Lily tried to push it back down. "You killed the king to kill the monarchy—and now you're killing the kingdom?"

This seemed to surprise him. "The state—it is not called the kingdom any more. Logically. What I did—what I do—is for the good of the state. Free of the superstitious customs embodied and upheld by the monarchy, we are at last free to make

efficient use of the resources available to us—to increase pro-
ductivity and grow the economy."

"I will stop you," Lily hissed, aware of how foolish this
sounded under the circumstances, but determined to be heard
all the same. "I will put things right."

He frowned. "Another instance of this foolish royal superstition. Do you really believe magic will save you, simply
because of who your parents are—or, rather, were?" Disdain
was not only in his face now, but dripping from his voice.
"That this invisible vegetable force will somehow defeat all
the power of men and steel that comes against you?"

She could only stare at him defiantly, trying to hold back
tears of rage.

"That was what your father thought—and you will pay the
same price for the same folly. The game is over. Checkmate."

"You forget," Lily said.

His eyes narrowed. "Forget what?"

"The king cannot be taken."

With that, she turned, and with one flying step, she leapt
over the edge. For one moment, her cloak fluttered, like the
wings of a falling bird, and then she was lost to sight.

⚜   ⚜   ⚜

Phelan took one long stride forward and looked over the edge.
The Wolf captain joined him.

"Did she say the king—" the captain began.

"Yes," Phelan spat.

"Isn't that what your bro—"

"Shut up!"

The captain did so, taking a prudent step back from the edge
for good measure. He watched his employer carefully.

Phelan's face worked as he struggled to regain control. Finally, he turned, and with a voice that was almost level, he
gave his orders.

"Post two guards. The rest and the prisoner with me."

"Guards?" the captain said, taking a dubious look at the frothing waters below. "You really think that's necessary?"

"Would I have ordered it if I didn't?" Phelan snapped.

"I'm not questioning your orders, sir," the captain began hastily.

"That is exactly what you were doing."

"I wasn't sure if you knew—she can't swim."

"And how do you know that?"

"There's a song going around," the captain said. "About her. It says she can't swim. Been causing her trouble." He looked over the edge again.

"Are you seriously suggesting that I make strategic decisions based on the content of a folk song?" Phelan asked, in a tone which made the captain give serious thought to his employment status.

"No! Of course not, sir. Silly of me."

"Yes." Phelan began to walk away, and then turned back. "The former take-alive order is rescinded. Tell your men they can shoot to kill—so long as they bring me the body."

⚜   ⚜   ⚜

Down in the cauldron of water, Lily struggled—for air, for movement, even to know which way was up. The unrelenting water hammered her down into the deep pool at the base of the waterfall. Up. Air. Away... Crossbows. They had crossbows. She fought her way out from under the crashing wall of water and, limp from the effort, let herself rise to the surface. Perhaps they wouldn't see her. She was deaf, she was blind...but she could breathe.

Painfully, she opened her tightly-screwed eyes, flinching as the arcing water splashed into her face. It was dim down here. The sun wasn't high enough to illuminate this stone chasm— but it would be soon. As soon as they left, she would find a way out. But, in the meantime, she must be invisible. Hidden.

Keeping close to the craggy stone cliff, Lily clawed her way around to the very edge of the waterfall. Here was the hard part. Hard? She had just jumped off a waterfall. A nearly hysterical giggle escaped her and she sternly censored it. Under the waterfall…

Her lungs burned till she could almost taste the smoke. But it had to be done. Three deep breaths, a fervent hope that the rocks were not too sharp, and she went under.

It was easier than she had expected, the pummelling less violent here at the side of the fall. She surfaced in even dimmer light, a faded white sheet of water curtaining her from the world outside. Tentatively, she put down her feet, and felt hard rock beneath them. As her eyes adjusted, she realized the darkness was depth. There was a cave behind the waterfall.

She crawled up into it and found Sennet was right about the slime, too. If he had told her, that day, that a time would come when she would lie down in a pool of slime without turning a hair, she would have thought his mind was going.

But here she was, down in the darkness, bereft of friends, family and home—but alive. A momentary panic was put to rest by finding the Horn of Vale and the Persimmon Key had survived the fall intact, though it took some time for the fluttering of her heart to subside.

Lily thought she slept, but could not be certain. The roaring waters were all she could hear, awake or asleep, and a thousand concerns filled her mind. Aunt Hortensia. Master Sennet and Holly. Woodward. Candra. Arcelia. Burnaby. Malin. Restoration Day.

At last, too heartsick to rest longer, she slid back into the water. The wall of water was bright, almost blinding where it splashed. Broad daylight. Paddling cautiously around the other edge of the falls, she looked up. It didn't seem so far from down here. Dark against the sky were two tall figures, the sun blazing on their yellow hair. Wolves. Sentries.

Silently, she slipped back behind the fall and sat down in her puddle of slime once more. Leaf and bud, but Uncle Phelan was thorough! Why couldn't he take something at face value for once?

Now she would have to wait for nightfall to make her escape, and the thought of trying to navigate her way down a rocky river in the dark did not appeal. Although trying to climb up the cliffs in the dark, wet and slippery, and probably with Wolves waiting even if she did reach the top alive...

No. The river it would have to be, rocks and all.

⚜   ⚜   ⚜

In the end, she did not wait for darkness, but only the dusk that makes the distance unclear. Trying to navigate her way blind through the frothing cauldron at the foot of the falls would be madness. She edged out and looked cautiously upwards.

The Wolves were warming themselves at a small fire. Lily smiled at the thought of Malin's disgust. Two men who had been staring into a fire would have no chance of spotting a person rippling across the water below.

By the time she reached the far side of the deep pool, the current had caught her, and she slid between the high rock walls of the canyon with a last smug look at the firelit faces of her would-be assassins.

The river was remarkably rock-free, the waters flowing fast and smooth, and she would have been almost enjoying herself, had it been less cold. It was, nonetheless, a welcome peaceful moment after the physical and emotional turmoil of the last few days.

True night fell, and she could no longer see where the river was taking her, but the stars overhead reassured her that the river flowed more or less north, down to the Norward Sea. It was a strangely quiet way to travel, with not even the subtle noises of a boat. All she could hear was the silvery giggles of the water as it tickled past the banks; all she could see was the star-scattered darkness.

Lily noticed that her heart had slowed. Past the danger, she reassured herself. She'd stopped shivering, too. She must be used to the cold of the water by now. Something stirred in her mind. Not shivering. A fire—a girl wrapped in white rabbit fur, sitting by a fire—or, no, was it Malin by a fire? Perhaps that was it. Malin by a fire, making her stay awake.

Lily's head jerked up. Malin's voice rang in her head. *You fall asleep, and you never wake up.* Too cold to shiver. Too cold. Out. She had to get out. She commanded her arms to paddle towards the edge, but they were slow and sluggish, and so, so heavy.

A hot bolt of panic shot through her chest. If she couldn't get out, she would die. Clumsily, she splashed towards the western bank, and felt along until she found a low place where she could clamber out.

The bank was rocky, and she was thankful her legs were too numb to feel the battering they received as she scrambled over the rocks, looking for higher ground. Smoother ground. The air was cold, and she knew she had to keep moving. It was bad to be so wet and cold. She stopped and took off her boots. The water poured out, and the socks squidged under her feet. Best to wring them out...

She went to put the socks on again, and stopped. Aunt Hortensia's oft-repeated strictures on keeping her feet dry echoed in her head. Even Malin agreed that wet socks would only give you blisters. She'd have to go barefoot, just for now, and hope no one saw.

Because that's *the worst thing that could happen,* said the voice in her mind, which sounded, now she thought about it, curiously like Malin. *Never mind getting killed; it's getting caught without your socks on you need to worry about.*

Voices aside, it took only one eye-wateringly painful stub of her toe on the abrasive rocks to decide that blisters were not so bad. The damp socks went back on, the soggy boots were wrestled over them, and she hobbled slowly on.

Her feet began to warm up, which only made them hurt more. She gritted her teeth and kept going, feeling the weight of her clothing slowly lessen as the water seeped away. She would be leaving a trail of drips, but they would dry before dawn.

Every time she was tempted to stop for a rest, she thought of Wolves, and of Malin lying crumpled on the ground, and kept going. She'd been walking for hours, but she couldn't have gone that far, since she had to feel her way round every obstacle.

The night wore on, and Lily kept walking. Once or twice, she thought she saw the welcoming glow of a fire in the distance, but she never seemed to reach it, and it disappeared from sight. A hallucination, perhaps. So long as she didn't hallucinate about where the edge of the riverbank was…

Dawn revealed that the river had curved in the night. Either that, or the sun had taken to rising in the north as well as the pedlar's moon. No harm done, she told herself. And then she saw the plume of smoke which rose black against the golden light of dawn, and misgivings filled her heart once more.

Argument and counter-argument flickered across her weary mind as she trudged across the thin and scrubby grass which covered the rolling northern country. It might be. It might not be. There was only one way to find out, and that was to keep putting one foot in front of another. She plodded on, head down, eyes heavy with sleep and blistered feet heavy with exhaustion. The tang of smoke drifted on the crisp morning air.

At last, she heard voices. She lifted her head, and stopped dead.

This, then, was the fire in the night. Devastation lay before her as far as she could see. The main building was a burned-

out, half-collapsed ruin, the outbuildings mere heaps of blackened stone on the scorched earth. A handful of people were
sorting through the still-smoking rubble.

To one side, carefully guarded by a homely-looking woman,
lay a shrouded form. And above all this, as though in mockery,
swung the inn's sign: a tarnished crescent moon in a smoke-
blackened sky.

The Last Quarter.

The Last Quarter

Lily stumbled forward and dropped to her knees by the shrouded form. "Who—?"

The homely woman gave her a piercing look. "I'm Gilly, my lady, and this is—was—my sister Hyacinth. Innkeeper at the Last Quarter these twenty years at least." She scrubbed her eyes fiercely with a handkerchief. "She wouldn't tell him where it was," she said, her voice quavering.

"Hyacinth." Lily said, "for *constancy*."

"And *sorrow*," Gilly added, and had a good sob into the handkerchief. "If I'd known where it was, I'd have told him myself, and that's a fact. Not that she would have thanked me for it." She blew her nose loudly and waved a hand at the rubble behind her. "Everyone's been searching for salvage since the first light, but there's nothing—nothing like what you're looking for. I'm sorry."

"*You're* sorry?" Lily asked. "For the suffering which loyalty to my house has brought upon you? I should be sorry, not you." She got stiffly to her feet. "And Phelan will be sorriest, if I can help it." She paused. "Did you see if the Wolves had a Burnabais with them? A prisoner?"

Gilly thought a moment, and shook her head. "It's not likely we'd have seen him anyway, my lady. Not in all the dark and confusion."

"Of course." Lily privately resolved to ask the rest. Surely, someone must have seen him!

"Will you stay for the burying?" Gilly asked timidly. "She'd be that pleased if she knew, and they're working on the box as fast they can find unburned wood for it."

"Of course I will stay," Lily said. And then, brow wrinkling, "The box?"

"The box for the burying," Gilly said. "Didn't you know?"

Lily shook her head in fascinated horror.

"The new ways," Gilly said with a sigh. "Buried in a box. Magister's orders."

"But, surely!" Lily said. "How would he know?"

Gilly wouldn't meet her eye. "Sometimes they check."

Lily's stomach heaved, and she was glad it was empty. How revolting! To box someone up like that, to prevent them returning to the earth! She supposed nature took its course, even so, but to keep it separate, as though you were storing something up for later!

> *When the dead cannot lie easy*
> *in the land that once was theirs…*

And as for digging it up—no, she wouldn't even think about it.

The outrage flowed through her like molten iron. Unconsciously, her spine straightened, stiffened; her chin took on that jut which, in earlier days, preceded throwing things.

"Bury your sister with all honour," she said, and Gilly looked up, startled at the change in her voice. With a few words of benediction on the departed Hyacinth, Lily turned away.

As she approached the remains of the inn proper, a weathered old man came up to her, limping on a shorter, twisted leg.

"It ain't here, my lady," he said, "and no use wishing for it. We've looked."

"You knew it was here, then?" Lily asked.

He shrugged. "There's always rumours. Could be they was put about by way of confusion, though, because any place hidden enough when the inn was alive—well." He flapped a hand at the desolation behind him. "It ain't so hidden now."

Lily stared at the blackened hulk, willing it to give up its secrets. There was a creak, and a shout of alarm; figures hurried out of the ruins with alacrity, and another piece of wall fell in, raising a great cloud of ashy dust.

"Tell me, Master, er..." she said, not taking her eyes off the fallen stones.

"Box," he said, "and not so much of the master. I'm just the oxtler here."

"A skilled profession," Lily said courteously. She certainly wouldn't fancy being caught in a burning barn full of panicky oxen. Those horns could be lethal. "Tell me, Master Box, have you a good working knowledge of the inns in this region?"

"Course I do," he said. "It's a network, see? Obviously, I'm more in touch with the ox side of things than the inside work, but you get to hear a lot, what with one thing and another."

"And how many inns are there in the north of Arcelia which have moon-related names?"

"One," he said, unhesitating. "Well, none, now."

Lily softly quoted the pedlar's song:

> The moon is rising in the north,
>   A sign for all to see.

"I know that one," Box said. "You reckon it means here, eh?"

"It has to," Lily said.

"Doesn't mean it's actually here, does it? Because it isn't. So it can't be."

"What else *could* it mean?" Lily asked hopefully.

"Well..." He rubbed his unshaven chin with a rasping sound. "Says it's a sign, right? So could be it's not the thing here; it's just something that points to the thing, if you follow me."

Lily considered this, and found it convincing. "Such as…?"

"That's what gums up the works," Box said, "because the only one in the know was Hyacinth, and she never told no one. Not even Phelan," he added with a hint of pride.

"A strong woman," Lily said, wishing she'd had the chance to meet her.

Box sighed. "She was a grand woman, she was. Knew every bit of the business like the back of her hand. I reckon he thought she'd told someone, and they'd be quick enough to spill once they saw what happened to her." He swiped at his eyes with the back of his hand. "I'm glad she didn't, in a way. At least he didn't get his way this once."

Lily heaved a sigh. She had come too far to give up hope now, however dark the outlook. "Thank you for your time, Box. I'm sure you're right, but if you don't mind, I'll just take a look around myself."

"If it makes you feel better. Just keep clear of the unstable bits, all right? I got my hands full without digging another grave."

⚜   ⚜   ⚜

Two hours later, Lily was as streaked with soot as any of them, and she reluctantly had to agree with Box's assessment. Wherever the Lunula was, it wasn't here. At least it hadn't melted in the inferno, but where did that leave her? Restoration Day was a mere handful of days away, and she had hit a dead end.

What was she to do? Wait for Hyacinth's burial, and then… what? With growing frustration, she strode around and around the blackened space, the salvagers tactfully keeping out of her way.

How could Phelan have done such a thing to these poor people, with so little evidence to go on? Her rage swelled. She turned the corner at what had been the front of the inn, and her grey glare fell on the sign.

It was a taunt, and she knew it. Even if Phelan was certain of her death or capture, it wasn't enough for him to destroy the inn; he had to display just which inn it was he'd dealt out death and destruction to. So he'd left it hanging there, an innless sign for all to see.

A sign for all to see...

Lily's skin prickled as her hairs stood on end. She looked closer, walked to the other side of the sign and looked again.

"Master Box!" she called, and he came at a jog-trot, startled by the urgency in her voice.

"My lady?"

"This inn is the Last Quarter, is it not?"

"It was."

"And will be again," Lily said, in a tone which brooked no disagreement. "So why does the sign display a crescent moon?"

Box screwed up his face in the midday glare and looked at the sign. "Dunno. Looks, probably. A proper last quarter'd sit there like half a cheese."

Lily was silent, staring at the sign.

"Does it matter?" Box asked, his tone suggesting he had enough to do elsewhere.

"I need a ladder," Lily said.

"Ladders all burned," Box said. "Sorry."

"Then we must make one," Lily said, "and quickly."

"There's no wood," Box snapped. "Except what we've managed to salvage for the box, and—"

"Then we'll use that," Lily said. "Hyacinth is to be buried properly, in the traditional manner."

"Why not? What else have we got to lose?"

She turned her grey eyes on him like gimlets.

"Restoration Day is coming, Master Box," she said, and her quiet tone was like a knife through silk. "The Horn of Vale is at my side, the Persimmon Key is next my heart, and if I have to cut down the inn sign to find out why the two sides are different, I will. Reluctantly, but I will."

"Different?" Box frowned.

"One crescent stands out from the wood," Lily said softly, "and the other does not."

Box looked. "Leaf and bud!" And he was off at a jerky run, calling for wood, nails, a hammer, hurry!

Lily stood and waited, not taking her eyes off the sign. The tiny rim of shadow faded and returned as clouds passed over the sun. Such a little thing to have tripped Phelan up at last. She stood, and waited, and smiled.

⚜   ⚜   ⚜

The ladder was swift but rudimentary; it was no more than two planks nailed end to end with offcuts along their length for rungs. Lily eyed it doubtfully.

"It'll hold," Box said confidently. "Looks a right mess, I grant you, but it'll hold."

She had no choice but to take his word for it. One of the young men leaned it up against the arm of the signpost and steadied it for her.

"Thank you," Lily said fervently.

"You'll be wanting this," Box said, and passed her his hoof knife. "In case it needs prising off."

Lily thanked him and tucked it handle-first under the edge of her cuirass, the hooked end pointing away from her. The ladder flexed beneath her as she made her ascent, but it was held firm. She forgot her nerves and looked only at the crescent.

Up close, she could see it was, indeed, a curve of tarnished silver, held in place with bent nails. But it was smooth, and the Lunula was ornamented with an inlaid pattern of the lunar cycle. She bit her lip. What if it wasn't...? No. It had to be. It *had* to be...

Moving slowly, Lily took one hand off the ladder and slipped out the hoof knife. One by one, she prised each bent nail open with infinite care. Scarcely daring to breathe, she slid the hoof knife back under the cuirass, and stretched out her hand to the metal crescent. It came loose at the top.

Her fingers slipped beneath and found the ornamentation. Of course, Hyacinth would have concealed the more distinctive side. Cautiously, she pulled it further away from the wood, until it jammed.

Lily hissed with frustration. One nail was still too bent, and she could not risk damaging the Lunula by yanking at it. She would have to let go of the Lunula, or the ladder.

She let go of the ladder. An indrawn breath from below told her that she was not the only one who considered this a risky move. Slowly, the hoof knife moved across to the stubborn nail and pushed at it. Stiff. She pushed harder, and the brittle nail broke away.

Lily lurched sideways, clutching at the heavy wooden arm to save herself. There was a clatter and shouts from below as she scrabbled to get her feet back onto the ladder's tiny perch. Willing hands moved it closer, and her feet found purchase. Heart thrumming, she pulled herself back upright. The Lunula was gone.

Her chest tightened, and her breath caught as she looked down. One of the inn maids had caught the Lunula and was holding it up with its terminals to the sky. From Lily's high vantage point, the crescent seemed to encircle the young woman's neck like a torc. Lily's heart turned over, and the next moment, the world turned over with it. *Like a torc...*

No, it wasn't the world; it was her. She was suddenly the other way up, and the world, which had been upside down since that moment of dark discovery in the Magister's dungeon, was finally the right way up again.

Mistaking her shocked expression, they were calling up to

her that it was all right, not to worry, it had come to no harm, and as for the hoof knife, well, fortunately, it had fallen handle-down and Woodruff's head was that solid, what difference would it make?

Lily took in none of this. She slid down the ladder, adding one or two nasty splinters to yesterday's grazes, and took the Lunula in her hands.

The illustrations had always shown it sideways, as with a crescent moon, and, naturally, she had always assumed—but was it naturally? Aunt Hortensia would have thought so, but now Lily wondered how she could ever have taken this for a crown. Now that it was free of its flattening imprisonment, it had curved back into its proper shape. It was never meant to be worn atop a head, of that she was sure.

Lily lifted the Lunula and eased the pointed terminals around her throat. They seemed to part, and then to spring together again, as she settled the cool weight of the torc into place around her neck.

Queen of Arcelia; Arcelia's thrall.

⚜   ⚜   ⚜

The Last Quarter's hospitality was barely lessened by the loss of its buildings. Food was provided at noon, and work was already underway to make at least one room habitable before nightfall. They pressed her to stay on for the night.

"It would be an honour for the new Last Quarter to have the queen be the first guest," Gilly maintained, "and only four days before Restoration Day, at that!"

"*Four* days?" Lily repeated, panic shooting up her chest.

"Five, counting Restoration Day," Gilly said. "Falls on Fallowday, and today's Landday."

Landday, Middweek, Martday, Launderday, Fallowday. Five days. Four left. Lily sat in silent shock. Somewhere along the way, she had lost a day, or lost track of the days. How could it be nearly a week since Murdock? Where had she—? No, that wasn't important now. She had to be in Denton by dawn on Restoration Day, and there was no knowing how long the journey would take.

"I am so sorry," she said, "but I mustn't stay. Restoration Day is sooner than I thought, and I—"

"No need to apologize, my lady," Gilly said. "Hyacinth would be the last to keep you. Not when she laid so much importance on keeping the hope of Restoration Day alive. You go, and I'm just sorry we can't be of more help to you."

Lily blinked away the tears. "I'll come back. If—if I can."

"And the Last Quarter will be ready to receive you," Gilly said firmly. "Won't it, Box?"

"That it will. Now, if you'll take my advice, my lady, you'll steer clear of the roads. Far too many Wolves passing up and down, and there's a garrison not two hours down the road, which is where the Magister passed his night, like as not. Much better if you cut across country. Not as smooth going as the road, to be sure, but you might save time going straight across country, and you're much less likely to run your head into trouble."

"Thank you," Lily said, and "thank you," again as a young woman pressed a packet of food into her hands.

"I'd set you on the way myself," Box said, "but, with my leg, I'd only slow you down. Woodruff'll show you."

Lily bid them a hasty farewell, wishing them all the best with their own restoration, and hurried away across the ashy field at Woodruff's side. At the top of the rise, she looked back to see them hard at work again already.

"This way," Woodruff said, putting his arm out for all the world as though he were a signpost. "Southwest it'll take you, straight as an arrow to Denton."

Lily thanked him, wishing she could travel as fast as the arrow would. He jogged back down the hill, and she started briskly on her way. She would keep this course till nightfall, she decided, then stop to eat and rest before she carried on. It was still not much past midday; she could cover a good distance. Sleep could wait.

What could not wait, she soon discovered, was the pain in her feet. Sure enough, Malin had been right. Wet socks caused blisters, and then they wore away at the blisters, and the result was sheer agony.

The pain forced her to a halt. She couldn't keep going like this—too painful, for one thing, and too slow, for another—but what was the alternative? Going barefoot, a thing a lady *never* did, and certainly not in public. And certainly not at night, where it was impossible to see what you were about to stub your toe on.

Another thought assailed her. Was travelling at night even going to be possible, without Malin to guide her? She'd managed last night, but that had been far too slow, and with time running out—!

The thought made her stride out again, and the pain made her stop. She forced herself to be calm, and considered the options. When only one remained, she faced it squarely: travel barefoot, and only by day. If anyone saw her—well, having her naked feet on view would be the least of her problems.

She sat down, pulled off her boots with a wince, peeled off her socks (both pairs) and stuffed them into the boots. Tying the laces together, she settled them over one shoulder, got to her aching feet, and set off southwest to reclaim her kingdom.

⚜   ⚜   ⚜

To her surprise, Lily did not see anyone all the rest of that day. She stayed off the roads, and passed by many farms which appeared abandoned. Where had everyone gone? To the towns and their manufactories? This was hard land from which to wrest a living; small blame on them if they had found it too hard under the new conditions.

The distant views of the eastern and western ranges were all she had to keep her on the right course, for there was no one from whom she could ask the way.

Lily slept that night in the open, tucked under a scraggly bush which formed the best shelter she could find. She wrapped her cloak tightly about her and hoped she would pass for a puddle of shadow, should anyone come by.

The night passed as quietly as any night outdoors, with the movement of the land's night-dwellers heard in little scratches and flutterings all around.

The sunrise pried her eyelids open and revealed a millipede prospecting across her cloak. Lily grimaced, flicked it off into the bush, and got to her feet. At least a millipede couldn't chop her head off.

She shook her clothes out carefully, however, and gave her face and hands a good scrubbing in the first water she came to: a shallow stream trickling aimlessly across the heath.

She thought, though she was not certain, that she was still heading in the right direction. The uncertainty grew as she went on, from a hesitating niggle—surely Candra, atop Mount Covell, wasn't quite in the right line for Denton?—to an almost paralyzing doubt. What if she was on the wrong bearing? She could end up miles out of the way, and not have time to make her way back. If only there was someone she could ask!

Nonetheless, Lily forced herself on as fast as her abused feet would go. She had to keep moving, even if she wasn't going quite the right way.

Her heart leapt when, at last, she saw another human figure come over a rise, heading north to the main road, and then another. Her mouth was already open to call out when a shadow fell across her mind and she thought better of it. No more Laurels. She crouched down in the scrubby growth where it was still shadowed from the morning light, and waited for the figures to pass nearby.

The voices arrived first. Two men, travelling together by the sounds of it. Lily quieted her breathing, and listened. Arcelian voices, yes. She strained to catch their words.

"—but he doesn't look certain to me."

"Reckon she's still alive, then?"

They were close to her now. She could even hear as the first man sucked his teeth doubtfully.

"Doesn't seem likely," he conceded. "But you never know."

This had to mean her, and the waterfall, and Phelan. So they'd seen him recently—they might have news of Malin. If only they would declare their loyalties! But perhaps people had got into the habit of keeping their views to themselves, and how could she blame them, in the circumstances? She felt a sudden rush of sympathy for these two men, afraid to say what they thought, even out in the middle of nowhere.

"Takes a lot to make him certain," the second man agreed.

"Imagine he'd pay quite a lot for proof," the first man said.

Lily's sympathy ebbed. That...did not sound so innocent. She stayed low, and listened. All the way until they passed out of her hearing, they spoke of how they would spend such a princely sum.

Lily waited, chafing, until they were out of sight, and then set off again, her indignation lending briskness to her pace. It was two hours before she realized the boots had fallen off her shoulder as she hid, and she had forgotten to pick them up again. There was no time to waste going back for them. She would just have to face her uncle—and the world—with bare feet. She groaned once, and then walked on.

The land changed from hour to hour as she passed across it. Not simply the changes of light and heat wrought by the sun as it climbed overhead, but the very nature of the land. She was leaving the stony, barren lands behind. The soil felt softer and deeper beneath her feet, and trees were no longer isolated and unusual.

Lily conscientiously warned herself to redouble her caution. Where the land was good, there were invariably people.

It was not yet noon when she found herself approaching what looked very much like a lattie. The chequerboard of fields had been ploughed, and probably planted by this time, though she could not see any new life springing up yet. Yes— definitely planted. There were dozens of birds hanging about, rising, settling to feed on the seeds, and then rising again in a sudden flutter.

Her heart lurched. Down in a waste corner of the field stood a sturdy dwarf figure, which seemed to wave to her. She began to run. How had he—? And then she stopped, her heart sinking down to her feet. It was a stranger, not waving, but throwing stones at the birds to scare them off the fields.

Trying to contain her disappointment, Lily drew closer. The dwarf heard her approach, turned, and got the shock of his life. He stood there, his mouth opening and closing, and, then, with a sudden panic, he gave a jerky bow.

"My lady!"

"Oh, please don't!" Lily burst out. "Burnabaise don't use titles..." She stopped. Where had that come from?

The dwarf was staring at her now.

"I'm a friend of Malin's," Lily said, and this seemed sufficient explanation for the both of them. "Have you seen him?"

"Here? I wish."

Lily noticed for the first time the dull gleam of metal at his throat.

"He was captured by Phelan yesterday—no, the day before. Taken prisoner, but—" She swallowed painfully. "But no one's seen him since."

The dwarf kept silence, though his face was set in an old despair.

Lily pulled herself together. "In that case, can you please tell me if I'm going the right way for Denton?"

The dwarf turned to follow her line of sight. "You're a bit south, I'd say. Make a bit more west, like so. Don't go over the fields, though. Take this line, along the edge of the fields, and keep going till you come to an old broken tree. Then—you see that mountain over there?"

Lily sighted along his arm. Mount Covell. Candra. She swallowed, and nodded.

"Head for that mountain, and you should be about right."

"Thank you."

She smiled and turned to the path he had indicated. Only a few steps along, she turned back to him.

"This Fallowday is Restoration Day," she said. "Which will be the last day of thralldom, or the last day of my life."

His face did not hold much hope, but she was glad she had said it, just the same. Never before had she put it that plainly, not even in the privacy of her own head. She held the thought in her mind as she strode along the field's edge. Fallowday. The last day of Phelan's rule—or the last day of her life. And the life of Arcelia.

⚜   ⚜   ⚜

Lily's meagre foraged lunch was fortified a few hours later by the family she met at a pool in the slow-moving stream which crossed her path. Their laundry—two days early to avoid crowding—was spread out drying on the bushes as the woman and her children rested and sported, respectively.

There wasn't much food left, for which the woman apologized: "You know what children are like, m'lady, hollow legs the lot of them."

But there was enough to share, as there always would be with such a woman, Lily suspected, however little she had. Afternoon tea… She'd almost forgotten what it was like, this most pleasant of meals. She could spare a few minutes. She'd be faster for having a rest.

The woman, it emerged, was a widowed dressmaker, Laburnum by name; her children were Fern, a dark-eyed slip of a girl not yet nine, and an older boy called Hawkweed ("eyes like a hawk and grows like a weed," according to his mother). The two children clambered out of the water to sit dripping in the sun as they ate their seed cake. They eyed her, Fern openly and Hawkweed with surreptitious curiosity.

"If you're a princess," Fern asked, "why aren't you wearing nice clothes with lace and that?"

"Fern!" her mother squawked. "That's no kind of a question to ask—oh, I'm so embarrassed, I don't know where to put myself!"

To ease the undoubted awkwardness of the question, Lily asked one of her own. "Did you bake this seed cake yourself? I do believe it's the best I've ever tasted."

Laburnum flushed again, but this time, Lily hoped, with pleasure.

"I did, my lady, and I'm glad you like it. It's a family recipe, as a matter of fact, but seeing it's you…"

"Thank you," Lily said, "although perhaps you had better hold on to it until…" She looked sideways at Fern. "Until the events of the next few days resolve themselves."

She caught Laburnum's eye, and a look of understanding passed between them.

"Very wise, my lady, and I'm sure I wish there was more we could do for you. Have you got somewhere to stay for the night?"

Lily was tempted. But it was only tea time, and she couldn't afford to lose the rest of the day's walk.

"I'm afraid I must hurry," she said. "I don't suppose you've seen Evi—I mean, the Magister pass through these parts lately?"

"Happy to say I haven't," Laburnum said firmly.

"I have," Hawkweed volunteered, the first words he'd spoken so far.

"What? And you never told me? You know I like to have plenty of warning—"

"He wasn't stopping," Hawkweed said defensively. "Just passing through, yesterday it was. Heading for Denton, and he'll have reached it by now, pace they were going." He tried to look grown-up and knowing.

"Did he—?" Lily took a breath and got her voice under control. "Was there a dwarf with the group? A prisoner."

Hawkweed avoided her eye.

"Answer the lady, Hawkweed!"

"I've heard that song," Hawkweed said, still not meeting her eye. "About you and Malin of Burnaby. Was that who you were meaning?"

"Yes!" Lily leaned forward, agog. What feats had Malin done that marked him out to Hawkweed's eye as the dwarf of story and song?

"Then I'm sorry," Hawkweed said frankly. "He was tied over the back of an ox, and…well, he didn't look good."

Lily forced herself not to break down, to keep her voice level as she asked, "Dead?"

"I dunno. I'm sorry, I wish I—I dunno. He didn't look good."

Lily looked down, so that he could not see her expression, and a tear splashed onto her skirts. Then Laburnum's hand appeared in her field of vision, and patted her arm gently.

"Don't you worry, my lady. I've never yet known the Magister start carting dead bodies about, and I doubt he's started now. Roughed up a bit, your friend may be," she conceded, "but too soon to be ordering the black armbands, I'd say."

Lily forced a smile.

"Thank you so much for your hospitality, Mistress Laburnum," she said, getting hastily to her feet, "and for your information, Hawkweed," which took the downcast look off his face, "but I'm afraid I really must be going. I've a long way to go still, and I *must* be in Denton for Restoration Day."

Laburnum nodded and smiled, Fern dipped a sweet little curtsy that would have impressed even Aunt Hortensia, and Hawkweed lifted a troubled face.

"Just a minute, miss—I mean, my lady. He was in a hurry, Magister was. Big hurry." He stumbled as three pairs of eyes tried to read his meaning in his face. "The sort of hurry where you don't wait around for prisoners with short legs keeping up."

"Oh! I hadn't thought of that," Lily said, and relief washed over her. "Thank you!"

"Let me show you the way!" Fern said, taking Lily's hand.

Lily allowed the little girl to lead her to the stream, and followed her from rock to rock across the flow until she landed dry-footed on the other side. Fern scampered back again, and Lily turned to smile and wave goodbye.

⚜   ⚜   ⚜

The accuracy of Hawkweed's observation was soon proved when Lily encountered the trampled trail of a Wolf Pack. No ordinary patrol, either: moving too fast to wreak their customary devastation, and with the tracks of an ox intermingled with the booted prints. No sign of wheel marks, so a riding ox, and, by the length of the tread, a giant one.

It had to be Phelan and his men, leaving the road for the speed of the straight line. She looked closer. The grass was starting to spring back. Yesterday's trail. For better or worse, Malin would be in Denton by now.

On Lily went, somewhere between a walk and a run, as the sun rolled down to the west and the gloom gathered. The terrain became harder and harder to see.

Looking up, she found with a start that a derelict farmhouse was looming out of the dusk. She had become so intent on the trail, she had stopped being observant. A quick look around reassured her that she had not been caught, but she scolded herself for her carelessness. To come so close, and then to risk being caught so easily!

She made up for it with the caution of her slow and silent approach to the farmhouse. She could not have been more careful if it had been full of Wolves with sentries at every window, which made it something of an anticlimax when she found it completely empty. But, from the looks of it, they had passed the night in these rooms.

Lily hesitated. On the one hand, she needed a rest—but was this a prudent place to stay? On the other hand, there were no furnishings or provisions to suggest that Wolves stopped here regularly. She decided to take the chance, sleeping by an empty window frame to allow for a quick escape should the necessity arise.

The morning light revealed the details of occupation which she had not seen the night before. There was some very stale bread, which she pocketed in case of need, and a wide disturbance of the dust round one leg of the rusted bedstead, up against the wall.

Lily realized, with a spurt of anger, that it marked where Malin had been tied to the leg of the bed—as though he were a dog on a leash! He didn't appear to have slept much. But at least he was alive, and moving.

There was also a piece of broken stone within the semi-circle of disturbed dust. Lily spent some time trying to elucidate the significance of the stone—its type, its placement and so forth—before realizing, with embarrassment, that the stone itself meant nothing. Malin had just been using it to scratch a pattern on the wall.

She crouched down and looked closer. It was not the finest of artistic mediums, and had probably not been executed under the most favourable conditions, but it appeared to be a violet.

Lily sat back on her heels and contemplated this. A violet. *Faithfulness* or *modesty*. Or it could be a reference to Gran Vi. Or just a sign of Malin getting bored. Perhaps not—he wouldn't have gone to the trouble of carving something into the wall. It must be meant for someone to see. Someone who would understand its message.

Lily bit her lip. Had Malin guessed that she would be following his path? Or hoped? Enough that he thought it worth going to some trouble to leave a message for her. But what was it? She tried to remember what she'd told Malin about violets.

She stared at the rough flower, willing it to give up its secrets, and then her gaze sharpened. She looked closer, nose practically pressed against the wall. The scratching was shadowed by the bedstead, but, looking close, she could clearly see that there was only one petal pointing down, not two. One central petal. Which meant it *wasn't* a violet. It was a heartsease flower. *You occupy my thoughts.*

Lily gazed at it until she could see it even when she closed her eyes. *You occupy my thoughts.* Of course, she reminded herself, he might well be thinking about the nearness of Restoration Day—as should she. Time to be going.

She shook the dust out of her skirts and stepped out of the door, to be confronted by chaos. The garden, seen by day, was overgrown and full of weeds, with self-seeded vegetables pushing through here and there. Flowers, cultivated and wild, ran riot over all. And added to this was trampling, broken stems, hacked branches—and blood.

Dried blood, dark on the trampled leaves. There had obviously been a struggle here, of some dimensions. It wasn't a lot of blood, but it was enough to make her feel uneasy. Someone had been injured here. She looked closer. Those bootprints...she'd seen them before. She'd followed them over half the kingdom. Malin—on his own two feet! An escape attempt, perhaps.

She could see the scrapings of mud off his boots where he'd climbed into the rhododendron. Had it broken under his weight, or was that a slashing cut from a Wolf? Below lay a handful of torn-off oleander leaves. Climbing the tree to get away was understandable, although it didn't seem to lead anywhere. The oleander made less sense. He could hardly expect to have a chance of poisoning his captors with the leaves.

She stared at the dark leaves, with the rhododendron dangling over them, and remembered the heartsease. Malin was leaving messages for her.

Rhododendron, oleander. *Danger. Beware.*

Harm's Way

Lily took the warning seriously. If Malin believed she was alive, Evil Uncle Phelan might very well be of the same opinion, and what could be more dangerous than following him into the very centre of his power?

Caution must be her watchword, and she must make sure that no one saw her. She could not take the chance, even if their speech showed them the truest of loyal subjects—it could so easily be a trap.

Privately heaping elaborate confections of abuse on her uncle for thus driving a wedge between people and creating an atmosphere of mutual suspicion and mistrust, she paced on.

> *And the people shall fall silent*
> *in the shadow of their dread...*

This was all just like the Fate. No—wait. Lily stopped dead, chills crawling across her skin as the Fate slowly unwound in her mind.

> *When the round of life is broken*
> *with the breaking of the year;*
> *When the orphan and the widow*
> *weep in darkness and in fear;*
> *When the kin of Vale have weakened*
> *till they cannot bear the load;*

When the heartless masters beat them
to their knees under the goad;
When the people are divided
from each other and the land;
When their holdings are abandoned
into few and grasping hands;
When the land cannot lie fallow,
but is stripped of all it bears;
When the dead cannot lie easy
in the land that once was theirs;
When the poor man's debts shall drive him
into thralldom for his bread;
And the people shall fall silent
in the shadow of their dread;
Then, in hunger, crops shall dwindle
under flood and slip and frost;
To a foreigner's dominion
shall the land at last be lost.

This wasn't *like* the Fate; this *was* the Fate. She saw it clearly, end to end, through the past fifteen years and on to the future, when Uncle Phelan would eventually die, and his place would be taken by one of his Wolves.

"To a foreigner's dominion shall the land at last be lost," Lily whispered.

Unless…unless the land could be restored. Restoration Day wasn't just needed for the health of the land and its magic—it was the key to Arcelia's continued existence. Realizing just what rested on her shoulders, Lily hastened on.

The combination of Aunt Hortensia's dancing lessons and Malin's more recent guidance had given her a talent for walking silently, and she used it to the full, moving as fast as she could, and stopping neither to rest nor to forage.

So much for being the cynosure of all eyes, she reflected once more, as she waited in the shelter of a spreading shrub for a plodding traveller to pass by. Although one would hardly wish to attract attention in this condition, with bare, muddy feet and ill-fitting clothes that hadn't been washed in…far too long.

At least they were holding up well to the rigours of travel. She blenched at the thought of what her shell-pink satin dress would have looked like by now, and then flushed with embarrassment at the memory of her ungracious response to Malin's thoughtful provision of wearable clothes. Malin…

She got up and walked on. He had come to her rescue. She had not gone to his. Had there ever been a chance? Would he have expected her to take it if there had been? Or wanted her to? Restoration Day was the main thing, of course, but could she have helped him, and still reached Denton in time? It was too late now. Malin was in Denton, and though she would be there in time for Restoration Day, it was more than likely that it would be too late for Malin.

Angrily, she told herself that it was foolish to be so upset; that Malin had known what he was doing, and had always been willing to die for his cause.

That she would never see him again should not make her so distraught; she had only known him for two or three weeks, and she had not enjoyed either the experience, or his company, for a large part of that time. She would go back to her world, and he would be remembered only as a loyal son of Burnaby who had done his part for freedom.

Life would go on. She would marry—

She cut the thought off. She was only eighteen. There was no rush. As queen, she could not be proposed to; she would have the freedom to wait until she was ready. But she could not wait forever. Arcelia would need an heir to follow her.

One day, she would have to choose someone. One of those faceless princes of her childish dreams? She snorted, unladylike as it was. There was the problem. She wasn't a little fairy-

tale princess any more; she was Lily, queen of an all too real
and troubled kingdom, and whomever she married would be
a real person, too, and try as she might, she couldn't bring herself to think about it.

She sighed. There was no point in lying to herself, but nor
was there any point in dwelling on what could never be. Better
by far to keep her mind on what was passing about her, and
the task that lay ahead.

The clumps of trees had been thickening for some time
now, Arcelia's natural covering of forest asserting itself in
little patches which became more and more common. Evil
Uncle Phelan may have been harvesting trees at an unsustain-
able rate, but at least the destruction had not yet ranged all
over.

Lily avoided the hamlets, which grew more common the
closer she drew to Denton. And she was drawing close, of
that she had no doubt. These low, rich soils were the flood-
plain of Parsifal. By what would have been tea time—had she
had anything to eat—she could hear the rushing of his waters.

Suddenly, the battered trail she had been following for
nearly two days swung away to the left. Lily stopped and
stared at it. So Phelan had turned away, to ride parallel to the
river. She must still be to the north of Denton, then. Should
she keep following his trail? Or would it lead straight into a
trap?

Lily moved into the deeper coolness of the trees, rested her
head against rough bark, and tried to ignore the gnawing in
her stomach. She must think clearly. She was close to Denton
now, and Restoration Day was not till the day after tomorrow.

There was no point marching up to the gates again. She
would have to plan how and when to make her entrance, try
to find out what was happening and plan accordingly, and
she had one clear day to do it. All that haste had served her
well—so long as she was not discovered in the meantime.

But, first, she had to get across Parsifal. No doubt the bridges would be guarded; she couldn't just walk across, as Evil Uncle Phelan's cohort had no doubt done. She sighed. Swimming again. Best to get the lie of the land first; that's what Malin would have done.

She slipped from shadow to shadow among the trees, following the sound of the water. She stood on the bank, her feet slowly sinking into the expanse of silty mud, and took a quick and cautious look along the river.

Just as she had thought, she noted with satisfaction as she pulled back into the shelter of the trees. There was a bridge upstream, towards Denton, where Uncle Phelan would have crossed. But it was closer than she had anticipated and heavily guarded to boot. They were on the lookout, without a doubt, and, even at this distance, she doubted she would make it across the river unnoticed.

Lily hissed with frustration. She would have to wait for dusk, *again*. And then she stiffened. There were voices in the forest behind her; Easterling voices. Her eyes darted about, seeking a hiding place. No branches low enough to climb. No chance in the river. She looked down.

At least, she told herself, it was good Arcelian mud, the very earth she was struggling to reclaim. When she had thoroughly coated herself, she slid on her belly into the shadow of a tree and lay still, scarcely daring to breathe.

A voice called in the distance—were they leaving? But the reply came from close at hand; they had spread out, and were combing the woods for her.

The hair on the back of her neck struggled to stand up under the cold blanket of the muddy cloak. A lady's breathing is never audible, Aunt Hortensia's voice reminded her, and she compelled her burning lungs to start a slow intake and exhale.

A Wolf splattered through the mud to the riverbank (*footprints*, Lily thought, *I must have left footprints!*) and shouted up to the bridge. A shout came back. Nothing seen. He swore and splattered back again, complaining about the state of his boots. The voices died away, and, after waiting another age, to be sure they weren't coming back, Lily lifted her head and looked at the mud where the Wolf had trod.

There were his deep prints, coming and going, and there—there was the mark of her rolling, which must have wiped away her prints. Good Arcelian earth! And it was only another hour, if that, till dusk. Then she could swim across Parsifal—losing most of the mud on the way, she hoped—and then she would...she would...

Lily lay on her face in the mud and looked at the situation. She had no one to turn to, nowhere to go, and no idea of what to do next.

⚜   ⚜   ⚜

By the time night fell, Lily had made up her mind. She would cross the river and try to find out what was happening in Denton. Eavesdropping was not very ladylike, but a lady could do a great deal in defence of her country that would be most unsuitable in general social situations.

Stifling a groan at the stiffness of her joints—not to mention the stiffness of her cloak, which had dried in a sort of muddy carapace over her—she slithered down to the water and slipped in as silently as she could manage.

Parsifal was deep—that was how the *Scintilla* could have sailed right up to Denton—and his current was fast, under his deceptively smooth surface. But at least he was carrying her away from the bridge, and not towards it.

She paddled on, careful not to splash, and kept a wary ear turned towards the bridge. Sound travelled over water, and if she could hear them, they would certainly hear any noise she was foolish enough to make. Her ears picked up a slow, dull tramp of boots, nothing more. They had not noticed her—yet.

Her aching limbs protested, but she made them keep moving. The night was dark and she could not see the other side, but surely she would reach it in time, if she just kept moving...

It was unexpected when it arrived: a sprawling tree root which somehow avoided her reaching hands and banged her in the face. She let out a yelp, and then froze. Had they heard her?

There was no point waiting around, either way. Her instinct told her to haul herself up and flee, but she controlled herself, and slowly, oh, so slowly, pulled herself up out of the water and onto the muddy, tree-ridged bank. She lay still for a moment, the water running off her in streams.

Must. Keep. Going.

Lily could feel the weakness in her limbs, the result, she supposed, of too much travel on too little food. Well, it couldn't be helped now. She pushed herself up into a sitting position and looked back across the river. Cold as she was, the sight chilled her further.

The Wolves were back, and they were searching with chemical lanterns, a light from which there was no hiding, a sun that could circle a tree and strip every shadow.

Devoutly thankful that she had wasted no time in crossing, she clambered to her feet and slowly squelched away from the bank, feeling her way through the trees. A flicker of light troubled the corner of her eye, and she shook her head. Perhaps she was seeing things. A twig cracked in the same direction, and this time she turned her head. The unearthly blue light of a chemical lantern glared between the distant trees in the direction of Denton.

Casting caution aside, she turned and fled, colliding with trees, tripping, falling, crawling, running away from the light. Crashing behind her told her that she was discovered, and being pursued, and she ran the faster, her breath coming in ragged, tearing gasps. She could feel blood trickling down her face from a collision with a particularly angular tree, but she did not stop to wipe it away. Already blinded by the darkness, what was a second blinding?

But what if they could track her by the blood? She staggered to her feet again, and there was an unexpected moment of silence. She froze. It was dark; all she could see were the fading after-images of that first terrified look at the chemical lantern's glare. She was alone. She took a sobbing breath, and a hand reached out of the darkness and seized her by the shoulder, spinning her around.

Lily shrieked, and was blinded by the sudden glare of the unshuttered lantern. It swung away as she gazed in mute terror, and illuminated the face of her captor. It was Holly. Holly a long way away in the bubble of light, and then only darkness.

⚜   ⚜   ⚜

"Lily!" a voice hissed. "Princess! Er, queen! I mean, my lady!"

Lily blinked and sat up, her head swimming. Holly. It *was* Holly, his face scrunched with anxiety.

"I'm fine," she said, shaking her head. "I just need…a bit of a rest…"

"Not here," Holly said, helping her to her feet.

"What happened to—"

"Not here," Holly repeated. "Like as not, they'll be searching this side next."

The thought of this was enough to get Lily to her feet, and she staggered away, leaning on Holly's supporting arm.

"I've found a sort of disused outbuilding," Holly whispered as they came to the wide pourstone road, crumbling and overgrown at the edges. He checked for any unwelcome eyes, and hurried her across to the shelter of a shadowy wall. "It's not quite what you're used to, but…"

"You wouldn't believe what I'm used to," Lily said with the ghost of a laugh. "As long as we won't be found."

"Safe as houses," Holly said briskly, leading her around a corner and down an overgrown lane, bordered on one side by the patchy trees still fringing the dump, and on the other side by the walls and fences of workshop yards. "Safer, really, because houses have people in them."

"It's awfully quiet," Lily said, looking about warily. "There wasn't even anyone on the road, and it's not that far past dusk."

"Curfew," Holly replied, squeezing his bulk between two palings of a rather dilapidated fence. "All clear. Phelan's making sure there's no one around to see you except his men."

"And you," Lily said gratefully, following him through the gap.

"Well," Holly said, with just a trace of smugness, "these chemical lanterns make surprisingly good cover. People see it bobbing about in the distance, assume you're a Wolf, and don't stay to ask questions. They're awfully clever, too, the design—in here, my lady."

It was a tiny shed, barely long enough to lie down in, and not much wider. But it was quiet, and Holly said it was safe, and she was so tired... She dropped to the floor and leaned against the wall.

"Tell me everything."

"I'll just turn this down." He squinted at it, stuck out his tongue by way of concentrating, and twiddled a little knob on the side of the lantern.

The light flared, hurting her eyes.

"Whoops! Wrong way..." This time he succeeded in lowering the light to a dim blue glow, and set the lantern down. "Right. Where to start?"

"Candra burned," Lily said. "Start there."

"That was the Hedge, actually. Dried out like a husk after you left, so, of course, it went up like anything. Never been so hot in my life. And then we were besieged, and Sennet was a hero, and—"

"Besieged?" Lily sat up. "You don't mean to tell me that the two of you tried to hold Candra against Phelan and his Wolves?"

Holly puffed out his chest. "Tried, and succeeded." The chest deflated a little. "For a while, anyway."

"But why? You must have known it was no good! Candra's a summer palace, not a fortress!"

Holly looked a bit abashed. "Sennet's idea, really. We thought, what with Phelan charging up the hill and all, he must think you were there, so…"

"So you thought you'd sacrifice yourselves just to buy me some time?" Lily could feel the tears welling up.

"More or less. Though we didn't have to, in the end. Obviously. I, um, played a bit of a trick to get Sennet out safely, and he was that cross!"

"What? And why? And where is he, and…?"

"One at a time! He was all for a last stand, thought he'd fall on his sword or something, and then he came to in Renwick and wasn't best pleased about being carried out of the castle like that. No retreat! You know. He's a bit old-fashioned, is Sennet."

"But where is he now?"

Holly sobered. "Phelan has him. They were neither of them fit to run, and they told me to go, so I did, but the Wolves got them, and word is they're locked up in Denton, in the dungeons."

"They?" Lily asked, not daring to hope.

Holly smiled hugely. "The Lady Hortensia. We happened across a cave, and…"

"You managed to wake her up? Oh, thank you!"

Holly coughed. "Not me you should be thanking. Not to say I didn't try—in a purely medicinal manner—" he hastened to add, "but, no, it was most definitely Master Sennet who did the waking, if you take my drift."

"You mean he—?"

"I wasn't there exactly," Holly admitted, "but I could see which way the wind was blowing."

So there was hope. Hope—and, with it, the fear of hope lost again.

"Now, tell me all about what you've been up to, you young scamp of a runaway! Which is to say, my lady. Not that I haven't heard a few things in my intelligence-gathering sorties," he added.

"Have you heard anything about Malin?" she asked hopefully. "He's a dwarf, he—" She saw the look on his face and fell silent. "He's dead, isn't he?" Her heart sank within her.

"No, no. Prisoner. Closely guarded. I'm afraid…I'm afraid Phelan's planning something."

"When we first met, he said Phelan was saving him up to execute on Restoration Day," Lily said miserably. "And now he can, because I can't stop him—can I?"

"No, I don't think you can," Holly said sorrowfully, and Lily burst into tears.

When she finally lifted her head, Holly's handkerchief was on her knee, and Holly himself was drying his eyes with his sleeve.

"I'm so sorry," he said, "but if you try, you're sure to get killed—you wouldn't believe how tight security is at the gate, I saw them pulling an old woman's hair to see if it was real, I give you my word—and he'll be just as doomed if you're dead. And so will the rest of us," he added lugubriously.

"It's just—" Lily gulped. "He saved my life so many times, and then he let himself get caught so I could get away, and—" The tears threatened to overwhelm her again.

"Now, now, none of that. You've had your cry out. Now, supposing you tell me all about it."

So, taking a deep breath and pulling her shaky self together, Lily told him all the long tale of her travels: the cave, meeting

Malin, the explosion ("That's my girl! Er, queen!"), the Council of Burnaby, Woodward being so nearly dead—that made him suck his teeth thoughtfully—the slip, the song, finding the horn, losing the horn (Holly punching the air vigorously to show just what he would like to do to this Millipede fellow, if he caught him), the riot, the gentleman pirate, Laurel's trap and the explosive escape from it ("This Malin sounds like my sort of, er, dwarf,"), and the run from inn to inn as Phelan closed in.

By the time she reached the events at the waterfall, his eyes were round and fixed on her face, and he leaned closer and closer as the tale wound on through the desolation of the Last Quarter, the double discovery of the Lunula, and the long run towards Denton.

"And, then, there you were," Lily said, and leaned back, conscious, at last, of how weary she was, and realizing just how much she'd put herself through, especially in the last few days.

Holly drew a long breath. "*Well.* You do live, don't you?"

Lily managed a wan smile. "It's a nice change from people telling me I'm dead. But, Holly, I feel like such a fool. Nearly every step along the way, I've done the wrong thing, or said the wrong thing, and—" she burned with shame to admit it, but the time for pretence was long past, "—I don't know what to do. I don't know how I'm going to make Restoration Day happen."

"My dear lady," Holly said, "you're alive, and you've got all the Requisites. If that's your idea of being a fool, you're not very good at it."

Lily considered this. "But I've needed so much help! All the way along I've—"

"We all need help," Holly said. "You'd be daft not to accept it."

"But I—" She froze, and dropped her voice back to a whisper. "Did you hear that?"

Holly's eyes widened. They had both become so caught up in each other's stories, they had forgotten to be cautious. And, now, most distinctly, there was the sound of someone approaching the door. Someone wearing heavy, hobnailed boots.

Lily blanched. There was no way out. Holly set his jaw, got up, and prepared his fist for the newcomer. Lily held her breath.

The door was flung open. Holly's fist arced through the air, and, with a dull clonk, he sank to the ground. Lily's jaw dropped.

Standing in the doorway was an old woman wielding a washing dolly, a thing like a three-legged stool on a stick. She was wearing an old coat over a nightdress, and a grim look.

Holly groaned. A young head appeared at the old washerwoman's side and surveyed the scene.

"Oh!" the girl said, and her mouth formed a perfect O of astonishment.

"You stay in the house like you were told, Sweetie," the old woman scolded.

"That's the lady who helped when the nasty man grabbed me," Sweetie said, and, as she squeezed past the old woman, her face caught the light, and Lily recognized her.

"Oh!" she said. "I'm so glad you're safe."

She smiled warmly, and the old woman gasped, dropped the dolly and grabbed for the doorframe.

"Auntie Clo!" The girl stopped smiling at Lily and turned to support her aunt.

"Perhaps we'd all best go in," Lily said, and this seemed to decide the question. "I think my friend may need some help."

Holly got muzzily to his feet. The two pairs of helped and helper moved across the muddy yard, Holly slithering dangerously. So that was why the old lady was wearing pattens, Lily realized. She'd taken the clink of the metal rings for hobnailed boots.

She wiped her feet carefully before entering a large humid room which smelled so strongly of soap it had to be a laundry room. They passed through it to a small though warm and cheerful kitchen, where Sweetie deposited her aunt in a chair. Lily did likewise for Holly, whom she could now see had a large bruised bump forming on his head.

"I'll get your vinegar," Sweetie promised her aunt, and, a moment later, she waved a little bottle under her aunt's nose.

Her aunt breathed in sharply and rose to her feet. "Clover and Sweetbriar at your service, my lady," she said, wavering as she stood, "and I'm terrible sorry about the dolly."

"Perfectly understandable under the circumstances," Lily said, "and do please sit down yourself. You aren't well."

"Nor is he," said the old woman with a hastily-stifled cackle. "Sweetie, get a cold cloth for the gentleman."

"Urghh," Holly said, and, then, as the cloth was applied, "Ow."

Lily swayed gently, the room seeming to sway with her.

"Best sit down before you fall down, my lady," Clover said, and Lily sank gently into a chair proffered by the ever-helpful Sweetbriar. "And what can we do for you? You look like you could use a good meal and a warm bed."

"Oh, *yes*," Lily said faintly, surprised to find her head was on the kitchen table.

"And a bath, if you don't mind me saying so," Clover added, her voice coming from a great distance.

Food appeared in front of her, and she ate it. A bath appeared, and she got in. The last thing she remembered was Clover carrying her clothes away at arm's length, draped over the washing dolly. She sank into a deep unrestful sleep, dreaming of water and fire and terror and running, always running.

⚜   ⚜   ⚜

There was no peaceful moment of forgetfulness on waking, either. She woke with the first light through the worn curtains, and it was all there: her aunt and Sennet prisoners, the Wolves combing the banks for her, Malin a prisoner under sentence of death—and Restoration Day tomorrow.

A quick, panicked look reassured her that the Key and the Horn were still safe—and had been given a clean, by the look of them. The Lunula was still around her neck, incongruous against Sweetbriar's best pink nightgown with its sprinkling of little embroidered flowers.

There was a brisk knock at the door and Clover came in, carrying a pile of clothes. Lily's clothes, clean and pressed.

"How did you do that?" Lily asked, half afraid that she'd slept a day away and it was Restoration Day already.

Clover's thin lips bent into a smile. "Craft secrets, my lady. Your friend's better this morning, asking if he can see you."

"Oh! I'll come down," Lily said, pushing the covers back and getting to her feet.

"There'll be some breakfast in a minute," Clover added, and left Lily alone to dress.

The cuirass was stiff and hard to fasten, but she wasn't going to risk going without. Not today. She was closer to danger than ever before, and there was nothing to do but wait, and try to think of a plan.

You have a day, she reminded herself, as she slung the Horn across her chest and slipped the Key back into its concealment. A lot can happen in a day.

❧   ❧   ❧

A lot did happen that day, and little of it good. Sweetbriar was sent off after breakfast to deliver yesterday's clean laundry to the garrison in Denton. Holly went along as a spare pair of hands and ears, as he put it. Lily felt adrift without him, but seeing how the tension drained from Clover when Holly volunteered to keep an eye on her niece, she restrained the urge to recall him.

"I'd go myself and spare her," Clover said apologetically, as Sweetbriar set off with Holly pulling the basket-laden hand-cart, "but I'm not so young as I once was, and with my back, I can't lift the baskets the way I used to. But..."

"But?" Lily asked. There was something significant here, something not to be blurted out.

"I'm a loyalist," Clover said. "Have been since before there was need of a word for it, and I don't see myself changing now. But I know how to keep my mouth shut. Sweetie...she thinks all the world's her friend. You know how it is. Some are just born like that. Particularly to the older mothers, I've noticed, and Sweetie's mother was—well, she was too old, that was the way of it, and that was how we lost her." She stared hard at the old iron stove.

"I'm sorry," Lily said. It didn't do any good, but you had to say something, to show that the other's pain had not gone unnoticed.

"She's been a joy to me all her life," Clover said, "and I had her from two, when her father went to the War and never re-turned. But she doesn't know when to keep her silence, and that's a fact. I'm not blaming her, but there it is. She said what she oughtn't to have said in the hearing of some of them high-ups, and I heard it got to the Magister himself. Whichever way it was, they sent me that." She gestured to a shadowy corner of the kitchen.

Surprised, Lily got up and looked. It was a box, long, nar-row, and dark, just large enough for a person to lie down. A burying-box.

"He's not one for what you might call the crude threat," Clo-ver said, "but he got his message across, clear enough."

Lily suppressed a shiver.

"Since then," Clover continued with a sigh, "I've had to tell

Sweetie she's not to talk to anyone about anything but laundry, doesn't matter who they are. It's hard on her, poor girl, because she can't talk to her friends any more, but what else can I do?"

Lily considered this, and admitted that there did not appear to be any alternatives.

"If it wasn't for Sweetie," Clover said, melancholy mantling her thin face, "I'd face it out and damn the consequences—pardon my language, my lady—but if something happens to me, what'll happen to her? Doesn't bear thinking about." She got up from the table and busied herself with the breakfast dishes.

Lily silently took up a cloth and dried as Clover washed, treating each piece with the same care Aunt Hortensia had insisted on for each piece of the Queen Magnolia tea set. Clover looked sideways at her, but ventured no comment.

They had finished the dishes and begun work in the laundry room ("Best you keep away from the windows, my lady,") when they heard the patter of feet, and Sweetbriar came rushing in, pink in the face and nearly out of breath.

"Sweetie!" Clover cried.

"Holly?" Lily cried, fearing the worst.

Sweetbriar flapped a hand behind her. "He's too fat to run fast."

"Sweetie!" Clover said, scandalized.

"He said to run home fast and tell you, so I did," Sweetie said.

"Tell us what?" Lily asked, a dark hand clenching at her vitals.

"The little man is tied to the big pole in the square, and people say Magister's going to chop him dead."

Lily sank to the floor, her legs losing all their strength. She had expected this, but, somehow, now that it had arrived, she could not bear it. There was a pounding of feet approaching, and Holly burst in, red and sweating.

"Did you tell them?" he puffed.

"She told us," Clover said, her face grim.

"Quick, then," Holly panted. "They'll be here any minute!"

"Who will?" Lily asked sharply.

He stared at her for a moment. "Wolves! Didn't she tell— never mind that. They're doing a search, house to house and they're not far away."

Lily sprang to her feet and looked about the room for a hiding place.

"Not in here, my lady," Clover said. "Leastways, not unless you can hold your breath in a cold copper for as long as it takes."

"But where…"

"They're going through the yards as well," Holly said, his breath returning.

There was a moment's frozen silence.

"The box," Clover said decisively, leading the way into the kitchen. "They'd not think of looking there."

Lily looked at the shadowy box with a cold horror prickling her skin.

Holly looked over her shoulder and shuddered. "I don't ever want to see you in one of those, Lily, my lady."

"Better alive in a box than dead out of one," Lily said, climbing in.

Holly helped Clover settle the lid precisely into place again, and, as they did so, there came the sound of banging on the front door. Lily drew in her breath and reminded herself to keep breathing, slow and sure.

The door opened, and harsh voices sounded over the trampling of feet. The sounds came to Lily clearly, though they seemed at a greater distance than she knew they could be. The Wolves were in the room with her. There was no running now.

They were making a thorough job of it, she could tell. Every room in the house was turned upside down; crashes and bangs came from the yard. There must be a Pack, or more than one, combing the area. Looking for her.

It seemed she lay in the dark box for an hour or more, but she was sure it could not have been more than a quarter of an hour before the Wolves were once more in the kitchen. They were no gentler there than they had been anywhere else, and Lily heard more than one piece of crockery smash.

Footsteps. Closer. Closer. Stopping by her head, standing over her.

"Look at this, boys!" a rough voice shouted. "What do we have here?"

Clover's voice replied, tight and hostile. "You know very well what that is."

The Wolf roared with laughter. "A present from the Magister! Better remember to be a good girl, hadn't you?"

The other Wolves joined in his laughter, adding a few coarse suggestions which made Lily's ears burn. Then they tramped away, slamming the door behind them, and were gone.

A strange, high-pitched, jerky sound remained behind, and, after a moment's focus, Lily identified it. Clover, trying her hardest not to cry. Lily's eyes filled with sympathetic tears.

"Have my hankie," Holly said, "and a chair. I'll just pop the kettle on. Best stay put a bit longer if you can bear it," he added, his tone unchanged. It took Lily a moment to realize he was now talking to her.

"Better alive in a box than dead out of one," she whispered, and, at that moment, the idea bloomed fully-formed in her mind. Now, at last, she knew how she would get into Denton.

⚜   ⚜   ⚜

Holly took some convincing, as she had known he would. It was not, he was adamant, the danger to himself that bothered him. He'd been prepared to lay down his life for his sovereign before, and he was ready to do it again. But he couldn't stom-

ach the possibility of Lily laying down her life. They argued it
back and forth.

"I won't do it," he said, wearing his most mulish look. "After
all these years of helping keep you safe, you think I'd just hand
you over to your worst enemy? What kind of loyalist do you
take me for?"

"The kind who does what his queen tells him," Lily said,
and the mulish look slipped.

He sighed heavily. "All right. I still don't think it's a good
idea, but if you order me, my lady, I will do it."

She smiled. "Thank you, Holly."

He sighed again. "It's Deni, actually."

"*Deni?*" Lily repeated. "You mean—you're—but—"

"Must've been that clong on the head last night," Holly, or,
rather, Deni, said. "It all just popped back. Even Da dying,"
he added miserably.

"Oh, Holly—I mean, Deni…" Lily's eyes overflowed again.

"Call me Holly," he said. "I'm used to it."

"Your family," Lily said in consternation. "You must go back
to them!"

Holly straightened his back. "Not till after tomorrow."

"But, Holly!"

"No," he said, and Lily had never heard such strength in his
voice before. "I went to war to see Phelan put in his place, and
I'm not going home till I do. And if I don't make it home, well,
it's no difference to them now, is it?"

He wiped his eyes on his sleeve, having distributed all his
handkerchiefs, and chopped the vegetables for the soup with
more than necessary force.

"Holly—"

"We'd better be thinking through tomorrow while we have
the time," he said, and Lily let it drop.

There were only a few preparations to be made—Clover
offered the use of their handcart and Sweetbriar suggested

flour—and then there was nothing she could do but wait.

Holly muttered his way back and forth through his story while pottering about the kitchen; Clover and Sweetbriar busied themselves with the day's laundering; and Lily sat in the corner by the box, ready to clamber back in at a moment's notice. There was no use trying to plan further ahead. She would have to improvise as the situation unfolded. That left only one avenue for her mind to pursue, fruitless as it was.

"Did you see him?" she asked.

"Hm?" Holly turned from the stove, where he was stirring lunch. "Who?"

"Malin."

"'Fraid so. Chained to a pillar in the square."

"How did he look?" She didn't want to know, but she had to.

Holly sighed. "Black and blue. A bit bloodied. But no bones broken, if I'm any judge."

A pang went through her. "Holly, isn't there some way I could—"

He put the wooden spoon down and turned to face her fully, arms folded across Clover's striped pinny. "Now, you listen to me, young lady. Queen you may be, but fool you aren't, and if you don't know a trap when you see one, it's time you learned."

"A trap?"

Holly rolled his eyes. "If Phelan only wanted him executed, he'd execute him, no messing about. All this display—it's there to get the attention. Your attention. He's trying to lure you into the open, and Malin's the bait."

"I—I just can't help thinking how he must be feeling. Chained there, waiting, and wondering if I'm going to just leave him there to—to die." She had another weep into Holly's spare handkerchief.

"If he's the person you've made him out to be," Holly said,

"he's more likely standing there hoping like mad you'll have the sense to stay away. What price the bait once the trap's sprung?"

This was undeniably true, and it steadied her.

"He's made his grand gesture, my lady, and if you waste that, you'll be making a fool of yourself *and* him."

Lily told herself to be sensible, dried her eyes, and composed herself again.

"While there's life, there's hope," Holly encouraged her. "He's no use to Phelan dead, and Phelan's not one to waste his resources unnecessarily."

"Hope is a good deal less than certainty," Lily said, forcing a watery smile. "I only hope Phelan's famous efficiency is not on peak form tomorrow morning."

Holly grimaced. "No use worrying till we get there."

No use, true. But all through that long and weary day, Lily's mind kept drifting to a stocky figure, lashed by chains to a pillar of cold stone. She watched night fall, at last, with a weary patience. If all went according to plan, she would not see Restoration Day dawn.

Restoration Day

Lily lay in the pre-dawn darkness and wondered if she would even know when light began to dawn. The box was sturdily made, and the lid had been well nailed down. Was she the first to know how loud nailing sounded from inside a burying-box?

The handcart jounced suddenly—a pothole?—and her elbow banged painfully against the side. She suppressed a gasp, and hoped it was not much further to the gates.

The damp of her freshly muddied clothes clung clammily about her. It had gone very much against the grain for Clover to dirty clean clothes, but Sweetbriar had helped with a will, and Lily now looked as filthy as if she'd dragged herself through every mudpuddle in the kingdom.

Her face was likewise muddied, with a deathly pallor courtesy of Clover's best baking flour. The Requisites were concealed from view by the artful draping of her cloak, which, she ardently hoped as they bounced over another hole, would not be shaken loose too soon.

"Approaching the gate," Holly muttered.

Lily understood. There would be no more communication from Holly, and she must be as silent as the dead.

"Who goes there?" the call went up.

"Holly, the cook—former cook—of Candra. The Magister told me to come—said I'd be rewarded."

"Open the box," another Easterling voice said. Authoritative. The guard captain?

"No!" Holly sounded too defensive. Lily tried to remember to breathe, but gently. "No."

"What does a cook bring the Magister in a burying-box? A very big cake?" They laughed.

"I'm bringing him what he's been looking for," Holly said significantly.

The laughing stopped. There was a silence so complete Lily could hear a bird singing in the far-off distance.

"We'll take it from here," the captain said.

"And steal all the credit?" Holly said. "No—I'm not turning coat for nothing."

"You'll get your reward. Pass it over."

"No! I'm taking this to the Magister and no one else," Holly said stubbornly. "And he won't be happy you kept him waiting for good news from a key ally."

"A key ally?" The captain snorted. "A fat cook?"

"I'm a valuable informant," Holly said. "In deep with the royalist's counsels. The Magister's man on the inside, that's me. Someone they trust."

"*Do* they trust you?"

"*She* did," Holly said, and the captain laughed. It was not a pleasant laugh, and Lily felt the hairs rise on the back of her neck.

"Open the gate for the fat cook," the captain called. "And escort him all the way to the door."

"That's more like it," Holly said, and, the next minute, they were moving again, rattling over paving stones to the accompaniment of marching feet.

Lily's heart beat faster. Her plan had succeeded. She was in Denton—and in the greatest danger of her life.

There was no sound in the streets but the scrape of the hand-cart's wheels and the ring of the nailed boots on the cobbles. The streets were empty. Lily felt a twinge of fear. The Restoration Day rite needed the presence of the people. Could Phelan thwart her so easily?

The echoes changed as they moved into an open space. The square already? She tried to remember what little she had seen of the layout of Denton on her previous visit.

"Hey!" The sudden shout, close at hand, made her start, and she fervently hoped the movement would be taken as a wobble of the cart. "Hey, shorty, guess who we've got here?" And a fist banged on the lid of her box.

Lily's straining ears caught a clink of chains, and a hoarse, croaking voice which poured out denunciations, execrations, and a positive diatribe of vivid threats. And despite the language—which would have made Aunt Hortensia blench— Lily's heart sang, because, hoarse and choking as the voice was, it was undoubtedly Malin's, and no dead dwarf could shout like that.

The Wolves laughed derisively and moved on. Fear closed around her again. Malin was closer to death than ever before, now that he was no longer needed as bait. With every fibre of her being, she willed Phelan to have left no standing orders for Malin's execution. Malin might yet survive. But only if she succeeded…

"You can't take that cart inside," one of the Wolves said. "We'd better carry it from here."

Lily was thankful for the warning as they swung her suddenly into the air. They quickly fell into step, and she began to feel rather ill as the box swayed from side to side atop their shoulders. Tilting—they were going up the stairs. There was a creak as the door opened, and hurrying footsteps came towards them as they moved through the entryway.

"What's this?" a fretful voice enquired. "Here is not the place for burying-boxes, and you know it!"

"Special delivery for the Magister," a Wolf replied significantly.

"You mean...oh! Well, I dare say he's at work already. Today of all days," the fretful voice muttered.

"There is nothing special about this day," the Wolf reminded him. "Business as usual." His voice was faintly threatening.

"Of course," the fretful man replied, on the defence. "But you know as well as I do, it takes effort to keep it that way."

"We'll go straight up," the Wolf said, and they moved sickeningly into motion again, although at least they were on the flat—for now. This must be the great hall with the chequered floor, Lily thought. We shall have a ball here, she told herself, trying to distract her uneasy stomach. When all this is over, a ball...

The box tipped again; they were going up the great stairs. The stairs down which, she told herself fiercely, she would make her entrance, *alone,* regardless of what Aunt Hortensia thought.

Aunt Hortensia, who was probably in this very building, she realized. What Aunt Hortensia would think of her current method of ascending the stairs, she didn't like to think, but at least she could say she wasn't unaccompanied!

Lily fought down the urge to giggle hysterically and focussed on keeping her breathing smooth and even. It seemed to help the nausea, which surged as the Wolves carried her around the hairpin turn of the great stair.

Not far now... They were on the flat, and—yes, there was the knock at the door.

"Come!" a distant voice barked, and Lily went cold all over. Memories of the waterfall rushed in on her.

The door opened, she swayed forward, and stopped.

"You?" Phelan said.

"I...I thought about what you said, sir," Holly said, and Lily could see, in her mind's eye, the servile wringing of the hands that would accompany the cringing voice. "About progress, and the way things go, and..."

"Get to the point."

"Well, I didn't want to get left behind," Holly gabbled, "and so I've made my choice and I hope you'll see I don't lose by it."

Silence. Lily waited, forcing herself not to tremble.

"I see. Put it down there," Phelan instructed. "I trust you have not left the gates unguarded?"

"No, sir!" The Wolves deposited the box on the floor with more haste than care, before rapidly retreating from the room, closing the door behind them.

"Crowbar?"

"Er, no…" Holly sounded flustered.

"The gate guards may be gullible enough to take your word for the contents," Phelan said. "I am not. Vetch!"

There was someone else present, perhaps the secretary who had seen her in this very office the first night she arrived. So Phelan was not outnumbered. Not yet. A dull scrabble in the corner was followed by a clonk.

What kind of person keeps a crowbar in their office? Lily wondered as Holly began prising the lid loose. *A very prepared person,* the answer came back. She shivered and closed her eyes all but a crack, going limp all over. Thankfully, the cuirass would cover the faint signs of her breathing—as long as he didn't hold a mirror to her lips…

With a groan, the lid came loose, and Holly, panting from the exertion, set it down beside the box. A harsh light testified to the presence of chemical lanterns in the room. A shadow fell across her face.

"Yes," Phelan said at last. "Where did you find her?"

"In the woods alongside the river, a ways north of here," Holly said, as planned.

"The Easterlings searched there."

Holly coughed tactfully.

"Disappointing," Phelan said, and his tone promised no good to those who had disappointed him. "Vetch, a chit for the disbursement office. Now."

"Here you are," Vetch said. "The disbursement office is to the right as you come down the stairs. They will see to the, ah, financial aspects of the, er, occasion."

Lily waited for Holly's reaction. Should she reveal herself now? No—Phelan must be alone; there were too many variables at present and she could not expect to control them. They had agreed that Holly should stay if he could—what would he do?

"Don't just stand there," Phelan said. "You've done what you came to do."

"Um…" Holly said. "About the, er, the, er…" He flapped a hand at the box.

"No longer your concern," Phelan snapped. "The door is behind you. I advise you to use it."

"But—I thought—proper burial," Holly said, emotion leaking into his voice. "For old times' sake…"

"Vetch, ring the bell," Phelan said. "Have this person removed!" A distant shrill echoed in the cavernous silence of the building.

Interesting, Lily thought. Emotion disquiets him. She filed this away for future reference and focussed her attention on the scene playing out around her.

Holly was blubbing, Phelan's slamming of drawers and slapping down of files revealing his intense irritation.

Running feet sounded in the hall and the door opened.

"Sir?"

"Get him out of here," Phelan said, and, the next moment, a loud "*oof*" indicated that Holly had no intention of going quietly. A mêlée ensued, the progress of which was impossible to follow by ear, one "*oof*" sounding much like another.

"Get out, you incompetents!" Phelan shouted, and the mêlée receded towards the door. "Vetch, see to it he's dealt with properly. I don't need lunatics bursting in on me today of all days."

"Yes, sir," the secretary murmured deferentially, and the door closed, lowering the noise level significantly.

Her heart thudded. Holly had done it. She was alone with her uncle. Her enemy.

Lily prepared to make her move, everything in her poised for the right moment. A creak announced that Phelan was getting up, and a glaring blue light came closer. Coming to gloat? He'd regret that soon enough, she promised herself. She lay in wait. He came closer, until she could practically feel his breath on her cheek.

"Check—" Phelan murmured.

"Mate," Lily replied, her eyes flicking open.

Phelan fell back with a cry, the chemical lantern clanging onto the floor and sputtering out. Lily rose to her feet, towering over him for a moment as he leaned against his desk. His face was pale, she noticed, and his breath was coming quickly.

"Traitor," she hissed. "Regicide! Fratricide! Warmonger! Murderer! Despoiler of your native land!"

He made a visible effort to pull himself together, and pushed himself to his feet. He was considerably taller than her, though he would appear short next to an Easterling, and having to look up at him put a dent in her confidence.

"Call me what you will," he said, and his voice was not quite steady yet, "at least I am not a fool." The imputation was obvious, and Lily's fury blazed.

"Not a fool? To destroy the peace and prosperity of your own land, to subject it to the intimidation of a foreign force, all in the name of profit?"

This cut him on the quick, evidently. Two red spots appeared on his cheeks.

"And what do you understand of prosperity? You and your foolish fairy-tale belief in magic! I can see how it must look to you, of course," he said, and he seemed calmer now, to Lily's disappointment. "You have, no doubt, been taught to regard me as the big bad uncle, the evil usurper. But what I did, I did for the good of Arcelia. I took the people from subsistence to profitability, and, yes, there have been casualties, but that is the price of progress. I did what had to be done. And not for my own power, whatever you may have been told. I am no king."

"Not for your own power?" Lily said, rage bubbling over at his obstinate blindness. "When you have killed, destroyed, laid waste, simply to enforce your own views?"

He opened his mouth to reply, but she cut him off.

"Perhaps in all your evil you meant well. I am prepared to be merciful. But this ends here. Restoration Day has come."

With an effort, he controlled himself. "There will be no restoration." He gave a sharp yank on the bell pull. "Dreams of magic are no match for the force of reality—as your father found to his cost."

They glared at each other in silence.

"The forces of reality appear to be delayed," Lily said, silently blessing Holly for once more buying her time. "Whatever you're paying them, they're not worth it."

Phelan snorted.

"Your first mistake," Lily needled, "was a very simple one, and all your other mistakes flowed from it."

"I never make the same mistake twice," Phelan snapped.

"Nonsense," Lily returned. "You've been making the same mistake for the last fifteen years or more. You've been *wrong*," she dwelt on the word, "about one crucial fact. Magic *is* reality."

"And I suppose," Phelan sneered, "that you're going to trot out onto the balcony and tell all the people—who aren't there, I might add—that magic is somehow going to put everything back the way it was, in complete defiance of the facts."

"No," said Lily, with a sweet smile she hoped would irritate him more, "I'm going to go out on that balcony and make Restoration Day happen."

She unfastened her cloak and let it drop to the floor, revealing the Lunula, the Horn of Vale, and the Persimmon Key on a cord about her wrist.

There was a moment of silence as Phelan's face worked with rage.

"You're frightened of Restoration Day," Lily said softly, "or you wouldn't have gone to all this trouble."

"Encouraging foolish beliefs makes trouble," he snapped back, "that is all."

A patter of footsteps ran up to the door.

"Come in!" Phelan shouted.

"Sir?" the Wolf asked, and then gasped as Lily turned her gaze on him. "Sir, it's—!"

"Shut up," Phelan said. "Get the Hortensia woman brought up from the dungeon. And try not to make a mess of it."

"But, sir—"

"Go," Phelan growled, and the Wolf went, closing the door behind him.

Lily looked at the tall glass windows that opened onto the balcony. It was light outside. Restoration Day.

"Locked," Phelan said, "or did you imagine your magic key would open them?"

"I hadn't thought of that," Lily said candidly.

She stepped out of the box and crossed the floor with a light, almost dancing step. The Key did not open the lock. Phelan laughed quietly. Lily picked up a plain wooden chair which stood against the wall, and hurled it through the window.

As the tinkling of shattered glass died away, she could hear a voice shouting in the distance, deep within the building. It sounded like Sennet, if one could imagine him shouting. She turned.

"Did you say something?" she enquired politely.

Phelan was staring at her as though she had suddenly grown another head.

"Clever," he said, "but ultimately futile. Do not make the mistake of underestimating me. That I have not simply had you arrested should give you cause for concern, not confidence."

He smiled. It was not a pleasant smile. A cold wind gusted through the broken window, and blew down Lily's neck.

Lily's ears pricked up at a familiar tread coming along the passage, and she turned to see her aunt brought in. Her clothes were torn and soiled, but her head was held as high as ever, and, judging by the way her escort was limping, her spirit was undaunted.

"Lily!"

"Don't worry, Aunt Hortensia," Lily said soothingly. "I am quite all right."

"You!" Aunt Hortensia cried, fixing Phelan with a dreadful look.

"I understand that this woman is responsible for your upbringing," Phelan said, addressing himself to Lily and ignoring Aunt Hortensia's flood of vitriolic accusation entirely.

There seemed no point in denying it. "Yes," Lily said.

"That being the case, you would no doubt find it distressing to cause her death," Phelan said calmly, and Aunt Hortensia stopped mid-tirade with a gasp.

Lily looked her uncle in the eye unflinchingly.

"I see we understand each other," he said.

"Aunt Hortensia taught me," Lily said, with careful deliberation, "that a royal lady does not act with consideration for her own feelings, but in accordance with her duty towards others."

"Quite so," Aunt Hortensia said, with quiet dignity.

Lily felt she had never loved her aunt so much as she did at that moment. But the sun had risen, and she must do what she came for. Carefully, she slipped through the broken window and out on to the chilly stone balcony. The square was empty, but for a huddled mass at the bottom of a stone pillar. Malin in his chains.

"I must admit, I am somewhat impressed," Phelan said, and there was a note of grudging respect in his voice. "I had no idea you could be so...ruthless."

Lily turned back to see his pale face smiling in the dim room. Ruthless? Was she—ruthless?

"You are my flesh and blood, after all," Phelan remarked, and moved closer to the window. "Perhaps I have been over-hasty—tried to bring about change too soon. Perhaps," his eye held hers, "there is room for royalty after all, in this new Arcelia. After all," he gave a little deprecating laugh, "I will not live forever, and who better to succeed me at the helm of state than my own niece? You have..." he seemed to be selecting his words carefully, "...qualities, which would stand you in good stead. And, of course, it would please the people."

His voice was so smooth, so gentle, she found it hard to believe that this was the man who, mere moments ago, was threatening the life of her aunt.

"Naturally, great care would be taken of you," Phelan went on. "And of your friends, of course. I am sure you must have endured great hardships of late..."

"Lily!" Aunt Hortensia uttered, scandalized. "Your shoes!"

"Indeed," he said, flicking Lily's bare, muddy feet an amused glance. "As Arcelia's royal princess, you would be provided with appropriate clothing. The best accommodations, every comfort. A life of ease and refinement, with the comforting knowledge that you have done your best for your country, and saved Arcelia from another war..."

His words formed an image which blossomed in her mind. It would be just like being home again. Maybe she could go home. And she would have saved Aunt Hortensia, and Sennet, and Holly—and Malin.

"And Restoration Day?"

Phelan looked deprecating again. "I have made a good many concessions already."

Lily looked at him, trying to see past his face into the hidden mind behind. It was possible that this was a trap, that he had no intention of making his promises good.

"Oh, Lily, please," Aunt Hortensia said, breaking down and weeping for the first time in Lily's memory. "I ask you not for my own sake, but for yours! It is just what I would have chosen for you—a ladylike life—a life of safety…"

Her mother had not chosen safety. Lily forced herself to confront the fact that her mother had, therefore, died.

"I can assure you," Phelan said, holding her gaze, "that I am entirely in earnest." He fished a key out of his pocket, unlocked the broken window, and held it open for her to enter.

She looked at him doubtfully.

"Come," he said, and his voice woke a faint memory of her father's voice, long ago. "Come back to your family, where you belong."

"Please, Lily!" Aunt Hortensia cried, gasping with sobs.

Lily looked at her uncle, and saw why some had followed him. There was character there, and strength, clarity of purpose, strength of mind. The Lunula hung heavy about her neck, its weight a burden at the base of her throat. He looked so gentle, so kind…

Lily looked long and hard, and made up her mind.

⚜   ⚜   ⚜

The long, low note of the Horn of Vale rolled out across the empty square like a cow calling her calf across a foggy valley.

Phelan's face twisted with anger, the gentle mask falling away. "Stop! This is your last chance!"

Lily thought she could hear shouting, far in the distance. She sounded the Horn again, and into the square the people poured, the odd Easterling caught up in the tide. The crowd boiled around the square before settling into place and staring up in silence, a sea of watching faces.

There was a flash beside her and she leapt away just in time to avoid the long sharp dagger that had appeared in Phelan's hand. Aunt Hortensia shrieked and crumpled.

Lily flung herself away from her uncle, leaping up onto the very edge of the decorative stonework balustrade. She gasped in once, and blew the Horn one last time. From the corner of her eye, she saw Phelan's face, contorted with rage, lunging towards her.

There was a searing pain in her leg; it gave way—and she fell.

⚜   ⚜   ⚜

A myriad of hands reached up to her from the single great body of the crowd, and she was gently lowered to the cold, damp pourstone of the square.

"The earth!" she gasped, and the crowd made way for a burly man in a blacksmith's apron, carrying a sledgehammer.

With one firm blow, he cracked the pourstone, and willing hands seized the broken edges, prised the pieces loose, and bared the sweet, dark soil below.

Her head swimming, Lily seized the Persimmon Key as it swung at her wrist, and plunged it into the ground. A tingle went through her hand as the Key took root, lengthened, and put out twigs which were almost instantly garnished with perfect little leaves.

Lily's head cleared, as though the air were somehow fresher. She sat up, and noticed three things at once. Her wrist was still tied to the Key Tree, her bare foot lay in a pool of blood—and Evil Uncle Phelan was lying in a pool of his own, strangely huddled.

"He fell," she said, stating the obvious but trying to take it in.

"Lost his balance slashing at you, my lady," said a woman at her feet, already applying a clean cloth to the wound to slow the bleeding, "and who'd catch him?"

"Is he dead?" Lily asked.

"Not bleeding like that, he ain't. Well, not yet," the woman conceded.

The blacksmith pushed forward, sledgehammer raised.

"No!" Lily cried, beginning to feel weak again. "Please, smith—the chains on the pillar."

The smith scowled, but he went as he was asked.

Lily felt dizzy and slid down to rest her light head on the cool ground again. Someone was calling her name...

Holly pushed his way out of the crowd. "You're hurt!" He dropped to his knees at her side.

"Not as bad as it looks," the healer said, "but I've sent for poppy draught before I do the stitching. You don't look any too good yourself," she added with professional candour.

Lily looked up at him. He had a black eye, a split lip, and bruises deepening as she watched.

"Holly!"

"You should see the other fellows," he said, and put up his hands in a shadow-box. Split knuckles too, Lily noticed.

"Best if we carry you away somewhere quiet, my lady," the healer said. "No call for you to stay tied to the tree that I know of."

Holly whipped out a paring knife and slit the cord.

"I can't go now," Lily said desperately. "There's too much to see to! Phelan..."

Holly turned and looked thoughtfully at the fallen Magister. "Tricky. You could just leave him there. No? But if his wounds are tended, he'll probably live, and then what?"

"Well, don't look at me," the healer said promptly. "I've got her ladyship to see to, and then there's that Malin needing care, if I'm any judge. I've got no time for *him*," and her tone made it clear she had no intention of finding time.

"Poppy draught," a curly-headed youth called, darting through the crowd with a small flask in his hand.

The healer poured out a measure and Lily obediently drank it, wondering how long she had before its enchanting sleep claimed her.

"Oh!" she said, eyes widening. "Holly—get Sennet out. Tell him…Phelan…to the cave." Her words moved slowly and languorously as the heavy sweetness of the draught spread through her.

Holly laughed, a rich, rolling sound. "That'll do it. Who'd kiss him?"

"Then *go home.* Order!" Lily got out.

The world swung as Holly bowed extravagantly, and then he and the world went away.

⚜   ⚜   ⚜

Six months later, Lily stood at the window of what was now her reception room, and looked down over the dusky garden in the square below. Fifteen years of neglect had done little for the soil, but at least it had not been worked without rest. There would be something to show for her gardening efforts, tonight at the Harvest Ball.

She brushed a speck of dust off the midnight-purple velvet of her ballgown. It was considerably less ornate than the concoctions she had dreamed up in Candra, but it set the Lunula off to perfection.

In any case, her taste had changed. Just as well, considering her life as a working queen. Clothing had to be considerably more practical than she had anticipated. It wasn't just the gardening; it was the immense amount of travel she found herself doing. She had seen more of Arcelia in the past six months than she had on her quest, though travelling openly by ox or cart certainly provided a much better view than running and hiding did.

There had been the Wolves to sort out; that had turned out to be a relatively simple matter of promising them their back pay in return for reconstruction work until Midsummer, although there had been a few flare-ups of violence, fuelled by resentment or opportunism.

Then there had been the more difficult matter of balancing the Restoration of family lands with the appropriate penalties for thrall-holding, and restitution for the thralls.

And then there had been the seemingly endless negotiations with Burnaby on the legal agreement giving Burnaby the status of an autonomous region within Arcelia. The latest demand had been for permanent positions on the Great Council for the Old Man and Old Woman, a demand Lily had been only too happy to accede to.

She had been present for the talks—held alternately in Burnaby and Denton—as often as she could be spared from other duties, but she still hadn't seen Malin.

By the time she had come round from the healer's poppy draught, he had gone, leaving only a note: a mere scrap of paper with a rough drawing of a jasmine flower. This was the cloud that had hung over her for the past six months, even as she worked ceaselessly to get Arcelia back on its feet.

Jasmine could mean *I attach myself to you*—or it could mean *separation*. And as time went on, with Malin apparently avoiding her, it started to look more and more like the latter. He was around; others had seen him—but, somehow, he always managed to be somewhere else.

Yet she was sure he had cared for her; it hadn't been all for Burnaby's sake. She didn't know what to think. Even if she had seen him, she wasn't sure she would've wanted to come straight out and ask him what he'd meant.

Turning back to the window with a sigh, she saw a steady stream of people coming through the twilit square, arriving for the ball. Indeed, one man was already dancing, picking up his wife and swinging her around on the broad path which bordered the garden. Lily recognized the bouncy movement: Holly (or, rather, Deni), and his beloved Corrie, married for five months now and expecting their first child in early spring, to Gran Vi's delight.

She smiled. She would be glad to see them again; it had been a while since her duties had taken her to the Leaf and Bud.

"A cheering sight," said a creaky voice beside her.

"Woodward!" She put out a hand to his long green sleeve to assure herself that he was really there.

"In person," he said, wrinkles gathering around his eyes as he smiled.

"You're all right!"

"Thanks to you," he said soberly. "I am more sorry than I can say that such a burden should have been placed on you."

"I'm sorry I didn't listen more carefully," Lily said ruefully. But would she have had the courage to go if she had known what she would face?

"As the land regains its strength, so do I," Woodward said, "and I think I can promise not to leave you in the lurch again."

"You're not going to…go dormant over winter?" Lily asked cautiously. There were a number of issues she'd like to turn over to him, now that she thought of it.

"Certainly not." He stretched and breathed deeply. "Ahh… smell that good earth. No, I shall be around. I dare say we shall encounter each other quite often."

"Then—you're not staying?" Lily said, not even trying to keep the disappointment out of her voice.

His bright eyes regarded her keenly. "Do you need me to?"

Lily opened her mouth to say that of *course* she did, but the look in his eye told her this was not a question to give an unthinking reply to.

She closed her mouth again, thought carefully for a minute or two, and then sighed. "No, I suppose not. But…"

"Dandelions always pop up," he reminded her.   "Even where you least expect them."

"Will you at least stay for the ball?"

"Naturally, although I fear I am not yet strong enough to dance. Next year, perhaps."

Lily turned away from the window with a sigh. She picked up her cane from where it rested against the wall and limped towards a seat at the council table.

"We can be wallflowers together, then," she said, trying to sound cheerful.

She was eighteen, a queen, and this was her very first ball— but she could not dance. The healer had done all that was possible, and Lily was thankful that she could still walk, but running and dancing were out of the question. Not that she regretted the running, she thought with a wry smile. She'd had a lifetime's worth of that already.

A dry cough sounded from the doorway. "My lady?"

"Master Sennet," Lily said warmly, and turned to Wood-ward—who was gone, leaving a dandelion sprouting in the window box. She turned back to Sennet's anxious face. "Come in. Is anything the matter?"

"Nothing that can't wait for the next meeting of the Great Council," Sennet assured her. He was the head of that coun-cil, and represented her when she was absent from Denton. "But we mustn't think of business tonight! I did just wonder, though, if you'd had a chance…" He trailed off at the sight of her regretful face.

"She's been so busy," Lily explained. "First with the refur-bishments, and now with the ball. I've hardly had a moment with her that wasn't full of lists and plans and people rushing in and out."

"Indeed, we have all been rather busy of late," Sennet said. "Glad as I am to be attending a Harvest Ball again, I must ad-mit I will be rather pleased when it is—"

He broke off as Aunt Hortensia sailed into the room. He stood staring a moment at her resplendent deep blue ballgown.

"Aunt Hortensia!" Lily cried. It was the first time she had seen her aunt in anything but the purples and greys of half mourning, or the deep black of full mourning which she always resorted to on the anniversaries of bereavements. "You're wearing *blue!*"

A blush tinted Aunt Hortensia's cheeks a becoming pink. "I thought, as it was such an occasion…and, after all, it *has* been fifteen years…" She broke off, apparently flustered by the attention.

"An entirely appropriate choice," Sennet said, bowing courteously.

"I'm so glad," Lily said, taking her aunt's hand. "If you would excuse us, Master Sennet, I would like a moment's private conference with Lady Hortensia."

Sennet tactfully withdrew to linger by the door at the far end of the room. Lily drew her aunt closer to the council chairs. She had a feeling a chair might well be required at some point in the following conversation.

"If you had not requested this interview," Aunt Hortensia said, "I would have done, for there is a matter of great importance on which I wish to speak to you." She paused before announcing impressively, "Lily, this is your first ball. Among the attendees will be not only the cream of Arcelian society," (anyone who cared to come, as Lily well knew), "but some very eligible young gentlemen from here and abroad."

Lily froze, hoping very much this conversation was not going where she thought it was.

"You must give thought to the succession," Aunt Hortensia said, her cheek mantling a little at bringing up an almost indelicate subject. "For the sake of the nation, you must marry, and the sooner the better."

Lily saw her chance and leapt in before her aunt could provide her with an embarrassing catalogue of possible consorts.

"As a matter of fact, Aunt Hortensia," she said gravely, "I was wishing to speak to you on the subject of marriage."

Aunt Hortensia bent her lips approvingly.

"Master Sennet has asked me, as head of the royal family, to grant him permission to seek your hand in marriage," Lily began.

"But—" Aunt Hortensia gasped.

"Which I have been delighted to bestow," Lily continued serenely, and her aunt sank gently into the waiting chair.

"I have no doubt of your mutual affection, and have every hope of seeing you happily settled together. In fact," she went on, taking advantage of her aunt's temporary speechlessness, "I shall create him Castellan of Candra," (lest Aunt Hortensia feel she ought to decline for the sake of the family's rank), "with the castle forming your principal residence. Although, no doubt, the business of the Great Council will bring him to Denton regularly, and you may well wish to accompany him on those occasions."

Aunt Hortensia was still staring into space, with, Lily hoped, the tantalizing vision of a possible new life dancing before her eyes.

"It is, of course, entirely up to you to accept or decline," Lily added.

She waited a moment while Aunt Hortensia collected herself. A quick glance showed her Sennet was still hovering anxiously at the door, outside which some sort of rumpus was taking place.

"I must admit—I cannot deny..." Aunt Hortensia began, dabbing at her eyes with a scrap of lace which might be construed as a handkerchief. "But, no," she said, making a visible effort and pulling herself together. "I cannot begin to think of my own happiness until such time as you yourself are appropriately bestowed in marriage and my duty to you as guardian is complete."

Lily's heart sank. A vision of her future rose before her eyes, a future with a sad Sennet, a constantly advising aunt, and the eventual unavoidable acceptance of some man or other as her husband, with whom she must, for her land's sake, have children. Suddenly, laying down her life for Arcelia didn't seem so bad.

The disturbance outside escalated in volume, and the doors burst open, narrowly missing Sennet. The incomer turned to slam the doors in the face of the protesting voice outside before Lily could get a good look at him.

It was a dwarf: well dressed in new, though somewhat rumpled, clothes; a large parcel under one arm; and a thick thatch of hair in a sort of faded gold colour. Not someone she had dealt with over the negotiations, she was sure, and whoever he was, now was *not* a welcome time for uninvited guests.

"Now, I have a list here," Aunt Hortensia said, fishing it out of her reticule, "and I do feel you ought to give particular consideration to…"

But Lily was only half listening. The dwarf had turned back, with a cheery nod to Sennet, and was sauntering boldly up the room, tugging his clothing back into seemly order as he came. He looked up, grinned, and Lily's heart turned over.

There was no mistaking that green gaze, or that smile. It was Malin. Malin as she had never seen him before: not only well dressed, but *clean.*

"Of course," Aunt Hortensia was saying, "I am aware that none of these are what you might call *ideal* candidates, but in view of the circumstances…"

"That's quite all right, Aunt Hortensia," Lily said, without taking her eyes off Malin. "I'm going to marry Malin."

Aunt Hortensia stopped mid-flow.

"Aren't I?" Lily challenged him.

"That's what I thought," he agreed.

Aunt Hortensia, mouth open, turned to look at him and fell back swooning in her chair.

"Master Sennet!" Lily called, but he was already rushing to Lady Hortensia's side.

"Where have you *been?*" Lily demanded of Malin.

"I had to get you a wedding present," Malin said, as though this was a perfectly reasonable explanation for an absence of six months. "Here. Look out; it's quite heavy."

"So I see," Lily said, neatly depositing it on the council table.

"Go on, open it."

"But it's a wedding present," Lily demurred.

"Fine. It's an engagement present. I'll get you something else for a wedding present."

"Not if you're going to disappear for another six months, you won't," Lily said, untying the cords. "Without a word!"

"Didn't you get my note? *I attach myself to you*, right? See, I remembered."

"Jasmine also means *separation*," Lily said, but she was too happy to quibble.

"That's not what *I* meant," Malin said firmly. "I've done my bit for Burnaby, and I'm attaching myself to you. Permanently," he added, in case his meaning was not sufficiently clear.

Lily slid the last of the wrappings off. A smoothly finished wooden box was revealed, not quite square.

"The lid slides off," Malin said, and, in reaching to show her, their hands touched, but she did not pull away.

Together, they slid the perfectly fitted lid off, and Lily gasped.

In the centre of the box, taking up its full width, was a map of Arcelia in the form of a chess board. At each end of the box, nestled in green and grey velvet respectively, were the perfect little hand-carved pieces. The largest of the pieces on the green side caught Lily's eye.

"Malin—the queen! That's me!"

She balanced it on her hand. It was a tiny full-length statue of her in her questing clothes, carved of a fine-grained wood and not even the length of her hand.

"That's not the queen; that's the king," Malin said. "*This* is the queen." He put a matching statue of himself beside it.

"You're the queen?" Lily asked, puzzled.

"Most dangerous piece on the board," Malin said with a cocky grin.

Lily smiled, and put them back in the box, side by side. "Oh—and the Wise Man and Woman are Woodward and Aunt Hortensia! But where's Sennet?"

"Riding one of the Oxen—I figured since the siege, he counts as a soldier."

"And there's Holly on the other one—oh, and that *is* Candra, with Scholars' Tower—oh, and Gran Vi! And Sweetbriar. I must show her this one of her; she'll be delighted." Each pawn bore the unmistakable likeness of a friend made along the way. "You do realize I will never be able to *play* with this set. The idea of sacrificing even one of these!"

"That's all right," Malin said. "I can't play chess."

Lily turned her attention to the grey side. These pieces were not of wood, but of iron. Phelan as king, the top Wolf captain as queen, and Wolves for most of the other pieces. She made a face at the Wise Woman piece: Laurel.

"I know," Malin said, "but who else was there?"

"It's lovely," she said, sliding the lid back into place. "I'm not surprised it took you six months to have it made."

"Oh, the making was the easy bit," he said. "It was getting all the faces that took time. Not to mention the castles. I had to stalk your aunt for three days before I got a decent likeness."

"Did she spot you?" Lily asked anxiously.

"Of course not!"

"Just as well," Lily said, and turned back to her aunt.

Sennet's ministrations had obviously been effective, as Aunt Hortensia was sitting up, albeit looking rather pale. There was a whiff of smelling salts in the air.

"I have been explaining to Lady Hortensia the strategic value of the alliance," Sennet said gravely. "In the wake of such turmoil and foreign interference, it is naturally of the highest importance to strengthen the internal bonds of the country and emphasize unity within the region."

Lily smiled. Dear Sennet. Always dependable.

Aunt Hortensia sat up straighter, eyeing Malin. Lily leapt in.

"Aunt Hortensia—the time! They will be waiting for us in the ballroom. Perhaps you will have the goodness to open the ball with Master Sennet?"

This had the desired effect. Where duty was to be done, Lady Hortensia would never be found wanting.

As Sennet helped her to her feet, she turned to Lily for a moment and whispered, "About Candra...you'll see it done?"

"Yes, Aunt Hortensia," Lily promised, with a smile of heartfelt joy. "Tomorrow."

She watched as her aunt took Sennet's arm and sailed down the room and through the doors. A booming voice announced them, and the music struck up. This was it. She took up her stick again.

Malin took her arm and draped it over his shoulders. "Royal Crutch."

"What happened to *Burnabaise don't use titles?*" Lily teased, but she left the stick behind.

At the foot of the first flight of stairs, Lily stopped, still out of view of the thronged ballroom below.

"Nervous?" Malin asked.

"No. It's just...stairs. I was never allowed to, and then there was the injury and I couldn't, and..."

"Go on," he said, slipping out from under her arm. "I'll follow you for a change."

Lily looked across at the major-domo, waiting at the far side of the landing to announce her arrival. "Announce us both, if you please."

"Pray silence!" he boomed, and the room hushed. "Lily, Queen of Arcelia; and Malin of Burnaby!"

Keeping close to the rail for support, she turned the corner. A sea of cheering faces beamed up at her. Lily lifted her head, smiled, and walked down the stairs to the ball.

A Note from the Author

If you enjoyed this book, please consider leaving a review in the review-leaving place of your choice; or recommending it to others you think might enjoy it.

If you'd like to find out more, visit:

https://deborah.makarios.nz

where you can sign up to be the first to hear about new releases, read (or follow) the blog, or get in touch directly.

About the Author

Deborah Makarios was raised in the space between worlds and maintains an eccentric orbit.

She found her niche at the age of six when in short succession she read *The BFG*, her first Agatha Christie (*Why Didn't They Ask Evans?*), and encountered her first P. G. Wodehouse (*Something Fresh*—saying "Heh! Mer!" is enough to make her laugh, decades later).

Her personal motto is *tolle et lege*—pick it up and read it—regardless of whether *it* is a Bible, a book, or a jar of home-made marmalade.

Her mission is to write books, plays, and blog posts like cups of tea: warm, heartening, and restorative. She believes in happy endings, the ultimate triumph of good over evil, and always having a clean handkerchief. It is, however, against her religious principles to believe in "normal."

She lives among the largely unsuspecting populace of New Zealand with only two cats, and her brilliant, albeit marginally less eccentric, husband.

Acknowledgements

My thanks are due to many who have helped me along the long road to this finished book:

to my beta readers, including Nan Sampson, Ruth Fyfe, Kay McKenzie, Sara Litchfield, Ruth Gossner, Jess Trethewey, and Carol Carr, for their helpful and encouraging feedback;

to Sara Litchfield (again), for her enthusiastic work as an editor and her explanatory notes (a note of my own: any errors or inconsistencies remaining are due to my stubbornness and/or eccentricity);

to Eve Doyle, for her patience with a raw beginner as well as the wonderful just-what-I-wanted typography which graces the front cover and spine;

to my husband Timothy, for the years of endless encouragment, patient help and unwavering support: there isn't room to tell it all, and I really couldn't have done this without him;

to my Lord Patron, for everything.

Lightning Source UK Ltd.
Milton Keynes UK
UKOW04f0610090118
315800UK00001B/23/P